# Diamond

An historical fiction by

Cynthia Jordan

ISBN: 978-0-9886578-3-0

Published by
Emerald Eagle Publishing
5622 Woodbine Ln
San Angelo, TX 76904


Printed in the United States of America

*Diamond* is a work of fiction. While in all fiction the literary perceptions and insights are based on experience, the names of the characters are products of the author's imagination. No reference to any real person is intended or should be inferred.

This story is based on historical facts. References include: *Come Into My Parlor* by Charles Washborn, *Lulu* by Louise Brooks, *Goodness Had Nothing To Do With It* by Mae West, *Hollywood Posse* by Diana Serra Cary and *Flapper* by Joshua Zeitz. The majority of research references were obtained from Wikipedia. I want to extend a special thank you to my friends Susan Fowler and Pat Dreizler from Redondo Beach for their help and enthusiasm. Thanks Mom and Dad, Tita, Popu, Sport, Moe, and Ati and Emma Parvin for your inspiration and wonderful stories.

*Diamond* was edited by Kathryn Louie. Miss Victoria Pearl's photographs are of the great Edwardian actress, Lily Elsie. Photos of the "Lady Pearls" were created in the 1920's by Alfred Cheney Johnston. Photos of Redondo Beach today are by Cynthia Jordan. Special thanks to Doctor David and Janet Harvey who generously allowed us to photograph their home as Miss Pearl's Parlor and to Lee Pfluger for the beautiful photos of his Clear Creek Ranch in Menard County, Texas. Historical photos are public domain.

*Diamond* is dedicated to my dad
Roland Henry "Duke" Jordan.
He was born on November 4, 1928
at Universal Studios, where his father
Boder D. "Sport" Jordan
was an equestrian for silent western movies.
Thank you, Daddy, for giving us
a wonderful life in Redondo Beach, California

STATE OF CALIFORNIA
DEPARTMENT OF PUBLIC HEALTH

FULL NAME OF CHILD Roland Henry Jordan

# Preface

"Take your clothes off."

"I beg your pardon? I don't believe I understand."

"I said… take your clothes off. You want to be in the movies, don't ya?"

"I believe there must be some mistake. I was told this was an interview to set up a screen test for a part in the new western movie, *Rio Concho*. I am an actress and I also sing."

"Listen, Sweetheart… if you wanna play in the big leagues, you gotta play by the rules! Now take your clothes off!"

In the 1920's, courageous young women from all over America flocked to the studios in Hollywood and the theatres on Broadway with a dream of becoming a star. Some had talent. Some had good looks and nice bodies. Those who had it all stood a better chance to make it but every one of them was vulnerable to the sweet talkin' promise trap.

There were men who stalked bus stations. Many lied and made false promises, taking advantage of the inexperience of youth. Often this resulted in transforming big dreams into broken hearts.

Women helping women is the theme of the *Gem Series* by *Cynthia Jordan*. All of the books share two common themes. The first: ALL women have value. The second: Knowledge from experience and honest, trusting friendships are the greatest treasures anyone can have.

## CHAPTER 1

# Miss Pearl's Parlor

Miss Pearl! Miss Pearl!"

Panicked, Maggie, wearing a shimmering, blue satin dressing gown that cascaded like a banner in the wind flowing behind her, flew down the mahogany staircase of Miss Pearl's Parlor.

"My goodness, Maggie! What in the world…?" Pearl expressed with surprise.

Maggie was distraught. "I think he's dead, Miss Pearl! I think I killed him!" ozella came running into the room. It was her job to know everything that happened in the Parlor. Mozella's radar was keen and her reactions were swift.

"What happened, Maggie?"

"It's Mr. O'Hara, Mozella! We were having such a good time. He kept calling me his "Wild Irish Lassie." Then all of a sudden, after his springer had sprung, he quit moving. I believe he quit breathing too. He just wouldn't wake up. I even tried pouring water over his head!"

About a year after his wife had passed away, Mr. Michael O'Hara began patronizing Miss Pearl's Parlor. He had been delighted to learn that Pearl's parents were immigrants from Ireland. Every time Victoria Pearl would greet the charming, elderly Irish gentleman, Mr. O'Hara would gallantly kiss her hand and recite a favorite limerick. Less than an hour ago she had heard him say, "*May your thoughts be as glad as the shamrocks. May your heart be as light as a song. May each day bring you bright, happy hours that stay with you all year long.*"

The three women hurried up the staircase to the Green Room. Everyone knew it was Michael O'Hara's favorite, probably because he was Irish. All of the "entertaining" rooms at Miss Pearl's Parlor were decorated in themes and colors. Victoria Pearl had learned well working as a courtesan at the Everleigh Club in Chicago, where the entertaining parlors were spectacularly themed to create a den of sexual fantasy.

As Mozella slowly opened the door of the Green Room, Pearl could see Michael O'Hara lying comfortably on a large pillow and looking as if he were sleeping. His eyes were closed and he had the most glorious smile of contentment on his clean, shaven face. Maggie, biting her lip, was gravely concerned.

"Oh, Miss Pearl. Am I in trouble?" Maggie inquired.

"Actually, Maggie, this happened once when I was working at the Everleigh House," Pearl reassured her. "I remember Minna and Ada Everleigh handled the unfortunate incident promptly and seamlessly. Remember, Mozella?"

Mozella, a caramel colored woman with sparkling, blue sapphire eyes had been in charge of the colored help at the world famous Everleigh Club at 2131-2133 Dearborn Street in Chicago. She had run a tight ship and the Everleigh Sisters held her in high esteem. Victoria Pearl completely trusted Mozella and considered her to be a confidant and her best friend.

"I do remember," Mozella replied. "After we put the patron's clothes back on, Amos and Edwin carried the man down the servant stairs and loaded him into a cabby. The sisters gave the cab driver $50 to deliver the man to a hospital on the other side of Chicago. He told them to say that the man died in his cab. No one was ever the wiser. They saved the man's family from a lot of embarrassment. Miss Ada and Miss Minna were masters at covering up any kind of indiscretion."

"And that's exactly what we are going to do for Michael," Pearl declared. "San Angelo does not need to know how Mr. O'Hara passed. I know his wife died several years ago, but he does have children and I believe grandchildren as well."

Always a champ in a crisis, Ginger sauntered in acting sultry and cool. Nothing shocked her and she always seemed to have the perfect solution for any crisis. At 24 years old, Ginger had been a star student in the school of hard knocks.

"Just look at that smile. Good for you, Maggie. Looks like Mr. O'Hara met his Maker a happy man. I'll call Joe, Miss Pearl. We will take care of Mr. O'Hara and protect his dignity."

"Thank you, Ginger. Michael was such a nice man." Pearl sighed. "Thank you Ginger."

"I feel awful about this, Miss Pearl," Maggie expressed with regret.

"Are you kidding?" Ginger teased. "Can you think of a better way to go? Go get dressed, Maggie. We are going to the movies. It will help you get your mind off the unfortunate events of the afternoon. I want to see *The Hunchback of Notre Dame*. I read the book twice. We will ask Heather to come along. You know how she loves to go to the movies."

Mozella opened the closet and pulled out a crisp white sheet. When Mozella was growing up, her grandmother taught her the Bible and Mozella was known for punctuating any given situation with an appropriate Bible verse. Gently and solemnly, Mozella laid the sheet over the deceased Michael O'Hara. "Goodbye, Mr. O'Hara. You were a good man. *Ecclesiastes 7: A good name is better than fine perfume, and the day of death better than the day of birth.*"

"You always know just what to say, Mo. Mr. O'Hara died in the arms of an angel." Pearl sighed. "Isn't that just like the luck of the Irish?"

CHAPTER 2

# Miss Pearl's New Girls

Ever since the Santa Rita oil discovery in Big Lake, business was booming at Miss Pearl's Parlor in San Angelo, Texas. Victoria Pearl had learned well from the Everleigh sisters who had made millions of dollars providing female companionship to wealthy gentlemen in Chicago. Just like Ada and Minna Everleigh Victoria had high standards for her girls and conducted business at Pearl's Parlor with class, elegance and grace. When the young women who worked for the Everleigh sisters left to be a gentleman's bride Ada would always say, "So nice to see one of our butterflies find a new home." The business of entertaining gentlemen had a constant revolving door. For Victoria Pearl, saying goodbye to her girls was like losing family.

It had only been a few weeks since the women at Pearl's Parlor had said goodbye to Betsy, Redbird and Lucy. When Betsy's childhood sweetheart, Johnny Wayne, finally learned where she had been for two years, he had come to take her home to Kentucky to make Betsy his bride. Johnny Wayne had loved Betsy since the second grade. His unconditional love was genuine and he had built Betsy a house, never giving up on the fact he would find her again one day.

When Redbird's Aunt Gertrude had kicked her out of her house she came to Miss Pearl's Parlor looking for her friend Lucy who had also been told to leave her home in Houston. After two years working for Miss Pearl, Redbird received a letter telling her that Aunt Gertrude had died choking on a chicken bone and that she had inherited her father's company in Galveston. Redbird invited Lucy to come with her, and the two childhood friends moved back to Houston.

Although everyone at Miss Pearl's Parlor were happy for Betsy, Redbird and Lucy, there was a melancholy feeling throughout the house. Now Pearl understood how the Everleigh sisters felt when they said goodbye to her. Betsy was a sweetheart, Lucy was always making everyone laugh and Redbird had a heart of gold. All three women had taken a place in Victoria's heart.

The word was out that Miss Pearl had three spots to fill. This particular afternoon she was expecting two new candidates who had written to tell her they would be arriving on the afternoon train from Houston. Joe had just left with Mister O'Hara when the front doorbell rang

Seeing the two attractive young women standing on the front porch, Mozella greeted them with a big smile. "May I help you, ladies?"

"We are here to see Miss Pearl about a job," the shorter of the two expressed. "My name is Penelope and this is my friend Fifi."

Mozella took both girls into the great room, where Harmony was playing the piano. She had chosen a Chopin Nocturne to play, beautiful with a hint of sadness. Harmony always picked her music according to her mood, and it was obvious she was missing her friends who had recently left.

"You play so pretty," Penelope commented.

"Thank you," Harmony smiled, not wanting to waver from the flow of the musical composition.

"Pearl can see you now," Mozella announced. "Fifi, why don't we start with you?"

As the young French woman sat in the chair across from her, Pearl was impressed with how pretty she was. "What is your name, dear?"

"I am Fifi," the girl answered with her musical French accent.

# Fifi

Fifi was adorable. Her shiny, big, brown eyes were expressive and her French accent, divine. Fifi reminded Victoria of a girl from Paris who had worked a short time at the Everleigh Club. Another darling French girl with a musical voice, her name was Suzette, and the gentlemen in Chicago loved listening to her talk. To them, she was the epitome of exotic romance, and within a week, Suzette became quite popular at the Everleigh Club and was in high demand.

Three months after Suzette began working for Ada and Minna, she married a banker, and today is living happily ever after in a big, luxurious mansion on the north side of Chicago.

Pearl was delighted with Fifi's adorable French accent. Foreign women from other countries were rare in West Texas.

"You are a lovely girl, Fifi. Do you have experience?"

"Oui, Madame. I work at Chicken Ranch for two mont''.

"In La Grange?"

"Oui, Madame."

"I have heard of Miss Jessie in La Grange. We do things a little different here, Fifi. Our clientele is more exclusive. For this reason, I insist my girls dress well, stay clean, read daily and be creative in their work. Why did you leave if I may ask?" Pearl inquired.

"A nice man find me where I work for Miss Jessie. He take me to live in his big house and be his maid. He buy me a short black dress, white apron and funny white hat. Then he tell me not to wear panties when I clean the house. Only one hour every day. For this, he give me presents and $100 on Fridays."

"That sounds interesting," Pearl commented. She had met quirky men like him in Chicago. There was one man who frequented the Everleigh Club who paid well to watch the girls climb a ladder even though in those days the skirts always were long enough to cover their ankles. Pearl liked the fact that Fifi simply saw the situation as a job she was willing to perform.

"It was easy work. My room was nice and sometimes I cook for him. The man never lay me down. He give me feather duster and told me to climb ladders and reach high like dis."

Fifi stood up on her tiptoes and reached her right hand to the ceiling as high as she could. Pearl was amused.

"Sometimes he just like watching me go up and down the stairs. Easy job. He like it when I say, 'Oui, Oui and Ooh La La.' Sometime he like me to dance a cancan and sing French songs."

"What happened?" Pearl asked.

"His son come home for visit. Very handsome man. I like him. One day he take me for a walk and tell me I am pretty girl. He ask to see my breast so I show him. We make love. It was like magic. He was good lover. We make love at night and in the morning and at night again. We think his father asleep but he find us making love.

His father get angry. I do not know why," Fifi shrugged. "We were not lovers. The man and his son get in fight, so next day I leave and go back to La Grange. Penelope is my friend. She tell me she want to go to San Angelo to meet you. We take train and here I am. You have pretty house, Miss Pearl."

"You are a charming girl, Fifi," Pearl smiled. "As I said before, I run my business much different than Miss Jessie. My girls are clean and well mannered. Drugs and excessive alcohol are not tolerated."

"No worry. I do not do drugs," Fifi confirmed. "I do like champagne and wine but I do not like drunk women so I drink water when I feel too much happy."

Pearl was charmed with Fifi's perceived naiveté. Whether or not it was real would be determined, but, nevertheless, it worked well.

"I insist my girls read every day and I encourage them to expand on their creativity. Maggie is an artist and Katie is one of the best equestrians in West Texas. Harmony is an accomplished musician, Heather writes stories and wants to be an actress and Ginger sings in a way that will send chills up your spine. Sarah writes poetry and Annabelle loves to dance."

"I like to dance and I sing. I stay and work for you, Miss Pearl. Oui, Madame?"

"You remind me very much of a French girl I knew in Chicago. Her name was Suzette and the men loved her. Yes, Fifi, you will work out just fine, my dear."

"Thank you, Miss Pearl. You will like my friend, Penelope. She make me laugh very much," Fifi expressed enthusiastically.

"I am anxious to meet her," Pearl smiled warmly.

Pearl took Fifi's arm and led her to the tall double doors of the library. They could see Penelope, who was captivated by Harmony's music, sitting in a chair by the piano.

Seeing she was mesmerized with the music, Mozella gently patted Penelope on the shoulder. "Miss Pearl is ready to see you now."

# Penelope

As Penelope bounced into the room, Pearl thought about how much she reminded her of Lucy.

"My name is Penelope, but sometimes I am called Jezebel."

"Jezebel?" Pearl inquired.

"It's kind of a long story. Francine named me that when she caught me kissing Jimmy."

"And who are Francine and Jimmy," Pearl asked.

"Jimmy was our music director at church. He's real nice lookin'. I had a crush on him. Francine is a nasty old hag with lots of money. She's Jimmy's wife. That's why he married her, on account of she's rich. Francine is a mean woman, always telling Jimmy where to go and what to do.

"One night Francine caught Jimmy trying to kiss me after choir practice and started screaming at us like some kind of shrew. 'You Jezebel!' she yelled. Then she took hold of Jimmy's ear and marched him outside. A week later he tried to kiss me again, and I let him. It was real nice. One thing led to another and then…I surrendered to his passion, body and soul. We were in love, Miss Pearl…or at least, I thought so."

"I see," Pearl said, amused with the young lady sitting before her. "*I like her,*" Pearl thought.

"Got to be where I loved choir practice. We found a place to go where no one would ever find us. It was an old abandoned barn on the Farley place. I brought pillows and a nice quilt for us to lay on…some fresh hay… Sometimes he would end choir practice early and off we'd go. Then there were those days when Francine would take the train to Houston to go shoppin' and we'd sneak away to the barn.

"Jimmy was a real good lover, Miss Pearl. I even learned how to sing better. Jimmy never looked at me at choir practice much. In fact he kinda ignored me, on account he didn't want anyone to get the idea that we were in love. We had to keep it a secret but I wanted everyone to know."

"I understand," Pearl smiled.

"We made real good love, Miss Pearl. I know having sex with a married man is a sin, but somehow with Jimmy, it just didn't feel like we were doin' anything wrong. We sang church songs when we made love. Then lots of times, at the big moment, both of us would start yellin' *Amen* and *Alleluia*! Making love with Jimmy was just like heaven on earth, so the singin' seemed appropriate."

Pearl bit her lip to keep from laughing.

"When we made love, Jimmy liked to call me Jezebel 'cause that's what Francine called me that night she caught us. I found out Jezebel was a sinner woman in the Bible. I liked it when he called me Jezebel, 'cause then, when we did it, I pretended it wasn't really me doin' the sinnin', it was Jezebel. Penelope was a good girl."

"Very creative," Pearl remarked with a smile.

"Jimmy kept promising me he was going to leave that ol' bitch and marry me when I turned 18. For a whole year, he kept promisin'. When my birthday finally came, he quit promisin'. Then a month later, my grandma died. I'd been with her since I was three when my daddy died."

"What about your parents?"

"My daddy never married my Mama, and Lord knows what happened to her."

"I am sorry, dear." Pearl was beginning to understand the full picture of Penelope's plight.

"I kept askin' Jimmy when we was gonna get married. Then one day, a new girl joined the choir and I saw Jimmy lookin' at her the way he used to look at me. A week later after choir practice, he told me he couldn't see me anymore, on account of what we was doin' was a sin and he was feelin' guilty. Now I know it was all just a big lie."

"Uh oh," Pearl thought. "I think I know where this is going."

"Anyway, I got this feelin' when he started ignorin' the new girl the way he used to ignore me. So I followed them after choir practice one night. Can you believe where they went?"

"The barn?" Pearl answered.

"That is exactly correct, Miss Pearl," Penelope exclaimed. "I got to thinkin', I am going to help Jimmy, so he won't be a sinner anymore. The next Tuesday, after choir practice I took Francine to the barn. At first we could hear them singin', *in the sweet by and by; we will meet on that beautiful shore...* I knew what was comin' next! Sure enough, they started screamin' *Amen! Alleluia! Amen! Alleluia!*"

"Sounds appropriate," Pearl stated, trying not to burst out into laughter. She could see this was not at all funny to poor Penelope.

"Francine got real angry. She was mad as a hornet! Her face turned red like a beet and she started to breathin' funny, low and gravelly like. Miss Pearl, I swear it was if a demon had possessed her body! She was so scary I ran away.

"It was a big scandal on account that girl was only 16 years old. Jimmy blamed that poor little girl and brought shame to her family. Francine pretty much owned that church, so the folks took her side. After that, church goin' just wasn't the same. Grandma was gone, so I decided to leave town.

"I met Fifi working for Miss Jessie. Always did like sex so I made my work fun. I use the name Jezebel when I'm sinnin', and the rest of the time I am Penelope, the good girl. It just makes more sense to me to use another name."

"That is a fine idea," Pearl expressed.

"I still like singin' *Amen* and *Alleluia* at the big moment. Some men really seem to like it."

"We encourage creativity here at the parlor."

"A gentleman told me you might be looking for some girls, Miss Pearl. Told me all about you and how nice you are. I'd heard about you before. Miss Jessie's can sometimes get a little too crazy. Fifi was open for a different place to go, so here we are."

"I am happy you are here, my dear Penelope," Pearl smiled. "What was it like working for Miss Jessie?"

"It was okay. Before the war a crusade of reformers were trying to shut down her business in Houston. Miss Jessie decided it was too much trouble to stay so she bought a little 10-acre farm outside the city limits real close to the Houston-Austin highway. She was good at spreadin' the word. The girls sent letters and care packages to the local boys who were fightin' in the Great War overseas. Guess she figured they'd be pretty horny when they finally got home."

Pearl chuckled.

"From the front it looked like just a regular farmhouse with whitewashed siding and a few side buildings. After the war, it seemed more automobiles were passing on that road. Business got so good that Miss Jessie had to add extra rooms in the back. That's where the men would park their cars and horses. Always came through the back door."

"That makes sense," Pearl said nodding her head.

"Sheriff came over every night to learn the latest gossip. Funny what men will tell you after you're nice to them. Like you're some kind of priest hearing their confessions. Sometimes they'd talk too much."

"I know what you mean, Penelope. Sometimes women like us get information we do not want to hear. That's why secrecy is imperative."

"Not with Miss Jessie. She has a deal goin' with that sheriff. He has solved many a crime from what he learned from her. Miss Jessie took care of us girls. If she had even the slightest notion a man was giving any one of us a bad time, she would chase him out of the house with an iron rod in her hand. She didn't tolerate any sloppy drunks, either…men or women."

"Glad to hear it. That's how we do things here as well. Katie takes care of any bad behavior. She does not have an iron rod, but she can handle a rifle and it speaks loud and clear."

"Pearl's Parlor is so nice.. May I stay?"

"I will be happy for you and Fifi to join us, Penelope. A little polishing up and you will make a fine addition to our business. I will arrange for Doctor Ned to see the two of you in the morning. For now, Mozella will show you where you will sleep tonight."

"Thank you Miss Pearl. I won't let ya down."

"Will not, Penelope. I will not let you down," Pearl smiled.

"I will not let you down, Miss Pearl."

"Welcome to Miss Pearl's Parlor, my dear."

# Jolene

The next Saturday afternoon Mozella was cleaning the mirror in the foyer when through the beveled glass she could see a young woman struggling to climb the stairs leading to the front door of Pearl's Parlor. Opening the door, she could see the evidence of a harsh beating all over the woman's face.

"My Lord in heaven! What in the world happened?" Mozella exclaimed.

Before she could speak, the young woman collapsed in a heap on the threshold of the foyer. Just then Sarah's Aunt Katherine came running up the walkway behind her. "She told me her name is Jolene. I found her just over there at the river. She's in a bad way."

Pearl was in the library writing letters when she heard Mozella shout, "We need some help here! Someone call the doctor!"

Within seconds, Katie, Sarah, Maggie and Heather appeared. Carefully, the women carried the bruised, battered girl and laid her on the soft, green divan in the great room. Pearl was on the phone with the doctor. "Please come now, Ned. I believe she is hurt pretty bad."

Jolene woke up in a small room located next to the kitchen of Miss Pearl's Parlor to the smell of Mozella's cooking. Katie was sitting in a chair beside the bed, her 30-30 leaning conveniently against the wall.

"She's awake, Mozella," Katie called.

Mozella appeared, holding a glass of water. "The doctor will be here soon. Drink this, honey. *Psalm 41: The Lord sustains her on her sickbed; in her illness you restore her to full health."*

"A man?" Katie asked.

"Yes."

"Where is he?"

"I don't know."

"Don't worry, he can't hurt ya here."

Doctor Ned was familiar with Pearl's Parlor, in a professional way. Maggie liked to say he reminded her of Santa Claus, with his full white beard and twinkling eyes. The girls all loved Doctor Ned. His quiet, caring bedside manner was appreciated and his matter-of-fact humor always put the ladies at ease.

"Looks like your ribs are broken, my dear. I'll need to put a couple of stitches in that eye. Let's put some ice on your mouth. It's swollen pretty badly. The good news is... you still have all your teeth."

After giving Jolene a dose of morphine, Doctor Ned gently tended to her injuries. Although her soft green eyes were bloodshot and her ivory skin was purple and blue, it was obvious Jolene was a lovely girl. Her disheveled auburn curls were shiny and soft and her slender body was lovely indeed.

"Is she going to be all right?" Sarah anxiously inquired.

"She needs to rest, Sarah, but I believe she's going to be just fine. That is, if she stays away from the monster who did this to her."

"Thank you, Doctor Ned," Pearl said, as she walked him to the door. "I appreciate you coming."

"I will be by in a couple of days to check on her." Putting his hat on his head, Doctor Ned sighed. "I've seen this before, Pearl. I can tell by her scars this was not the first time," he said, shaking his head with disgust. "For some reason, they go back. I do not understand it."

"Some of them have nowhere else to go, Ned."

"My Mama kept going back to Stan," Sarah shuddered. "He'd beat her up and hurt her just like Jolene. Then he'd cry and tell her how sorry he was, making promises he was gonna change. Yeah, right. Mama killed him with her frying pan when she learned what he'd done to me. Stupid son-of-bitch was bragging to her about it. Can you imagine? And he was a cop!"

Tears began streaming down Sarah's face. "Mama shot herself. Most horrible sound I ever heard. It still haunts me to this day."

Katherine gently placed her arm around her niece. "My poor sweet sister. Our daddy was a mean son-of-a bitch. I still have nightmares about the things he used to do to us."

"These ladies and my Aunt Katherine are my family now. Don't worry, Doc, we'll take good care of Jolene," Sarah assured him.

Later that afternoon, a man appeared on the front lawn of Miss Pearl's Parlor. Wearing a blue shirt and denim pants, he was relatively handsome. "Jolene! I know you're in there. I'm sorry. Jolene…"

Katie stepped out on the porch and aimed…

BOOM!

The man felt the vibration of the bullet scream between his legs.

Looking up, he saw a pair of intense, shiny deep blue eyes staring at him down the barrel of a 30-30. Beside her was a black and tan German shepherd, growling with his lip curled, waiting patiently for his master to give him permission to strike.

"Like to beat on women, you sorry son-of-a-bitch? You best leave town now. That is, if you have any reverence to that thang hangin' between your legs. Now get the hell outta here, you goddamn coward, before I turn you into a gelding!"

"ONE… TWO…"

BOOM!

BOOM! BOOM… BOOM… BOOM!!

Another shot buzzed between his legs. The other bullets hit so close to his feet that they made him dance. Squealing with terror, the man ran away, never to be heard from again.

Pearl learned that from the time she was a little girl Jolene had been abused. When her mother learned she was pregnant with little Jolene, it brought great shame to the family and her parents told her she had to leave town. When Jolene's father learned her mother was pregnant he moved away. Jolene was born with her mother resenting her.

When Jolene was five-years-old, her mother married. For years, her stepfather had abused her, making horrible threats if she ever revealed the truth. Finally, when she was 15, her mother caught them in the barn. Blaming Jolene, her mother kicked her out of the house, banishing her never to return again. Since then, Jolene had been with three different men.

When Jolene recovered she began her new life at Miss Pearl's Parlor. Never before had she ever been treated like a lady. Now, at 19 years old, Jolene was wearing beautiful clothes and learning how to read. She found refuge and a sense of value with the girls at Miss Pearl's Parlor. As far as experience, she had plenty, and none of it was good. Now for the first time in her life, Jolene felt appreciated and loved. She had finally found a family and a home.

CHAPTER 3

# Happy Harvey

Reading was mandatory and a daily occurrence at Miss Pearl's Parlor. Most late mornings, the ladies could be found on the front porch of the mansion, reading a variety of literature. Heather was particularly fond of movie and theatre magazines. Becoming an actress and living in Hollywood was her secret fantasy and deepest desire.

For over a decade, the movie industry had been producing new glamorous stars and memorable stories that were developing a free-spirited culture throughout America. The old fashion ideals of the

Victorian Age were fading away, as young women imitated the new exciting fashions and trends being displayed bigger than life on the magical silver screen. The movies were telling America's story and the 20's were roaring with prosperity and change.

Heather was admiring a photo of Alice Terry on the cover of the October, 1923 issue of Motion Picture Classic.

"Who's that?" Sarah asked.

"Alice Terry," Heather answered. "She has a new movie coming out in February. It's called *Scaramouche*. Look at how beautiful she looks. Ramon Navarro is the leading man."

"What in the world is a Scaramouche?" Maggie inquired.

"He's the one who wears the black mask in the Punch and Judy puppet shows."

"I saw a Punch and Judy show at a festival in Austin," Harmony remarked as she continued strumming on her guitar.

"What's the movie about?" Sarah inquired.

"It's a love story that takes place during the French Revolution. They call it a period piece," Heather revealed. "I love historical movies, especially love stories. They love, they hate, they win, they lose..."

"The French Revolution was a terrible time," Fifi remarked. "My country has had so much war."

Honk! Honk, Honk!

"Look, everyone! Harvey's here!" Maggie exclaimed, pointing at the shiny, new Rolls-Royce Silver Ghost pulling up to the mansion.

"Who's that?" Penelope asked.

"Harvey is our best girlfriend in a man's body," Ginger said. "The man has taste and style and we all adore him. Every visit from Harvey is a new adventure. C'mon. Let's go see his new car."

Harvey James Rochester was an attractive, wealthy, charming, witty man who cherished his Lady Pearls, as he affectionately called them. He never missed a birthday and loved to buy the girls gifts. An excellent eye for fashion and jewelry, the girls always looked forward to visits from Harvey. His generosity was overwhelming and the girls saw him in the same way a child looks at Santa Claus.

"How was your trip, Harvey?" Maggie asked.

"It was fabulous. I have so much to tell you ladies," Harvey exclaimed. The backseat of the glistening, silver automobile was full of white boxes tied with bright red ribbons. "Wait until you all see what I have for my Lady Pearls."

This time Harvey brought everyone a fashionable evening gown, each one carefully chosen to adorn his beloved friends. Dresses made with colorful brocades, beads, silks, lace, and lovely satin sashes were revealed as the girls excitedly opened their gifts.

"Miss Pearl, I believe I see unfamiliar faces," Harvey commented. "Now that Lucy, Redbird and Betsy are gone, I had a feeling there might be some new Lady Pearls I had not yet had the pleasure to meet."

"Harvey Rochester, may I present Jolene Fairchild, Miss Fifi Roux and Penelope Overjoy," Pearl graciously introduced.

One by one, Harvey kissed each of the girls' hands. Instantly he felt an attraction to Penelope. "Penelope? I do not believe I have ever met anyone by that name."

"That's my good girl name," Penelope whispered, raising her eyebrow and wearing a mischievous smile. "My other name is Jezebel."

In that moment, Harvey knew he had found his new playmate. Harvey was a one-woman man, and now that Lucy had gone back to Houston with Redbird, he was anxious to fill the void.

"How do you feel about costumes, Penelope?" Harvey asked with delight. "Something like a bright, red dress with a cape and little black horns ..."

"Sounds delightful," Penelope answered. "I bet you would look great in a pair of angel wings and..."

"Pearl, I believe Penelope and I are going to be great friends," Harvey smiled. "By the way, I brought extra gifts just in case I might have the opportunity to be introduced to any new members of our family here at Pearl's. Here you are, dear ladies." Harvey handed Penelope, Jolene and Fifi a white box with a red ribbon. Each box contained a lovely brocaded wrap with a fur trim.

"Thank you Harvey," Jolene graced with tearful eyes. "I have never had a lovelier gift."

"You are welcome, Jolene. It looks spectacular with your red hair, my dear."

Harvey smiled from ear to ear as Penelope gave him a sweet kiss on the cheek.

"Merci beaucoup, Monsieur Harvey," Fifi curtsied.

"Ah, vous êtes les bienvenus, Madame Fifi," Harvey bowed.

"Parlez-vous francais?" Fifi asked.

"J'ai besoin de pratiquer," Harvey replied. "Je vais certainement aller Paris."

"What in the world are y'all talking about?" Maggie asked, as she came to kiss Harvey on the cheek.

"Looks like Fifi is going to be my new French teacher. Oh, how I love my Lady Pearls," Harvey expressed.

Just then Mozella walked into the room. "I knew I heard the voice of the sweetest man know."

"Mozella!" Harvey cheered. "This is for you."

Mozella opened a large round box and pulled out a wide brimmed purple hat decorated with flowers and wispy feathers.

"*Corinthians 9: For God loves a cheerful giver,*" she bellowed. After Harvey placed the new hat on her head with precision, he took Mozella's arm and walked her to a large mirror hanging in the hall.

"You look exquisite, my dear," Harvey praised.

"I hope you are hungry, Mister Harvey. I have made up a mess of my famous..."

"Fried chicken?" Harvey guessed. "I love your fried chicken, Mozella."

As everyone took their place at the lunch table, Pearl invited Harvey to sit in her seat, positioned at the head of the table. Seeing he was fond of Penelope, Pearl told her to sit in the chair to his right.

Harvey turned to Annabelle who was sitting on his left. "I brought a new dress and baby doll for little Julie Marie. I believe I missed her birthday. It's hard to believe she is turning five."

"Thank you, Harvey. Julie Marie is in Christoval with my mother. I think I am going to open a grocery and supplies store there. I have saved quite a bit of money and..."

"That is a lovely idea, Annabelle," Harvey exclaimed. "Let's be partners. I will help you get started. Let's go to Christoval this week. I really would like to give Julie Marie the doll myself."

"Julie Marie would probably love to take a ride in that new car of yours," Pearl declared. "It's funny how life works. Annabelle met her husband, Billy, while he was working for his uncle in a grocery store."

"Julie Marie looks more like her daddy every day," Annabelle sighed. "Billy was the love of my life and I know I will never marry again."

"I know how you feel, Annabelle. Sometimes I wish I could spend just one more day with my Robert," Pearl smiled warmly. "God, I miss him. He had such a great laugh. For now I just have to settle for seeing him in my dreams."

Harvey reached over and warmly patted Pearl's hand.

"Let's say grace," Mozella announced. They all bowed their heads. "Heavenly Father, thank you for your many blessings. Watch and protect our Lady Pearls and we especially thank you for our friend Harvey. Thank you for the food for the nourishment of our bodies, in God's good grace, Amen."

"Tell us about New York, Harvey," Heather asked. "Did you go to the theatre?"

"Did I go to the theatre? Honey, I performed on stage," Harvey announced. "In fact I brought a photo."

"No way," Heather exclaimed. "Is that you, Harvey?"

"It depends on what you mean. You are looking at a photo of Harriet the Drag Queen."

"You have been holding out on us, Harvey. My goodness you look absolutely stunning," Ginger complimented.

"It's my secret life, Ginger."

"Ahh, so this is why you like New York," Heather hailed.

"I've been going for years and have many friends in the theatre. Thank goodness fashions have changed. Now that dresses are straight lined, a person no longer needs to have boobs and a small waist to look good. On this last trip my friends talked me into singing, and I made my vaudeville debut at a theatre on 42nd Street."

"I didn't know you like to sing," Harmony commented.

"My goodness, I was shaking like a puppy in a rainstorm. Then as soon as the music started a calm feeling came over me. Just like magic, I transformed into Harriet the singer and stayed in a state of suspended animation throughout the whole song. It was me, but then again, it was not me. Oh, and the applause! The beautiful, grand applause… like nothing I have ever known."

Tears began filling Harvey's eyes. "Approval is something I have never experienced with my own family, and they are the ones who are supposed to love me. These were perfect strangers. It was all so wonderful."

The table went silent as Harvey continued.

"I cannot help what I am. You ladies are my real family. Here I can be myself with no fear or judgment, only love."

Harvey began weeping and Pearl gently touched his arm. After a minute, Harvey produced a handkerchief and wiped his eyes.

"I know my Mother knew, but she never said anything. Our relationship was quite formal. She always seemed so emotionally detached," Harvey remembered.

"At least she didn't sell you to a house full of strangers," Ginger winced with painful bitterness.

"That must have been horrible for you Ginger," Harvey sympathized. "My father never showed my mother any affection. Always smoking those smelly cigars, drinking whiskey and chasing women. The man went to his grave never knowing that his only son preferred… preferred…"

Harvey began chuckling, quietly at first, and then his laughter became so strong, the handkerchief he was holding was used for tears of amusement.

"Oh my goodness. HA, HA, HA! In my crazy world of imagination I just saw a vision of my father rolling over in his grave. Oh well. I guess he knows now," Harvey bellowed. "Sorry, Father! Surprise, Surprise, SURPRISE!"

With that, the entire table exploded into laughter. Mozella's laugh was the loudest.

"I remember that first day he took me to Miss Hattie's. That's the day I met my Sugar. What a sweetheart she was. She told me to yell, 'yeah baby,' while she jumped up and down on that squeaky old bed. My father was sitting in the parlor, smoking one of his stinky cigars. He could hear everything. I'll always love Sugar for that." Harvey smiled.

"Sugar was yellin' 'ride 'em cowboy' at the top of her lungs. Then she told me to moan like I just hurt myself, as loud as I could. We were making quite a racket! Daddy was satisfied thinking I was a mighty stud and Sugar became my best friend.

"She never told a soul. That's how I got the reputation in town of being a treetop lover. I will tell you this, ladies. There is more integrity in a place like this than any other place I have done business. You at least are always honest."

"Silence is golden and every one of our clients knows it," Pearl bragged. "The Everleigh sisters ran their business the same way. I remember one particular afternoon when a wealthy client had a messenger deliver a $2000 payment to take care of his festivities the night before. Because the sisters did not recognize the man delivering the money, Ada refused the payment and denied knowing the client at all."

Harvey decided to get back to Heather's question. "Oh Ladies, the theatre is grand. Vaudeville, Burlesque, Broadway, the Ziegfeld Follies, and the George White Scandals are all spectacular. Dinner at '21', speakeasies, women dressed to the nines… I am telling you, it is virtually impossible to describe the excitement of New York City."

"I have never been," Pearl declared. "Minna and Ada live there now. I would love to see them again. My friend Madeline has invited me to visit her in New York. The Santa Rita Number One has turned out to be a great success for all of us, including Mozella."

"I have been talking to an oil company who wants to drill on one of our ranches," Harvey informed.

"Pearl's Parlor is doing exceptionally well, and we have learned much in the past few months from the oil men who visit the parlor," Pearl commented.

"I loved Madeline and her sister, Elizabeth," Harmony said. "Such fine ladies. It was a pleasure having them here."

"Don't forget crazy Aunt Rosey," Heather laughed.

"Remember the night she taught us how to do the Charleston?" Maggie expressed. "They were such fun."

"I was impressed with Elizabeth's psychic gift. It was so strange when said Billy was with me," Annabelle remembered. "At first I didn't believe her. Everyone here knows Billy was killed in the war. Then she mentioned that funny dance he did for me on our honeymoon. He was completely naked. How could she know? Do you think she could see him naked?" she chuckled.

"She saw my sweet David. How did she know *The Yellow Rose of Texas* was his favorite song? Damn war," Harmony grimaced.

"Elizabeth told me I was in danger," Heather shuddered. "Never in my wildest dreams did I ever think Tony would find me here."

"Tony's gone, Heather. Gone forever," Katie said. "You never have to worry about him anymore."

"That's the truth," Ginger affirmed.

"Tell us more about the theatre, Harvey," Heather asked.

"Now that I have told you about my secret life as Harriet, I feel free. In the theatre you can be anything you want to be. Men can be women, women can be men… the theatre is a glorious existence, a virtual reality. I have many friends in the theatre and they have welcomed me with open arms."

"I have never thought about the theatre in those terms," Heather expressed. "I only know I love it."

"One of the most fascinating acts I ever saw was Bert Savoy and Jay Brennan. Bert was big and muscular, whereas Jay was slender and more effeminate. Dressed as a woman, showing off an hourglass figure, Bert would glide across the stage always wearing some kind of outrageous hat. Jay usually wore a modest suit and straw hat. They were a huge hit in New York City. Audiences absolutely adored them. Several years ago I saw them perform in the Ziegfeld Follies with Eddie Cantor, W.C. Fields and Will Rogers. It was spectacular! Last year, I saw them perform in the Greenwich Village Follies."

"They say opposites attract," Heather commented. "It's probably what made their act work."

"Exactly," Harvey agreed. "Bert played a dominant strongwoman and flirted incessantly with the audience. Jay was more timid. I believe Bert was one of the funniest actors I have ever seen on stage."

"You say was? Did something happen?" Maggie asked.

"Last summer the most incredibly bizarre thing happened. Jay went to a resort in Indiana for vacation, and while he was gone, Bert and a friend went to Long Beach in Long Island. It is a fabulous place and a lot of vaudevillians like to go there.

"Anyway, Bert and three of his friends were walking along the water's edge when their perfect bright blue sky transformed into a thunderous dark rainstorm. Bert was obviously disappointed with the thunder, lightning and rain. His friends saw him put his hand on his hip, look up into the darkness of the clouds and scream, 'That will be enough out of you, Miss God!' The words were barely out of his mouth when a bolt of lightning crashed down, killing him and his friend, who was standing next to him, on the spot. All of Vaudeville is still grieving."

"Whoa!" Maggie commented. "Miss God? Whoa!"

"Guess you just never know," Harvey said. "When it's your time, it's your time."

"The older I get, the more I realize just how true that is, Harvey," Pearl commented.

Mozella entered the dining room with a pitcher of tea. *"Ecclesiastes 3: To everything there is a season, and a time to every purpose under heaven. A time to be born and a time to die."*

"Mozella, you are a treasure. Thank you for a delicious meal," Harvey declared with sincere sentiment. "I cherish every single minute I spend with all of you,"

"The feeling is quite mutual, Harvey," Pearl complimented.

"Have you heard from Redbird and Lucy? How is little Betsy? Any word?" Harvey inquired.

"Redbird and Lucy have moved into Redbird's family mansion in Houston. She pulled her little brothers out of boarding school and they are a family again," Pearl informed.

"That's wonderful news. I must go see them. I promised I would help redecorate the mansion. Now that Redbird's hateful Aunt Gertrude is gone, we need to make it all brand new. Kind of ironic she choked on a chicken bone. She had no right to kick Redbird and her brothers out of their home. God really does work in mysterious ways," Harvey said.

"Lucy stole her family's housekeeper away from her mean Mama," Sarah added. "One time Redbird told me, 'If it wasn't for Mary, Lucy's mother would have thrown her out with the bath water.' Mary is working for Redbird now."

"I don't expect to hear from Betsy," Pearl sighed. "When she left with Johnny Wayne, I told her to move forward and never look back. That young man has loved Betsy since they were in the second grade. Only a real man would find the woman he loved at an establishment like ours and bring her home. Johnny Wayne's love is unconditional. Poor little Betsy was so afraid her family would be ashamed. I know Johnny Wayne will keep her secret. I am very happy for her."

"Just like a fairy tale," Maggie sighed.

Harvey reached for Penelope's hand. "How about you and I take a little stroll down the river after lunch? I believe I would like to get to know you better."

"You can call me Jezebel," Penelope smiled coyly.

"I bet you look fabulous in red, my dear," Harvey flirted.

It was dusk when Harvey finally drove away in his shiny, new Rolls-Royce Silver Ghost. As always, it had been a wonderful visit, and Harvey was more than delighted that he had found his new playmate that day at Miss Pearl's Parlor.

CHAPTER 4

# Christmas 1923

Christmas at Pearl's Parlor was always a joyous occasion. Although she had come to love the new girls, Victoria often thought about the ones who had left and was elated when she received their letters.

*December 1, 1923*
*Dear Miss Pearl,*
*I hardly know where to begin. Two weeks after we returned to Kentucky, Johnny Wayne and I were married. The way he saw it, we have been engaged since that day he made me a grass ring and carved our names in the big oak tree when I was ten years old. It's still there!*
*Johnny Wayne built us a nice house and I have enjoyed fixing it up and making it our home. No one knows anything about my time away from the farm. Going to Europe, running away with a gambler and living at Miss Pearl's Parlor all seemed like a dream now. I often wonder what would have happened if Ginger had not found me sobbing like a baby at the train station.*
*I have no regrets. One thing is for sure, I will never again wonder if I am missing out on what the world has to offer. When I first came home people kept asking where I had been for the last two years. Johnny Wayne told them to mind their own business. Mama and Daddy never asked. They are just happy I am home again.*
*Johnny Wayne and I are expecting a baby in the fall. If it is a girl, I will name her Ginger Ann. If it's a boy he will be Johnny Wayne Jr. I am not showing too much, but the first few weeks I was sick as a dog in the mornings. I remember the day I left. It was Redbird's birthday and Emma Grace showed up to the party sick. Now I know how she felt.*
*You made all the difference in my life, Miss Pearl, and I am so very grateful for knowing you. I miss Mozella's cooking and the way she always quoted those Bible verses. It seems so strange to be back in Kentucky. Nothing here has changed but I sure have. I am happy, Miss Pearl. I am really happy. Thank you for telling me to write the letter to my family. Kentucky is where my heart is. Please tell everyone hello and that I am doing fine.*
*I miss and love you all!*
*Betsy*

*December 10, 1923*
*Dear Miss Pearl,*
*I hope this letter finds you well. Returning to Houston has been bittersweet. On a good note, it has been wonderful being with my brothers again. Anthony and Alexander have grown so much since the last time I saw them. Unfortunately the separation has left emotional scars that I am hopeful will heal in time. The spark is gone from their eyes. This makes me sad, and angry, at both my mother for deserting us and hateful Aunt Gertrude for forcing us out of our home.*
*Lucy can make anyone laugh. I do not know what I would do without her. Mary left the Armstrong house the day Lucy called. She just packed her things and told Lucy's mother, "goodbye." She lives with us now and takes care of the house. Harvey is coming in a few weeks to help us redecorate. This will help us get rid of the past and begin a fresh new start.*
*Business in Houston is booming and our company has invested in oil exploration. We are doing quite well. My uncle is a master at making money. He is teaching me the family business. As you may know, my brothers and I own half.*
*I am taking Alexander and Anthony to California for Christmas. Lucy and Mary are coming as well. We are going to the Hotel del Coronado in San Diego for two weeks. A lot of celebrities stay there as well. Maybe I will meet one.*
*I want you to know I will always be grateful to you for taking me in when I had nowhere to go. I have learned so much from my experiences at Miss Pearl's. Thanks to you, I have a good understanding of how men think. This will serve me well as I pursue my business ventures.*
*Lucy sends her love and says to tell Mozella we will miss her warm, homemade wine this Christmas. Give our love to the girls.*
*Lovingly,*
*Redbird*

The week before Christmas, Pearl gave the children at the orphanage a Christmas party. Santa Claus showed up and the children were thrilled. Sarah's Aunt Katherine was bursting with excitement as she shared her good news with Pearl.

"I spoke to him!"

"Spoke to who?" Pearl asked.

"I spoke to Joshua, my son! I saw him at the pharmacy. He told me he was buying medicine for his mother. Apparently she is pretty sick. I know his father passed away not too long ago," Katherine sympathized.

Pearl hugged her friend. "You have a son? That's wonderful."

Once a week, Pearl and Sarah's Aunt Katherine met at the orphanage to read and play games with the children who lived there. Katherine always brought a bag full of candy and Pearl brought books to read and money for supplies.

"My heart was beating so hard I thought it might jump right out of my chest. It was the first time I had spoken to him since that day I said goodbye. Those three wonderful weeks I had holding my baby and feeding him from my breast, were the most satisfying experience I ever had as a woman. How I loved him…I still do, more than ever. I was so young, Pearl.

"After I left my baby, I cried for weeks. When I was seven months pregnant, I went to church and prayed to God to give me a sign what to do. I knew I couldn't take care of him. God was already answering my prayer. The woman sitting next to me asked me when my baby was due. She was real nice. Then she told me she and her husband were not able to have children. I took it as a sign. Giving that nice couple my baby just seemed like the right thing to do," Katherine winced.

"It was a loving gesture, dear. I know it must be hard."

Katherine wiped the tears away. "It turned out all right. I was so happy when they adopted him. I watched him grow up but I've never spoken to him…that is until today. I even said hello to my little grandson. Looks just like his daddy. His name is Joshua too. His daddy calls him Josh. You should see him…three years old now…he's so cute. "

"How did you manage to talk to them?"

"We were both waiting for prescriptions."

"Sounds like God put you there for a reason," Pearl smiled.

"What do you mean?" Katherine asked.

"Think about it. If the woman he knows as his mother passes, maybe it will be a good time for him to know about you."

"Oh God…I don't know."

"Do you know where he lives?"

"He lives in the same big house where I left him 25 years ago. I believe he moved in with his mother after his wife died."

"Oh dear, what happened?"

"She died when little Josh was born. I'm not sure why."

"That is sad," Pearl commented.

"I wonder if he knows he's adopted or that I left him on the doorstep in a basket. I left a note. It said, HIS NAME IS JOSHUA. I didn't want to take him to the orphanage like other girls do. I wanted him to have a good life."

"At least you didn't get an abortion."

"My father was the meanest man that ever lived. He did horrible things to me and my sister. I ran away from home and ended up in San Angelo, working for Miss Hattie. It was much better than living in that crazy house. Always felt bad about leaving my little sister behind. He kicked my sister Bethy out when he learned she was pregnant with Sarah. It's a miracle he didn't kill her. I swear he was insane."

"Sarah told me about him shooting her boyfriend. She said your father aimed his gun at her and Michael jumped in front of it. Poor kid… She still has nightmares."

"I'm glad she is with you at the parlor."

"We all love Sarah. I see her sadness every day."

Katherine decided to change the subject. "Let's go see the children. I brought a big sack of lollipops and Hershey bars."

When Pearl returned to the parlor, she was delighted to see the girls decorating the Christmas tree. Harmony was playing traditional Christmas carols on the piano, and everyone was enjoying cookies and a cup of Mozella's spicy, warm, homemade wine.

"Your molasses cookies are just like my Granny's, Mozella," Maggie said. "Yummy."

"Glad to see everyone is getting in the spirit for the Christmas Party tomorrow night," Pearl expressed. "The cowboys are coming next Friday. We will celebrate Christmas with them then."

"We sure love our cowboys," Maggie exclaimed.

Oui," Fifi agreed. "Joe Bob should be in the sexy Olympics. Ooo la la! He is much fun."

"I like the cowboys," Penelope chimed. "All of them acted like perfect gentlemen when they were here."

"They better act like gentlemen. There are no second chances with Miss Pearl, and they know it," Katie said.

"Katie, you are my hero," Jolene declared. "This is all so new to me. I feel like I have a family."

"You're going to be all right, Jolene," Katie said. "No one's gonna hurt you on my watch."

The Christmas party was a huge success. The girls looked lovely in their fancy evening gowns and they all received lovely gifts from their favorite clients. Some of the men gave Pearl an extra bonus.

"You know how to do it right, Miss Pearl," one gentleman said, as he handed her a check for $5000.

Graciously, Pearl accepted the money and smiled. "Thank you Smitty. It is nice to be appreciated."

The next week, Katherine showed up at Miss Pearl's with the morning newspaper in her hand.

"She died," Katherine said as she pointed to the obituaries. "This is her, Pearl, the woman who raised my Joshua."

"Oh my word," Pearl expressed. "What are you going to do?"

"What's going on?" Sarah asked, seeing her Aunt Katherine talking to Pearl in the Great Room.

"I don't know what to do, Sarah. Remember I told you about leaving my baby with those nice people who couldn't have children?" Katherine reminded her."

"Yes. You told me you threw rocks at their door."

"That's right. This is the woman," Katherine said, pointing at the newspaper. "Her husband died last year."

"Oh my goodness, Aunt Katherine. Are you going to tell him you are his mother?" Sarah asked.

"I am terrified, Sarah. I don't even know who his daddy is. What would I say? Oh, Lord have mercy. I never thought about ever telling him. I don't know…I don't know," Katherine said, clearly distressed.

"If I might make a suggestion," Pearl said. "I remember when Betsy was so distraught about missing her family. I told her to write a letter. You can do the same. Write Joshua a letter and tell him your story. Be honest with your feelings; leave the rest to him. Do it with love in your heart. If you do not at least try, you will never know."

"I can do that," Katherine said with some hesitation.

"Let's go in the library and do it now," Pearl suggested before Katherine could change her mind.

*December 18, 1923*
*Dear Joshua,*
*I am sorry about your mother passing. She was a good woman and I know you loved her very much. I realize it is hard to lose someone we love, especially at Christmas. I would like to tell you a story.*
*Once upon a time there was a very young girl who had a beautiful baby boy. For three memorable weeks, the girl nursed him, danced with him and sang songs and lullabies to him. Every moment she held her baby was precious, because she knew she could not keep him.*
*The girl was alone and had no money and no family. She knew she would not be able to care for her baby but refused to take him to the orphanage in town.*
*A few weeks before her baby was born, the young girl went to a church to ask God what to do. As it happened, the woman sitting next to her asked when her baby was due. "That's wonderful," she said. "We have not been blessed with a baby in our marriage." The young girl knew that God had intervened. It was the answer to her prayers.*

*The next week, the young girl returned to the church and very cleverly, learned where the couple lived. One evening she wrapped her baby in a blanket and gently placed him in a big basket. She went to their home and could see the couple was inside enjoying a warm fire. The young girl hid behind a bush and threw small stones at the door. The man saw the baby sleeping peacefully in the basket and brought him inside. The couple adopted the baby and raised him as their own.*

*The young girl never stopped loving her baby and watched him grow into a fine young man from afar. She saw him play in the park and went to his high school graduation. Most Sundays she went to that same church, just to see the family who adopted her baby walk in.*

*For 25 years his mother's arms have ached to hold her baby again. Every day she prays for his happiness and wellbeing.*

*If this letter makes no sense to you, please disregard.*

*However, if you wish to respond, light a candle and put it in your window on Christmas Eve.*

*Merry Christmas,*

*A Friend*

"I don't know, Pearl," Katherine said.

"It will go one of three ways. If they never told Joshua he was adopted, the letter will make no sense. If they did tell him, he will either want to see you or not. If you do nothing, it will all remain the same. It takes courage, Katherine. I believe it was not just some random coincidence you spoke to him at the pharmacy," Pearl said. "That is the way God works. Now let us put a stamp on it."

The next few days were full of Christmas festivities and celebration. On December 22nd Mozella prepared a beautiful Christmas dinner for the ladies at the parlor. There was turkey, ham, mashed potatoes, greens, carrots, hot fresh bread and apple pies for dessert.

"I have never celebrated Christmas before," Jolene expressed. "Mama was usually drunk through the holidays and slept most of the time.

I remember one of her boyfriends gave me a doll once, but she threw it away when he left."

"Dang, Jolene," Maggie said. "You really have had it rough."

Tears filled Jolene's eyes. "I'm just so very thankful I am here with all of you now. Merry Christmas, everyone."

"Merry Christmas," the ladies repeated in unison.

"I will be leaving for the ranch in the morning, ladies. The boys are home for Christmas and will be disappointed if Santa does not put something in their stockings."

"How old are those boys?" Mozella asked.

"It does not matter, Mozella," Pearl grinned. "Santa has always brought David and Michael something for their stocking."

Christmas Eve was magical. Happy Harvey brought gifts for everyone; the girls exchanged presents and Mozella read the Christmas story from the Bible. Ginger made warm toddies and everyone sang Christmas carols well into the night.

That evening at the Five Star Ranch, Maria Rosa and Angela had prepared a lovely dinner to celebrate Noche Buena in their Mexican family tradition. Everyone on the ranch gathered together in the big house as they did every year. Victoria kept thinking about Robert and how proud he would be of their two boys. "They are so much like their father," Victoria thought, as she watched Michael and David talk about college and how big the dome was at the state capital building in Austin.

"It is even bigger than the one in Washington D.C," Michael bragged. "I like going in there. Maybe I can be a Senator one day."

"I am not sure about that, dear. You might be too honest to be a politician," Pearl teased.

That Christmas Eve Katherine's prayers were finally being answered. From the street she could see a dozen lighted candles blazing in the front window of Joshua's home. Katherine had spent hours getting ready. Wearing a lovely, cream-colored dress and fur lined cape, she slowly walked up to the porch, where she laid down a large bag full of presents. As she rang the doorbell, Katherine's knees began shaking uncontrollably.

When the door opened, she could see Little Josh playing with a train set by the Christmas tree in the front room. His father greeted her with a warm smile. "Hello, Joshua," Katherine managed to say.

"Please come in," Joshua invited, taking her bag.

"Thank you," Katherine replied.

"Let me take your wrap. Josh… come say hello."

With outstretched arms, Little Josh ran over to his grandmother and gave her a big hug. It seemed as if he instinctively knew exactly who she was. Katherine's heart was full and she felt a warm rush fill her body.

"Are you my other grandmother?" he asked.

Katherine looked at Joshua, who nodded in response.

"Yes, honey, I am," Katherine replied in an effort to conceal the lump in her throat.

"Your letter came as a surprise," Joshua said. "I liked your story. I have heard a similar story all of my life. However, I believe you left out one important detail."

From the side table, Joshua produced an envelope. Inside was a piece of paper that had yellowed with age. The edges were frayed from being handled so much. On it, in Katherine's handwriting, were the words, HIS NAME IS JOSHUA.

As Katherine stared at the paper, warm tears trickled down her cheeks, remembering the night she gave her baby away.

"Merry Christmas, Mother."

CHAPTER 5

# Ella May Comstock

"She's back," Mozella announced.

Pearl was in the barn brushing her mare, Bluebonnet, after taking her for a morning ride down the river.

"Who's back?" Pearl asked with curiosity.

"Miss Ella May Comstock. *Philippians 2: 'Do not merely look out for your own personal interests, but also for the interests of others.'*"

Miss Pearl smiled a curious grin, "Well then, Mozella, let us see what in the world is on that dear lady's mind."

This was not the first visit Miss Ella May Comstock had made to Pearl's Parlor. A few months prior, Ella May had come to Miss Pearl requesting she educate her husband Henry on what she referred to as, the magic love button.

Ella May had informed Pearl that her sister's husband Jimmy had learned about the magic love button from a sporting woman in La Grange, Texas. Dora May told Ella May that when Jimmy found her magic love button she shivered, shook and burst into a howling frenzy. Ella May confessed to her sister that she had never experienced such things before. Therefore, she commissioned Miss Pearl to give her Henry an education on how to find the magic love button and had paid her with one dollar to do it.

As Pearl and Mozella walked into the great room of the mansion, they heard a strange yet familiar sound coming from inside the library.

"Mmm ahh! Mmm Ahh! Mmm AHHH!"

Pearl and Mozella stood at the doorway, watching sweet little Ella May in ecstasy, sniffing the Italian leather journal that usually sat on Miss Pearl's dark brown, mahogany writing table.

"Good morning, Ella May. So nice to see you again," Pearl graciously announced.

"Oh, Miss Pearl, I just have to get one of these Italian journals. I do so love the smell of good leather."

Ella Mae took one more, deep snort, "Ahhhhhhh!" Ceremoniously, she closed her eyes, held the book to her bosom, and then gently laid it down in its proper place.

There was something endearing about this little woman. Barely 5 feet tall, Ella May's carefully pressed, periwinkle dress had a crisp white collar and white buttons down the front. Her hair was short, dark and curly and she held in her dainty-white gloved hands a small cinched bag, clutched in front of her.

Ella May whispered, "Can we have a private conversation, please? This is top secret!"

These were the same words she had spoken on their last visit.

"We can do that," Pearl smiled. "Kindly leave us Mozella, and please shut the doors."

*"Proverbs 25: It is the glory of God to conceal things, but the glory of kings is to search things out,"* Mozella said, winking at Pearl.

Ella May pulled a carefully folded dollar bill out of her bag. "Miss Pearl, I have saved one dollar. This is for you. As you recall, it was the amount we exchanged the last time I was here."

"Thank you, Ella May. Now how can I help you?"

"First I want to thank you for giving my Henry an education on the magic love button. Ever since that day you spoke to my sweet husband at the river, our sexual experience has improved. When Henry finds my magic button, I go to shakin'! Then a quiverin'! Goose bumps all over my body! Then my breathing changes just like this."

Ella May started breathing long breaths and moaning "ahhs" that gradually grew in intensity. Stifling her laughter, Pearl watched as Ella May's breaths got shorter and shorter, while the "ahhs" got louder and louder. It was all she could do to keep a straight face.

"Then from the depths of my being, I make a big ol' loud sound just like a coyote on the Texas plains howlin' at the full moon above just like this! Ahhhhhhhhhhhh OOOOOOOOOO! Ahhhhhhhhhhhh OOOOOOOOOOO!"

"I am very pleased to hear that, my dear. It sounds like Henry paid attention to my suggestions. A very good student indeed."

"Yes, Ma'am. For weeks I kept pullin' him into the bedroom, two, sometimes three times a day. I think I was wearing him out. It got to where I believe he was hidin' from me when he saw me comin'. All those things you taught him… I just never knew I could feel like that. I especially liked that you told him it takes seventeen minutes to awaken the goddess. He watches the clock and never once has he ever stopped kissing my lips, my nippys or my tummy or tending to my magic love button until seventeen minutes have passed. Then when we connect, it is heaven, Miss Pearl,

ABSOLUTE HEAVEN. We owe it all to you and for your great wisdom, I am forever grateful."

"Your Henry is a special man, Ella May. You are a lucky woman to have a man who cares about you so much."

"Miss Pearl, I've been thinkin' that maybe I could use an education. I love my Henry so much and I want to make him happy. It just doesn't seem fair that I get all the attention. I was wonderin' if maybe you could teach me what you know."

"My dear Ella May. You really are a delight," Pearl smiled.

"Just a minute." Ella May reached into her bag again and pulled out a notepad and pencil. "Ok, Miss Pearl. I am ready."

"Many years ago, when I lived in Chicago, I met a woman who taught me what you are asking me to teach you."

"Chicago? Are you a Yankee, Miss Pearl?"

"Would that be a bad thing? I have been in Texas now longer than I lived in Illinois. I met a cowboy who brought me to his ranch and made me his bride. I love Texas and my twin boys were born in Texas."

"Oh my. I had no idea, Miss Pearl."

"My boys are in college, Ella May. This is the business I know and I like working."

"What about your husband, if I might ask?"

"He died from the Spanish flu 5 years ago, dear."

"I'm so sorry, Miss Pearl. I didn't mean to pry."

"It was a beautiful love story, Ella May. It's still not over. I will love Robert until the day I die." Pearl's eyes welled up with tears.

"Dang, sometimes it seems the only time I open my mouth is so I can change feet. I can really stick my foot in it. I didn't mean…"

"No, no, Ella May. Please do not feel bad. I will tell you what my friend Madeline told me. When I started in this business, I had only been with one man. He proposed to me and, when I said 'yes', he took my virginity that very same night. When he learned I was with child, he left town. I lost the baby. No longer a virgin, I felt soiled and used. Then as fate would have it, I met the Everleigh sisters and Mozella. My parents were both gone, so they became my family. "

"That is sad. I am sorry for you, Miss Pearl."

"Life always seems to work itself out. I am grateful that I have known real love in my lifetime. Let us now talk about your Henry."

"Yes Ma'am," Ella May exclaimed, raising her pencil in the air.

"Your Henry's male part is like a larger version of a woman's magic love button. It is a glorious sight to behold when it is firm and strong."

"Oh no, Miss Pearl... I mean, I like the way it feels but I really don't look at it too much. It's kind of embarrassing."

"My friend Madeline told me it is all a matter of perspective. When you look at a man's erection as the bearer of the seed, the staff of life, the rod of creation, it can actually look magnificent and even glorious. Most men are extremely proud of their prize possession and some will even give it a name!"

"My husband calls his Little Henry. Sometimes he'll say 'Little Henry is lookin' for some lovin',"" Ella May giggled.

"I knew a man in Chicago who called his The Gladiator and another man called his Ivan the Great."

Ella May threw her head back and laughed, "Wah hah ha ha, Wah Ha Ha Ha, WAH HA HA HA!!"

"Sex comes in all different forms, my dear Ella May. It can be passionate, playful, silly, creative, spiritual and, above all, the most wonderful way to communicate love between a man and a woman. In that way, I believe sex is a gift from God."

"I never thought of sex like that, Miss Pearl. Putting sex and God in the same sentence sounds kind of strange," Ella May expressed.

"Making love to your Henry can be a beautiful experience. Men love it when they know they are wanted. Come to him wearing only a gown or a robe with one shoulder exposed. With a lighted candle in your hand, tell him you would like him to draw you a bath. If the tub is big enough, invite him to join you. Slowly and sensuously wash each other. Let the conversation focus on love. Do not talk about anything else than the fact you adore each other. Conversations about broken farm equipment or the new quilt you are making can wait."

Ella May was enthusiastically writing on her pad. She was completely captivated with the subject at hand.

"Smile at Henry, and tell him it's time for bed. Dry him off slowly. Remember the slower you move, the more sensuous the experience. Hold his hand as you lead him to the bed."

"Miss Pearl, I don't mean to interrupt, but I don't ever have to get Little Henry ready for anything. I'm the one who needs preparation and thanks to you, Henry is very good at that. When my husband's got lovin' on his mind, Little Henry is ALWAYS ready. Some mornings all I have to do is bend over and take biscuits out of the oven and there's Little Henry ready to go!"

"Spontaneity can be fun, Ella May. Robert and I experienced that many times. What I am describing is a sensuous kind of ritual where the two of you can use the sexual act to express your love. It is what I like to call the sacred dance," Pearl gleamed.

"I knew you could help me," Ella May smiled.

"Invite Henry to sit across from you on the bed. Gently take his hand, and as you put it over your heart, look deep into his eyes and put your other hand over his chest. Sometimes Robert and I would exchange breath. He would inhale as I exhaled, making our breath as one."

"This is very beautiful, Miss Pearl."

"Love expressed can be sensuous and wonderful, Ella May. What I am sharing with you today does not usually happen here at the Parlor. The eyes are the mirrors to the soul. Connecting as one before the act begins is a soulful experience that can only happen when the couple has an emotional bond. Feeling the pulse of each other's heart, sharing the same breath and looking for your reflection in his eyes are lovely preludes to the sexual dance."

Victoria Pearl's eyes were bright as she basked in the memory of making love with her Robert. Up until now it had been an intimate secret between two lovers. Knowing how much the Comstocks loved each other, she found herself happy to pass their experience on.

"I will share a couple of tricks of the trade that can make your love making playful, if you'd like."

"Yes, yes, please do," Ella May expressed eagerly.

"One of our girl's is known as, 'Heather with her feather.' Do you have a plume?"

"As a matter of fact I do."

"Then use it, my dear. Very lightly stroke different parts of Henry's body. He will probably want to do the same for you."

"It sounds delightful," Ella May commented as she wrote in her notebook.

"Tasty condiments can be fun. For instance chocolate syrup on your nippys…"

"Jam! My homemade strawberry… peach…Oh my goodness! Henry loves my orange marmalade!"

"Very good, Ella Mae. Now you are getting the idea."

"We could lay a blanket under the stars!"

"Yes, my dear. Yes."

"Oh, Miss Pearl. This is so exciting!"

"You know there is something you can do for your Henry on those womanly days that intercourse might not be appropriate."

"Oh, you mean during the monthly?"

"Did you know that we strongly discourage intercourse at Miss Pearl's Parlor? Our girls use creative techniques to accomplish their goal of producing a fountain of pleasure."

"Really?"

"When you go to bed, tell Henry you want to give him a present. You will need a towel and a bottle of lotion." Victoria picked up a piece of paper from her desk and rolled it into a long tube to demonstrate.

"Gently take Henry's sack in your hands and for several minutes, lightly stroke his manhood, and tell him it is the most gorgeous thing you have ever laid your eyes on. Then as it becomes firm, stroke the underside just below the head, very lightly with your fingers. Sometimes that's all our girls ever have to do, especially if it has been a while since the last time the gentleman had his pipes cleaned."

Ella May was surprised. "Really?"

"Yes really! You can skillfully use your hands with oil or lotions. Remember the longer he can sustain, the more powerful his orgasm. The more experience you have, the more you will know when to stroke it slowly, stop for a few seconds, and then stroke it a little more quickly, each time bringing him higher and higher into his ecstasy. Be playful and encouraging. What is most important is that you be sensuous. When his pleasure is fulfilled, gently wipe him clean."

Pearl watched as the young farmer's wife wrote in her notepad. When she finally finished, she looked up and, with the most radiant smile, Ella May announced, "Miss Pearl, I am going to have a baby,"

"Oh, Ella May…that is wonderful!"

"I haven't told Henry yet."

"So that is the glow I see all over your face. I knew there was something different about you. Congratulations, my dear. I am truly happy for both of you."

"My sister, Dora May is also pregnant. She told me she and Jimmy are still havin' marital bliss and she's seven months along. Our Mama told us a real gentleman does not bother a lady who is in the family way. That is one of the reasons I have not told Henry about our baby. It seems these days I want sex more than ever!"

"Robert and I made love the day before our twin boys were born. As my belly grew, we had to shift positions. Finally, the only way sex was even possible was when I got on my knees. I remember feeling so-not-sexy, but like you, I was full of desire. I remember how he kept telling me how beautiful I was. I felt like a cow. In fact, sometimes when I got on all fours I Mooooooooooed!"

Again, both women laughed hysterically.

"Miss Pearl. I don't know how I could ever thank you enough for this wonderful visit. I so want to make my Henry happy."

"You are very welcome, my dear. Savor every single day, every single hour and every single minute with your Henry, Ella May."

"Mama never talked to us about sex. It's nice to be able to talk openly to another woman about such things."

Pearl reached into her desk, pulled out a twenty-dollar bill and handed it to Ella May. "Please take this gift and buy something for your precious little one."

"I don't know what to say, Miss Pearl...thank you."

Mozella knocked at the door. "A gentleman is here for Miss Ella May, Miss Pearl."

The two women hugged and held on an extra few moments.

"Hello, Henry. It is nice to see you again," Pearl smiled.

"Good day, Miss Pearl," Henry grinned.

Pearl watched from the porch as the happy couple drove away. With a longing in her heart, she went to her room, picked up the photograph of Robert from her dresser, and sat on the bed. "I miss you, my love."

Victoria Pearl tenderly picked up a small, wooden music box she kept on the nightstand beside her. Robert surprised her with it when she was pregnant with the twins. Victoria wound the key, opened the lid and listened to the delicate tune that always warmed her heart. *Meet Me in Saint Louis, Louis, meet me at the fair*. Tearfully, Victoria remembered a glorious, star-filled night in 1904, when Robert McKnight asked her to be his bride. The view was spectacular at the top of the Ferris wheel at the Saint Louis Fair. To her it would always be the happiest, most memorable moment of her life.

## CHAPTER 6

# Springtime

It was the spring of 1924, twenty years since Robert McKnight had asked Victoria Pearl to be his bride. As the car entered the ranch, Victoria remembered how she felt the first day Robert had brought her there. Today, as she reflected on that special time, Victoria's memories were especially vivid.

Although part of her felt empty and sad, Victoria felt a sense of satisfaction thinking about what her life would have been without Robert McKnight. Shifting to thoughts of appreciation, Victoria realized how grateful she was that she had the privilege to experience true love in her lifetime.

Victoria thought of how so much had changed since that first day she entered the gate at the Five Star Ranch. For the first time in America's short history, young men were sent across the Atlantic to fight in The Great War. Automobiles had replaced carriages and it was illegal to buy champagne. Victoria's long, thick hair was now bobbed and curly, and the corset that bound her so tightly had been replaced with fashions that no longer required a waistline.

There were also things that had not changed. The ranch was a luscious green from recent rains and the oaks and tall pecan trees were full with leaves. Two spaniels waving their tails were there to greet Victoria with happy barks, just like Honey and Barkley did that first day she and Robert had driven the carriage through the gate. Angela, now in her 50s, walked out on the porch, smiling and waving her hand to welcome her.

Even though it had been five years since Robert died, it was still difficult to be at the ranch without him. Everywhere Victoria looked, she could see her cowboy laughing, riding his horse, playing with his boys and loving her. When Victoria's mother passed away, less than a year later, her father died of a broken heart. Victoria might have done the same if not for her loyal friend Mozella and the idea of opening Miss Pearl's Parlor.

Victoria was literally living a double life. After losing Robert, having a new business venture helped pull Victoria out of her deep depression. At first, she went to San Angelo a few days a month. Michael and David still needed their mother and she needed them. For this reason, Victoria had taken her time decorating the mansion and getting Miss Pearl's Parlor ready for business. Losing Robert made her more aware that time spent with loved ones should be appreciated and not taken for granted. Knowing it was only a few short years before they would go away to college, Victoria savored every precious moment she had with her sons.

Like her husband, Victoria considered the Mexican families that lived and worked for the McKnights loyal friends. They loved the twins and Michael and David loved them. Victoria knew the boys were well cared for when she was gone, and, for this, she was extremely grateful.

To Michael and David, the Five Star Ranch would always be home. As far as their father was concerned, his sons were as much a part of the land as the natural springs that flowed from the ground. The

McKnight family had homesteaded the Texas land five generations before. Robert often said, "one day this will all be theirs." It was the twins' birthright and, although the ranch reminded her of how much she missed her beloved husband, Victoria would always honor Robert's dream for their sons.

Now that Michael and David were in college, they were becoming more independent. Although they looked very much alike, they were different in many ways. Michael was aggressive and outgoing. He was extremely intelligent and a master at reading people, and Victoria was impressed with the way he handled the family business. Although Michael was always cautious, he could instantly put anyone at ease in a conversation. People liked him and this served him well when it came to negotiating sales.

David, on the other hand, was a man of few words. Since he was a small boy, he viewed the world with spiritual eyes, curious of everything around him. Victoria remembered a day when the twins were five. As the family enjoyed a picnic by the springs, Michael was describing the frogs and dragonflies hopping around the lily pads. David, with his inquisitive nature, was simply observing them. Always in a world of his own, David was the dreamer.

Spring was Victoria's favorite time of the year to be at the ranch. Lovely shades of green and soft pastels offered the land its annual promise of renewal and fresh beginnings. It was Wednesday afternoon. Victoria was expecting David and Michael to come on the weekend. After settling in, Victoria decided to walk the grounds and visit her memories. "Twenty years ago today, I was making arrangements to leave the Everleigh Club and move to Texas to be a June bride," she thought. "Robert and I were so happy."

Moving to Texas had been the happiest time of her life. As Victoria walked towards the bluff to the peacefulness of the natural springs, she thought about those last days in Chicago. The Everleigh sisters had given her a lovely going away party, complete with an Irish fiddler and bubbly champagne. Victoria remembered the tears when she said goodbye to Mozella, Minna and Ada Everleigh and her friend Madeline.

In those days, Victoria had been alive with anticipation and the excitement of being with Robert every day. She had never before known such a feeling of love and elation. It seemed like forever ago, and at the same time, it was as if it just happened yesterday.

The springs on the ranch were magical. Before Victoria had come to Texas, Robert had created a colorful, fragrant rose garden for his new bride. It was in the Rose Room, an exquisitely decorated chamber at the Everleigh Club, where Victoria and her cowboy spent their first time together. After that, everyone knew the Rose Room belonged to Victoria and Robert whenever he was in Chicago.

Victoria had made the rose garden Robert's final resting place and had arranged that when it was her time to leave this life, she was to lie beside him. Roses entwined together were etched in Robert's headstone.

Thinking of her days to come without Robert made her sad; remembering their days together filled her soul. Knowing she would see her sons in a few days brought it all together, making her feel content and fulfilled as a mother and a woman.

Victoria went to the springs at the Five Star Ranch and sat below the live oak, where dark green leaves cascading down created a comfortable cool shade. The fresh scent of roses seemed to be especially fragrant this day.

With her eyes closed, Victoria listened intently to the soft, gentle flow of water and the breeze dancing in the leaves. The sound of happy birds chirping created nature's soothing orchestrated melody making Victoria's spirit feel light.

Victoria allowed the memories of her loving days with Robert to fill her heart, mind and soul. For a long time, Victoria sat, relishing the peacefulness of the springs. For a moment, all was quiet and still.

Suddenly from a distance, Victoria could hear the galloping tread of a horse approaching her. She saw a man who looked like Robert riding towards her on a magnificent white stallion. As the rider came closer, Victoria gasped in amazement and her heart jumped with joy. It was Robert!

Handsome and virile as ever, Robert's smile was soft and loving. He was wearing a white cowboy hat and suit, an iridescent glow of light surrounded around him like a mystic halo around the moon. Dismounting his white steed, Robert came towards her.

"I thought I would find you here," he grinned.

"Robert?" Victoria asked. "Oh, Robert, my love. How I have missed you, my darling."

"I have never left you, Victoria. Our love is eternal and strong. I am always close."

"You look like you did that first night I met you."

"And you are beautiful as ever, Victoria."

"The roses are especially lush and fragrant this year, Robert. I love coming here. I am drawn to the enchantment of the springs. I believe it is truly heaven on earth."

"It is heaven, Victoria, because it is a place of beauty, peace and love. It is our magical place. We spent many happy times here, Victoria. I know you are drawn to the enchantment of the springs."

"Sometimes, I can feel you with me…"

"That is because I am with you, Victoria. Not just here. Whenever you think of me and your heart is full, I am with you."

Robert and Victoria were meshed in a glorious essence, where time does not exist, only the pure spiritual experience of two loving souls being together. Victoria could hear beautiful music and saw bright vibrant colors she had never before seen.

A glorious celestial waltz began to play, the same music that they danced to that first evening they met at the Everleigh Club. Blessed in a state of magical bliss, Victoria was dancing with her beloved Robert again."

"Is this real? Am I dreaming, Robert?"

Robert smiled at his bride. "Yes, my love. This is real. Heaven is everywhere when you look at the world with loving eyes. I love you, Victoria."

"I love you, Robert McKnight, with all my heart."

Robert held Victoria in his arms until the music stopped.

"It is raining, my love," he whispered. "Better go to the house."

Victoria awoke to the sound of gentle raindrops falling. Quickly she closed her eyes. If it was a dream, she did not want to wake up. Victoria had been blessed with a glimpse of heaven, where Robert was only a loving thought away.

From that day on, Victoria felt content knowing that Robert was with her every time her heart surged with love for him. She began to look at the ranch with different eyes. Instead of a giant graveyard, Victoria saw the Five Star Ranch as the land Robert loved, and the future home of generations to come.

After spending a glorious week with Michael and David, Victoria Pearl returned to her other life in San Angelo, Texas.

"Mozella, I had a dream at the springs," Victoria shared, as the two friends sipped their nightly cup of chamomile tea. "I saw Robert. We spoke to each other. It felt real… like nothing I have ever experienced before. Robert looked like the night I met him, so handsome, so strong..."

"That was not a dream, honey. That was a gift. Like it says in the Lord's Prayer, 'on earth as it is in heaven.' You can't really explain it, but then you don't have to."

"I feel different now, Mo. I am not sad like I was. I have my children and the best friend anyone could ever want. I have decided to spend the rest of my life counting my blessings while I am still here. I know I will be with Robert again."

"Your work is not finished, Victoria. You make a difference in people's lives, especially the girls at the parlor. Think of where each of them would be if not for you. The world is a place full of both the light and the darkness. You are the light in their darkness."

"I love the girls, Mo. I truly do want the best for them. So much has changed since that first day I met you. I am blessed and my life has been full."

"I loves you, Miss Pearl," Mozella smiled.

"And I loves you back, Mo!" Victoria laughed.

Gazing into the endless West Texas night, the two women finished their tea in silence. Best friends can do that.

CHAPTER 7

# Hollywood in Texas

"Hollywood? Here? Where are they?" Heather squealed.

"I believe they are downstairs in the speakeasy," Sarah informed her friend, knowing she would be excited. Everyone knew Heather loved going to the picture show and dreamed of one day being a star in the silent movies.

"Oh, my goodness. I need to be gorgeous. Ten minutes, tops. Do not let them go anywhere. I will be right down."

Heather picked a royal blue dress from her closet, simple with just enough cleavage to be interesting. Seven minutes later, she had changed, primped her hair, added a little more drama to her eyes, and applied a deep shade of red lipstick, forming a perfect Cupid's bow any man would be tempted to kiss. Selecting a long, bright orange plume from her collection, Heather hurried down the stairs to the first floor. Then with a sassy stride, sauntered down the stairs to the speakeasy located in the basement of Pearl's Parlor. She made her way to the Hollywood men at the bar.

"Hello…I am Heather with my feather. I can tickle your ears, I can tickle your nose, I can tickle your fancy, I can tickle your toes," Heather flirted. "Welcome to Pearl's Parlor, gentlemen."

"How do you do? Pleased to make your acquaintance," one of the men said. "My name is Rex and this here is my friend Jake."

"I hear you are from Hollywood," Heather cooed. "I go to the picture show every time a new movie comes to town. What brings you to San Angelo?"

"Actually, we're working, Ma'am. Just finished shooting a film in San Antonio, and came through to do some research on Fort Concho," Rex informed her. "We heard Pearl's Parlor has the prettiest girls in town."

"That's a nice thing to say," Heather flirted. "Tell me, what is it like to make movies? Do you know any movie stars?"

Raising their eyebrows, the two men looked at each other. Instantly, Heather wished she could swallow her predictable questions back into her mouth. "C'mon Heather," she thought. "Don't be so silly and over anxious. You know better."

Intuitive to the situation, Pearl walked up to the bar. Somehow she always knew when she was needed to polish up uncomfortable rough edges with her charm.

"Good afternoon, gentlemen," Pearl expressed. She was very aware of Heather's desire to be an actress and was a master at seizing an opportunity. Pearl nodded her head for Heather to leave the bar and began engaging in small talk with Rex and Jake. Acknowledging Pearl's gesture, Heather joined a gentleman sitting across the room.

Duke had been playing a soft slide piano in the corner of the room, creating a perfect ambience for the patron to relax and have a drink with friends. An expert at working the room, Pearl engaged in light conversation with the movie makers until she felt the time was right to show off Heather's talents.

In an effort for Jake and Rex to see Heather in a different light, Pearl made a request. "Heather, honey…why don't you sing us a song? You know how much I like, *My Buddy*."

It was one of Heather's best performed numbers. She always sang *My Buddy* with compassion for Annabelle, who had lost her husband in the Great War. Closing her eyes, Heather became lost in the depths of emotion. With great sadness and dramatic pauses, she delivered the first line of the song a- cappella, and when she did, the room became quiet.

"*Nights are long since you went away, I think about you all through the day, my buddy, my buddy, no buddy quite so true. Miss your voice the touch of your hand, just long to know that you understand, My buddy, my buddy, your buddy misses you.*"

As Duke played the melody through, Heather looked up and saw Annabelle standing at the foot of the stairs. Heather had told her that every time she sang *My Buddy*, she secretly dedicated the song to Billy, Annabelle's lost love.

In that moment, for the two young women, it was as if they were the only two people in the speakeasy. When she finished the song Heather smiled warmly at her friend as Annabelle gently wiped the tears from her face. Those who knew Annabelle's story were also deeply touched with Heather's performance.

Rex broke the silence with grand applause, followed by Jake and then everyone else in the room.

"She's really good," Jake expressed. "Put a lump in my throat."

After singing two more songs, Heather called Ginger to the stage. "Ginger, give us some of that sassy New Orleans jazzy-blues," she requested.

As Ginger approached the stage, Duke started playing a slide piano in G. Ginger grabbed the microphone, closed her eyes and began swaying to the steady, walking rhythm of the bass. "*Won't you come along with me…down the Mississippi…*"

As usual, all the men in the speakeasy were mesmerized by the display of self-assured, feminine sexuality being displayed on the small stage in the corner of the room. Ginger and Heather were excellent entertainers and both were aware of the power they held over men when they sang.

Pearl took Heather to the side. "I want you to avoid those men tonight, honey. You don't want them to see you as anything else than the talent that you are. There are hundreds of girls in Hollywood that will do anything to be a movie star. Be mysterious and secretive. I will speak to them on your behalf and see if there is a legitimate opportunity for you."

"Do you think that maybe…?" Heather asked.

"You already know how these things work, Heather. Remember Chicago? Tony hired you as a singer when what he really wanted was to own you as his mistress. You had no idea you were getting involved with a hot-tempered, jealous gangster. Lord knows what would have happened if I had not taken you away from there that night. Frankly, my dear Heather, you are lucky to be alive. Trust me on this."

"Thank you, Miss Pearl," Heather said. "I do trust you."

"I want the best for my girls, Heather. Fortunately I have enough experience to know the ropes," Pearl grinned. "Some things never change."

Within an hour, all the girls were in the speakeasy and the party had begun. Fifi did a cancan and charmed the men with her adorable French accent. Miss Pearl was congenial to all, as it was her business to make sure everyone was having a good time.

"We are going to Fort Concho tomorrow," Jake said as he was leaving. "Do you ladies know any ranchers we might be able to talk to? We are looking at the possibility of doing some filming around here and we are always looking for local cowboys who can ride."

"Come back tomorrow night," Pearl suggested. "It's Friday night and our cowboys are coming to town."

"Sounds good. You can bet we will see you tomorrow, Miss Pearl," Rex assured her. "I believe I would like to see Fifi again. She is a lot of fun. Love the way that gal says, *Ooh la la* at the most appropriate times."

"Maggie told me I was the best lover she ever had," Jake bragged. Miss Pearl did not have the heart to tell him Maggie told all the men they were the best.

"That's why they always come back," Maggie liked to say. "They like to be told they are the best!"

The next afternoon, Heather was feeling a little distraught. "Miss Pearl, I thought about what you said and I feel so stupid. Everything you tell us about keeping our composure went right out the window yesterday when I was talking to those movie men from Hollywood. It's just that I was so excited."

"A lesson learned, my dear. So many pretty young girls want to be starlets. I read that one Saturday 1500 young women stood in line in the rain to walk across the stage for Florenz Ziegfeld, just for the opportunity to play a part in his Follies.

"If you want people to see you as a star, you must act like one. Stars twinkle brightly from far away, making them exquisitely beautiful, like diamonds. At the same time, they are untouchable. The less you speak the more mysterious and intriguing you will be. Smile, as if you know something they do not know and use those beautiful eyes of yours."

"I have wanted to be an actress since I was a little girl, Miss Pearl. The front porch of our farmhouse was my stage, and my dolls and pets were my audience," Heather exclaimed.

"Rex and Jake are coming back later on tonight to recruit. They are looking for cowboys to hire, not pretty girls. Remember that. People usually don't buy what they don't need, that is, unless they find a good enough reason to buy it. Men like a good hunt. I will let you know when it would be appropriate to speak with Jake and Rex, and when you do, let them do all the talking," Pearl advised.

It was just before dusk, when the sun's light produces rich golden shadows over the West Texas land. As promised, Jake and Rex showed up at Miss Pearl's Parlor and saw the girls were excited. Although cowboys were not the wealthiest of clientele, they were virile and strong. Pearl saw them as sexy and good for morale. As long as the cowboys treated her girls with appreciation and respect, they were welcome.

"Here they come!" Maggie squealed.

As the cowboys got closer and closer, the girls could see a huge dust cloud growing bigger and bigger. They were men on a mission focused on their destination: Miss Pearl's Parlor.

Whoopin' and hollerin', the cowboys finally reached the mansion and, as they always did, formed a single file with hats in hand, promenading for the ladies who stood on the porch in ritualistic fashion. Everyone knew it was going to be a good night.

"Impressive," Jake commented.

It was always a good time with the cowboys. Mozella had made fried chicken, mashed potatoes, greens, a plate of fried green tomatoes and cornbread. After shining their boots, washing up in the barn, and replacing their dusty clothes with clean shirts and pants, the cowboys were ready. As always, the food was delicious, and the music was fun. The cowboys knew it was a privilege for them to be able to visit Miss Pearl's Parlor and they were usually always on their best behavior.

Tonight, the food and music seemed exceptionally good. Heather was sensational, Ginger was sexy and Duke's easygoing piano style kept the ambience calm and easy. Rex and Jake were interviewing cowboys, soliciting their talents as riders in some local western footage they planned to shoot in the next few weeks. Dusty and Jesse were particularly interested, especially when Rex told them they were good-looking enough to be movie stars.

"Tom Mix, Hoot Gibson, they all started out as extras," Rex informed them. "Most of the cowboys you see in the movies come from the rodeo circuit. Hollywood loves a man who can handle a horse. They are like gold. Even better if they can rope too."

"Workin' every day at the ranch, we might as well be in a rodeo. Breakin' horses, ropin' up calves and roundin' cattle are what we do most days. Difference is rodeos don't always pay. Personally I like the steady work," Jesse said.

"How'd you like to be in movies?" Jake asked.

"Never really thought about it," Dusty answered.

Pearl, overhearing the conversation, decided to join in.

"Excuse me gentlemen. I heard you say that cowboys are in high demand in Hollywood?" Pearl asked.

"Good ones are," Jake answered.

"Everybody thinks the movie business is glamorous and exciting," Rex said. "Truth is, it's hard work. Not only that, but sometimes it can be dangerous. Did you hear about what happened in San Antonio last November? It was when we were working on a picture, *The Warrens of Virginia*, with Martha Mansfield."

"Such a nice lady," Jake commented.

"Is that the woman who was burned?" Pearl asked.

"Tragic. We were shooting a Civil War movie. Martha was wearing a hoop skirt with all kinds of frilly ruffles on it. She had just finished shooting her last, outside scene and decided to rest in the backseat of her car. She was pretty exhausted.

Someone flicked a cigarette in the window and her costume burst into flames. Will, her leading man, put out the flames with his overcoat. That's why her neck and face didn't get burned. Martha's driver had bad burns on his hands trying to take the burning skirt off her. She was burnt badly. Died a few hours later in the hospital," Rex said, shaking his head. It was obvious the memory was vivid in his mind.

"I am sorry," Pearl commented.

"I remember seeing her in *Doctor Jekyll and Mr. Hyde*," Heather commented.

"They had to get another actress to fill in the parts they had not filmed. That's what Hollywood does. We tell stories, and one way or another, we make it look real and get it done," Jake said.

"Sometimes people get hurt," Rex added.

"The closer we can get to authentic, the better we do our job. That's why we need you boys," Jake said. "Think you might be interested?"

"You need an answer now?" Dusty asked.

"Just let us know by Thursday. Pay is better than what you are making now. The day is long, but it can be fun."

Pearl took Rex to the side. "Our Heather wants to be in the movies, Rex. What would you suggest?"

"Pearl, there are hundreds, maybe even thousands, of pretty girls in Hollywood who want to be in movies. Like I said, it can be a rough business, but at the same time, rewarding and fun. Heather is beautiful."

"She put a lump in my throat," Jake expressed.

"To tell you the truth, I don't know if it's fate, timing, or just plain luck, that gets a girl in the movies," Rex commented.

"A fact I am well aware of," Pearl acknowledged.

"I'll tell you what. I can arrange for Heather to take a screen test. I can't promise anything, but at least I can do that much for her."

"That would be much appreciated," Pearl smiled.

"Now, if you will excuse me, I need to find my little, *Ooh la la,*" Rex grinned rolling his eyes. "You sure do have a nice place here, Miss Pearl."

"Thank you, Rex." Pearl nodded. "You boys have fun."

Pearl decided to wait until the next day to tell Heather about the conversation she had with Rex. When she did, Heather's shrieks of excitement could be heard throughout the Concho Valley.

"I'm going to Hollywood! I'M GOING TO HOLLYWOOD!!"

# CHAPTER 8

# A Screen Test

Ever since she was a little girl, Heather had dreamed of being an actress. While growing up in Illinois, the porch of the farmhouse had served as her stage. With homemade props and costumes, she impersonated different characters from made-up stories and sang songs for her dolls, pets and enthusiastic younger siblings.

Setting up a screen test was relatively easy if the girl was pretty enough. As promised, Rex called Bill Stein and arranged for Heather to meet with him. Bill could certainly make the screen test happen; the rest would be up to Heather.

"I am going with you to California," Ginger insisted. "Screen test? You and a thousand other girls. You might not need me, Heather, but I want to be there for you in case you do."

As the train travelled through the vast terrain of the southwest, Heather was overflowing with a sense of adventure. She thought of the brave souls who crossed this untamed land not that long ago with their dreams of a better life, just as she was doing now.

"Thank you for coming with me, Ginger. I can't help thinking my life is about to change forever."

After finally pulling into Los Angeles, Heather and Ginger took a cab and checked into the Pink Palace Hotel. She could hardly sleep the night before her meeting with Bill Stein and was up before dawn the next morning. Walking on the grounds, Heather felt exhilarated as she watched the brilliant colored sunrise, transforming the sky into another blue-sky day in Southern California.

After examining herself carefully in the mirror, and trying on seven different outfits, Heather finally decided the royal blue was best. Simple and elegant, the dress showed off Heather's shapely figure, as well as the fact that this homegrown farm girl was a lady with class.

Feeling confidant and worthy, Heather walked into the Hollywood office of Bill Stein.

"Shut the door."

Unlike the gentlemen Heather was used to, Bill Stein did not stand when she entered the room. She watched as his smirk slowly transformed into a devilish smile.

"Take your clothes off."

"I beg your pardon? I don't believe I understand."

"I said… take your clothes off. You want to be in the movies, don't ya?"

"I believe there must be some mistake. I was told this was an interview to set up a screen test for a part in the new western movie, *Rio Concho*. I am an actress."

"Listen, Sweetheart… if you wanna play in the big leagues, you gotta play by the rules! Now take your clothes off!"

Leaning forward, the man rested his elbows on the large oak desk standing between him and his newest conquest. He knew she wanted to be a star. They all did. His eyes glared at Heather's breasts with appreciation and desire as he chewed on his smelly, unlit cigar.

"Oh…I see," Heather affirmed. "May I please sit down for a moment, Mister Stein?"

"Ok, but just for a minute. I am a very busy man."

Heather had heard the Hollywood stories of casting couches and girls being put in compromising situations. She had rehearsed this scene for months. Looking down at her soft creamy hands gently folded on her lap, Heather slowly bit her bottom lip. After a moment, with her shiny, expressive soft brown eyes, Heather dramatically looked straight into the dark pupils of a man who had the power to make her dreams come true.

With full confidence in her ability to charm, Heather smiled. Locking the man into her hypnotic gaze, she spoke slowly and deliberately. "So this is business? What are your terms? What do I get when I take off my clothes?"

This one was different. Welcoming the challenge Mister Stein folded his arms and leaned back into his chair. "It depends on how friendly you want to be," he smirked, licking his fat lips. His lines had been predictable and Heather was more than ready to perform her part.

Heather blinked a few times and made her eyes big. "Don't you want me to read for you or sing you a song?" she cooed with profound innocence.

"Take your clothes off, Missy. We'll start there."

"Will you guarantee I get a part? If this is business…"

"I can make you a star, Sweetheart!"

For a long moment Heather stared at the man behind the desk. A woman with experience, she was a master at reading most men and knowing their deepest desires. Coyly, Heather grinned and began speaking seductively in a slow, sultry voice.

"All right then, Mr. Stein. Today is your lucky day. I brought a girlfriend with me. Ginger wants to be in the movies too. Can I ask her to join us? Ginger can be extremely friendly. In fact together we can give you quite a show. She is waiting for me just outside the door."

The man quickly laid down his slimy cigar. "Yes in-deedy! Invite her in!"

"I'll be right back," Heather smiled.

A minute later, Heather and Ginger entered the room. Carrying a large, fashionable leather bag, Ginger was dressed in a bright red dress, revealing every sensuous curve on her body. Maintaining her mysterious confidence, Ginger was always cool and rarely smiled. Her body danced to her own sensuous, sexy, lustful song with the pure intention of stimulating delicious, sexual desire.

"This is Mr. Stein, Ginger. He's going to put us in the movies!" Heather declared.

"Why don't you girls call me, Bill?" the man invited as he drooled on his smelly cigar.

"He said all we have to do is take off our clothes!" Heather chirped.

Ginger cocked her head to the side. "Really?"

Raising her eyebrow, Ginger looked the man up and down. After a long moment, she finally spoke in her slow, husky, southern drawl. "Ok, Bill. You say if we take off our clothes we can be movie stars?"

"Yes, yes, yes!" Bill blasted with excitement, his cigar falling out of his mouth, landing on the floor by the desk.

"That seems easy enough."

Ginger slowly removed her shoes and wriggled out of her red dress. It was all she was wearing. Bill Stein stared at Ginger in awe. Like the statue of Venus de Milo, her body was curved with perfection.

"Your turn, Big Boy. Take off those pants so we can get this party started," Ginger demanded.

Taking the cue, Heather opened her dress to reveal two firm, milky white breasts. Reaching into her purse, she pulled out a large purple plume that had been coiled up inside. Beginning with her neck, Heather slowly stroked her luscious, smooth skin, sensuously forming a circle around each nipple. Approaching the man, she deliberately pointed her feather at him and then recited the rhyme that made her famous at Miss Pearl's. "I am Heather with my feather. I can tickle your ears, I can tickle your nose, I can tickle your fancy, and I can tickle your toes!"

Hastily, the man unbuckled his pants and dropped them on the floor around his feet. He even pinched his leg to make sure he wasn't dreaming. This was Bill's fantasy. Standing before him were two of the most gorgeous women he had ever seen, ready and eager to please him behind the closed doors of his office. Breathing hard, with perspiration beading on his forehead, Bill's manhood proudly bounced to full attention.

Ginger was sensuously swaying back and forth, dancing to the music playing in her head. Again, Heather locked Bill into her gaze as she methodically opened his shirt and began caressing his chest and then hers with the long purple plume. Bill was on fire, anticipating the pleasure he was about to receive.

"Look what I have," Heather cooed as she suddenly produced a black sleeping mask. Gently and without protest from Bill, she brushed the hair away from his eyes and carefully blindfolded him. "Lean back and relax, Mr. Stein," she whispered. "You are going to love my feather!"

"Have you two girls done this before?"

"Don't talk, Honey. Jussst relax..." Heather instructed. She began stroking the inside of Bill's thighs with her feather. Teasing with long, gentle strokes for several minutes, Heather expertly worked her way up to the top of Bill's manhood. Smiling, he moaned and whimpered with delight. Heather was in complete control.

"Oh, baby... Yeah baby..." he moaned. "You are making me crazy. I love it!" he breathed. "I want you to kiss it. I want you both to kiss it," he moaned.

FLASH!!

"What the??"

FLASH! FLASH! FLASH! FLASH! FLASH! FLASH!

The man quickly pulled the sleep mask off his face. Ginger's red dress and shoes were back on and both girls were standing at the door. Ginger put the camera back in her bag. Heather quickly finished buttoning her dress. The large purple plume was lying on the big oak desk.

Bill was unable to move. While Heather had been expertly stroking her sensuous feather on his thigh, Ginger had quietly slipped his belt around the foot of the chair securing his foot to one of the legs.

"You can keep the feather as a souvenir, Mr. Stein," Heather offered.

"See ya later, Bill. Thanks for the photos. You really were adorable!" Ginger complimented.

"Goodbye, Mr. Stein. So nice of you to let me be in your movie. You'll see. I am perfect for *Rio Concho.* You are going to love what I can do. I promise I will not disappoint you."

Bill watched the door shut and sat for a few moments in silence. Freeing his belt from the leg of the chair, he slowly pulled up his slacks and buckled the buckle. Shaking his head, he buttoned his shirt. "Didn't see that coming," he said to himself. "Creative.... I like that. I really liked that."

Heather and Ginger had played their parts well. Tittering in defeat, Bill reached for the phone.

"Hey, Eddie. I found our leading lady for *Rio Concho*. Beautiful girl and a great actress."

The next day Heather received a call.

"Bill Stein says you have talent, Heather. We want to see you at the studio next Monday morning at 10 AM."

"Thank you. I will be there."

Heather hung up the phone in the Pink Palace bungalow and ran outside to find her friend, who was basking in the warm, Southern California sunshine.

"Ginger! You are a genius! Let's call Pearl!"

## CHAPTER 9

# Let's Go to the Beach

"I feel like celebrating. Let's go to the beach!" Heather exclaimed. "We can leave today and come back on Sunday."

"I'm game," Ginger replied. "I will speak to the concierge and find out where we can go."

Like a model on a runway, Ginger glided through the lobby of the Pink Palace, turning every head in the room. Men loved looking at her and women either hated her or nodded in appreciation. Ginger's movements were deliberate and her body language was expressive, clearly saying, "self-confidant and sexy; trespassers will be punished."

Amused, the hotel manager could see the people in the lobby had a "who-is-she" look on their faces. He was curious himself.

The concierge, a well-dressed, professional man, smiled as Ginger sauntered towards him. Ginger did not smile back. She never did. Instead she lifted her chin, tilted her head and raised her right eyebrow.

"May I help you?" he inquired.

"My friend and I would like to go to the beach. We will be checking out for a few days and plan to return on Sunday."

"May I recommend Redondo Beach, my dear? There is much to do there. It has the largest heated indoor saltwater pool in the world, and a Pavilion where you can dance the night away. Here is some information."

Taking the brochure, Ginger slightly stroked his hand in a friendly gesture. The man blushed. Still, she did not smile. That might appear as an invitation. It was just her way.

"You can take the Red Car," he offered. "There is a pickup station just outside. Redondo Beach is less than twenty miles away."

Eager to speak with Ginger, the hotel manager joined the conversation. "My brother Stewart manages the Hotel Redondo. Would you like me to call him and make you a reservation? I will tell him to give you and your friend a room with a view that overlooks the ocean."

"That would be lovely. What is your name?"

"Edward."

"Thank you, Edward. I believe Heather and I will enjoy Redondo. I have never seen the Pacific Ocean before. I lived in New Orleans for several years. It is quite different there."

"Would you like me to hold your bungalow, Miss…?"

"Ginger, Edward. My name is Ginger Dubois."

"Yes, Miss Dubois."

Like most men Ginger encountered, Edward was mesmerized. He felt like a 7th grader with a schoolboy crush. From the day the Pink Palace first opened its doors, Edward had managed the front desk and had met several celebrities and movie stars. He was not the type to be star-struck, and many times felt the movie stars were more impressed with themselves than he was of them.

In his experience, Edward found that the friendliest patrons were usually the most successful. He could not help but appreciate this lovely woman standing before him. Ginger knew her power and she used it with class and style.

"Yes, please hold the bungalow. It looks like my friend is going to be in the movies. She will be staying here until she finds a place to live."

"What about you, my dear? Any plans to be in the movies? I can certainly see you on the big screen."

"I sing Edward. I am not an actress. Silent movies are for girls like my friend Heather."

"I look forward to hearing you perform someday."

"Thank you, Edward. Maybe someday you will."

"Good-day Miss Ginger," he smiled.

Ginger winked and as she did, Edward felt a flash of heat rush to his cheeks. As Ginger exited the lobby, a man glanced up from his newspaper to sneak a look, prompting the woman sitting next to him to nudge him in the ribs. Ginger just had a way that made men take notice and she knew it. It was her business to know.

When she returned to the bungalow, Ginger found Heather in the midst of packing. Clothes were thrown all over the bed and Heather was dancing around the room singing, "*By the sea, by the sea, by the beautiful sea! You and me, you and me oh how happy we'll be! When each wave comes a-rolling in, we will duck or swim, and we'll float and fool around the water!*"

"Ginger laughed. "Look at you, little Miss Movie Star."

"Oh, Ginger! Thank you for coming to California with me. I will never forget you for this. I am a little nervous about seeing Mr. Stein again. I wonder if he will be at the studio on Monday."

"I am sure he will be, Heather. In a way, I think he appreciated what we did. I'm pretty good at reading men. You have to, if you want to survive in our world. Don't worry. Mr. Stein was not angry when we left his office. He just looked like a man who had been beaten at his own game. He'll be fine, especially when he sees what you can do. I believe in you, Honey. It won't be long before you become a household name."

"Really, Ginger?"

"Sure thing. They will all go to the next Heather…"

Ginger paused and looked curiously at her friend.

"What is your last name anyway?" Ginger laughed. "I only know you as Heather with her Feather."

"Smith. My name is Heather Smith."

"Oh no. That will not do. Your stage name needs to glitter and shine like a star. It must be something memorable."

"*Twinkle, twinkle little star, how I wonder who you are,*" Heather giggled.

"*Like a diamond in the sky,*" Ginger sang. "That's it Heather. You can be Heather Diamond. I love it."

Heather twirled around to look at herself in the mirror. "Hello, Miss Heather Diamond! You are going to be a movie star!"

"Lucky for Mr. Stein that you do have talent. They are going to love you," Ginger complimented. "Wait until they see what you can do! The camera is going to love you."

The two friends took the Red Car to Redondo Beach. It was a clear, beautiful day in Southern California. To the east they could see the San Bernardino Mountains towering in front of a bright, blue sky. As the car travelled westward, the air became cooler and the girls became more aware of the smell of the ocean and the salty air. When they finally reached their destination, Heather was like a little girl going to the circus.

"Look, Ginger!"

Heather stepped out onto the platform and took a deep breath. As she gazed at the vast beauty of the Pacific Ocean for the first time, Heather was overcome by a settling peace she had never known before. It was a feeling she could not explain, almost like she had come home. The sparkling blue ocean glistened as the sunlight danced on the surface and shone brightly through the curl of the waves. Heather watched, as one by one, the waves broke on the shoreline, singing her ancient song.

"Madame Pacifica, you are exquisitely beautiful," Heather breathed.

Walking into the lobby of the Hotel Redondo, a gentleman scurried from behind the desk and welcomed the girls with open arms.

"You must be Ginger and Heather. My brother Edward called and told me to expect you. I have a lovely room with a spectacular view of the ocean ready for you. The waves will put you to sleep at night. Scotty here will take your bags. My name is Stewart. Please do not hesitate to call me if you need anything… anything at all."

Stewart was right. With the windows open, the gentle rhythm of the waves sounded like nature singing a soothing lullaby, "All is well, all is well…"

"Look, Heather!" Ginger pointed.

The girls watched as a pelican swooped down with a great splash, retrieving its evening meal.

"Lots of pelicans on the Gulf. It's been a while since I have seen one. Fascinating creatures," Ginger recollected. "I used to watch them for hours."

"Let's go to the beach," Heather announced. "I feel like we have walked into a brand new world. It reminds me of Alice in Wonderland when she passed through the looking glass. This is all so exciting. Thank you again for being here, Ginger."

Dressed in simple cotton frocks, big brimmed hats and sandals, Heather and Ginger headed towards the beach. As they strolled down to the Boardwalk, the men who passed by tipped their hats and smiled with approval. Those accompanied by a lady usually just shifted their eyes slightly to take in the view.

"Let's go to the water, Ginger!"

Off came the hats and sandals as the two women instantly became two little girls who wanted to frolic and play. As they ran to the foamy, white water along the shoreline, they could feel the warm gritty sand squish between their toes. It was a sensation neither of them had ever experienced before. Heather squealed with delight when she felt the coolness of the water circling around her ankles before retracting once again to join the vastness of the sea.

"Isn't this just the bees knees, Ginger?" Heather exclaimed. "I love it here."

Beside them, a young mother and her three-year-old daughter were playing tag with the water that blanketed the sand. Long red curls cascaded down the little girl's back. Ginger watched them with a longing and tenderness in her heart. Not once in her childhood was there a time Ginger's mother ever played with her. When her mother was home, she was usually drunk and treated Ginger as if she were invisible. Ginger thought about how fortunate the little girl was to have a mother who loved her.

As if she were reading Ginger's thoughts, the toddler reached down, picked up a shell that the ocean had deposited on the wet sand and handed it to Ginger.

"Her name is Angelina," her mother smiled. "She likes picking up shells and giving them to people as presents. She is very particular with which one she chooses to give."

Heather saw Ginger's eyes fill with tears. This was unusual. No one ever saw Ginger cry.

"Angelina? What a lovely name and so appropriate for such a beautiful little angel," Ginger said.

Little Angelina pointed at the cold, wet shell in Ginger's hand. "Budder-fwy!" she smiled.

"You are right, Angelina. This shell looks just like a butterfly," Ginger agreed.

The little girl reached down and picked up another shell and gave it to Ginger.

"That's enough dear," her mother said. "She will not stop. Angelina loves giving presents."

Ginger bent down to speak to the little girl. "Thank you, Sweetheart. I will keep my butterfly shell forever!"

Angelina quickly kissed Ginger on the cheek. "Bye," she smiled. Dancing down the shoreline, the little girl found another group of shells to collect.

As Heather and Ginger walked along the wet sand, they marveled at the cool, white foam caressing their feet. When the edge of the wave retreated back into the ocean, Heather pointed out the hundreds of small holes made by the sand crabs burrowing in the wet sand to prevent being eaten by the birds or washed out to sea.

Patterns of small, colorful seashells and seaweed decorated the coastline, as if they had been placed there as a gift from the ocean, revealing clues to the mysteries hidden depths below her shimmering waters.

"Let's make a wish and write it in the sand, Ginger."

Heather picked up a stick and wrote the words, FAMOUS ACTRESS. Satisfied with her statement, she handed the stick to her friend.

"C'mon, Ginger, write something!"

Ginger looked at the wet sand for a moment, as if it were a canvas on which she could magically manifest her deepest desires. There was only one wish Ginger had ever wanted. Slowly, in big letters, Ginger wrote the word, LOVE.

Heather warmly took her friend's hand and tenderly squeezed it. Now she understood why Ginger was always cool and distant. She was protecting a broken heart that had shut down. Mothers are supposed to love their babies, not sell them to a brothel in New Orleans and never return.

Just then a strong wave covered the sand and washed their words away. It was as if the ocean claimed their wishes and carried them out to the magic of the sea.

"We have made our dreams known," Heather affirmed. "Now all we have to do is watch our wishes come true."

The two women sat on the sand and gazed at the warm colors of a brilliant sunset filling the sky. At first the yellow and oranges were soft. Within minutes, brilliant colors of magenta reflected off the clouds, creating a pink fluffy hue so breathtaking, words could not describe.

"I believe this must truly be a glimpse of heaven, Ginger. I have never seen the sky look so beautiful," Heather proclaimed.

So many events had occurred to bring these two women together in this memorable moment. As the sun sank closer and closer to the horizon, it changed into a brilliant ball of reddish orange. Touching the perfectly straight, dark blue line, the sun quickly disappeared as if it were melting into the coolness of the ocean. In the dim light of dusk, the seagulls transformed into flying silhouettes and the lights on the pier brightened up the darkness.

"I want to remember this day forever," Heather proclaimed. "Ginger, do you ever think about where you would be if you had not come to Miss Pearl's?"

"I don't want to think about it, Heather. Miss Pearl's Parlor is the first real home I have ever had," Ginger answered.

"Pearl saved my life. If she had not rescued me from Tony that horrible night in Chicago, I would have been fish bait. I shudder to think about it. My family would still be wondering what happened to me. That would have been awful for them."

"Family. What a nice word," Ginger sighed. "Let's go eat, Heather. I believe the salty air has made me hungry!"

When Ginger and Heather walked into the lobby, Stewart greeted them with a big smile.

"Will you ladies be dining with us this evening? I took the liberty to save you a table by the window."

"That would be lovely, Stewart. Thank you," Heather answered.

An hour later, with the two women dressed in elegant evening gowns, Stewart led them to their table by the window and gave each a corsage of pink carnations with a white ribbon tied neatly around them.

"How nice of you, Stewart," Heather commented. "What a lovely fragrance."

"Beautiful women should have flowers. There is a huge field of carnations not too far from here," he said.

"Ginger noticed only a few tables in the dining room were occupied. "Stewart, where are all the customers?" she inquired. "I would expect the dining room to be overflowing with people. The Hotel Redondo is such a charming place."

"Prohibition has really hurt our business. Not too long ago Redondo Beach was Southern California's premium resort. Not too far offshore, the floor of the ocean falls deep, and for many years, steamships brought thousands of people into port here. Now the big ships go to San Pedro. My brother Edward and I grew up here."

"You grew up in Redondo Beach?" Heather asked.

"Yes Ma'am. My father was a desk clerk at this very hotel the day it opened. Edward and I were just kids, but I remember like it was yesterday. Father was so proud… always dressed in a nice suit. We grew up in a house facing the ocean and the beach was our playground. Those were happy times."

"That's quite a playground, Stewart. This is the first time Heather and I have ever seen the ocean."

"We walked on the beach and wrote in the sand. We had a marvelous time. Tomorrow I believe we will visit the pier. I want to see the largest heated indoor saltwater pool in the world, like the brochure says," Heather smiled.

"Yes, we are very proud of our Redondo Beach Plunge. As a matter of fact, there is going to be a bathing beauty contest on the pier this Saturday. It is exciting to see pretty women all lined up in a row. You girls should enter it. You certainly could win."

Heather and Ginger quickly glanced at each other. In New Orleans, Madame Georgia always put Ginger in a line-up with her other girls. Most of the brothels in Storyville operated that way. One night at dinner, Ginger asked Pearl why she did not do line-ups at her parlor.

"My dear Ginger, it is all about perception. The Everleigh sisters always said, 'Gentlemen are only gentlemen when properly introduced.' Lining you up like cattle in a stockyard sale would take away your dignity. No one outside of yourself has the right to determine what you are worth."

"Thank you, but I think we will just watch, Stewart." Heather answered. "Sounds like fun though."

Sitting at the next table, an attractive older woman, wearing an elegant black velvet dress and an exquisite diamond and ruby necklace, was listening to the conversation.

"Now Stewart… do you really think these young ladies need to be in a beauty contest to determine whether or not they are pretty? Just look at them. Both of them are no less than stunningly gorgeous."

Stewart smiled. "Good evening, Ruby. May I present to you Miss Ginger Dubois and Heather…"

"Diamond! My name is Heather Diamond."

"Very nice to meet you ladies," Ruby said with a friendly nod.

Ginger instantly liked her. "Would you care to join us, Ruby?"

"Thank you. I would be delighted."

Although she was not a tall woman, when Ruby stood she carried herself like a queen ready to hold court. Her smile was radiant but Ginger could see there was deep sadness in her eyes.

"*I wonder what her story is*?" Ginger thought with curiosity.

# CHAPTER 10

# Ruby

"Is Heather Diamond your real name?"

"No. My last name is really Smith… Heather Smith."

"Heather Diamond," Ruby repeated. "I like it. My name is really Anna Maria. My girlfriend, Josephine, convinced me to change it when I ran away to Tombstone. She called it a pretend name. In Arizona the people knew her as *Sadie*."

"Ginger helped me think of it," Heather said. "It is my new stage name. I am going to Universal Studios this Monday to be in the movies."

"Really? My friend Wyatt Earp is a consultant for western movies. In fact Josephine is his wife. He works with Universal Studios sometimes."

"Are you talking about the gunfighter Wyatt Earp?" Heather exclaimed.

"The one and only. Where are you girls from?" Ruby asked.

"I grew up on a farm in the Midwest," Heather answered.

"Everybody has a story," Ginger commented as she lit up a Lucky Strike.

"Would you like to share yours?" Ruby asked insightfully.

"Maybe," Ginger answered, as she took a long drag of her cigarette.

"There is so much pain in your heart, Ginger. I can see it in your eyes. Sometimes it helps to talk about it."

Ginger could feel her soul connect and her heart soften as she looked long and hard into Ruby's compassionate eyes. For some reason she felt like Ruby was a lifetime friend she had just never met. Ginger took a deep breath and slowly put out her cigarette.

"Really not that much to tell. Mama came home one day and asked me if I still had my cherry. I didn't know what she meant. Mamie was really upset when I told her what Mama asked."

"Who's Mamie?" Ruby asked.

"I grew up on the bayou in Louisiana. Mama and Daddy were hardly ever home so the black folks there kind of adopted me. Daisy was my best friend and Mamie was her grandmother.

"Anyway, the next time Mama came home, she gave me a pretty dress and told me she was taking me on a trip to New Orleans. I should have been suspicious when she was being so nice to me. I remember I was very excited; never been out of the bayou before. When we got off the train at Basin Street, Mama took me to Madame Georgia's and sold me for a thousand dollars. That night they auctioned me off for $3500. Madame Georgia got a good price because I was still a virgin," Ginger said, as she put out her cigarette.

Heather's eyes filled with tears. She had heard about Ginger's story but never from her. Ruby's heart was filled with compassion.

Seeing Heather's tears, Ginger decided to take the edge off. "Aw…it wasn't so bad, Heather. I grew up white trash in the bayou. If it hadn't been for Mamie and the rest of the colored folks, I probably would have starved to death. In Storyville I smelt like jasmine, wore clean dresses, ate well, took warm baths, and slept in a real bed with two sheets. All I had to do was be nice to the men."

"Nice to the men," Heather repeated. "Always the men, the men, the men..."

"I learned how to sing at Mamie's church. Even sang with Jelly Roll Morton a time or two. He told me that I might be white but I have a black soul when I sing," Ginger smiled, recalling one of her favorite memories.

"You should hear her, Ruby! Ginger is amazing," Heather bragged.

"When Storyville closed down, I kept a few wealthy clients on the side and started making a little money singing in clubs in New Orleans, mostly jazz and blues. When Prohibition hit the city, I sang in speakeasies with a piano player named Duke. One day I got a wild hair to move to Texas. Duke's sister, Mozella, is Miss Pearl's best friend. I've been working for Miss Pearl's Parlor a few years now."

Ruby liked Ginger. "That's quite a story. I like to sing as well. I even did some theater in my younger years. Mama was from Italy and taught me songs from her homeland."

Dinner was delicious. The halibut was fresh and the vegetable medley was sautéed to perfection. Stewart had made sure the three women were well taken care of. Elegant women eating in his dining room made the Hotel Redondo that much more attractive. After the plates were cleared, Stewart appeared with three pieces of angel food cake on a silver tray.

"Angel food cake for three lovely angels," he proclaimed, as he laid the dessert, garnished with fresh strawberries, on the table.

"Why don't you bring a bottle of my secret stash, Stewart? I want to share some with my new friends. Oh yes, and put the dinner bill on my tab."

"Will do, Miss Ruby. Enjoy your dessert, ladies."

"Thank you, Stewart. And thank you, Ruby. That is very generous of you," Heather exclaimed.

"Yes, thank you, Ruby," Ginger expressed.

"What is your story, Heather?" Ruby asked.

"Like I said, I grew up on a farm in Illinois. Mama kept having babies and I took care of the little ones. We couldn't afford much. The boys helped on the farm and, even though Daddy loved all of us, you could see he was a little disappointed every time Mama popped out another girl.

I love to read and would tell stories to my little brothers and sisters by acting out the different parts. Sometimes I would make them up. I used the front porch of our farmhouse as my stage."

Ruby smiled, "Sounds like you are a natural for the movies."

"I guess I am," Heather agreed.

"You have to be an actress to do what we do at Miss Pearl's Parlor," Ginger remarked. "We live in a world of pretend."

"Tombstone was full of women who did what they had to in order to survive. It's an easy business to get into when you don't have a man to take care of you. The pretty ones made good money but it can be a hard life."

"Yeah..." Ginger sighed, lighting another cigarette. "Miss Pearl is different. She's...well...it's just different at Miss Pearl's."

"If it wasn't for Miss Pearl, I would be dead. She saved my life!" Heather exclaimed.

"What happened?" Ruby asked with curiosity.

"I also like to sing. One night, the most handsome man I had ever seen saw me perform at our annual Harvest Dance. He talked me into going to Chicago to sing for him at his speakeasy. I knew Mother and Daddy could use the money so I said, 'yes.' He bought me beautiful clothes and expensive jewelry and perfume. I had a gorgeous apartment with a spectacular view of the city."

"Uh oh...I think I know where this is going," Ruby remarked.

"I didn't know that he was married and I surely didn't know he was a gangster. All I knew was he was a fantastic lover and spoiled me."

"Italian?"

"Yes. How did you know?"

Ruby just smiled. "What was his name?"

"Tony."

"Ah...Antonio!"

"That's right. One afternoon, he told me he had some business and would not be coming to see me at the apartment. I decided to surprise him. I bought him a real nice necktie and brought it to his restaurant. The speakeasy, where I sang, was in a big room downstairs."

"Pasta and pizza, right?"

"Yes. How did you know?"

"I'm Italian."

"Oh. Anyway, when I walked in, Tony was sitting at a table full of people."

"Let me guess. You showed up and his entire family was eating spaghetti; wife, aunts, uncles, grandparents, in-laws, kids and all."

"How did you know that?"

"He always had a car for you and he didn't like you leaving the apartment. Am I right?

"Yes, you are, Ruby. That's incredible."

Ginger grinned. Obviously Ruby had been around the block a time or two.

"I walked in the front door and waved at Tony," Heather continued. "Harry, he was our bandleader, got up from the table and pretended I was his girlfriend. He rushed me out of there and that's when I learned Tony was married. I felt betrayed and cried all afternoon. How could I be so stupid?"

"You were in love," Ruby assured her. "Love really can be blind."

"That night, when I came to work, I talked to some of our regular customers. Maybe flirted is a better word. I knew how they always looked at me. I was so angry and hurt. I wanted to make Tony jealous."

"Oh no, Heather, you broke his rules and made him jealous. Lord have mercy child, how in the world did you get out of Chicago alive?" Ruby asked.

"That's when Miss Pearl showed up in my dressing room and got me out of there. Later she told me she had known Tony when she worked at the Everleigh Club. They kicked him out for getting rough with one of the girls. Pearl told me Tony liked to cut up women. At first I didn't believe her. Then I realized I had never seen Tony so angry before. We ran out the back door where she had a car waiting for us. That night we drove for hours and then caught a train to Texas."

"The Everleigh Club? I've heard of that place. My husband knew people in Chicago. Very swanky, as I understand. Pearl was an Everleigh Butterfly? I am impressed," Ruby complimented.

"I owe Miss Pearl my life," Heather exclaimed.

"Last year, Tony showed up in San Angelo looking for Heather," Ginger added. "He kidnapped Pearl and tied her up. Had a big Bowie knife he bought in town."

"Oh, my Lord. What happened?" Ruby asked.

"Let's just say, Tony is gone forever," Ginger answered, laying her hand on Heather's. "One of our girls, Katie, is our resident sharpshooter, and she and her dog, Rusty, know how to take care of the bad guys."

Heather looked at Ginger. No one had told her what happened the night Tony showed up in San Angelo and she never asked.

"Miss Pearl sounds like a fascinating woman."

"She is. Actually you remind me of her in many ways," Ginger stated.

"It sounds like Pearl looks after you just like Consuelo looked after me when I came to Tombstone. I met her on the stagecoach riding into town. When I told her my parents had died she told me she had lost her daughter and invited me to stay at her house. She was a great friend. Left me a fortune when she died. God I miss her."

Stewart appeared and presented Ruby with a blanket and a bag. "Enjoy yourselves ladies," he grinned.

In the bag was a bottle of red wine and three glasses. "Consuelo and I built a winery in Temecula," Ruby smiled, holding up the bag.

"I took the liberty to open it for you so it could breathe a bit."

The three women walked down the steps to the sand and removed their shoes. The sand felt cool as they made their way closer to the water's edge to sit down.

"Listen to those waves, ladies," Ruby said. "One by one they appear, then go back into the sea. Just like a mysterious woman, the ocean lets you see her, hear her, smell her, taste her saltiness, and feel the coolness of her water, but never does she reveal her deepest secrets."

"I like that, Ruby," Heather remarked.

"The ocean always brings me such peace. Sometimes life's craziness can, well, it can make you crazy," Ruby laughed.

"Tell us your story Ruby. By the way, your necklace must be worth a king's ransom! I have never seen a ruby that size or a necklace with so many diamonds!" Heather exclaimed.

"This necklace has quite a story. It was my mother's. She gave it to me the day she died. Her name was Carlotta."

"What a pretty name," Heather commented.

"My father died a few weeks later. I was seventeen when they passed. My friend, Josephine talked me into running away with her to Tombstone. That's where she met Wyatt Earp. Those were different times. Cowboys... saloons...gambling... gunfights. It really was the Wild West."

"Sounds like downtown San Angelo," Heather commented.

"Those clean cut, strong cowboys in the movies, who love their horse and always save the girl were not the cowboys I knew in Tombstone. They were bad hombres."

"Bad boys, huh. I've known a few," Ginger commented.

"Our cowboys are sexy and strong," Heather smiled.

"I'm surprised Pearl lets them come. Cowboys are not what I would call upper-class men with lots of money."

Ginger smirked. "Pearl says she lets the cowboys come for morale. As long as they respect us, stay clean, and act like Texas gentlemen they are allowed."

"It's always a good time when the cowboys come to town."

"Do you ever have any trouble with them? Cowboys can get rowdy you know," Ruby asked.

"We have Texas Katie. She doesn't miss when she shoots and everybody knows it," Heather laughed.

Ruby smiled. "Texas Katie? The one who took care of Tony?"

"One in the same," Ginger smiled.

"What is Wyatt Earp like?" Heather asked.

"Wyatt is no nonsense, soft spoken and not afraid of an-y-thing! Wyatt did well with the land boom in San Diego. Had four gambling businesses in the Stingaree. My friend Consuelo loved going to the Oyster Bar and play cards with him like she did in Tombstone. Mickey and I loved Consuelo. Both of them are gone now. Mickey was my husband."

"What happened to him? It's none of my business but..."

"He died," Ruby whispered.

"Oh no. When did that happen?" Heather asked.

"It was a little over two years ago. Dumbest thing. He was in a store buying me a diamond bracelet for our 40th anniversary. The clerk had just finished wrapping it when in comes a man with a gun to rob the place. Mickey tried to be a hero and pulled out his gun. That was it. The man shot and killed him. Shot the owner too. Just so happened a law officer was outside and heard the shots. He caught the man running out of the door."

"That's horrible," Heather sympathized.

"The owner was hurt, but he lived. The officer gave me this bracelet when they told me what had happened to Mickey."

Ruby proudly displayed a lovely diamond bracelet, glittering like the twinkling stars in the night, for the girls to gaze upon. Staring at her bracelet, Ruby's face became very sad and her lips began to tremble.

"I love my bracelet...but... I lost... I lost my Mi- Mi-Mi-ckey," Ruby wailed.

Poor Ruby began weeping profusely. Heather pulled out a handkerchief and both women tried to comfort her with warm, loving hugs. As Ruby wept and sobbed, Heather and Ginger rocked her in their arms. They didn't let go until she stopped. Gaining her composure, Ruby patted both girls on the arm.

"Thank you...thank you... thank you..."

Ruby wiped her eyes and then blew her nose with a honk so loud it made all three women laugh.

"You know that's the first time I have really cried since he died? For a long time I was in denial. Sometimes I still pretend he's on some kind of business trip, and anytime, I'll be seeing him walking through the door. God, I loved that man."

"Sounds like you love Mickey the way Miss Pearl loves her Robert," Heather commented. "I hope I find a love like that someday."

"The man who shot him was executed at San Quentin. 'Hung by a rope until dead,' just like the judge ordered. I was there. His Mama was there too. I actually felt sorry for her. Poor little thing wailed and sobbed.

It was horrible. Strange, after it was over, it didn't make me feel any better. What a waste. Good lookin' kid too."

For a while the ladies sat in silence, drinking Ruby's wine and watching as the waves gently broke along the shore.

"When I think about my Mickey, I like to picture him laughing. He had a great laugh. 'Come here to me, Amore,' he'd say. Oh, and the way he would say it." Ruby smiled. "How 'bout you Ginger? Have you ever been in love?"

"I don't know, Ruby. I don't know if you'd really call it love or lust. His name is Sam. Good – lookin', sweet – talkin', hot – lovin' Sam. Only man I have ever known who can make me feel like I might even have a heart. I know, because it jumps when I see him and it aches when we say goodbye."

Soft moonlight and the peaceful song of the ocean made a perfect setting, as the women spent the evening sharing stories of their lives. Sometimes the conversation would break out in boisterous laughter, breaking the silence of the peaceful night. Ruby especially liked the story about Heather's interview with Bill Stein.

It was after midnight when the ladies finally called it a night. Three different women, with three different stories, were now three trusting friends for life.

## CHAPTER 11

# Salty Dog

"Ginger, are you awake?"

"No."

"Let's go to the beach."

Standing by the open window, Heather took a deep breath, filling herself with the fresh, salty ocean air. Raising her arms in gratitude, she shouted with joy, "Thank you, God. I have never felt so alive!"

Gazing out into the horizon, Heather thought of how the massive ocean she saw before her was connected to every part of the world. Realizing this gave her a profound feeling of exaltation. Looking down, she saw the early morning sun cast a giant shadow of the Hotel Redondo over the golden sand below.

"Camelot," Heather exclaimed.

"What in the world are you talking about, Heather?" Ginger yawned.

"The Hotel Redondo looks like a giant castle on the sand and we are ladies of the court," Heather announced as she danced around the room.

"Ladies of the court? I can go with that," Ginger said, stretching her arms. "Any sign of Lancelot?"

"I don't know, Ginger. Being near the ocean makes me feel free. I want to dance, and sing, and make up stories about knights in shining armor rescuing beautiful women who adore them. It's a glorious morning. Let's go down to the water."

Putting on colorful sundresses, sandals, lipstick, sunglasses and big, brimmed straw hats in 10 minutes, the girls were ready and headed out the door. As the two friends entered the lobby, Stewart greeted them with open arms.

"Good morning, dear ladies. Ruby likes to get up early. She is already on the beach. You might see her if you are going that way."

"Thank you, Stewart," Ginger replied.

Heather and Ginger both made their way down the concrete stairs that led to the sand below. When they took off their sandals, the sand felt cool, not yet warmed by the morning sun. The sea was much different this morning than yesterday when they arrived. She seemed calm and relaxed, not as restless as the afternoon before. The waves were smooth, like glass reflecting the soft light of the morning sun.

Fishermen were lined up along the pier. Others were fishing along the shoreline. Some were holding their poles; others had stuck them in the sand. Ginger and Heather headed south along the water's edge, walking towards the Palos Verdes Peninsula.

"Is that Ruby down there?" Heather thought aloud.

"I believe it is," Ginger smiled.

Wearing a rolled up pair of blue overalls, a white shirt and a big straw hat, Ruby was sitting on the sand looking out into the water. Even without her diamonds and make-up, anyone could see that the woman had class. Ginger and Heather both watched as an older man walked away from his fishing line to visit with her. The man had a bushy white beard and was wearing a red cap and faded dungarees. As he sat beside her, it was obvious Ruby knew him. Side by side, the two of them were sharing the view of the ocean.

Sensing the girls' presence, Ruby turned and looked their way. She waved her hand and motioned to Heather and Ginger to come to her. Seeing the girls, the man stood up and took off his hat.

"A gentleman," Heather thought.

"Heather, Ginger, This is my friend, Salty Dog."

"You can call me Salty," he smiled.

"Salty has lived in Redondo Beach since before it was a tourist town," Ruby informed them.

"Yeppers, I worked for the Pacific Steamship Company. We used to stop here in Redondo four times a week on our run from San Francisco to San Diego. Redondo was the first port built in Los Angeles County. The steamships brought folks here by the thousands," Salty reminisced.

"I met Salty at the Oyster Bar in San Diego," Ruby said. "He was good friends with Mickey."

"I really liked taking Wyatt's money," Salty chuckled.

"Wyatt didn't like to see Salty or Consuelo comin' through the door," Ruby laughed.

"Truth is… Wyatt kept trying to get his money back."

"Sounds like you are a lucky man," Heather remarked.

Salty grinned with all the teeth he had left. "Luck? Maybe. I just always expected to win," he laughed. "Where are you girls from?"

"We are here from San Angelo, Texas," Ginger answered.

"Some men in the movie business came to town looking for cowboys," Heather chirped. "I told them I was an actress and they invited me to California."

"That happens a lot to pretty girls," Salty said, a little concerned.

Ruby picked up on Salty's protective nature. "Don't worry, Salty. Heather knows the ropes," she assured him, winking at the girls.

"Ginger came with me for support, and I am very glad she did. I am going to Universal on Monday."

"I see, young lady. Well you came to the right place for a little R and R before your big day. Redondo Beach is a lot of fun. Not so busy here now since they built a seaport in San Pedro."

Salty pointed towards the pier. "There was a roller coaster right over there they called 'Lightening Racer.' A big storm destroyed it a few years back. The Casino and Bathhouse is over there. You girls going to the plunge today?"

"Maybe," Heather replied. I'm really not much of a swimmer."

"There is a shallow end, honey, largest indoor heated saltwater pool in the world. It's four stories tall and has three pools and two diving boards. Even has a trapeze in the main pool area. It's not as cold as the ocean. The Pacific Light steam plant heats the water."

"Redondo Beach is absolutely charming," Ginger said. "I was in New Orleans for a while but the Gulf is nothing like this. I like watching the surf and listening to the waves break at night. It makes me not want to think. I just want to look and listen."

Salty pulled out his pipe and began preparing it for his morning smoke. "Redondo Beach used to be packed with tourists every weekend. Prohibition has really hurt business in the last few years. There's talk that they might take the Hotel Redondo down."

"That would be a shame," Heather winced, "a real shame."

"Mickey loved to bring me here," Ruby reminisced. "It was our favorite place. I have many fond memories of the Hotel Redondo. That's why I like to come. I feel close to Mickey when I am here."

"Lots of movie stars have come and stayed at the Hotel Redondo over the years, Heather," Salty said.

"I've seen Mary Pickford here a few times," Ruby shared. "Once I saw Charlie Chaplin in the dining room. Stewart had to tell me it was him. He looks different without his baggy pants, funny little hat and mustache. Not only that, he speaks with an English accent."

"One day people will be talking about Heather Diamond staying at the Hotel Redondo," Ginger bragged.

"Maybe so," Heather smiled. "It's hard to imagine."

Ruby beamed at her old friend. "Salty and I have been friends a long time. He's another reason I come to Redondo.

"Just as lovely as the day I met you," Salty said with affection. "Mickey was a good friend of mine. He got me out of a big jam one time. I will be grateful to the both of you for that, Ruby."

For a moment the two old friends smiled at each other. Whatever their friendship was, it was obvious Salty was especially fond of their new friend Ruby. Maybe even a little in love with her.

"You girls hungry?" Ruby asked. "I'd like to invite you to breakfast. Don't worry about making yourselves up girls. We're at the beach. Your sunglasses will do just fine. See ya later, Salty."

After breakfast Heather and Ginger decided to explore Moonstone Beach. As they walked north, they passed Tent City where, for $10 a month, a small family could rent a tent with a hardwood floor and electricity.

The pier was full of men and women fishing. Flags and banners were waving from the Pavilion by the Redondo Beach pier, creating a festive ambiance for the girls to enjoy.

Heather was dreaming aloud to her friend. "I've never been to a place like this, Ginger. I am going to become a famous actress and make lots of money so my family will be able to come visit me."

"Reach for the stars and you will land on the moon," Ginger encouraged her friend. "All the business savvy you will ever need, you have learned at Miss Pearl's. This industry is run by men and that is to your advantage. A smart woman lets the man lead the dance, and when you want to change the rhythm, convince him it is his idea."

"I am still a bit nervous to see Mr. Stein again, Ginger. That really was classic," Heather giggled.

"Don't worry, Heather. He'll be okay. We will give him the camera film as a present sometime after you begin shooting the movie and everyone has been wowed by what you can do. The camera is going to love your big brown eyes."

Ginger stopped walking and reached out her arms to hug her friend. "You are like a sister to me, Heather. I will always be there for you."

As the girls walked north along Moonstone Beach, they saw several people bent over the shoreline, looking for the smooth, iridescent white moonstones.

Heather grabbed Ginger's arm. "Isn't that Mae Marsh?" she asked, trying to contain her excitement. "I read about her in one of the movie magazines. She was in that movie *The White Rose* last year. She's married to Sam Goldwyn's publicity agent and has a sister in the movies as well. Let's go talk to her."

The lovely, young actress looked quite content as she strolled along the shoreline, occasionally stooping down to pick up one of nature's smooth white treasures lying on the wet sand.

"We don't need to bother her, Heather," Ginger cautioned.

"She looks nice. C'mon."

As the girls came closer, it was Mae who spoke first. "Don't you just love the beach? This is where I do my best thinking."

"This is our first time and, yes, we do love the beach, Miss Marsh," Ginger expressed.

"So you recognize me?" Mae smiled. "The hat and sunglasses didn't fool you? Most people don't, you know. I guess they don't expect to see movie stars on the beach picking up moonstones. Do I detect a southern drawl?"

"I grew up in Louisiana," Ginger informed.

"Really. Fascinating place. We filmed parts of *The White Rose* there. I especially liked New Orleans."

"I worked there a while. I am a singer," Ginger said.

"Jazz? I loved the music in New Orleans. The crew spent some time at the French Quarter. It was fun. Do you girls live around here?"

"I hope to move to Southern California soon. My name is Heather and this is Ginger. We came here from Texas."

"Texas? We rode through Texas on the train. It seemed endless. Do you girls want to get a drink?" Mae asked. "I'm thirsty."

"Sure," Heather replied.

Although Mae was a well-known movie star, it seemed she was enjoying the company. Heather was making a huge effort not to act like a star-struck schoolgirl.

"I am just starting in the movie business, Miss Marsh," Heather blurted. "Do you have any advice?"

"Call me Mae, honey. I can tell you how it happened for me. When I was six, my great-aunt brought my older sister Marguerite and I to Los Angeles. We were told my stepfather died in the San Francisco earthquake and mother needed help. Found out later he never died at all."

"That is strange," Heather commented.

"My aunt was in show business and was able to get us on the movie sets as extras. Marguerite worked on films before I did. I used to tag along with her when she went to the studio and watch. My big break happened when I was 15. Guess you can say I was in the right place at the right time. One day, for some reason, Mr. Griffith noticed me hanging around the studio and put me in the picture *Ramona,* with Mary Pickford."

"Mr. Griffith the director? I saw that movie," Heather exclaimed. "Great story."

"That got my foot in the door. My big break came when Mary Pickford refused to put on a grass-skirt and show off her legs when she was playing the role of Lilly White in *Man's Genesis*. Mr. Griffith was not happy and told her in front of everyone that, if she refused to do it, she would not play the lead in his next film, *The Sands of Dee.*"

"Uh oh," Ginger commented.

"Everyone was there, including Mary Pickford, when he called the first rehearsal for *Sands of Dee*. For some reason he turned to me and said, 'Well now, Miss Marsh, you can rehearse the lead.' Mary was shocked. We all were."

Ginger shook her head. "Don't mess with the man in charge."

"When Mary questioned Mr. Griffith, he reminded her of his promise to give the lead to someone else. Everyone wanted that part and he gave it to me. That's how this business works. Of course, I was thrilled but I never showed it. I felt bad that Mary was hurt. When people asked me about it, I just acted as if I was some kind of lamebrain, doing what the boss told me to do."

"Sometimes acting like you don't know what's going on works well," Ginger commented.

"I guess my best advice to you, Heather, would be, don't cross the man in charge," Mae stated.

Heather was captivated with every word. "You've been in so many movies, Miss Marsh."

"I love my work, Heather. After Lee and I married, I wanted to have a family. Now I only do a picture once a year. We are getting ready to film a movie called *The Rat*."

"From the stage play?" Heather asked. She was always up to date on anything to do with stage and screen.

"That's the one," Mae smiled. "Oh my, look at the time. I need to meet my husband for dinner and I have a thousand errands to run. It was nice visiting with you girls. Good luck to you, Heather. I wish you well on your career. Maybe I will see you again sometime."

"I hope so, Miss Marsh," Heather said.

The rest of day was spent exploring the promenade. Ginger and Heather were like schoolgirls eating ice cream, cotton candy, corn on the cob and drinking soda pop. Late that afternoon, after a well-deserved nap, they walked along the shoreline again witnessing yet another spectacular sunset as warm colors filled a seemingly endless sky.

It was Friday night and the Redondo Beach pier was alive with music. Because of the beauty contest, the Hotel Redondo was completely booked and from the beach you could hear the sound of laughter echoing throughout the night.

Walking back towards the hotel the girls saw Ruby standing alone soulfully gazing out to the sea. Her long white hair was blowing softly in the night breeze and her eyes were shining bright as if she was looking at something only she could see. Heather called out to her but she just kept staring into the abyss.

"I think we should leave her alone," Ginger suggested.

"She must be thinking about Mickey."

"Yeah… Mickey… I wonder what it would be like to know love like that?"

## CHAPTER 12

# Bathing Beauties

The next morning the pier was buzzing with crowds of people. A long platform had been built in front of the Pavilion, and the crowds, consisting mostly of men in straw hats, were gathering to take their place as spectators to view the Redondo Beach Bathing Beauty Contest.

Although the year was 1924, there were still many who did not approve of the new fashions in beachwear and considered them disgraceful. It had not been that long ago when women wore full-length dresses and long sleeves to the beach. With a spirit, lively and free, the flappers had drastically put a new look on style. Over the last decade, bathing outfits were requiring less and less material. One local church minister called the bathing beauties, *vampires of the flesh*.

Thousands of people always showed up for the Redondo Beach Beauty Contest. Although the contest was advertised as "girls in bathing suits", the clothing they wore was not suitable for swimming. The young women wore colorful costumes, many of which were homemade. There were still restrictions for modesty for the ladies to follow. Their outfit must completely conceal the view of each leg from the hip joint to an imaginary line one-third of the way to the knee.

Because of its popularity, the movie industry saw the event as an effective publicity tool. Famous movie stars and artists usually judged the contest and everyone knew it. This year they managed to get the cowboy star Tom Mix, who was promoting his new film *Trouble Shooter* to be a judge.

The bathing beauties consisted of models and want-to-be starlets. Mack Sennett, the movie producer and creator of Sennett Studios and the Keystone Cops, would sometimes send girls from his modeling agency to be in the beauty contests. "Mack Sennett's Bathing Beauties" served as pinup girls in World War I and were great publicity for his movies. Also, using beautiful women in advertising had only recently caught on. Men from car dealers turned up at the contests to scout for young, pretty girls to show off their new car models at various festivals and parades held all over Southern California.

Ginger and Heather decided to dress to the nines to view the contest. They looked like fashion models from Paris wearing soft pastel colored dresses and matching broad brimmed hats. Heather had never seen so many people in one place before. The weather was perfect, the ocean was majestic and excitement was weaving throughout the crowd.

Today the Hotel Redondo was full of people, mostly men wearing suits and straw hats. As Heather and Ginger both sashayed across the lobby, every gentleman they passed smiled and tipped his hat. Ruby was sitting at a table in the dining room when Heather and Ginger arrived for breakfast.

As soon as they sat down, Stewart appeared with a tray full of coffee and juice. "Good morning, ladies, you look absolutely stunning. Will you be attending the beauty contest today?"

"I believe we are. I've never been to a beauty contest before," Heather answered. "I know it will be interesting. Ever since the Miss America Pageant started three years ago, they seem to be a popular new trend."

"Enjoy your breakfast, ladies," Stewart chirped as he walked away.

Ginger leaned across the table to Ruby. "I don't really see the difference between lining up at a beauty contest or lining us up at Madame Georgia's. The men never saw us as real people with real names or feelings. To them we were purely fantasy girls for sale, to serve their needs with no expectations."

"Pearl never lines girls up. Neither did the Everleigh sisters from what I understand," Heather added.

"Everyone loves looking at young pretty women," Ruby offered. "Unfortunately, most of them don't realize what kind of power they have. Think about it… if all the women were to disappear from the earth today, it would be the end of the human race. But if all the men were to disappear, the human race would still go on."

"Because there are pregnant women?" Heather asked

"Exactly," Ruby affirmed.

"You sound like Miss Pearl," Heather smiled.

"Unfortunately, most young women do not realize the power they possess," Ruby sighed, "and they give it away.

"Things are so different now from when I was young. There was no such thing as film or models in magazines. Many of the women in today's beauty contest hope someone will spot them and make them a star. There will be men who will approach them, compliment them, get their contact information and then totally take advantage."

"I had that experience with Mr. Stein."

"Good thing I was there. At least Miss Pearl's business is more honest," Ginger said. "Everyone knows what to expect. One time a Jewish man told me, 'You have the perfect product. You sell it and you still got it,'"

All three women laughed again.

"Stewart is right. You both look stunning today. Your "you can look but do not touch attitude," makes you even more intriguing."

"Thank you, Ruby," Heather said.

That afternoon, Heather and Ginger watched the Redondo Beach Beauty Contest from the top of the Pavilion, where they had a good view of the crowd that consisted mainly of men lusting after the damsels in their bathing costumes.

When they finally announced the winner, Heather couldn't help but feel a little sorry for the other girls standing on the platform. "The message, not good enough, is a hard reality and can mess with a young woman's self-esteem," she thought.

After the contest, Heather and Ginger strolled down the promenade; they watched as a man approached one of the girls in the contest. "You should have won," they heard him say. "You were the most beautiful girl up there."

That evening, the coolness of the air gradually bade farewell to another lovely day. Heather, Ruby and Ginger enjoyed another evening of good food, Ruby's wine and girl talk. The white foam of the sea shone like a neon light, making each wave visible as it broke before the shore.

Ruby took a deep breath. "I love the way the ocean smells at night, with her salty, intoxicating fragrance. No wonder the sailors call her, she. The goddess sings with every wave, and every wave, unique in her own beauty, is part of the magical essence of the sea."

When it came time to pay the bill, Stewart told the ladies that a gentleman had anonymously paid for their dinner. "He told me to give you this," Stewart said, handing Ruby a small envelope.

Ruby opened the note and smiled. "Looks like we had an admirer. It says, *Thank you for the spectacular view, ladies*."

"Look what I picked up today, Ruby." Heather reached into her purse and pulled out a seagull's feather that had been lying on the boardwalk. "I am Heather with my feather, I can tickle your ears, I can tickle your nose, I can tickle your fancy, and I can tickle your toes."

"Very good, my dear," Ruby applauded. "Feathers are good luck. I know we are going to be friends for a long time."

The next morning when Heather and Ginger came downstairs for breakfast, Ruby was gone.

"Ruby took care of your bill," Stewart informed them. "She told me to tell you, she will be in touch."

"Ruby is quite a lady," Ginger complimented. "One of the finest I have ever known."

"Yes, indeed," Stewart smiled. "It has been a real pleasure having the three of you here."

"Salty told us there is talk of taking the Hotel Redondo down. That would be a shame," Heather remarked.

"The Hotel Redondo was a wonderful place to grow up. Right now I am finding the joy in every day I am here as if it were the last," Stewart sighed. "Edward told me he can put me on at the Pink Palace but I will certainly miss the sound of the ocean."

"It is beautiful," Ginger smiled.

"I know you will do well, Heather. You have everything it takes to be a star. Please come stay with us again, ladies."

"Thank you, Stewart. You can be sure I will be back."

CHAPTER 13

# Lights Camera Action

Heather was born to be an actress. As far back as she could remember, she created characters in her exclusive world of make-believe. Villain, victim, lover, snob, sweetheart, innocent, guilty, and even comedian, Heather had played them all.

Beautiful, adoring, playful Heather was an expert at creating exciting, sexual fantasy. Performing the part of an adoring mistress to the clientele at Miss Pearl's Parlor had served her well. Though sometimes challenging, she made her work a game of pretend. With every client, Heather imagined she was performing in an erotic play starring "Heather with her Feather." As a result, her co-star, whoever he was, usually left Miss Pearl's Parlor a satisfied customer feeling ten feet tall.

Because of her unique talents, Heather had acquired an impressive collection of diamonds and fine jewels, as well as money she had stashed away. Miss Pearl had taught her well and, for this, she would always be grateful. Now she was in Hollywood and, as far as she was concerned, she was destined to be a star.

Monday morning, Heather was awake before sunup. Unable to fall back to sleep, she decided to take a walk and let Ginger sleep. Heather watched as the warm glow of the sun first appeared over the San Bernardino Mountains. Gradually, bright colors of orange and pink painted a masterpiece throughout the morning sky. Brilliant rays of sunshine shot through the clouds; a perfect beginning to her new career.

"Are you sure you want me to come along?" Ginger asked.

"You are my good luck charm, Ginger," Heather said, hugging her friend. "I am so happy you came with me to California."

"Just wait until they see what you can do," Ginger praised.

As promised, Bill Stein had arranged for Heather to make a screen test to appear in the western *Rio Concho*. Although it was her first time, Heather began what would be an everlasting love affair with the camera. Skillfully, Heather laughed, pouted, flirted, and raged on cue. When she was asked to cry, she produced warm, salty tears that flowed like a fountain down her face.

Later that afternoon, Bill Stein and Richard Morris, the assistant director, sat in a viewing room to watch their new leading lady ravish the screen. Richard, a tall, exceptionally attractive man with dark wavy hair, was especially impressed.

"Where did you find this girl, Bill? She is perfect for *Rio Concho.* The camera absolutely loves her! My Lord, look at those eyes."

Chewing on his unlit cigar with great satisfaction, Bill Stein folded his arms and leaned back in his chair. Looking at the screen, he nodded his head and smiled as he silently agreed. Richard was right. Heather's charisma was refreshing and the camera adored her.

It was June 20, 1924, a glorious morning in Southern California and the first day of rehearsals for *Rio Concho*. The night before, Heather slept like a baby. Like a captive animal returning to the wild, Heather felt she was exactly where she belonged. She now had a sense of purpose that brought peace and contentment to her soul.

At 9 o'clock sharp, Heather and Ginger entered the lobby of the Pink Palace. As promised, a man wearing a brown suit and cap greeted them with a dramatic bow. "Miss Heather Diamond? I am here to escort you to Universal."

"What is your name?" Heather smiled.

"My name is Steven. I will be your driver."

Steven led the ladies to the car and opened the back door. Heather embraced Ginger with a long, warm hug.

"Thank you for everything, Ginger. It meant the world to me for you to be here. Give everyone my love."

Ginger gently squeezed Heather's two hands. "We believe in you, Heather. You are going to be fabulous. Call if you need anything. One of us will be on the next train. They might not know what they've got yet, but they will soon enough."

Happy and a little sad, Ginger and Heather looked at each other the way good friends do when one is about to embark on an exciting new adventure. Heather gave Ginger a final squeeze. Then like a princess entering her carriage, she took her place in the back seat of the limo.

"Let's go, Steven. It's show time," Heather sang.

"Yes, Ma'am," Steven smiled.

As Heather entered the gates of Universal Studios, she felt like Cinderella going to the ball. Richard, looking distinguished and handsome, was waiting for her when the car drove up. Heather was impressed with this well-dressed man smiling at her with pearly white teeth. Tall and lean, his dark, wavy hair glistened in the sun.

"How do you do, my dear? This truly is an honor, Miss Diamond. I am Richard Morris, the Assistant Director for *Rio Concho.* May I say, your screen test was impressive and I am looking forward to working with you. We will begin rehearsals in a couple of hours. In the meantime, I will give you a tour of our movie studio and then show you to your bungalow."

It had been nine years since Carl Laemmie first opened the gates to Universal City. With the help of nearly 300 movie hands and actors, he had erected makeshift buildings, set up cameras and had begun producing hundreds of one- and two-reel silent western movies.

After World War I, Carl created jobs at the movie lot for soldiers returning to California. Other studio chiefs laughed and called Universal "Laemmie's Folly." Carl got the last laugh. He knew the power of word-of-mouth promotion and because of his connection to the audience, his 230-acre ranch, now known as Universal City, became a huge success. He was the first to create the "star system" and, although he was not aware of it yet, Heather Diamond was about to be his newest star.

Heather blushed with excitement as she climbed into the front seat of Richard's open-air touring car. Everyone they met seemed friendly and waved as they rode by.

"Universal City is a 230-acre movie lot, Heather," Richard informed. "It really is an actual city. We have our own police force, fire department and a street cleaning crew, all with uniforms that say Universal City. We also have libraries, schools, greenhouses, a hospital, mill shops, forges, an immense reservoir and two wonderful restaurants that, combined, can feed over 1200 people."

"It is all so impressive, Richard," Heather exclaimed.

"We even have apartments and small houses on the studio lots, where workhands live with their families."

"Are those train tracks I see?" Heather asked.

"Yes they are, Heather. The Southern Pacific Railroad tracks run right through Universal City."

As Richard drove through the movie lot, the barns and corrals seemed endless. He showed her where the cowboys stayed in a bunkhouse close to one of the main stables.

Richard took Heather into an enormous tack room that had enough gear to put the entire U.S Calvary in the field and an Indian army to fight it. Near the bunkhouse was a big actors' lounge; cowboys could be seen at all hours of the day playing cards at round tables.

Universal had four mammoth stages, eighty dressing rooms and a vast prop department. Behind the stages and wardrobe sprawled the outdoor sets. The New York Street was made up of brownstone fronts and brick tenements. Just beyond were the narrow lanes and slate roofs of Paris.

"That's where Lon Chaney made *The Hunchback of Notre Dame,*" Richard said. "They are working on his new film *The Phantom of the Opera* there now."

The Western Town set lay further still.

"This is where you will be filming some of your scenes," Richard told Heather. "Let's get out and look around."

The Western Town set consisted of mostly building fronts supported by wooden frames, creating the illusion of a town in the Old West. Some of the buildings reminded Heather of Concho Avenue in San Angelo.

Heather could see why the Western Town facade was positioned so remotely at the edge of the Universal City lot. Just beyond the western set were miles and miles of open country where herds of horses, sheep, mules and cattle by the hundreds grazed when not needed for a picture that was being filmed. A big buff-colored knoll that formed a backdrop for the lot also doubled as a handy location for Westerns. Conveniently, all of it was less than ten minutes from Universal's front office.

"It's pretty much an everyday occurrence to look up and see a band of outlaws in hot pursuit of a galloping stagecoach, or Indians chasing a lumbering covered wagon around the flanks of this little hill. No one is shooting today but you'll see plenty of action soon enough," Richard said. "Universal's western heroes and extras are real cowboys. We like to be as authentic as we possibly can."

"I believe two of my cowboy friends from Texas were recruited for *Rio Concho*. Their names are Dusty and Jesse," Heather informed.

"I have not met them yet," Richard said. "It's hard to keep track of all of the extras who work on the movies."

"I met a woman who is a friend of Wyatt Earp. She told me he sometimes serves as a consultant for movies about the Old West."

"That is true, Heather. He often comes to the studio and helps us out, quite a fascinating old gentleman. Now, let's go see where you will be living for the next few weeks."

When Heather saw HEATHER DIAMOND above the star on the bungalow door, her heart jumped with delight. "This is happening… it's really happening," she repeated to herself.

For the next few days, Heather spent her time getting to know the movie crew and becoming more familiar with the streets, bungalows and sets of Universal City. She especially liked seeing the buses full of excited tourists who would come to observe movies in the making. For 25 cents, the public was allowed to enjoy a hillside picnic or sit in the viewing stands while observing the illusionary magic of moviemaking of Universal's latest films.

Although Heather was thrilled about her new life, she often thought about her friends in San Angelo, especially Pearl. This was the life Heather dreamed about and she was going to do whatever it took to keep the dream alive.

Richard had become Heather's new best friend and it was easy to be around him. He was different. Unlike most men she knew, he never indicated that he was even remotely interested in her, at least not sexually.

At first she assumed Richard was just keeping their relationship professional. Then on the afternoon before her first shoot, Heather was enlightened. While eating lunch with Richard at one of the restaurants on the lot, a young, attractive man approached the table and passed a note to Richard. It was the way they looked at each other that told the story.

"Charles, may I present to you our new star, Heather Diamond," Richard proclaimed courteously.

"So nice to meet you," Heather smiled.

"How do you do," he responded.

"Charles works in wardrobe and make-up," Richard continued. "You will be working with him."

"I look forward to it, Charles," she charmed.

"It will be an honor to work with a goddess as beautiful as you, my dear," Charles replied, kissing her hand. "Need to run."

"I will bring Heather over for her fitting at 2:30. See you then," Richard confirmed.

In a way, Heather was relieved. She knew sex between friends could change things and now she knew for certain the subject would never arise. Richard preferred men and that was just fine with her.

It was 10 AM when Richard knocked on the door of Heather's bungalow. "I have come to escort our princess to her first day of shooting," he exclaimed with a dramatic bow. "Your carriage awaits you, my dear."

When they drove up to the set, Heather was impressed how the facades designed to create the illusion of the town of San Angelo actually reminded her of Concho Avenue. As Heather joined the cast and crew, she was delighted to see two of her favorite cowboys on the set.

After working for them in Texas, Jake and Rex invited Dusty and Jesse to work on some upcoming projects and arranged for them to come to Universal.

"You are exactly what we need out there," Jake told them. "Try it. If you don't like it you can always go back to Texas." They had already been working as extras for several weeks.

"Jesse! Dusty! Hey!" Heather waved.

Both cowboys smiled and took off their hats. Heather couldn't help but admire the fact that they stood out as two of the most virile, handsome men on the set. There was just something about those Texas cowboys that put a fire in her womanly parts. Likewise, Dusty and Jesse were pleasantly familiar with the talented Heather and her feather.

Dusty picked Heather up and swung her around in a big circle. Jesse gave her a big squeeze. Dusty and Jesse were so happy to see a familiar face from home that they just couldn't help themselves. It was like being reunited with family.

The first day of production ran smoothly enough. When Heather heard the director yell, "Action," it was as if a switch had flipped inside her. Heather maintained a professional attitude and, as always, her charming attitude impressed the gentlemen both behind and in front of the camera. Heather was graceful, charming and self-assured and those who watched her work were mesmerized by her performance.

Heather loved the *Rio Concho* storyline. She had rehearsed her lines day and night, working hard to successfully create her character. For the last few days she was Jenny, a young girl who had been captured by the Comanche as a child, learning to live in a white man's world.

Heather's tears brought tears and her laughter brought smiles to both the movie crew and the tourists who were there to watch her work. By the end of the first day of shooting, Heather had developed an intimate relationship with the camera, bringing her deepest, most burning passions to life.

For days before the first shoot, John, the main director, had heard Richard singing Heather's praises. After the last take of the day, he commended his associate for his insight. "You were right, Richard. I like her; as a matter of fact I like her a lot."

After what seemed to be an endless day of shooting, Heather invited Dusty and Jesse to her bungalow. Respectfully, the three friends sat outside to defer any kind of gossip. Richard had provided their new leading lady with Applejack and the three friends drank to their future and to the success of the film.

"This is fun," Jesse remarked. "Pays lots more than being a ranch hand but seems kinda fake."

"Yeah, hard to explain," Dusty agreed. "It's like being a cowboy is some kind of hero thing. Damn. It's hard work. But like Jesse said, it's fun and pays a lot more than what we were making at home. One thing for sure, there's lots of poontang hangin' around the Waterhole."

"What's the Waterhole?" Heather asked.

"It's a hangout for cowboys working or looking for work in the movies. The women who come around are mainly extras and girls who want to be movie stars," Jesse said.

"Not exactly Miss Pearl's standards but will do in a pinch," Dusty smiled.

"Girls eager to please," Jesse said. "Always sayin' somethin' 'bout the way we walk and talk. They think cowboys are sexy or somethin'."

"Women do love cowboys. That's why Pearl lets you boys in the parlor. Athletically speaking, she knows it is good for morale."

Dusty and Jesse both smiled.

"Cowboys might not be rich but they sure are sexy. A good, strong cowboy lover beats a soft skinned poochy rich man on any day," Heather grinned.

"Yeah, we sure have had some good times at Pearl's. Always liked the way you used that feather," Dusty smiled.

"People out here don't know what I did at Miss Pearl's, boys, and I don't want them to."

"Your secret is safe with us," Jesse assured her.

"Thank you, boys. I always have appreciated a true Texas gentleman," Heather said with a warm smile.

Jesse was contemplative. "It's different out here all right. Cowboys from all over stay in the bunkhouse. Some of them want to be movie stars."

"You need to meet our new friend, Sport," Dusty suggested. "Met him in the stables. He takes care of the horses. Moved here from Missouri with his family and they live on the studio lot. His wife is expecting a youngin'."

"Sport says his wife can make bathtub beer without blowin' anything up," Jesse laughed. "He told us sometimes on days off, they have mini-rodeos with the ranch hands. Real nice guy."

"Sounds like fun," Heather remarked. "I'd like to meet him. You know Annabelle is from Missouri."

"Heard she's moving to Christoval," Dusty said. "She was one of my favorite ladies at Miss Pearl's. Didn't talk much, but quite a lady and real nice. Always seemed a little sad 'bout something."

"Annabelle has a little girl, Julie Marie," Heather informed them.

"What the..." Jesse commented. "Why in the world is she at Pearl's with a little girl and all?"

"Annabelle lost her husband in the war. She has a Mama and baby to support. Working at Pearl's made her enough money to purchase a little grocery and supply store in Christoval."

"Dang," Dusty expressed. "I never knew."

"Everybody has a story, boys, and ours just got better! Here's to *Rio Concho*!" Heather cheered.

Meanwhile back at Bill Stein's office, a frustrated pretty, petite, young blonde woman quietly opened his office door.

"What are you still doing here?"

"You promised me the part in *Rio Concho*! You said if I..."

"Sometimes things just don't work out, Sally Jean. That's the way this business is. I had nothing to do with it."

"I heard you on the phone! I heard you telling someone you had found the new leading lady for *Rio Concho*. That was supposed to be me!" she sobbed.

"Stop crying!"

"I don't want to be a secretary! I want to be a star, like you promised!"

"I got you in…"

"As an extra. That's no big deal!" she said folding her arms and falling on a chair with a pout.

"You have to be present to win, my dear. Hang in there. You'll have your day," Bill assured her, as he chewed on his cigar. "Now slide off your pretty panties and be nice to me. I'm horny as hell."

CHAPTER 14

# Hollywood Cowboys

By the time Heather arrived, Dusty and Jesse had already settled into their new life style and were consistently getting work. It was not easy to find “real cowboys” in Hollywood, California.

Universal Studios came up with a unique way to recruit cowboys. A large pen, fenced with wire, was installed just inside the studio gates. Here, cowboys looking for work could pass an hour, or an entire day, waiting for the appearance of a director who needed them. Sometimes a director would act purely on a vague notion that they might need cowboys and would shoot with no script at all. In fact, very often, they wouldn’t know if they might need a posse, or riders chasing a runaway stagecoach, until they get on top of the scene.

Hollywood had an over-abundance of pretty young women who wanted to be movie stars. There were also plenty of people available to play an extra, just to say they were in the movies. On the other hand, expert horsemen were hard to come by. Directors like Thomas Ince, D.W. Griffith and Cecil B. DeMille desperately needed what cowboys had to offer. Fearless men with nerves of steel willing to execute the most perilous stunts were precious treasures to producers and filmmakers.

When Jesse and Dusty arrived at Universal City, they had no idea what to expect. Early that first morning of shooting, the foreman came into the bunkhouse and yelled, "Roll out or roll up, you sons-o-bitches."

Jesse looked down at his friend, who was sleeping in the bunk below him. "Dang, Dusty. For a minute I thought I was back in Texas."

After breakfast in the cookhouse, the cowboys saddled up and strung out in single file along the edge of the road, headed for the location of the day. It would be several hours before sunrise.

When they arrived at the location, they were told to push their horses up the opposite side of a steep, small knoll all the way to the crest. When given the signal, the cowboys were scheduled to descend the knoll at top speed. In the meantime, the director ordered half a dozen stand-by cars to back up in a long row, with their rear bumpers facing the knoll.

Directly in front of the parked cars, prop men set up a solid wall of silver reflectors. When the director yelled "Action!" through a short megaphone, the stand-by drivers switched on their headlights. This empowered the reflectors to cast a bright glow of instant daylight on the down slope, where the cowboys were to make their first pursuit of the day. Several scenes were shot in this manner before the sun finally burned through the haze. They shot the scene again the same way after sundown, in order to snatch a few more feet of film from the impending darkness.

It had been a long day of hard riding when the cowboys put their weary ponies back into the barn. Somehow the group seemed satisfied. Every morning for the next few days, the cowboys were awakened the same way, "Roll out or roll up, you sons-o-bitches."

It seemed they were either running like crazy, or as one cowboy put it, "It feels like sometimes we just hurry up and wait." Dusty and Jesse didn't mind. Although the work was different, the pay was all right.

The next Saturday afternoon, Dusty and Jesse found themselves at the Waterhole, a friendly establishment they had discovered close to Universal, where a cowboy could find cold drinks, a friendly poker game and, sometimes, a friendly woman.

Conversations at the Waterhole ranged from old-time ranch memories to the day's activities on the studio lots. The cowboys were not impressed with fame or dazzled by wealth. To them, a Western star was just another man who had to step into his pants every morning.

Real cowboys turned movie stars liked hanging out at the Waterhole because it kept things real. One could easily lose his soul when caught up in the illusion of Hollywood fame.

The movie business was not easy. Cowboy stars were usually referred to as "White Hats." Pressured by producers, directors, bad horses, leading ladies and ex-wives, many saw the White Hats go from eating stardust to finding their only comfort in a bottle of whiskey or any woman who might say "Yes."

The White Hats who claimed to be authentic might fool women, the front office and movie fans, but the cowboys who rode in their shadow could read them better than anyone else alive. To a real cowboy, the one way to judge any man, from the greenest of the green to the most powerful director in Hollywood was: "Is he the kind of man you'd want to ride the river with?"

While sitting at the bar, Dusty and Jesse saw a familiar looking man wearing a white cowboy hat enter through the swinging doors. His eyes were black and blue and there was a white bandage stretched across the middle of his face. His demeanor was deliberate and strong, making one think, "Wonder what happened to the other guy?"

Jesse and Dusty could feel respect for this man emanate throughout the room. The cowboy sat down at one of the poker tables and bought $20 worth of chips.

"What in the hell happened to your nose, Yak?"

"Broke it fallin' off a 12-foot cliff workin' on *Branded a Bandit*. Doc had to reset it. The studio put a delay on shootin' the film for a couple of weeks."

"Damn, ya look like a raccoon."

"Yep. Looks like I've been in a helluva bar fight. Doc says I'm gonna be even better lookin' now that he's straightened out my nose. Same doc fixed my lip last year after that damn Brahma bull tore it open. Gave me back my kisser," Yak grinned, kissing the air three times.

Irma, a fiery redhead with bright green eyes, sauntered up behind the rodeo champ and wrapped her arms around him. Rubbing her oversized breasts across his shoulders, Irma licked his ear as if it was a giant sucker you buy at the fair.

"You are a real good kisser, Yak. Best I ever had."

"You say that to all the boys," someone yelled from the bar. "You even said it to me."

"That was before I kissed Yak," Irma announced. "Yak's a better kisser than you could ever hope to be, ya big goon."

Everyone in the room laughed as the cowboy, who had obviously had some kind of previous sexual encounter with Irma, turned three shades of red.

"Now don't be startin' any trouble, Irma" Yak corrected. "That's a friend of mine. We're all friends here. You go on now."

"What the hell! You weren't shooing me off the other night. In fact you kept callin' me your 'Wild Strawberry Roan!'"

"Sorry darlin', but I'm afraid I don't remember too much about that night, except for the fact at one point, I felt like I was on a pretty good ride."

Laughter filled the Waterhole. Fuming, Irma slapped Yak's hat to the floor and stomped out the front door, causing a crescendo of laughter to blare throughout the room.

"I like fire in a woman," Yak beamed. "Irma's as feisty as any bronc I ever rode. Hey Joe, give that man a cold drink, on me."

Dusty and Jesse, both new to the Waterhole, were sitting at the bar next to the cowboy who obviously knew Irma more than a little bit.

"Who is that?" Dusty asked.

"That's Yakima Canutt," the cowboy answered.

"Yak?" Jesse exclaimed. "I gotta go say hello."

Jesse jumped off the bar stool and Dusty followed. As they approached the poker table where Yak was sitting, the two friends watched as the legendary rodeo champ produced a pair of fives.

"Damn!" one of the cowboys at the table cursed.

"Sorry, boys," Yak smiled as he collected the chips. "Should have hung in there with that three of a kind, Joe."

"Are you the same Yak that won the saddle-bronc competition in Fort Worth in '21, '22 and '23? Rodeo called it, 'Yak Days', as I recall," Jesse asked.

"Yessir. That is correct. I am one in the same. You boys from Texas?"

"How'd you know?" Dusty inquired.

"You been around rodeos as long as I have, you get to recognize a Texas cowboy pretty easy. Are you workin'?"

"Yessir," Jesse answered. "Some movie people came to San Angelo and offered us a job. Makin' more money at Universal than we were in Texas. So far it's been pretty fun, although they work us pretty good.

"That's good," Yak commented. "A good cowboy can always find work in Hollywood. What's the name of the film you're working on?"

"Right now we are working on *Rio Concho*," Dusty answered. "A friend of ours is one of the stars. Her name is Heather. Calls herself Heather Diamond since she came to Hollywood. Real pretty girl."

"Can she act?" Yak asked.

"Sure she can," Jesse boasted. "I heard Richard the AD (Assistant Director) say she has camera eyes. He and John seem to be real happy with her."

"That's good, that's good," Yak commented.

"Who'd ever think we'd meet Yak Canutt in California," Jesse remarked. "How long you been ridin' on the rodeo circuit, Yak?"

"I started in major rodeos in 1914, and went through to last year. We had a good group traveling together. Always had special railroad cars and cars for the horses. We'd play anywhere from three to ten-day shows. Bronc riding and bulldogging were my specialties but I also did some roping. Started my career in Hollywood doubling for Tom Mix after he saw me in a rodeo in Los Angeles."

"Tom Mix wouldn't make a wart on a real cowboy's ass," somebody yelled. "He's all show. Got 6-foot letters on top of his house that say TOM MIX like anybody gives a shit. Hell, I heard he went AWOL after the Spanish-American War."

"Can't argue with success, Bubba. Mix has been good to me; gave me my first job in Hollywood. I stunted for him on two movies. After we shot *Lightening Bryce* I decided to go back on the rodeo circuit. Thought I'd had enough of this crazy town but now I'm back, this time in front of the camera as an actor. That's why they had to delay shooting on this film. I don't look so good for the camera with these two black eyes. How 'bout you boys? You want to be movie stars?"

"Never really thought about it," Jesse answered.

"Me either," Dusty said. "It's different being a cowboy in movies. I know we ride and all but it just doesn't seem real somehow."

One of the cowboys joined the conversation. "Ain't no long-term contract; still it pays five times more what any of us made punchin' cows. Besides you work in the saddle, not on your feet. And who'd go back to dry-nursin' cows inside some barbed-wire pen anyway when you can ride your tail off just as easy out here and for better pay?"

"I'll say," another added. "That paycheck at the end of the day looks as pretty as a speckled pup. Sure beats the hell out of digging wells and cuttin' poles."

"That's right. Riding as an extra can be long and brutal but compared to the trail drives or round-ups I've been on, it seems pretty mild," someone commented

"You gotta be careful Hollywood doesn't swallow your soul, boys. It's not so bad as long as you are working," a man who looked to be in his 40's said. "I'm getting too old for this kinda work. Lately I've had to find work in between jobs to support my family. Thinking 'bout going back to Texas. There ain't nothing more degrading to a cowboy than a job that you do on foot. It carries a stigma bordering on shame only another cowboy can appreciate."

"I hear ya," someone added. "Stunt work ain't somethin' you want to be doin' the rest of your life, but it's all right for now. At least the pay is good."

"Yeah, as long as you don't get hurt," a man with a sling on his arm said.

"What happened to you?" Jesse asked.

"They gave me a stallion not quite broke in. Did somethin' to my elbow. I'm seein' the doc tomorrow."

"Let me see what ya did, son," an old timer said, looking at his arm. "Hell we can fix that; done it for many a hand."

Pulling up a chair, the old man sat in front of the hurt cowboy and took off his right boot. "Take your wrist in my two hands; put my foot like this against your chest and- p-u-l-l…" The cowboy leaned back while the old timer pulled.

Crack…

"Ahhhhhh!" the man screamed. "Hey wait. That's amazing", he said, moving his arm around. "Popped right back into place. Thanks."

Just then, Irma walked into the Waterhole with two men following behind her. "There he is," she yelled, pointing at Yak.

"Goddammit," Yak cursed. "Already got my nose broke. Sure don't need this shit. Damn woman!"

"Don't worry, Yak. We got this. C'mon Jesse!" Dusty yelled.

Charging towards the bigger of the two with his head down, Dusty tackled him to the ground before he could react. Slamming his elbow onto his neck, Dusty paralyzed the man from any chance of fighting back.

At the same time, Jesse ran to the other man and, reaching up, punched him square in the jaw, knocking him out cold. The man rolled his eyes and fell backwards, breaking a chair on his way down.

Irma screamed and jumped on Yak's back. "You goddamn son-of-a-bitch! I'll teach you to screw me then treat me like trash! Who in the hell do you think you are, you damn asshole??"

More dangerous than the two men she brought with her, it took six men to pry Irma off Yak's back. Biting and kicking, she fought the men with all of hell's fury, until throwing her into the horses' water trough outside finally cooled her off.

Meanwhile, the man Dusty had tumbled to the ground surrendered. The cowboy who had been sitting at the bar poured a bucket of water on the man Jesse had temporarily put to sleep.

Joe the proprietor of the Waterhole walked outside to find Irma struggling to get out of the water trough.

CHAPTER 15

# Wyatt Earp

It was the last week of filming for *Rio Concho*. Heather was told to be up and ready at 4am for a sunrise shoot. The film called for a lover's kiss, followed by a dramatic retreat into the sunset. The director wanted mountains. Because it was sunrise, they shot the lovers riding off first and then the kiss.

Everyone on the set prepared for that spectacular instant the sun would reveal itself in the first crack of dawn, before the golden glow of light that would spread over the rolling hills of the San Fernando Valley. The timing was perfect and Heather was sensational as Jenny, surrendering to her lover's kiss.

It was a magical moment that directors dream about. Brilliant colors lit up the sky and the entire crew cheered when the shot was complete.

"Too bad this isn't a color film," Richard commented. "The colors in the sky are breathtaking."

Satisfied with her performance, Heather went back to her bungalow to grab a short nap and change. She was scheduled to shoot a few more short scenes at one of the corrals later that morning. When Heather arrived at the set, an older gentleman wearing a suit and cowboy hat was sitting straight and proud on a bench, talking to Richard. Heather watched as a young, good-looking man, about 17 years of age, eagerly approached the elderly gentleman whose regal demeanor made it seem as if he were holding court.

"Good morning, Mr. Earp," the young man said. "Can I get you some coffee?"

"That would be fine, son. What's your name?"

"My name is Marion, Marion Morrison. Some people call me 'Duke.' When I was a kid, we had an Airedale named Duke. He went everywhere with me. Some firemen friends started calling me "little Duke" because my dog was so big. The name kinda stuck."

"If I were you, son, I'd just stick with Duke," the man grinned. "You're too big a man to be called Marion. Duke suits you well. You play sports?"

"Yessir. I play football. Looks like I'll be getting a scholarship to USC next year."

"That's real good, son. I like my coffee black."

"That's got to be Wyatt Earp," Heather guessed.

When Richard looked up and saw Heather, he walked over and reached for her hand. "Come with me, Heather, there's someone I want you to meet."

Heather remembered Miss Pearl's words and smiled. "Gentlemen are only gentlemen when properly introduced."

As Richard and Heather approached, the man slowly stood up tall and put his hat over his heart.

"Mr. Wyatt Earp, may I present to you our newest star Heather Diamond," Richard bragged.

With a twinkle in his eye, Wyatt kissed Heather's hand. "Very pleased to meet you, my dear."

"It is an honor, Mr. Earp. I have heard many great things about you."

"Please, call me Wyatt."

"This is Heather's first movie," Richard said. "She is a wonderful actress."

"Thank you, Richard," Heather gleamed. "I believe we have a mutual friend... Ruby? I met her a couple of weeks ago at the Hotel Redondo."

"Ah, yes," he beamed. "I met Ruby in Tombstone. She and my wife have been friends since they were kids. You are right, Heather. Ruby is a good friend."

Wyatt looked into the air as if he were watching a movie screen. "Ahh, Ruby. That woman is good as gold. How is she?"

"She is good," Heather charmed. "It turns out she and I have a lot in common."

Wyatt's eyes twinkled. "I'll bet you do, little lady. I'll bet you do."

Looking at each other, Heather and Wyatt smiled as if they could read each other's mind.

"Mind if I watch you work, Heather?"

"I'd love it, Wyatt."

Just then Duke returned with coffee in hand.

"Thank you son. Duke, this is Heather Diamond. I believe we are going to be seeing a lot of her on the silver screen."

"How do you do, Ma'am?"

"Hello, Duke. What do you do here?"

"I work for a man who owns a soda shop. He is the farrier here. Sometimes he lets me come along and I help shoe the horses."

"Do you know Sport?"

"Sure do; real nice guy. Strong too."

"I hear his wife is pregnant. I'd like to meet them," Heather said.

"We are ready for you, Heather," Richard instructed.

"Very nice to meet you, gentlemen. Maybe we can visit later, Wyatt. I bet you have some great stories. I'd like to hear some."

Wyatt smiled and tipped his hat.

Heather flashed her eyes and winked.

Wyatt watched as Heather turned around and glided away like a swan on a crystal clear lake.

"If only I was 40 years younger…" he thought.

By mid-morning, the crew had completed filming for the day. Richard and John, the director, were reviewing the raw footage on a small screen in one of the editing rooms.

"Too bad it's in black and white," Richard remarked. "The colors were spectacular! At least the lightening is good."

"Look at those eyes," John exclaimed. "Those big, beautiful, expressive eyes. The close-ups are fantastic. Where did you say Bill discovered her?"

"I believe our movie scouts found her in San Angelo, Texas, when they were on that research trip to visit Fort Concho. Heather is a friend of some of the cowboys they recruited to shoot some footage. She told them she was an actress and wanted to come to California. One of them set up a meeting with Bill Stein and here she is."

"Hmm. That's not like Bill to take a chance on a new girl like he did with Heather," John remarked.

"I don't know…Stein seems to have good instincts," Richard replied, desperately wanting to change the subject. He knew about Bill Stein and how he was with girls who wanted to be movie stars.

It was no secret. Bill Stein took full advantage of the fact that Hollywood was full of women who would do anything to be in the movies. Usually, when an aspiring young actress gave him sexual favors, Stein would put her in as an extra, giving the girl hope of being discovered and making her famous. Richard was not sure how Heather was able to land the leading role in *Rio Concho*, and part of him did not want to know. However, he was curious.

Because Heather was confident and talented, Richard saw her as a professional from the first day she came to work. Unlike other girls he had worked with, Heather was a hard worker and took direction well. True to her craft, Richard could tell Heather was not in it for the fame; she was born to be an actress.

After the shoot, Wyatt had agreed to meet Heather at the stables. Watching her work, he was impressed with how easily she transformed into her character Jenny.

Not wanting to waste a minute, Heather hurried to her bungalow. Quickly she changed into a skirt, boots and a white Mexican peasant shirt she had purchased on Olvera Street, when she and Ginger went on an excursion to explore the city.

As Heather neared the big barn, the smell of the horses made her think of home. It had been almost two years since she began sending money to her family on the farm in Illinois. She wondered about her little brothers and sisters. "They must be getting so big. I wonder if they even remember me."

"Hey, Heather," Dusty waved.

They were all there: Wyatt, Duke, Dusty and Jesse. "This is Sport," Jesse bragged. "Sport, this is our friend Heather. She's the leading lady in *Rio Concho*."

"Howdy do Ma'am," Sport said, flipping his hat.

"Nice to meet you, Sport. Jesse and Dusty say you have made them feel right at home."

"It's been fun," Sport exclaimed. "We're going to play with the horses in a little while. Kind of like a little rodeo. Why don't you come watch? My wife will be there. I believe Hoot Gibson is going to join us as well."

"Sounds great," Heather agreed. "Hello, Wyatt."

"Good day, Dear Lady," Wyatt said with a gentlemanly bow.

"Wyatt has some great stories, Miss Heather," Duke exclaimed.

"Let's go sit under that tree," Wyatt said with authority.

Several yards from the stables, the cool shade of a majestic white oak beckoned the group to sit on the benches below its branches.

"You know, Heather, there is a reason they call it the "Wild West." I have been trying for months to convince Hollywood to tell my story. There was a time when the law was ignored, and a man had to have balls made out of steel to survive. Funny how life is. At one time, I was a highly respected man of the law. Things change. Now, I am an unpaid movie consultant."

"Tell the story about what happened in Tombstone at the OK Corral," Duke eagerly requested.

Heather watched as Wyatt became somber and his eyes glistened with intense emotions of sorrow, anger and strength.

"Goddamn Cowboys. Stupid, goddamn Cowboys wouldn't give up their guns. Pride can be a killer. What a waste."

Wyatt pulled out his knife and picked up an oak branch that was lying on the ground. Whittling seemed to calm his mind, when the darkness of his memories would overtake him.

"Like I said before, things change. In Tombstone, cowboys were not heroes like in movies today. Cowboys were known as a band of cattle rustling, horse thieves. Even stole some mules from the U.S. Calvary and laughed about it. They were a bad lot and sometimes killed folks just for the fun of it. Wore red sashes. People were afraid. The law was weak on the frontier; too much open space to cover. Made it easy for the Cowboys to do whatever the hell they wanted."

A light breeze was blowing through the oak tree leaves, creating a peaceful atmosphere. The small group listened with full attention and respect, as Wyatt Earp reflected on a time when a man could not be fearful and survive.

"My brothers and I came to Tombstone when it was a new mining town to make money. Virgil was hired to be the U.S Deputy Marshal for the region. When we first came, the town had just over 100 people. It was mainly tents, some buildings, silver mines and a few saloons with friendly ladies." Wyatt stopped and looked at Heather. "That's where I met Ruby," he smiled.

"Tombstone was becoming a mining boomtown and, for me, a perfect place to set up gambling saloons. It was rough in those days. My brothers and I did what we could to keep order in the town. Tried to be fair. In fact, I was the one who stopped the town from lynchin' one of the Cowboys. They called him 'Curly.' Dumb fool accidentally shot the Tombstone Marshal, Fred White. Crazy, stupid son-of-a-bitch, but it was an accident.

"By 1881, Tombstone was the largest boomtown in the southwest. All kinds of people with dreams and high expectations were moving there. Poor folks, rich folks, businessmen and merchants ...most of them brought their wives and kids. There were even groups of Mexicans and Chinese. It seemed like hundreds turned into thousands overnight.

"It was hard. Tombstone had gotten pretty rough. Virgil was in charge of keeping the law. Town shootings were common and there were horse rustlers and bandits robbing folks.

"Tombstone had gotten so bad, the City Council finally decided to pass an ordinance, 'no deadly weapons in town.' That included bowie knives, dirks, pistols and rifles. Anyone coming into town had to leave their weapons at a livery stable or saloon. As you can probably guess, the Cowboys ignored the new law.

"Tension had been building. The trouble started when those boys robbed the Benson stagecoach. The drivers were both killed. Made a deal with Ike Clanton to tell me who shot 'em. He told me it was Frank Stillwell and his partner, Pete Spence. Virgil arrested them. Frank was in with the Cowboys and came up with some bogus witnesses to support their alibis. Judge let them go. There was no question it was Frank. I saw his boot print at the scene of the robbery.

"Not too long after that, Virgil arrested Frank Stillwell again for another robbery. Started telling folks the Earp brothers were picking on him like some bratty little kid. That's when the threat came. While Virgil and I were in Tucson at the hearing, Frank McLaury told our brother Morgan, the Cowboys would kill us if we arrested Stillwell, Spence or any of the McLaurys again.

"A few days later the McLaurys and Ike Clanton came to Tombstone to sell some beef stock. That night at the Alhambra Saloon, Doc Holliday accused Ike of lying in his testimony and the conversation got hot. Both men were drunk. Virgil showed up and told them to stop fighting or he was going to put them both in jail.

"That's when Ike started making his threats. 'I'm putting an end to all this bullshit in the morning! I'll be ready for you in the morning, Holliday.' I went looking for Morgan. I knew there was going to be trouble."

Heather was fascinated. She had never heard anything like this before. As Wyatt continued his story, her heart was on fire with excitement.

"You gotta understand. This was a long time comin'. It wasn't just about the guns. The Cowboys hurt a lot of people. These boys had no regard for the law and it had to be stopped. The whole town was talkin' about it. There were folks who heard the Cowboys say they were going to kill us. Some asked if we needed help but Virgil said, 'no.' Saw it as our fight. He had deputized Holliday that morning. Morgan and I had already been deputized. It was time for the bullshit to end."

Wyatt laid his stick and knife on the ground, leaned forward on his seat with his elbows on his legs and paused. For a long moment, it seemed the birds stopped chirping and the horses became quiet. The only sound that could be heard was the soft summer breeze rustling through the oak leaves, whispering the memory of a timeless moment that to Wyatt seemed like yesterday. Unattached to anything around him, Wyatt Earp continued his story as if he were watching a small screen in front of him. His voice became quiet and strong.

"I remember it was cold and windy that day. Virgil had picked up a double-barreled shotgun at the Wells Fargo office and hid it under his coat. Gave it to Holliday who put it under his coat. The Doc was already wearing a pistol holder. My brothers and I had revolvers in our coat pockets and waistbands.

"We heard the Cowboys were next to Buck's boarding house where Holliday was staying. The four of us walked in a line down Fremont Street.

"'Let's get 'em, boys,' Virgil said.

"Holliday was ready. 'All right,' he said.

"When we first spotted the Cowboys, Sheriff Behan was with them, trying to get 'em to give up their guns. He came towards us, nervous as hell. Kept lookin' back.

"'For God sake, they're gonna murder you,' he told us. Tried to tell us he had taken their guns away but we knew better.

"'Throw up your hands. We want your guns,' Virgil yelled.

"Ike Clanton had been bragging all over town he was going to kill me and my brothers. He ran up and grabbed me. Told me he was unarmed and didn't want a fight. 'Go to fighting or run away,' I told him. I pushed him away. Damn coward ran into the boarding house. Damn coward with a big mouth.

"Billy Clanton leveled his pistol at me. I knew Frank McLaury was the best shooter there, so I aimed at him and shot him in the stomach the same time Billy shot at me.

"Billy missed.

"Tom's horse jumped to the right. He jumped behind it and fired over its back. Holliday stepped around the horse and shot Tom in the chest with the short double-barreled shotgun. Tom was tough. Stumbled to the foot of a telegraph pole before he met his Maker.

"Holliday dropped the shotgun, pulled out his revolver and commenced to shootin' at Frank McLaury and Billy. Kept shootin' even after they were hit. One of those boys hit Morgan in the back. Morgan went down for a minute then got back up. Virgil was shot in the leg but got a shot off at Billy. I just stood there shootin'. Never did get hit.

"Frank shot at Holliday. Hit him in his pistol pocket then headed down Fremont with his horse. Holliday was hurt just enough to piss him off. 'That son-of-a-bitch has shot me and I am going to kill him!'

"I'm tellin' you, those boys were stout. None of them died right away. Ike Clanton, that yellow-bellied coward who started the whole mess, was still running. Heard he had a pistol hidden under his coat and shot at us a couple of times.

"Lots of folks called us murderers. Over 2,000 folks at the funeral. A couple of months later, Virgil was ambushed at the Cosmopolitan Hotel. They shot him in the arm and crippled him for life. Doc pulled out twenty pieces of buckshot from his side. I remember when the Doc was patching him up, Virgil looked at his wife and said, 'Never mind, Allie, I still got one arm left to hug you with.'"

Wyatt smiled for a moment and, like a storm cloud blocking the sun, his expression turned very grave.

"Next spring the sons-of bitches killed our little brother, Morgan. It was my 34th birthday."

Heather watched as soft tears glazed over Wyatt's eyes.

"After that there was more killin'. When the score was finally settled, I left Arizona."

Dusty, Jesse, Sport, Duke and Heather watched as Wyatt picked up the piece of oak he had laid on the ground. Coming back to the present, he commenced to his whittling.

It was Duke who broke the silence.

"It's an honor knowing you, sir."

"Thank you, son," Wyatt responded. "Thank you."

Suddenly the roar of a truck sped up to where the group was sitting, breaking the solemnity of the moment.

"Sport! Sport! You gotta get to the house! Opal's ready to pop out a youngin'!"

"Looks like I gotta go," Sport grinned.

"Congratulations, my man," Wyatt exclaimed as Sport jumped into the truck.

Before he entered the house, Sport could hear the wailing cry of his third born singing the song of new life that puts pride in a daddy's heart. Walking in the door, he saw the midwife wrapping a blanket around a handsome, healthy baby boy. Small in stature and with such a big baby, it appeared as if she were holding a toddler in her arms.

"You have a strong healthy son," the midwife announced, handing the swaddling infant to his proud father. "Quite a set of lungs on this one. I believe he will be a singer one day. What is his name?"

Sport looked into the baby's face, his heart bursting with pride. "Roland. His name is Roland Henry Jordan."

"A good, strong name, Mr. Jordan. Very fitting for such a big boy. There is someone tending to Opal right now. Do you have a scale? Let's see how much this boy weighs."

"In the kitchen," Sport answered.

Sport laid his new son on the kitchen scale. "Looks like he outweighed the scale. Only goes to twelve pounds," Sport declared.

"He must be 13 or 14lbs! Biggest baby I ever delivered. Thank God the labor didn't take long," she said.

"I want to see my wife. Where's Bobby and Dodie?"

"They're fine. They are playing with the kids next door. We barely got here in time. Happens a lot with the third baby. Three big pushes and Roland was here."

"Think the little guy is hungry?" Sport grinned, as he swaddled little Roland Henry back into his blanket."

"I am sure he is," the midwife smiled. "I believe Opal is ready to see you now. Let's go check on her."

"Hey, Baby. You doin' ok?"

"Tired, but I am ok," Opal replied.

"I just realized, today is Will Rogers' birthday. Are you sure you want to call him Roland Henry?"

"I promised Mother."

"Well I'm going to call him Duke."

"Duke?"

"Met a kid today named Marion. Told us some folks call him Duke on account of the fact when he was a kid, he had a dog named Duke that was so big, folks called him 'little Duke.' He's a big kid, plays football. Wyatt Earp told him to stick with the name Duke 'cause it suits him better. Roland here is gonna be a big kid too. I like Duke. That's what I'll call him," Sport boasted.

"I like Duke just fine," Opal agreed as she offered her new son her breast.

As Sport gazed upon his wife and son, his heart filled with pride. "Thank you, Opal. You are by far the most beautiful woman in the world. I love you."

"I love you, Honey. Guess you better get back to work. I'm fine. I have plenty of help."

When Sport returned to the barn, everyone was still there. "Did your wife have her baby?" Heather asked.

"She did. A big boy. Outweighed the kitchen scale. His name is Roland, but I believe I'm going to call him Duke, just like you," he said, looking at the football star.

"I do like Duke better than Marion."

"And I'm sure he will like it better than Roland," Sport grinned.

"Guess I better get back to the house and see what Sadie's cookin'," Wyatt declared.

"I heard your wife's real name is Josephine," Heather inquired.

"They called her Sadie in Tombstone. My Sexy Sadie," Wyatt smiled.

"Sadie was Johnny Behan's girlfriend till she found him in their bed with another woman. He was a real asshole... full of himself. She even took care of his kid. Made promises to Sadie he never kept. First time I saw her that woman had me. Prettiest girl in town. My wife Mattie was so loaded up with laudanum most of the time, she never knew if she was comin' or goin'. Sadie and I became friends and then...well...we became close," he smiled to himself nodding his head.

"Mattie moved to California with my family. Drugs finally killed her," he sighed. "She never was a happy woman. Sadie always felt bad about it."

"I'm sorry," Heather offered.

"Mattie was a sporting woman and Sadie was an actress. Guess I just have a thing for the friendly type." Wyatt winked at Heather in a way that made her hot with flush. "*I could easily fall in love with this man,*" she thought.

"Someone should tell your story."

"I've been talking to Billy Hart about making a movie about my life. We shall see what the future holds. Good day, Miss Heather...Good day, boys. See ya around."

*(Note: Marion Morrison chose the name John Wayne when he became an actor and later claimed that he imitated Wyatt Earp's demeanor when he made his films.)*

## CHAPTER 16

# Universal Tours

Strong friendships were easily cultivated between the cowboys who frequented the Waterhole. Most of them were drifters. Ranch hands, ropers and rodeo riders from different parts of the west were the most common. Seeing them as heroes on the silver screen, women loved the cowboys and most days there were a variety of "buckle bunnies" ready and eager to engage in free sexual activity.

Dusty and Jesse liked their work all right. Unlike working on the ranch in Texas, there were days when there was nothing to do but hang out at the Waterhole. They were handsome and, because of Miss Pearl's insistence on having good manners, they knew how to act like gentlemen. This quality made them especially attractive to the ladies.

Working at Universal City in the San Fernando Valley, it was not unusual to run head on, at any time, into three or four big stars working on their western serials. It usually only took five days to film a chapter which gave the boys plenty of work.

One of Dusty's favorite cowboy stars was Art Acord. Art was one of the few cowboys to have ever ridden the legendary bucking horse Steamboat. He had worked for a time performing for the Miller Brother's Traveling 101 Ranch Wild West Show. It was during that time he made friends with Tom Mix, Bronco Billy and Hoot Gibson, all cowboy stars of the silver screen. At first Art worked as a stuntman. When Cecil B. DeMille gave him the lead in Squaw Man, he became an overnight sensation.

Dusty and Jesse had made friends with a stuntman named Jack, who knew of Dusty's admiration for whom some referred to as the "Mormon Cowboy."

"How'd you boys like to meet Art Acord? I'm working with him tomorrow afternoon. Might need a few extra hands."

"Sure Jack," Dusty answered.

"He's working with a Mexican knife thrower named Ortega. I've never seen a man so quick and true with a knife as that chili-dipper and I've seen plenty in my time. Meet me tomorrow at the Western street around one."

"We'll be there," Jesse affirmed.

The next afternoon Jack met the boys on the set. Sport was there, securing a saddle on one of the mares. "Hey Dusty, Jesse. You workin'?"

"Jack said he might need some extra help," Dusty answered. "I'm a big fan of Art Acord."

"Hello, everyone," Heather greeted

"Hey, Heather, what are you doing here?" Dusty asked.

"I have nothing I have to do today so I thought I'd come watch you work. I am also a big fan of Art Acord. How's that new baby boy, Sport?"

"That boy can eat!" Sport said. "He's doing just great. Sleeps pretty well through the night. Gave me a big ol' smile this morning. Thanks for asking."

"Who is this pretty lady?" Jack asked.

"Jack, may I present to you our friend from San Angelo, Miss Heather Diamond. She is the leading lady in *Rio Concho*."

"Pleased to meet you Ma'am," Jack said, tipping his hat.

"Hello, Jack" Heather smiled.

"Did I hear y'all are big fans of Art?" an older gentleman asked.

"Yessir."

"This is Gillis," Jack introduced.

"I've known Art since he was a green kid on his first ranch job. Never known any other man quite like him. Why I once seen a bronc take him right through a six-strand barbed-wire fence, and I mean they was wrapped up together like a Christmas package. But damn, if Art didn't stop that bronc, got them both unwound. When we got back to the barn he patched up that poor pony as good as any good vet could've done."

Gillis continued, "The man's tough. Hell, I've seen Art with no clothes on, and there ain't a patch of hide bigger 'n a silver dollar on him that don't have a knife wound, a gunshot scar or some other kinda brand. C'mon, I'll introduce you myself."

Just as they started over, three busloads of tourists pulled in, including a group of chattering women from Rhode Island attending an out-of-state convention.

"Holy Cats!" Gillis groaned. Art hates the studio tours like the devil hates holy water. He calls these groups of ladies, 'heifers in heels.' This always puts him in a bad mood. Says it makes it hard to work with all that talkin' and squealin' going on. We better wait till they leave."

It was a well-known fact the tourists loved the studio tours but for those who were trying to work it was nothing less than terribly annoying. Although everyone complained, their pleading fell onto deaf ears.

"The tourists are driving us crazy!! Those tinhorn guides yellin' at the top of their lungs and tourists wantin' autographs in the middle of a scene…how the hell can we work?"

Everyone at Universal referred to the owner of the studio as Uncle Carl. He had installed viewing ramps on every stage, allowing the tourists to watch "movies being made." He saw the tour as folks paying him for word of mouth publicity. Tourists were his "brainstorm good-neighbor policy" and there was nothing anyone could do to change his mind. Today, Art and Ortega would go on the warpath to change all that.

Although there was no question Art Acord was built as solid as a brick wall, Dusty was surprised to find he was shorter than he appeared on the big screen. Today he was dressed in authentic Levis and a blue work shirt, with a .45 slung, butt forward, on his left hip. Waiting for the prop man to get set up, Art strolled over to a false-front sheriff's office where he had a bottle of spirits stashed behind one of the uprights.

Ortega, about 3 inches shorter and much stockier, was dressed in tight vaquero pants and a clean white guayabera shirt from the Yucatan. He was killing time practicing his knife throwing, hitting a bull's eye every time. The Mexican had joined Acord in sharing the bottle. Although at first the two men seemed friendly enough, a quarrel suddenly erupted between them.

Gillis was familiar with Art's explosive temper and decided it best to step in before real trouble began. "Say boys, how 'bout a round of poker with me and my new friends here while you are waiting to shoot the scene."

Acord started cussing as loud as he could with the most vulgar language he could think of exploding from his mouth. That's when the director came over and tried to calm him down.

"C'mon, Art. Cool down. Let's be sensible. There are people watching and we don't want to give them a bad impression."

The director's comment was like throwing gasoline on a fire. Art was out of control.

"I don't give a goddamn if Saint Peter himself is leadin' that bunch of Rhode Island Reds. I'm gonna run this chili-dipper off the lot or kill him tryin'!"

Angrily, Ortega spun around and pushed the director out of the way. Then with a fury, yelled, "No yellow filthy gringo bastard calls me that!"

"Maybe I was wrong," Acord smirked. "I reckon you're just a buck-nun Mexican sheepherder!"

Fuming, Ortega pulled a huge knife out of the red sash cinched around his waist. In the same instant Acord's right hand whipped out the .45 in a cross "border draw."

"Now Art," Gillis said, backing off.

"Everyone get the hell out of my way. I'm gonna fill this greaser so full of holes he won't even float in the brine."

Ortega made two dragging steps towards Acord then leaped like a cat, the blade of his knife blazing in the afternoon sun. Art fired his gun and hit the Mexican in the shoulder. As Ortega clutched his wound the red blood spread across the front of his white guayabera shirt.

With superhuman strength, the Mexican jumped forward, wrestling with the cowboy star and rammed his knife into his chest several times until both were drenched in each other's blood.

"Oh my God!" Heather screamed.

Realizing this was not a movie but a real confrontation, the tourists began screaming with horror and scattered like turkey hens in a hailstorm. Fear had taken over the crowd as they ran in chaos, bellowing and falling over each other trying to find a safe haven. Some crawled under the tour buses. Others were able to make their way inside.

Miraculously, Acord had enough strength to fire three more bullets into Ortega's body. Unable to stand, Art dropped the pistol from his hand and fell face down on top of the Mexican's lifeless form. For what seemed like an endless space in time, nobody moved. In a fierce frenzy the tour busses roared away.

The crewmen, actors and extras slowly crept out of their various sanctuaries, moving towards the middle of the street where the two lifeless bodies lay.

Gillis was distraught. "I always feared that boy would end up this way."

Hats in hand, Dusty, Jack and Jesse respectfully approached the circle that had gathered around the cowboy hero who had tragically met his doom. All that could be heard was the quiet murmur of men speaking softly in the presence of death.

All of a sudden a cackling laugh broke through the silence of the somber moment. "Hell, it was the only way we could think of to stampede that bunch of broomtails and their wranglers!"

Gillis was speechless as he watched the knot of mourners doubling over with laughter fall apart. He watched Art and Ortega rise from the ground within the center of the mourners like two bloody ghosts. Tears celebrating their accomplishment were streaming down their faces as they held on to each other's shoulders, rocking back and forth with laughter.

Ortega was gasping for air. "When you busted that fist full of blood capsules we stole from the prop man, I didn't know which one of us was going to drown in gore first!" he cried.

"And you…flashin' your goddamn rubber knife! I thought you were going to finish me off before I dropped you with my roll of blanks."

Gillis, still caught up in the general hysteria of relief, was slowly coming into the reality that the whole event was just a ploy to get rid of a bunch of tourists.

"Art, you damn son-of-a-bitch! You scared the holy shit out of me! I don't know whether to kiss ya or punch your lights out."

Gillis hugged Art like a daddy would hug his son who just returned from war. "This is Dusty and Jesse, Art. These boys are from Texas."

"Pleasure to meet you boys," Art grinned. "Ma'am," he said, looking at Heather.

Heather smiled at Art, holding her hand on her heart with relief.

"Sorry Gillis. Didn't mean to scare ya," Art told his old friend.

In light of the events of the afternoon, it was decided that shooting would resume the following day.

"Seems like an appropriate time to visit the Waterhole, boys," Art announced. "Drinks on me!"

When the guides heard it was all just a horrific joke played on them, they were furious. With raging contempt they marched into Uncle Carl's office and informed him they would never take a tourist bus to observe another Art Acord film.

Later, when Art heard about the boycott, he solemnly replied, "I guess the punishment fits the crime."

It brought great satisfaction knowing he and his compadre Ortega had not "died" in vain.

## CHAPTER 17

# Poor Fatty

Richard was excited when he knocked on Heather's bungalow door. "It's a wrap. You are finished, my dear," Richard said, kissing Heather on the cheek. "I just came from the editing room and everyone is singing your praises. There is talk the studio is considering you for the film *Blue Midnight*. I have read the script and it is spectacular! You are perfect for the role. You'll be working with Hoot Gibson."

"I really don't know what to say, Richard. It is like I have walked into a dream." Heather smiled. "I have met so many wonderful people."

"Let me take you to lunch. There are some places I want to show you. I will be back in an hour to pick you up."

Richard arrived, as promised, behind the wheel of a green, 1924 Dodge Touring Convertible. As they drove through the studio gates, Heather breathed in the freshness of another beautiful day in Southern California.

"I want to show you Pickfair," Richard said.

"I've read about Pickfair," Heather exclaimed. "Douglas Fairbanks bought it for his wife Mary Pickford as a wedding gift."

"Only the elite, who's who of Hollywood, gets invited to Mary Pickford's home. They are giving a party to celebrate the completion of Pickfair next week. The invitation says, 'and guest.' I would like you to come with me, Heather. It is time you started meeting the important people in this town. I truly believe it won't be long before you get on the "A" list."

"I don't know what that means but it sounds good to me," Heather smiled.

"I first worked with Mary back in 1914 on *Hearts Adrift*, when she was with Zukor's Famous Film Company. Back in those days she was known as 'America's Sweetheart' and 'the girl with the curls.' I was at the party where she met Douglas. He was married at the time. So was she. We all sold war bonds together with Charlie Chaplin. Our friendship had developed over the years. I don't believe any of us ever dreamed the movie industry would explode like it has. We were just having fun making films."

It could not have been a more perfect day. The land looked fertile and green in the new Beverly Hills real estate development. Richard had the top down on his touring car and Heather held her chin up high, feeling exhilarated with the warm September breeze blowing across her face.

"This used to be a lima bean field, Heather. I believe it won't be long before we see hundreds of new homes being built throughout this area. Mary and Douglas are trendsetters. Ever since they formed United Artists with Charlie Chaplin and D.W. Griffith, they are a powerful entity in this town."

"I met Mae Marsh at Moonstone Beach when my friend Ginger and I went to Redondo. She told me what happened with *Sands of Dee*, when Mr. Griffith gave her the lead because Mary Pickford…"

"Yes, I was there. I felt bad for Mary. It really hurt her when Griffith gave her lead away. You have to be a forgiving woman in this town if you want to survive, Heather. Mary is a smart lady. Right now, she is the most powerful woman in Hollywood."

There it was in all its majesty. Heather had seen photos in magazines but looking at Pickfair in its full glory was quite different. Again, she thought of Camelot."

"Here we are," Richard announced. "Oh look, there's Mary and Doug coming down the driveway. How is that for timing?"

Richard beeped his horn and waved. Seeing them, Heather was humbled.

"Hello, Richard," Douglas greeted warmly. "Beautiful day to drive with the top down, isn't it? Couldn't ask for better weather."

"Hello, Richard," Mary echoed. "Who is that lovely young lady you have with you?"

"Douglas and Mary, this is Heather Diamond," Richard announced proudly. "We just finished shooting a western at Universal. Thought I'd show her Pickfair."

Heather waved. "Hello," she said, barely able to speak, being in the presence of the king and queen of Hollywood.

"I am bringing Heather to the party next weekend," Richard informed them.

"Good, good," Mary smiled. "We look forward to seeing you there. Everyone is coming. It should be fun."

"Congratulations on completing Pickfair. It is simply spectacular," Richard complimented.

"Thank you, Richard. We are certainly proud of it. See you then," Douglas cheered, beeping his horn as he and his bride waved goodbye.

Richard and Heather sat for a few minutes, enjoying the view. "Douglas brought me here when it was a hunting lodge and told me he was going to buy it for Mary. They have been renovating and decorating Pickfair for five years. There is a beautiful pool in the back."

"I cannot wait to see it, Richard," Heather expressed.

"Buster Keaton is building an Italian Villa not too far from here and Charlie Chaplin is building a home next door. Pickfair is just the beginning. Beverly Hills will soon be the residence of the stars," Richard said.

"Can we go by the Pink Palace? I'd like to say hello to my friend Edward," Heather requested.

Seeing Richard and Heather in the lobby, Edward burst from the front desk and greeted them with open arms. "Heather! Richard! How wonderful to see you!"

"Hello, Edward," Heather greeted. "You know Richard?"

"Everyone knows Richard," Edward exclaimed.

"We just finished filming *Rio Concho*, Edward. Heather was superb. I just drove her by Pickfair. Looks like Beverly Hills is getting ready to expand."

"That is correct my friend. Beverly Hills is looking at approving plans for a new University. Pickfair has made the area a more desirable place to live. Most of the real estate transactions happen here at the hotel," Edward said. "So many changes since the movie business came to town. People are moving here in droves because there is so much work."

"I'd like to stay here again for a few weeks while I decide where I am going to live, Edward," Heather said. "I believe I'm going to purchase a beach home in Redondo. Ginger and I loved it there."

"Excellent choice, my dear. Just let me know when you want to come. I am at your service," Edward bowed.

"How about next Thursday," Heather inquired.

"I will have your bungalow ready," he smiled.

When Richard and Heather entered the Blue Front, a local hangout for people in the movie industry, everyone turned to stare at the new girl in town.

With a dramatic flair Richard announced, "Don't just goggle everyone, put your hands together and welcome Universal's brand new starlet, Heather Diamond."

Everyone stood and clapped. Like the professional she was, Heather humbly smiled and made a dramatic bow as if she had just received a standing ovation for her performance in a Shakespearean play."

"Well done, my dear," Richard commended her.

Heather nodded her head, accepting his approval.

"Hollywood is an exciting place, Heather, but it is important to play the game right," Richard started.

"The game?"

"Yes, dear Heather, the game. It is not easy to be an overnight success, but it is very easy to become an overnight failure. No matter who you are in your personal life, when you are in public or working at the studio, you are Heather Diamond. Try to see yourself as two different women in one body. One is Heather Diamond, an illusionary product that belongs to the world. The other is just Heather, a farm girl from Illinois. It is the part of you that dreams, hurts and likes to go a little crazy sometimes. Am I making sense?"

"Yes, Richard. I am listening. I actually do know what you mean. I have been "two girls in one body" for a long time. In fact there might even be more like a dozen of me when I count being a sister, a daughter, a friend, a dreamer, a child… and then there are the character roles like Jenny in *Rio Concho*. Kind of like when Shakespeare said, "And one man in his time will play many parts," Heather quoted with a dramatic flair.

"Bravo," Richard applauded. "You do get it."

"Overnight failure? Heather repeated. "Is that what happened to Fatty Arbuckle?"

"Roscoe should never have let those girls in his hotel suite. Everyone in Hollywood knew both of them were trouble."

"Roscoe? Sounds like you know him." Heather remarked.

"I have worked on several pictures with Roscoe. He is such a talent. Did you know the man can sing like a bird?" Richard bragged. "One of the nicest men you'd ever want to meet. Funny? He is so funny! I'll never forget shooting that pie in the face scene with Mabel Normand. We were all hysterically rolling on the floor. Roscoe invented that gag."

"I loved the Fatty Arbuckle movies," Heather said.

"For a big guy, Roscoe is pretty agile. He can skip upstairs light as a feather and do a backward somersault as graceful as a girl tumbler. Roscoe did some great movies with Charlie Chaplin and he actually discovered Buster Keaton in a vaudeville act. Not only is he a talent, he knows talent when he sees it."

"Buster Keaton and Charlie Chaplin? Wow!"

"Such a nice guy, too; generous to a fault. That's what got him into this damn mess. Roscoe had just signed his new million-dollar-a-year contract with Paramount Pictures. On a whim, he gathered up some friends and drove his brand new car to San Francisco to celebrate." Richard lit up a cigarette, obviously upset.

"He burned his butt accidentally when he leaned on a hot light on the set, so he had to use a special pillow to sit on," Richard smiled. "Later he told me, "I couldn't have had sex with anyone if I wanted to, Richard. My butt was too sore.

Roscoe was married to a wonderful girl. Her name is Minta; tiny little thing. I don't think she's half his size."

"What happened to her?"

"They were in vaudeville together. They had a great act. When she learned she wasn't part of his million-dollar-a-year deal, it broke her heart. Minta starred in several comedy roles back in the day. She just wasn't part of the new package.

"That's what I'm talking about, Heather. This business is hard on a marriage and then there's the drinking, drugs and screwing around…lots of that going on.

"I'll admit Roscoe likes his liquor and loves to throw parties. That's why he drove his friends to San Francisco that day. They rented the 12th floor of the San Franciscan Hotel, called a bootlegger and the party was on. Somehow Virginia Rappe and her sorry-no-good-trouble-making friend Maude found out about it and crashed the party."

"All I know is what I've read in the newspapers, Richard," Heather said, "Pretty morbid stuff. They said he used a piece of ice, then a coke bottle, then a champagne bottle…"

"Lies, Lies, LIES! Damn Hearst. Roscoe didn't rape Virginia; he was trying to help her for god sakes. Hearst made a fortune distorting the story. While the trials were going on, all anyone had to do was tell the press they had some dirt on Roscoe Arbuckle and Hearst would put their picture in the paper. It completely ruined Roscoe's career. People believe what they read. Too bad they didn't tell the real story."

"What is the real story?"

"Virginia Rappe had the cards stacked against her from the start. Her mother was a prostitute in Chicago and she had already had five abortions before she was 16 years old."

"That's horrible!"

"No kidding. Apparently Virginia was prone to infections. She had her 6th abortion the day before she showed up to Roscoe's party with that damn bitch. I still cannot believe Roscoe let Maude into the party. Everyone in Hollywood knows she is a demon."

"You mean Maude Delmont?"

"Exactly. Better known as Bambina. What kind of a name is Bambina? Sounds like some kind of female mobster. Maude is a blackmailing bitch from hell. Told everyone Roscoe raped Virginia and, just to add insult to injury, she told the press he was impotent and fell on top of her, rupturing her bladder.

"The press had a field day with it. They put her ugly mug all over the newspapers. Poor Roscoe – such a nice guy. He was trying to help Virginia that night. Found her in the bathroom puking her guts out. The woman drank like a fish. Roscoe just thought she had drunk too much. He even got her a room to recuperate."

"The newspapers made it sound like Fatty Arbuckle is some kind of monster… how sad."

"I went to all his trials. Minta was at every one as well. After everything that happened, she still supported him."

"She sounds like a good woman."

"Minta is a sweetheart. The San Francisco DA went after Roscoe like a wolf looking for blood. He was using the incident to further his political career. Blew it way out of proportion. He played dirty and forced people to lie. Roscoe's true friends never believed he was guilty of such a horrendous crime.

"At the party, Virginia was writhing in pain, delirious with fever. There were a few witnesses who heard her yell, 'He did this to me. Get him away from me!' when Roscoe walked in the room. He was just putting ice on her abdomen trying to ease her pain. The whole thing was taken totally out of context but the DA ran with it.

"The only real evidence was a torn blouse. They said Roscoe tore it, but there were witnesses who saw Virginia tearing at her clothes. What a damn mess!"

The more Heather heard, the sadder she became.

"The doctors in the hotel let Virginia stay there two days before they finally took her to the hospital. She died from an infection, probably from a botched up abortion. Poor kid.

"Weirdest thing… the DA never put Maude on the witness stand, and she was the one who said Roscoe raped Virginia. The first trial Fatty got a 2-10 guilty verdict.

"At the second trial, the DA got some ex-convict to say Roscoe bribed him. Roscoe's lawyer told the court the man had been in jail for sexually assaulting an eight-year-old girl. The man was a scumbag! Roscoe's attorney was so confident he was going to win; he didn't give a closing argument or let Roscoe testify. It all backfired with a 10-2 verdict. I guess when Roscoe didn't speak up for himself the jury saw him as guilty.

"By the time the third trial came, the press had printed more distorted stories about Roscoe having alleged orgies and weird sex. Sold a lot of papers but totally ruined Roscoe.

"Like I said, anyone who had a story got their picture in the paper whether it was true or not. Maude, the bitch from hell, was making a small fortune touring the country doing one-woman shows as the woman who signed the murder charge against Fatty Arbuckle and was lecturing about the evils of Hollywood. Imagine the nerve. She was the evil of Hollywood!"

Richard lit up another cigarette. Talking about his friend Roscoe always made him agitated at the unfairness of it all. After a long drag, he continued.

"In those days, Hollywood was getting a bad reputation. Two months before Roscoe's third trial, the movie director Bill Taylor was murdered. The press was having a field day. You've got to be careful in this business, Heather, or the press will swallow you up and take you away to a dark place of no return."

"I'm beginning to see," Heather said with appreciation.

"At the third trial, Roscoe's lawyer took no chances and tore the DA's prosecution apart. He called Maude, 'the complaining witness who never witnessed.' They found out later Maude tried to get money to change her testimony. That's why the DA couldn't put her on the stand.

"It was a glorious victory, but too late for Roscoe to get back into the good graces of the public. Too much had happened.

"It only took the jury 6 minutes to deliver the not-guilty verdict. They even wrote a letter of apology to Roscoe. It made me cry when they read it at the trial. After all was said and done, Roscoe ended up with a $500 fine for having a party with booze. The lawyer cost a fortune and Roscoe lost his house, his movie contract and the most tragic loss of all, his adoring fans. Minta divorced him last November."

"I had no idea, Richard," Heather said, sadly shaking her head in sympathy.

"A couple of days after Roscoe's acquittal, the Hollywood censor board banned him from ever working in movies again. There was just too much heat.

"Damn Hearst. Later he had the nerve to tell Roscoe it was never personal. He just wanted to sell newspapers. Can you believe that? Roscoe is one of the greatest, most talented men who ever lived. In just one bad night, his life was ruined. Sometimes I think about all the laughter that could have been, that will never be. It breaks my heart, Heather.

"Buster Keaton has been a good friend… prince of a guy. Always gave Roscoe the credit for getting him in the business. Buster gave Roscoe 35 percent of all the future profits from his production company, to help him out. Roscoe has been co-directing under another name for Buster. Right now they are working on the Sherlock, Jr. project.

"Although Buster's generosity has helped, everyone knows Roscoe is depressed and hitting the bottle more than ever. Can't say I blame him. Even after he was found innocent, people still believe he raped Virginia Rappe. Damn media."

"I'd like to meet Fatty, sometime," Heather said.

"What would you do if you met Roscoe Arbuckle, Heather?" Richard asked.

"I'd give him a great big hug," Heather smiled.

"Well then, now's your chance. Look who just walked in," Richard smiled.

Heather turned around to see Buster Keaton and Fatty Arbuckle walking through the door.

"It's them!" Heather exclaimed. "What a coincidence."

"No such thing as a coincidence, Heather. C'mon, let's go to their table. I will introduce you," Richard grinned, taking her hand.

As Richard led Heather to the table, she felt an array of different emotions. Excitement, sadness, respect and compassion all filled her heart. Heather could see profound sadness in the man she knew as Fatty Arbuckle. His bright light she had fallen in love with on the screen, had turned to solemn darkness.

When Roscoe saw Richard, he broke out into a big smile. He appreciated Richard supporting him through all three trials and valued his friendship when so many had turned their backs on him. "Hey, Richard, great to see you," Roscoe cheered.

"Hello, my friend," Richard answered.

Being perfect gentlemen, Fatty and Buster both stood when they saw Heather. Buster tipped his hat. "Who is this lovely lady with you, Richard?"

"Gentlemen, may I present to you, Heather Diamond."

"A pleasure to make your acquaintance," Heather graced. For the second time that day, she felt humbled to be in the presence of greatness.

"Heather is our leading lady in *Rio Concho*," Richard bragged. "We just finished shooting. She was fabulous. A real pro and hardworking."

"Good for you, my dear," Buster commented. He reached for Heather's hand and kissed it.

"*Oh my gosh*," Heather thought. "Buster Keaton is kissing my hand!"

"I wish you much success in your career," Buster encouraged, maintaining his famous stone face.

"Thank you, Mr. Keaton," Heather respectfully replied.

Heather offered her hand to Roscoe. "Mr. Arbuckle, may I please tell you how sorry I am for all of your misfortune."

Roscoe kissed her hand, like gentlemen do. "Thank you, dear lady. Thank you."

"*Buster Keaton and Fatty Arbuckle both kissed my hand today,*" Heather thought. "*If I am dreaming I never want to wake up!*"

Buster Keaton and Fatty Arbuckle

CHAPTER 18

# Pickfair

By the early 1920's America had fallen in love with the glamour and excitement of Hollywood. Most towns had movie theatres providing entertainment for local citizens and people from rural communities. When the lights went out and the screen lit up, for a short time, a person could get lost in a brand new and sometimes even timeless, reality they never had experienced before.

Most Americans went to the movies at least once a week to escape their day-to-day humdrum lives. For less than a quarter, moviegoers across the nation could sit in the darkness and become totally engaged, as their favorite stars provided them a story in a fashion that was bigger than life.

Stimulating the imagination, movies made people dream of far-away places, engage in historical adventures, and participate in passionate love stories. Unlike theatre, close-up shots filled the screen with emotions, enabling the audience to see facial expressions that made them bellow with laughter or cry with tears of sadness and joy.

Ultimately it was the movie fans that created the stars. The more fans a star had the more money the studios would make. Women across America fantasized being held in the arms of Rudolph Valentino. Young farm boys pretended they were cowboy heroes like Tom Mix and a young city girl could imagine herself as the brave and beautiful Mary Pickford.

At twenty years old, Heather had enough life experience to handle just about any situation that was handed to her. Classy, confident, beautiful and naturally talented, Heather was ready for her destiny. As far as Richard was concerned, Heather met every qualification to be a great star. Although they did not know it yet, Heather Diamond was about to be Hollywood's newest sensation.

As far as life's lessons, Pearl had been Heather's best teacher. In the two years she had worked at Pearl's Parlor she learned how to be the epitome of a lady and knew the importance of projecting the image of an elegant woman with grace and style. Heather could be anything she wanted to be. A prisoner, a princess, a shrew, a carefree flapper, Heather could play any role and do it well. Her passion and empathy of the human spirit ran deep and the camera loved her.

It would be several weeks before Heather would be making personal appearances and giving interviews to promote her new film. The next Wednesday, Richard helped her move back into the Pink Palace. Edward was more than accommodating.

"Welcome back, Heather. We will take care of your things," he greeted warmly. "You will be in the same bungalow as before. Hello again, Richard. Good to see you."

"Hello, Edward. I am taking Heather shopping today. We have been invited to Pickfair this weekend and we need to make her absolutely stunning. I will make sure of it," Richard bragged.

"You remind me so much of my friend Harvey, Richard. I bet you have exquisite taste. Let's go," she cheered.

Heather knew she could always be herself with Richard. Carefree and excited about life, the two friends shared a memorable day of shopping. Heather allowed Richard to choose everything. He was like a grown man playing dolls. They laughed all day and sang in the car.

"You can sing," Richard complimented.

"I have a few tricks up my sleeve, Richard," Heather teased. "You never know. One day movies just may have sound and there will be roles for singers."

"Funny you should say that. It is a technology the studios are seriously looking at. Up until now, it has been challenging to match the voice with the actor and keep it in sync. It is a strong possibility. It may even be sooner that we think," Richard grinned.

When Richard picked Heather up on Saturday, even he was impressed. She had applied her make-up light, not too much around the eyes, making her look youthful and fresh. As far as he was concerned, too much make-up always made women look like they were trying too hard.

Sitting next to Richard in his shiny convertible, the two were a striking couple for anyone to behold.

"You are about to meet the A-list, my dear. Not just anyone gets invited to a party at Pickfair. You will see stars, famous producers and directors, as well as film photographers and editors. It's not what you are; it's who you are. Mary only invites people she likes. Her most treasured friends are the ones who knew her when she first got into the business. I am one of those friends," Richard smiled. "I guess you can say we grew up together."

"She seems very down-to-earth," Heather remarked.

"Make no mistake, America's Sweetheart knows exactly who she is. Just be your charming self, Heather. You belong with these people. I know Mary is going to love you. The two of you are very much alike and she will see that."

Driving through the gates of Pickfair, Heather felt like Cinderella going to the ball.

Located at 1143 Summit Drive, the renovation of the 25-room mansion was finally complete. There were tennis courts, stables, servants' quarters, several garages, a large guest wing, a billiard room and even a bowling alley.

Entering the grand hall, Heather wanted to memorize every detail. "Pearl would love this," Heather thought.

There were ceiling frescos, fine mahogany wood, bleach pine paneled halls, gold leaf and mirrored niches, and parquet floors. The rooms were filled with antiques including 18th Century English and French period furniture and notable pieces from the Barberini Palace and Baroness Burdett-Coutts estate in London. Heather was most impressed with the collection of Oriental artifacts the couple had collected on their many trips to Asia.

"C'mon, Heather. I want to show you something," Richard coaxed.

To Heather's amazement, Pickfair had its very own Old West style saloon, complete with an ornately carved burnished mahogany bar that had been purchased from a saloon in Auburn, California. Remington paintings decorated the walls and there were even women dressed as dance hall girls, serving spirits to the guests at the party.

"Oh, my goodness. This reminds me of Texas," Heather exclaimed. Turning around, she saw a familiar man with a beautiful smile had joined them

"Richard! It's about bloody time I see you. How have you been, old boy? And who may I ask is this very charming young lady?"

"Heather Diamond, may I present to you my good friend, Charlie Chaplin," Richard introduced.

This time Heather was prepared. Unlike the other day when she was caught off guard, she was not going to allow herself to be star-struck at this event. If she was going to be a star, she needed to act like one.

"Hello, Mister Chaplin," she graciously smiled.

"Oh, please call me Charlie," he answered.

Heather knew he had a reputation with the ladies. She had already made up her mind she would not be like the others. Respect was important to Heather. Besides, as far as anyone was concerned, she was with Richard.

"Your first time at Pickfair?" Charlie inquired. "It is grand, don't you think?"

"Everything I have seen thus far is quite lovely," Heather graced.

Obviously impressed with Heather's choice of words, Charlie felt he was in the presence of a woman with high breeding. In that moment, Heather was grateful for the lessons in etiquette and speech she had learned from the two years she had lived with Miss Pearl. Although she was bursting with excitement on the inside, her calm demeanor gave the illusion of elegance and class. In turn, Charlie, who grew up one of London's many impoverished children, felt the desire to claim his nobility.

"Right now I am planning to build a new home next door," he said. "Beverly Hills is a beautiful area."

"I am sure it will be grand, Mr. Chaplin… excuse me, Charlie," Heather smiled.

"Heather just finished a picture for Universal," Richard bragged. "Not only is she lovely, Heather is very talented and takes direction well. She even had a few ideas we used."

"I believe I would love to see more of Miss Heather," Charlie flirted, looking into her eyes as he kissed her hand.

Just then D.W. Griffith walked over to the group. "Hello, Richard. Sorry to interrupt. Charlie, I must discuss something with you. Please excuse us, my dear," he said graciously.

Charlie nodded his head and winked. Heather gave him a glorious smile.

"Let's go outside, Heather. I want to show you the pool," Richard suggested.

The grounds of Pickfair were perfectly manicured, displaying colorful flowers and greenery equivalent to the royal courtyard of any king and queen. White chairs and tables were filled with people, chatting about their newest projects and quietly sharing the latest Hollywood gossip.

Ironically, unbeknownst to anyone else besides the hosts of the party, the latest scandal was being discussed in a private corner of the estate.

"What were you thinking, Charlie? For heaven's sake, she's only 16," Charlie's business associate inquired. "You can go to jail for this! The press would have a field day…"

"Don't worry, D.W. I am taking her to Mexico in a few days. We are going to Sonora. It has all been arranged. Congratulate me. I am going to be a father," Charlie winced.

"What about an abor…?"

"No. Lita won't do that. We already discussed it. She has been working for me since she was 12. Lita's a good kid. If it's a boy she wants to name him Charlie Chaplin, Jr. I really have no choice here, D.W. It will be all right," Charlie claimed.

Fake compliments, genuine compliments, fear, admiration, jealousy, confidence, heartfelt friendships, and spiteful enemies… they were all here, smiling and laughing as if none of them had a care in the world. Some were drinking socially. Others were drinking too much. Mary's brother Jack Pickford and his actress wife Marilyn Miller were among the more intoxicated.

"Richard!" Jack slurred. "How are ya? Marilyn, say hello to Richard."

With Marilyn holding on to her husband's arm, the couple appeared as if they were attempting to hold each other up. "Hi…"

"We're going swimming," Jack announced. "Headed to the bath house now to put on bathing clothes."

"That sounds like a grand plan," Richard cheered as the couple staggered away.

"Jack Pickford?" Heather asked.

"The one and only. Poor Mary. She's always cleaning up after him and he constantly asks her for money. He was involved in a scandal when he was in the Navy. Seems he was taking bribes to help men avoid the military and getting young women for officers. Marilyn used to be in the Ziegfeld Follies."

"Wasn't his wife Olive Thomas the Ziegfeld girl?" Heather asked. "It was all over the papers when she died."

"Yes, Olive was a Ziegfeld girl. What a beauty she was and such a sweetheart. I worked with her on The Flapper. I cried for days when I learned she died," Richard expressed.

"What do you think really happened, Richard? There was so much speculation. Do you think it was suicide? Some say Jack killed her." Heather said.

"Jack might be a womanizer and a drunk but he's not a killer, Heather. His biggest problem is that his sister Mary is more successful. Olive was a big star as well.

"They had gone to Paris for a second honeymoon. Olive wanted the marriage to work. He was using mercury to treat his syphilis. I think she drank it by accident. He said she screamed when she swallowed it and woke him up. She was in excruciating pain and Jack got her help as fast as he could. One time, he told me he has horrible nightmares about Olive's screaming when the mercury started eating her stomach away."

Richard and Heather made their way to the slide by the swimming pool where Mary Pickford was playfully entertaining her friends.

"Hello, Richard," Mary called. "Nice to see you again, Heather. "Are you having a good time?"

"Yes I am, thank you. Richard has been showing me around. Your home is exquisite," Heather complimented.

"Thank you," Mary said, "Oh look, here comes Douglas. Hello, darling."

"Looks like you are having fun, my dear. Everyone loves America's Sweetheart," he taunted. Heather picked up on a hint of sarcasm she heard in his voice.

"Look who's here, my love," Mary encouraged.

"Hello Richard, Heather…"

"Hello Douglas. Great party like always," Richard said.

Heather was flattered the great star she knew as Douglas Fairbanks remembered her name.

"Nice to see you again. Lovely party," she complimented.

As Heather watched Mary interact with her guests, Heather could see Douglas was possessive of his wife and not particularly fond of her friendliness with other men. It wasn't what he said, or did exactly; Heather could just tell. Maybe because she had seen that same look on Tony's face, back in Chicago when any man spoke to her. She just wasn't aware of what it meant at the time.

While strolling through the party, it became obvious that Richard was well thought of in Hollywood. This was probably due to the fact that, as a director's assistant, his job was to make people look good. People who are good at what they do, make it look easy, and Richard was one of the best.

Richard dealt with everything from smoothing out hard feelings and temper tantrums to making sure the director had everything he wanted. Never losing his cheery disposition, even when a request seemed impossible to achieve, Richard would somehow manage to get it done. In times when he felt angry or frustrated Richard never showed it. That would be unprofessional to him. Having these admirable attributes was the reason everyone in Hollywood held him in high esteem.

Although some were suspicious, Richard kept his private life extremely private. Richard was an expert at working the room and Heather was the new object of his affection. He introduced her to people at the party as if she were a princess. Meeting Harold Lloyd, Lillian Gish and Gloria Swanson was a thrill. Even though her heart was thumping like an excited puppy, Heather managed to maintain her calmness.

To be seen on Richard's arm provided Heather with the credibility she needed to be accepted by the Hollywood elite. In truth this was the first time anyone had ever seen Richard with a woman he was so fond of. Since the first day they met there was a mutual feeling of friendship and trust. Something about Heather made him want to protect and mentor her.

"I feel like a schoolgirl in a candy store, Richard. Oh my goodness, is that…?"

"Rudolph Valentino. Yes," Richard acknowledged in a tone Heather had not heard from her friend before.

Richard lit up a cigarette. Heather had come to know her friend well enough that smoking calmed Richard's nerves.

"Do you know him, Richard?"

"I do. It's complicated Heather," Richard confessed.

Rudolph Valentino was the handsome, Italian heartthrob of America. Making eye contact with Richard, he made a slight two-finger salute and smiled. Richard, doing his best to compose himself lifted his chin in acknowledgement.

"I am sorry, Heather. I always need to breathe a little before I speak to Rudolph. We have history…"

"Say no more Richard. I understand. Let's just go over and talk with meaningless conversation."

Handsome, charismatic, and sexy as hell, Rudolph Valentino kissed Heather's hand. When he spoke to her, she felt she might melt into a pool of butter right there in the middle of Pickfair. She was almost relieved when she figured out his relationship with Richard. Alone with this beautiful, Italian-born man, Heather knew she would not hesitate at all to surrender to anything he desired. Apparently, he had the exact same effect on her friend Richard.

"Please call me, Richard. I would like to see you." Rudolph said. "Bellisima!" he exclaimed, kissing Heather's hand again. Richard lit up another cigarette.

"Is that Clara Bow over there? Who is that woman talking to her, Richard? They look like they could be sisters," Heather asked.

"Clara is talking to Barbara LaMarr. We call her 'the girl who is too beautiful' because, when she was 16, a policeman told her she was too beautiful to be walking about the city alone."

"Barbara LaMarr was in Three Musketeers with Douglas," Heather said. "She really is a beautiful girl."

"Unfortunately she has a drug addiction. I worry about her. She's a sweet kid and everyone loves her. I want you to promise me something, Heather. The mob has fingers everywhere. If anyone ever asks you to do drugs or wants to sell you any, do not do it. I have seen many wonderful girls in this business get hooked. Some have even died," Richard implored.

"Don't worry, Richard. Miss Pearl has told me stories of girls in Chicago that would curl your hair. I was involved with a gangster in Chicago. I don't ever want to mess with the likes of that again.

"Glad to hear it," Richard smiled.

"One day I will tell you the whole story, Richard," Heather said. "Actually it would make one helluva movie."

"The greatest movies come from real life stories, Heather. That's why Charlie Chaplin and Buster Keaton are so successful. Their stories are real, at least for the most part."

"What about Buster Keaton, Richard? Somehow I expected him to be here," Heather inquired.

"I am sure he was invited. He usually is. Buster is not one to socialize much, especially since Hollywood turned its back on his friend Roscoe. Even though they only banned him from working for six months, Buster is the only one who will give him a chance. I am sure they are having their own party somewhere."

At dusk, on a patio lit up with lanterns that had been purchased in Chinatown, an orchestra began to play. An excellent dancer, Richard was pleasantly surprised at how light Heather felt as he glided her across the dance floor.

"Heather, Heather, light as a feather," he chimed.

"Richard, Richard, pretty as a picture," she responded.

By the third dance, unable to watch any longer, Charlie Chaplin tapped Richard on the back, asking permission to cut in. Winking at Heather, Richard graciously allowed the Hollywood icon to intervene. Within five seconds another woman Heather did not recognize, insisted Richard dance with her.

Flattered but surprisingly not overwhelmed, Heather found herself dancing beneath the twinkling California stars in the arms of Charlie Chaplin. Those who were there and knew him saw Heather as another desired conquest. Charlie knew his power over women. They never said, "no."

However, Heather was all too much aware of this familiar protocol, and although Charlie Chaplin was charming, gracious and polite, she let it be known to everyone present that she was with Richard.

Richard and Heather were amongst the last to leave the party. While Richard and Douglas competed at the billiards table, Mary Pickford made it a point to engage Heather in a conversation, woman to woman.

"I like you, Heather. Something about you seems different than most of the young girls who I see get into this business," Mary acknowledged. "Why do you want to be an actress?"

"I don't believe I chose to be an actress, Mary. It chose me. I have been an actress since I was a little girl, performing plays for my little brothers and sisters on the front porch of our farmhouse in Illinois," Heather answered.

"Do you want to be famous," Mary asked.

"I thought I did. Reading about stars in movie magazines, it all seemed so glamorous. Now that I have actually worked on a film, I see things much differently. I want to be an actress because I want to make people feel; love... sadness... joy... victory... Movies stimulate the deepest of human emotions. That is the magic of the cinema, and I want to be a part of it," Heather revealed.

"And you will my dear. You will be a big part of it," Mary Pickford encouraged, patting Heather's hand. "I was especially impressed with the way you handled Charlie this evening. Most women throw themselves at his feet. Right now he has some personal issues you will learn about soon enough.

"You are a smart woman, Heather. This business can swallow your soul if you let it. Remember your actions must be impeccable."

Charlie Chaplin, Douglas and Richard had been standing by the bar, immersed in a lively discussion about the movie industry.

"Let's ask the ladies," Douglas suggested.

"Ask us what?" Mary replied.

"What do you ladies think of talking pictures?" Douglas asked. "Richard believes talkies will happen within the next five years."

"I don't think talkies could ever be successful," Mary answered. "How will people be able to appreciate the music? After all, it was Charlie's musical compositions that brought the audiences to tears in *The Kid*. Putting voices into movies would be like putting red lipstick on the statue of Venus de Milo."

"What do you think, Heather," Richard smiled.

"I do not know, Richard," Heather beamed. "All I know right now is, I LOVE HOLLYWOOD!"

For Heather, the party at Pickfair on that glorious day in Southern California was like a dream come true. Many of those in attendance only showed what they wanted everyone to see. Smiles and forced laughter masked the many dark thoughts of fear, judgement and insecurity on some who were there.

One of them was a pretty, young blonde woman whose heart was raging with jealousy for the new actress who had just finished filming *Rio Concho*. Her glorious smile was radiant as she reminded Heather in a short casual conversation that she was the secretary at Bill Stein's office.

*"It should have been me!"*

## CHAPTER 19

# A New Home

The next two weeks flew by like a whirlwind. Photo shoots, a private showing for the press and personal appearances were set up to promote *Rio Concho*, starring Universal's newest discovery Heather Diamond. The buzz on the street was "beautiful, charming and easy to work with."

Contracts were signed for Heather to star as Maria in the upcoming film *Blue Midnight* and Richard was delighted to have a gorgeous young starlet on his arm to show off at parties, premiers and social events. In turn, Heather felt protected and loved to be seen with her strikingly handsome, well-liked gentleman who seemed to know everyone who was anyone in Hollywood.

It was a Tuesday afternoon. Heather was exhausted from what Richard promised to be the last photo shoot before *Rio Concho* would be released.

"You think things are crazy now, Heather? Wait until *Rio Concho* is released to the theatres," Richard exclaimed. "It won't be long before America will fall in love with Heather Diamond and you become a household name. There are some who appear on the screen and then there are those who light it up. You, my dear, set it ablaze."

"I really don't know what to say, Richard. If I am dreaming, I never want to wake up. I want to go to Redondo Beach and see my friend Ruby. She told me she would be staying at the Hotel Redondo this week. Why don't you come with me? I'd love for you to meet her. Ruby is an interesting lady. She knows Wyatt Earp and his wife, Josephine. Ruby met Wyatt when he was a lawman in Tombstone. She and Josephine have been friends since they were teenagers in San Francisco."

"Somebody needs to tell that man's story, Heather. I have been trying to help him pitch it for a movie. Sometimes I believe Hollywood loses sight with what is fantasy and what is real. No doubt Wyatt is the real deal. They just don't realize what a treasure he is. The man has been in over a hundred gun battles. You'd think…"

"I like Wyatt," Heather smiled. "I really like him."

"When do you want to go to Redondo?" Richard asked.

"I told Ruby I would meet her for dinner tomorrow night. Then I plan to stay at the Hotel Redondo through the weekend. The ocean has a way of speaking to my soul, Richard. I can't really explain it. I just feel so much peace, especially when I look out to the horizon. It's like anticipating a magical voyage with endless possibilities, much like I feel about my career at this point."

"Beautifully said, my dear," Richard said with affection.

Entering the Hotel Redondo the next evening, Stewart greeted Richard and Heather with a warm hug. "How are two of my favorite people in the world?"

"Hello, Stewart. So nice to see you again," Richard exclaimed.

"What? You know Stewart, too?" Heather asked.

"The Hotel Redondo has been a favorite beach getaway for Hollywood for quite some time now, Heather. Stewart is great about maintaining privacy for the movie stars who come here. Depending on their mood, many respond with 'mistaken identity' when recognized in public. I know Chaplin and Buster Keaton like to come to Redondo as well as Mary Pickford and her husband Douglas."

"It's funny," Stewart chuckled. "One time I saw a woman insist one of our guests was Clara Bow. No matter how much the poor young woman insisted she was clearly not Clara Bow, the more the woman insisted that she was and wanted her autograph. Finally, the young girl gave in and signed, Clara Bow, on one of our brochures. It was a brilliant solution. The woman was quite satisfied."

"I like that story," Heather smiled.

"Most people don't recognize Charlie Chaplin without his black derby, eyebrows, and funny little mustache. Not only that but he speaks with an English accent," Stewart said.

"You know he's not physically a big man, but his talent certainly makes up for it. Composer, writer and actor… he is an absolute genius," Richard said with admiration.

"I have a message for you, Heather. Ruby told me she would meet you in the dining room at seven. I believe she and Salty went for a walk on the beach to watch the sunset."

"I think Salty is a little in love with Ruby," Heather smiled.

"No doubt they are great friends," Stewart said. "Funny how time changes things. I believe the older we get, the more we appreciate the people we love."

That evening Richard and Heather were waiting in the dining room when Ruby made her grand entrance. When she did, the room fell silent. Beautifully adorned with her diamond-ruby necklace, Ruby was wearing a long white chiffon gown that flowed with every graceful step. Her shiny white hair was neatly curled in the latest fashion and her smile was radiant. "*She looks like a queen,*" Heather thought to herself.

Respectfully, Richard stood and smiled.

"Richard Morris, may I present to you our most gracious Ruby Castalini," Stewart announced.

"Very nice to make your acquaintance," Richard greeted, kissing her white, gloved hand.

"The pleasure is definitely mine," Ruby graced.

"Hello, Dear," she smiled, kissing Heather on both cheeks.

"You look stunning, Ruby," Heather exclaimed.

Ruby gazed long and hard at Richard. "You forgot to tell me how handsome he is, Heather. I hear you know my old friend, Wyatt."

"Yes I do," Richard affirmed. "He is quite a man."

"Fearless and sentimental all in one package," Ruby commented. "I was there that day in Tombstone when the Earp brothers and Doc Holliday took down that sorry lot at the OK Corral. That was a different time," she said, shaking her head. "Wyatt's one of the finest men I've ever known. Tell me about your new movie, Heather."

"It's called *Blue Midnight* and I play the part of Maria. It's a story about a young heiress, whose husband tries to have her committed to a Sanitarium by convincing everyone, including her, that she is crazy. Finally, the husband tries to push her over a cliff to the ocean below, making it look like suicide. The gardener, who is secretly in love with Maria, comes to her rescue. In the midst of a fight, the husband loses his balance and falls over the cliff, plummeting to the boulders below to meet his doom," Heather ended with a dramatic flair laying the back of her hand on her forehead.

"Ramon Navarro is going to play the part of the gardener who rescues Maria," Richard said.

"As in the Mexican heart throb, Ramon Navarro?" Ruby exclaimed. "Any love scenes?"

"Yes, of course," Heather grinned.

"We will start shooting *Blue Midnight* in a few weeks. As a matter of fact some of the scenes will be shot next door on the Palos Verdes peninsula overlooking the ocean. They have fabulous cliffs there," Richard informed.

"That's wonderful, Richard." Heather exclaimed. "I have completely fallen in love with this whole area."

"There's a house for sale not too far from here, Heather. If you really love Redondo Beach that much, maybe you should..."

"Buy it? Yes! Let's go look at it tomorrow."

"We'll go after breakfast. Do you know when *Rio Concho* is being released?" Ruby asked. "I want to put it on my calendar."

"Middle of January," Richard informed her. "I will arrange your personal invitation."

"Wyatt promised me he will be there as well," Heather exclaimed.

"Good. I will look forward to seeing him." Ruby patted her hand. It won't be long before America falls in love with Heather Diamond."

"We are very proud of *Rio Concho*. The camera absolutely loves Heather," Richard bragged.

"And I love the camera," Heather smiled.

"That's what makes the magic," Ruby assured her. "Let's order. My walk on the beach with Salty has made me hungry."

The next morning after a breakfast of poached eggs, orange juice and toast, Richard, Ruby and Heather walked to the house on the Esplanade that was for sale. The ocean glistened with a soft blue hue and the surf was mild as the waves broke gently on the sand. Ten minutes later, Ruby stopped and pointed to the three-story Cape Cod style home set on the sand dunes looking over the golden beach below.

"There it is," Ruby announced.

"It is absolutely perfect!" Heather squealed, as she began running to the house she would soon call home.

"Love it. Love it, LOVE IT," Richard commented.

That afternoon, Heather bought a dream house overlooking the ocean in Redondo Beach.

"From now on, you can stay with me when you come to Redondo, Ruby," Heather remarked.

"Thank you, honey, but I plan to go down with the ship. I will be at the Hotel Redondo until the day it closes its doors. It's where I feel closest to my Mickey."

"This is a good move, Heather," Richard said. "It's close enough to Hollywood for you to stay involved with your work and, at the same time, it's just far enough away for you to disconnect from the craziness and drama that goes on. I'll take you up on that offer if you don't mind."

"Sure, Richard. I will make one of the bedrooms just for you. You can help me decorate," Heather grinned.

It was official. Heather was now a permanent resident of Redondo Beach, California.

"Now that you are a local, I'd like for you to come with me to a fancy dinner at the La Venta Inn next week. The real estate developers who have their offices here at the Hotel Redondo will be hosting it. I believe they are inviting movie stars," Ruby said. "Why don't you come too, Richard? I will make sure you are included on the guest list."

"Thank you, Ruby. I would like that."

"Look, you can see the La Venta Inn from here," Ruby said, pointing south toward the Palos Verdes hills. "Wear your black tie, Richard. The invitation says 4 PM, a perfect time to appreciate the view of the ocean and take in the sunset."

The next week, Richard, Ruby and Heather drove up the curvy dirt road to attend the real estate event at the La Venta Inn. Ruby was dressed in a simple black dress. Tonight she was wearing white iridescent pearls and matching pearl earrings. Richard was elegantly handsome in his white tux and Heather was dressed in a cream colored, chiffon evening gown with a handkerchief hemline. The neckline draped low enough to evoke curiosity and show off an emerald necklace she had received as a gift from a wealthy Texan in San Angelo.

The patio of the La Venta Inn was elegantly decorated with lanterns, ribbons and greenery indigenous to the area. As always, Richard was shaking hands with several men he knew and kissing women on the cheek. Heather recognized some of the guests from the party at Pickfair.

As they walked into the Inn, Richard, Ruby and Heather entered a room set aglow by a warm fire, evoking a welcoming atmosphere. Silver candelabra stood on the tables, on top of wheat-colored linen tablecloths accentuated with dark green napkins. The green color was possibly chosen because in Spanish, "Palos Verdes" means "green sticks."

A handsome young man carrying a silver tray made his way to where Heather was standing. "Hors d'oeuvre, Madame?" he grinned, causing the dimples in his cheeks to cave into a friendly smile that spread across his handsome, sun-bronzed face.

"Thank you," Heather said, flirting with her eyes in appreciation of the very fine male specimen standing before her. "Do I detect a French accent?"

"Oui, Madame. I am Francois."

"We were told to come early because of the view. It looks like the view inside this room is quite nice," Ruby playfully said as she took a cracker garnished with crabmeat and cheese from his tray.

"Madame," the young man blushed. Bowing respectfully, he turned to walk away.

Heather turned her attention to the magnificent view beckoning to her on the other side of the double French doors. "Look!" Heather exclaimed. "Oh my goodness, Richard, look!"

Walking onto the grounds outside, Heather felt a surge of joy she had never experienced before. "You can see the ocean forever from up here. Look how beautiful she is!"

Gazing upon the miles and miles of blue water before her, Heather felt her heart surge in awe and her soul dance with delight. In that moment, she wished she could fly like an eagle into the vast abyss of the ocean's mystic invitation to explore her sacred realms.

Watching Heather's reaction to the majestic view, Ruby thought of those days she and her mother visited the ocean in San Francisco when she was a little girl. Because of this her own appreciation of the beauty of the ocean was refreshed. The sea had been Ruby's only friend, in those first painful days when she lost her beloved Mickey. Listening to the waves singing her ancient song was the only thing that brought peace and solace to Ruby's broken heart.

The three friends watched as the sky subtly changed its patterns of bright orange, magenta and golden light like a magnificent, colorful slide show, highlighting the soft fluffiness of the clouds above.

Heather was in awe. "I have never seen anything so beautiful in my entire life. I believe this must truly be heaven on earth, Ruby."

The halibut garnished with lemon and capers was delicious and the fresh vegetables were sautéed to perfection. For dessert, delicious flaming cherries jubilee were eloquently served.

"...And the La Venta Inn will be an upscale dinner house," the speaker announced. "The Palos Verdes Country Club will open next week on the 15th of November and charter membership is now available. We have a beautiful golf course and tennis facilities. Palos Verdes is also known for its horseback riding. We are very excited about the Palos Verdes Project and we hope you will join us."

"Last week they took a group of us on horseback to see the lots that are for sale. I bought two side by side lots with spectacular views of the ocean," Ruby told her friends. "It was fun. I'm looking at house plans next week. I want something like an Italian villa, with golden stucco, a red tile roof, lots of arches and a circular stairway. One of the lots will serve as a garden. I might even get a horse. Mickey would have loved it."

"That's just swell, Ruby. We'll be like neighbors," Heather bubbled.

After dinner, Richard excused himself to look for the handsome young Frenchman, Francois, to engage in some friendly conversation and give him his calling card. Together Ruby and Heather strolled out to the garden to enjoy the night air before leaving the party.

"Don't look now, honey, but tall dark and gorgeous is headed this way. He's been looking at you all night long," Ruby whispered.

"Really?"

"Permit me to introduce myself. I am Lorenzo."

"*Lorenzo*?" Heather thought to herself. Something about this scenario seemed familiar.

"My name is Heather and this is my friend, Ruby."

"Very nice to meet you beautiful ladies. Heather, may I speak to you privately? Just for a moment."

"No problem. I need to take care of some business, Heather," Ruby winked.

"Lorenzo. That's a nice name. Where are you from?"

"I am Italian. My dear, you are by far the most beautiful woman in the room. Is Ruby your mother?"

"No, Ruby is a good friend."

"Oh," he responded, sounding a little disappointed then quickly smiled to cover up his calculated intention. He had been impressed with Ruby's flashy display of diamonds.

Heather suddenly remembered Betsy telling her the story of the handsome Italian man she met on the steamship to America who preyed on wealthy women. Betsy had been an elderly lady's traveling companion on a trip to Europe and fell head over heels in love. She was so much in love, she ran away from home to be with him. The Italian man, whose name was also Lorenzo, had told her his family was wealthy merchants that dealt in textiles.

"Lorenzo! No… that would be too strange a coincidence. If he is the same person, no wonder Betsy fell for him. This man is magnificent! He reminds me of a younger version of Tony; pretty but not to be trusted."

"Italy? I have always wanted to go," Heather cooed.

"For generations my family has done very well trading beautiful textiles throughout Europe."

"It is him! Son of a BITCH!"

Poor Betsy. This man had completely destroyed her life. As Heather felt the hostility inside her slowly rise to a boil, she thought it best to use her acting skills to transform into a naïve bimbo genuinely impressed with the lying asshole standing before her.

"Textiles? How lovely," Heather smiled, as she imagined herself pushing Lorenzo off the Redondo Beach pier.

"You are doing something to my heart, Heather. Your beauty…your face…your lips…"

Thinking about sweet little Betsy and those long nights she cried herself to sleep, it was all Heather could do to refrain from picking up a heavy object and hitting Lorenzo several times over the head with it.

"I see my friends, Lorenzo, and I really must go. Why don't you come see me tomorrow and we can have a late lunch? I am staying at the Hotel Redondo. One o'clock?"

"I will be there," Lorenzo said with his dazzling smile.

Greeting Richard and Ruby with a big, sparkling, plastic grin, Heather could feel herself literally shaking with disgust. "We need to go," she announced, gritting her teeth.

"What in the world?" Ruby asked.

"I'll tell you when we get in the car."

"What in the hell happened, Heather?" Richard said, starting up the car. "I have never seen you like this before. For heaven sakes, who was that guy?"

"Ughhhhhhh!! It's a wild crazy coincidence. OK…let me calm down for a minute."

Ruby reached into her purse and pulled out her flask. "Here honey, take a few gulps of this. It will make you feel better."

"Gulp…gulp…gulp, gulp gulp…"

"I have a friend; her name is Betsy. She used to work with me at Miss Pearl's. Sweet kid. Betsy was a farm girl from Kentucky who agreed to be this rich woman's traveling companion so she could see the world.

"Gulp… gulp, gulp.

"Anyway, Betsy fell for this Italian guy on a cruise ship. He thought she was wealthy and he told her his family was rich. She ran away from home to be with him. Turns out he was a lying gambling son-of-a-bitch.

"His name was Lorenzo!

"He told Betsy he had a wealthy family in the textile business. They were on a train headed to San Francisco when she woke up one night and he was gone. She found him in the gambling car in a high stakes game.

"When she wouldn't give him more money to gamble, he left her completely stranded and alone at the train depot in Dallas. Ginger found her sobbing hysterically and brought her to Miss Pearl's. He took her virginity, Ruby. She was too ashamed to go home and face her family in Kentucky."

"What happened to her?" Richard asked.

"One day at the parlor, when she was crying, missing her family, Pearl suggested she write a letter to her parents just to let them know she was alive and well. Two weeks later, Johnny Wayne, her childhood sweetheart, came and rescued her. They are married now and have a baby girl. They named her Ginger Ann."

"After Ginger?" Ruby asked. "That's nice."

"I invited Lorenzo to lunch tomorrow."

"Why in the world did you do that?" Richard asked.

"I want to hurt him like he hurt Betsy. I want to push him off the pier, stick toothpicks in his fingernails and set his hair on fire!"

"No, Heather, NO!" Richard exclaimed. "From now on, you need to avoid trouble, not invite it. You are about to become a famous movie star and you need to keep your nose clean."

"Richard's right, honey. Let me take care of Lorenzo," Ruby assured her.

The next afternoon, at precisely 1 PM, Lorenzo walked into the lobby of the Hotel Redondo. Ruby was waiting for him.

"Heather's gone," Ruby informed him.

"I don't understand. She told me to meet her here at one."

"Plans have changed. Let's go outside and have a little visit. I could use some fresh, salty air about now."

Ruby was wearing her diamonds to pique Lorenzo's interest. This was intentional. He took the bait.

"Miss Ruby," he smiled. "Heather is only a girl. I prefer mature women. They are much more interesting and…"

"You mean they have more money…" Ruby remarked speaking to him now in Italian.

"Older women are better lovers…"

That was it. Ruby began shouting to him in Italian. "It is time to get real, Lorenzo. You work for Capone don't you?"

Lorenzo looked like he just swallowed a peach seed. He could only stare. The hesitation gave him away.

"I don't know what…"

"Do not lie to me. Sadly my friend, you are more transparent than window glass. Mickey Castallini was my husband. I am sure you have heard of him or at least his reputation," Ruby said.

Lorenzo's eyes grew bigger than saucers.

"I know the cove in Palos Verdes where you deliver the booze, and where the caves are that you stash it. That's why you were at the party last night. You're a bootlegger. You're also a slimy snake who preys on little girls. Remember Elizabeth from the cruise ship? Left her on a train in Texas, I hear."

"How… do you know…?"

"You'd be surprised what I know. Now get out of town before I make a phone call to Capone's house in Fontana."

Fear cast its shadow over Lorenzo's face.

"ADESSO!!"

Lorenzo ran away and never looked back.

Satisfied, Ruby looked up towards Heather's room where she had been watching from the open window above. Smiling, Ruby held her thumb up then waved her friend to come down.

The two women spent the rest of the afternoon on the beach laughing and telling stories.

"I wish Betsy could have seen the look on his face! This has been a good day, Ruby."

"Every day is a good day, Heather. I am happy we are friends."

CHAPTER 20

# Hooray for Hollywood

"I need to talk to someone! Can I come over?"

"Of course, Richard. You sound upset," Heather responded.

"To say the least. I will be there within the hour."

Thirty-five minutes later, Richard pulled into Heather's driveway. As she greeted him at the front porch, he jumped out of his car, carrying a newspaper in his hand.

"It's awful, Heather. The very last thing Hollywood needs is another scandal. Thomas Ince is dead and the stories are buzzing around like a disturbed hornets' nest."

"I'm sorry, Richard."

"At one time Tom was one of the most powerful producer-directors in town. I just saw him a few weeks ago, Heather. A brilliant man and totally dedicated to his craft. MGM just bought the studio he created. There is a replica of George Washington's home at Mount Vernon on the lot."

"I've seen pictures of it. What kind of stories have you heard?"

"It was Tom's birthday and Hearst wanted to throw him a party on his yacht. Tom was busy in the editing room and wasn't able to join them right away so he took a train and met them in San Diego. Apparently Charlie Chaplin and Marion Davies have been too friendly lately and Hearst walked in on them…"

"Marion is Hearst's mistress, right?"

"That is correct."

"They say he built a huge mansion for her in San Simeon."

"Yes, he did. It's like Pickfair. Only the A-list gets invited. The man is crazy obsessed with her. Anyway, one story is Hearst found Ince sitting in the dark with her and he thought she was with Charlie and shot at him. The other story is Hearst caught her in a compromising position with Charlie and he shot and missed, hitting Tom in the head."

"Oh my…"

"The first Los Angeles Times headline read: *Movie Producer Shot on Hearst Yacht.* Now they are saying he died from heart failure, although some people said when they took him off the yacht, his head was bandaged with a gunshot wound. He's been known to have attacks with ulcers and bad digestion. It's because he works so hard."

"Wow, Richard. You are right. Hollywood doesn't need this kind of scandal. Charlie Chaplin just married that girl and…"

"The studios work really hard to create the illusion that Hollywood is a clean wholesome group. The stars live in a bubble and sometimes they do crazy things. I can't imagine the D.A will ever accuse Hearst of anything. He's just too powerful. They'll probably sweep the whole thing under the rug to hide their dirty little secret, whatever it is.

"It's not the truth that matters, it's what people believe is the truth that makes all the difference. People believe what they read. Roscoe

Arbuckle is a perfect example of that. Even after he was clearly declared innocent, people still believe he's guilty. It's a strange phenomenon."

"Let's have a drink Richard. The sunset will relax you."

Sitting on the balcony of her new beach home, watching the sun bid farewell to another day, Heather listened while her friend poured out his frustrations.

"Movie-making is a great industry. You've got to be strong or you'll get lost in the illusion. You know, Heather, when silent films first came out stage performers were embarrassed to be seen in them. Theatre people considered films pantomime and were afraid of ruining their reputation. To them silent films were just a step above carnivals and freak shows."

"Really?"

"Ahh yes…the theatre... a grand experience indeed. There is nothing like emotionally connecting to a live audience."

"Like the tourists at Universal Studios?" Heather teased.

"That's when it becomes a freak show," Richard laughed. "The star-system was created when audiences wanted to know actors names. Nowadays image is everything. Studios want their stars to be stylish when seen in public. The women are expected to wear make-up and act like ladies and the men like gentlemen. Some contracts even have morality codes written into them for all the good it does."

"I'm not worried, Richard. I've got you to look after me. I can play the game; I've done it before. I know how it feels when someone or something owns you."

"Poor Tom. Power is the most important thing in Hollywood. With all the changes and partnerships happening so quickly, he was slowly losing his status."

"Some birthday party…"

"I'm feeling restless tonight. Go get dressed, Heather, while I make a reservation for us at the Cocoanut Grove. Wear that little black, backless number I saw in your closet. I want you to be especially beautiful. I guarantee you the bees will be buzzing tonight."

Richard kept a small wardrobe that included a black tuxedo and freshly polished shiny black shoes in the room he declared his at the beach house. Both he and Heather had a spontaneous nature and he was always ready to dine at the La Venta Inn, take a walk on the beach or enjoy a casual game of golf.

"How do I look?" Heather asked, as she seductively turned around for Richard to take in the view.

"You look absolutely stunning, my dear," Richard marveled as he helped her with her white fur.

"This is nice," he commented.

"A gift," she winked.

"And the diamonds?"

Heather just smiled and winked.

It was a cool clear evening in Southern California. When Richard pulled up to the Cocoanut Grove, the valet was most accommodating.

"Good evening, Mr. Morris," he smiled.

"Hello, Freddie. How are those two boys of yours?'

"Very well, sir," he smiled.

Richard slipped Freddie a dollar bill. As another valet opened the door for Heather, Freddie winked at Richard and whistled. Crooking his elbow, Richard proudly offered his arm to his dazzling date.

"Let's do this," he smiled.

Coconut trees were etched on the double glass doors that served as the regal entry to the popular Hollywood nightclub. Feeling as if she had walked into a brand new world of excitement and beauty, Heather thought of the days when singing at the barn dance for the local October Fest was an enormously big deal. The Cocoanut Grove was certainly not a barn; it was a gorgeous place. Upon entering the gigantic room, guests had the feeling of actually walking inside a grove of real coconut trees.

Heather had never seen a room so grand. A big stairway led down to the dance floor framed by golden archways with colorful designs. Box seating was on the sides and tables with white tablecloths all around. A hundred couples were dancing to the music of Gus Arnheim and his Cocoanut Grove Orchestra.

A friendly maître d' with a carefully curled, black moustache greeted them with a strong Italian accent and menus in hand.

"Good evening, Mr. Morris. We have your box ready."

"Thank you, Giovanni. Bet on any good races lately?"

"Won the exacta last week for a couple of hundred," he grinned.

"Very good, my man," he said, patting him on the back. "This is Heather Diamond. She has a picture coming out in January."

"Molto Bella," he exclaimed.

Richard worked the room as they walked to their table. Heather put on her most seductive walk and loveliest of smiles. Together they were a striking couple.

Gus Arnheim waved at Richard from the stage. Mary Pickford and her husband Douglas Fairbanks were sitting with D.W. Griffith, probably discussing Charlie Chaplin's newest predicament. Gloria Swanson and Clara Bow both gave Richard a friendly wave.

"You have come on one of our best nights," Giovanni beamed. The Charleston Contest will begin in an hour. Lots of pretty girls wanting to become stars come from everywhere."

"Actually a cute little blonde girl named Jane just signed a contract with Fox films last month for $75 a week. She was discovered here. Her new Hollywood name is Carole Lombard. I met her at a party once. She's quite a character, cute and funny," Richard remarked.

"I want to enter the contest, Richard," Heather said excitedly. "I learned how to do the Charleston in Texas. I'm pretty good."

"No, no Heather. I have other plans for you tonight," Richard grinned, as he handed Giovanni a piece of folded paper. "Give this to Gus," he grinned.

"Yessir," Giovanni smiled.

Within a minute a sophisticated gentleman presented a tray with two fruity beverages, set them on the table then bowed.

"Your usual, sir."

"Thank you, Ralph."

Turning to Heather, Richard raised his drink. "To Hollywood's bright new star," he toasted.

"And new best friends," Heather responded, clicking his glass. "Whew, that's a bit strong."

"Sip it slow. After all it is Prohibition."

For a few minutes neither of them spoke as Richard cased the room. "I knew it. Everyone is here tonight except Chaplin. Poor guy. It's not like he does anything different than any other man in this town. It just seems that he's always getting caught. I was right. Everyone is here tonight, Heather. Sam Goldwyn... Cecil B. DeMille...Mary and Doug...That's Louis Mayer three boxes over. Hollywood is like a family. In a funny way, we all know we are here honoring our fallen soldier, Tom Ince. Look across the room. There's Valentino."

Just then, Heather heard her name being announced from the stage.

"I have a note here from Richard Morris. It seems we have a new star in our midst and apparently she's not just an actress...she can sing! Heather Diamond, would you be so kind as to grace us with a song?"

Heather stared at Richard with surprise.

"I've never heard you sing," he grinned. "Get up there kid and show them what you can do."

Curiosity flew through the room like a Texas wildfire as Heather sauntered to the stage. Her heart was beating hard, and her right knee was shaking so out of control, she felt as if she might fall on her face in the middle of the dance floor. No one seemed to notice as the noise in the room made a declining decrescendo until finally the room became quiet. With a big welcoming smile, Gus Arnheim reached out his hand and welcomed Heather to the stage. Could he see her lip trembling?

Heather's perfectly shaped naked back was facing the audience as she said, 'Oh My Man in the key of D'. Gus smiled. He instantly knew this wasn't this girl's first rodeo. She was a pro.

Heather slowly turned to face her audience. Stars she'd read about, directors and studio moguls; they were all there.

"This is just too surreal to be afraid. I am going to make these people feel... it's what I do."

Heather raised the microphone to her mouth, closed her eyes and stepped into the silent chamber of her mind where all of her memories danced. Peace overcame her as she allowed her soul to translate the deepest sorrows of her heart in song.

"Oh, my man I love him so, he'll never know."

There she was, laughing with Tony again, seeing the gifts and that look in his eye that said, "I need you, now."

"All my life is just despair, but I don't care."

A flashback of herself soaking in a lavender bath, waiting for him to show and then the phone call he wasn't going to make it.

"When he takes me in his arms the world is bright all right."

Never was there a lover who could set her on fire like Tony.

"What's the difference if I say, I'll go away?"

Even after she knew how dangerous he was, Heather's heart had ached for months after leaving Tony.

"When I know I'll come back on my knees someday."

Heather realized she was in love with the dream.

"For whatever my man is, I am his forever more."

Tony was the only man she had ever known who was able to stir her passions. Even after all that happened, thinking about the way he made love to her still moved something deep in her soul. It had all been an illusion. Tony was the devil himself.

As the orchestra went into the final pass, Heather opened her eyes and delivered the song again. This time she sang the lyrics with frustration and anger revealing her deepest sorrows, her passionate love story, and her darkest of nightmares.

Heather had completely forgotten who was in the audience. Her dramatic presentation drew the musicians and the entire room into an emotional sea of dramatic sensations. Both men and women were crying. Heather was in the zone.

In that moment, she realized a part of her soul still belonged to Tony. He was her drama…he was her pain. Belting out the final line, Heather looked to the ceiling then closed her eyes.

"For whatever my man is, I am his forever more."

When the music stopped, Heather, still lost in her memories of Tony, was deaf to the applause and the standing ovation before her. When she did finally open her eyes, she saw Richard on the floor, tears running down his face and clapping sensationally.

Heather humbly smiled and graciously curtsied, then kissed Gus on the cheek.

"Thank you, Gus."

"Anytime, little lady. Anytime!"

Proudly, Richard escorted Heather from the stage.

"There she is, folks. Heather Diamond. I am sure we haven't heard the last of this lovely starlet," Gus said. "The boys and I are going to take a little break. When we come back, we will begin our Charleston contest."

"You were sensational, Heather. My God, you belong on the stage. You belong on Broadway, my dear, where people can hear you sing," Richard praised.

As if on cue, a man walked over to the table and handed Richard a card. "Where did you find this little gal, Richard? I heard Fanny Brice sing that song once at the Ziegfeld Follies. She made the audience cry just like you did tonight. You should be in New York, Heather. You are a perfect fit. I'd like to tell Flo about her, Richard."

"Oh, Richard, the Ziegfeld Follies??"

"She's shooting another movie in a few weeks..."

"No one can hear those pipes in a silent film. Heather needs to be on stage, she needs to be recorded."

"Thank you, Christopher. We'll be in touch," Richard smiled.

"Can't I do both, Richard? After all movies are filled with vaudeville comedians and actors from Broadway."

"I don't see why not. You are not locked into anything major right now and I like New York. We won't start filming your next film until late in the fall."

"I've never been to New York."

"There are many people on Broadway who still look down their noses at Hollywood, but that seems to be changing. The more I think of it, the more I like the idea, Heather. Besides, if movies ever go to talkies... Uh oh...don't look now, but Bill Stein is walking over to our table."

"Looks like he has his secretary with him. I spoke with her for a few minutes at Pickfair. She's a real sweetheart. I cannot imagine what it must be like for her working for Bill Stein."

Considering herself a wonderful actress, Sally Jean put on her brightest smile to hide the seething contempt that was boiling inside.

"Bill! Good to see you my man," Richard gleamed.

"I am totally humbled by your talent, my dear. Heather, you were fabulous," he said, with hat in hand.

"Thank you, Mr. Stein. "Good to see you again, Sally Jean."

"I am happy for your success, Heather" Sally Jean lied.

Let's do lunch, Richard," Bill suggested.

"Absolutely," Richard said flashing his million dollar smile.

Dinner was delicious and Heather was pleased that Richard was such an amazing dancer. He didn't allow anyone to cut in.

"You are not someone to be passed around, Heather. Believe me… they will appreciate you more if you are just a little bit hard to get. By the way, I was watching Mr. Mayer watching you. He was quite pleased. They all were."

Richard and Heather stayed until Gus Arheim's orchestra played the last song. As Richard and Heather approached the stairs, she noticed three men and a very intoxicated woman still sitting in one of the boxes.

"Who's that woman, Richard? She looks familiar to me."

"She used to go by the name Margaret Gibson. Now she goes by Patricia Palmer. She's trouble, Heather. You stay away from her. She was arrested last year on felony charges. Seems she was part of a nation-wide blackmail and extortion ring. She's also gotten in trouble with drugs. Somehow she always gets the charges dropped."

"Those men kind of remind me of some of Tony's friends in Chicago. The gangster type…"

"Your instincts are right on, Heather. Movie people have money and they are perfect targets for drug pushers. You've heard of the William Desmond Taylor murder? Remember it happened during Roscoe Arbuckle's trial? Mabel Normand was one of the suspects… a sweet kid, but a holy mess. She has an expensive drug habit and Bill was trying to help her kick it. Even sent her to rehab. He really cared for her. She was the last one to see him alive."

"Don't worry Richard, I have had my fill of gangsters. It's a dangerous business."

## CHAPTER 21

# A Dangerous Business

February 1, 1922: Margaret Gibson, also known as Gibby, sniffed another line of cocaine then rubbed the residue on her teeth. "Nice, Lou. Real nice," she said with approval.

"You know Bill Taylor?"

"Yeah, I know him," Gibby answered as she reapplied her bright red lipstick.

"We hear you know him pretty well."

"We worked on a few pictures together. Even had a few romps in the hay. Nice looking guy…kind of the heartbreaker type. Love 'em and leave 'em, if you know what I mean. At least that's how it was when I knew him."

Gibby put her compact and tube back into her purse.

"We want him gone and we want you to do it."

"What do you mean gone?"

"Gone, Gibby. Forever gone. He's been shootin' his mouth off to the FBI. We want you to make him go away."

"What? Me? But..."

"You got two choices, Gibby. Get rid of him or suffer the consequences."

It was well known Gibby was no angel. She had been arrested for selling drugs and everyone knew she slept around with more men than even she could count... but murder? That was something different.

"Here's the deal, Gibby. This guy Bill has been talkin' to the FBI about turning in his girlfriend's suppliers... that would be us. Cocaine is a hard addiction to break. This is good for business. This guy wants to be a hero, a do-gooder. That would be bad for business. He's gotta go and you're gonna do it. We'll give you twenty grand."

"Tonight? What about me? What if I get caught?" Gibby asked. Bill had tossed her away like yesterday's newspaper but so did a lot of guys. But murder? Damn! That was a different story.

"It's simple. The boys take you to his bungalow and park down the street. You go inside and shoot him."

"I don't know..."

"You owe me, Gibby. Do what we ask or suffer the consequences. Now that we've had this little conversation, you are what we call a loose end. Capisce?"

"OK, Lou. I get it."

"I'll have the boys pick you up at 7."

Good looking, hot loving Billy Taylor had charmed many a young, pretty starlet into his bed, including Gibby. There had been rumors that he had a taste for men as well. Bill and Gibby had done several pictures together. It was natural for two stars to create chemistry off screen before bringing their scenes to life. When the director yelled "Action" a little intimacy beforehand made it more convincing, creating a better product.

By reputation, Bill had been with just about every new starlet who crossed his path. However, from the first day he met Mabel Normand on the set, something had clicked that was different from the others. Although Mabel was a master at comedy, something about her seemed vulnerable. When Bill learned the new object of his affection was addicted to drugs at the tune of $2000 a month, he tried to save her.

Mabel would get clean but then something would happen to make her start using again. This usually happened whenever she was in the company of others who used. It was hard for her to say no to the cocaine rush or the opium high and it wouldn't take long until she was again out of control.

It had been dark for several hours. At 7:40 PM Gibby watched from the side of the house as Bill and his good friend Mabel walked outside the bungalow. They had been discussing the new picture he was directing and he had given her a book as a gift. The two friends hugged. Mabel settled into the backseat of her lilac limousine, unaware that she would never see her friend again. She kissed the window and bid Bill farewell. She was later said to be the last one to see him alive. As the limo drove away, Gibby watched as the couple blew kisses to each other.

"What a chump," Gibby thought. "She's the reason he's gonna get it tonight. Hope she was worth it, Billy Boy."

Gibby looked around. The neighborhood was quiet; the residents had snuggled in and seemed to have called it a day. Gibby stepped on another cigarette butt and braced herself for the task at hand. After standing for a minute, she knocked at the back door, feeling as if her heart would jump out of her chest. I will play it as if I am acting out a sinister part of a murder mystery. It will be the performance of a lifetime.

It was rare Bill opened his door for anyone, especially unexpected guests.

It seemed Bill had a premonition of doom. Just days before his death he had told his lawyer, "If anything happens to me, I want you to take care of my affairs." Strangely, the day before he died, Bill withdrew $2500 from his bank account and deposited the same amount back into the account the same day. He kept a loaded gun on the bureau and proudly boasted he would be inclined to shoot any intruder. Lately, strange men had been seen snooping around his bungalow. Bill was receiving mysterious phone calls with no one on the other end, as if someone was checking on whether or not he was at home.

Knock, knock, knock…

No one ever knocked at the back door. Apprehensive at first, Bill peeked out the window to see who it was. When he saw it was Gibby, curiosity got the best of him. "What in the world are you doing here and why are you dressed like that? Rehearsing the part of your next leading man?" he joked.

"Hey there, lover boy. Aren't you gonna invite me in?" Gibby answered, trying to contain the nervousness in her voice. "Don't worry, I won't stay long. I need to talk to you. It's about your girlfriend Mabel."

"All right… come in, Gibby."

Bill turned around and walked towards the living room. "Can I offer you a drink?"

Gibby knew she had to act fast or she would surely lose her nerve. Slowly, she pulled the revolver out of her purse. Bill turned around and gasped when he saw his fate pointing straight at his heart.

Although Gibby was shaking so hard she felt her knees would collapse, the revolver remained steady in her hand. She was about to play the most spectacular role of her lifetime, only this time she wrote the script and Bill would be the only one to see it.

"You pissed off the wrong guys, Bill. Damn, I hate this but ya pissed off the wrong guys! Now I gotta kill ya."

"Gibby?"

"Shouldn't have gone to the FBI, Bill. Put your hands up and turn around. I don't wanna see those baby blues."

Bill slowly lifted his arms and turned around. Far be it from him to argue with a woman with a gun.

Looking over his shoulder, he pleaded, "Gibby? Can't we…"

BOOM!!

Gibby saw Bill fall forward onto the floor, as if she were watching a film played in slow motion. For an endless moment all she could do was stare as the reality of her sinister actions crept slowly into her troubled mind. Very carefully Gibby turned Bill's body over to make sure he wasn't breathing. To her horror, he looked at her with confusion and disbelief.

"I'm sorry, Bill," she whispered. "I'm really sorry."

Gibby watched as Bill gradually transformed into a sweet surrender. Then with a giant rattle, Bill stopped breathing.

Gibby had performed well the most difficult role of her career. For a short time, she went completely into character, pretending she was the murderess and Bill was her victim. She knew doing so was the only way she would be able to go through with her unsavory assignment. In the movies when an actor is murdered and plays dead, the director yells out "cut," and the victim gets up, brushes himself off and walks away. A part of her had expected Bill to do just that. Not this time. His body lay still… very, very still.

The house was eerily quiet. Bill's eyes were wide opened, staring at the ceiling. As usual he was impeccably dressed and not a hair out of place. Gibby reached into her purse and pulled out a carefully folded napkin that contained three blonde hairs. She carefully laid them on his lapel.

As the blood began flooding the floor, reality began to seep in and fear completely consumed her. What if someone saw her? What if she got caught?

Suddenly, Gibby felt like she was in a horrible nightmare. Bill was dead. Every day, for the rest of her life, Gibby would replay this murder scene, the darkest of memories, over and over again.

It had been less than 10 minutes since Bill let Gibby inside.

Gibby walked out of the bungalow. Remembering she had left the revolver on a table, she quickly went back inside to retrieve it. As she was leaving, she encountered one of Bill's neighbors. The neighbor assumed Gibby was a man and the two acknowledged each other. She would testify later "the man had an effeminate walk and was acting a little funny." Right on cue, Lou's men drove up and Gibby jumped into the car.

"Did you see that? I almost got caught!" Gibby exclaimed.

"Is he dead?" the driver inquired.

"He's dead," Gibby whispered.

"I hope so, for your sake," he threatened.

"He's dead."

"We need to let the movie studio know."

The car drove up to a phone booth. Lou's man jumped out and made two phone calls. One was to his boss and the other was to his contact at the movie studio.

The last thing the movie studio needed was another scandal. Everyone was just getting over the Fatty Arbuckle ordeal and women's groups and religious leaders were trying to boycott people from going to the movies. A "cleaning crew" was put together to search Bill's bungalow to remove any bootlegged liquor or personal letters that the press could get a hold of.

For the next week, Gibby did not leave her house in Santa Monica. Lost in drugs and opium, the whole event seemed surreal. The night after the murder, one of Lou's thugs delivered a suitcase containing $20,000 with a note that said, "Good girl."

"Good girl?" she read aloud. "That's a joke. Good girl?"

Gibby started laughing hysterically and poured herself a glass of straight, bootlegged gin. "Here's to you, ya big chump!"

The booze was gone in one big swallow but the darkness slowly crept back in. Gibby began sobbing incessantly. No amount of drugs or liquor would ever erase that horrific moment when Bill looked at her before he passed.

They knew he would let her in. Bill trusted her and that was his demise. Every day the events of that horrible evening remained fresh in her mind. As the darkness of the memory tormented her soul, Gibby began to realize she would never be free.

Gibby was never questioned or even considered a suspect. The Mob had chosen its assassin well and no one would ever be the wiser. In less than a week, the detective in charge of the investigation was told to *lay off* and no one was ever convicted.

Although Gibby was never a suspect, the heartbreaking image of the way Bill looked at her before he died haunted Gibby often. Sometimes the guilt would be overwhelming and even make her a little crazy. "*They knew he would let me in. The poor sap trusted me.*"

*December 5, 1924*
*Dear Miss Pearl,*
*The premier for "Rio Concho" is going to be on January 14 at Grauman's Egyptian Theatre. I want to extend an invitation to you or any of the girls to attend. Shooting for my new film, Blue Midnight, will begin the following week so please come early.*
*My life has changed so much in these last few months. I bought a home with a beautiful view of the ocean in Redondo Beach. It has been exciting meeting the famous movie stars, directors and producers I only before read about. Really, they are all just people living their lives like everybody else.*
*I love my new friend Richard. I worked with him on Rio Concho and he has taken me under his wing. We are the perfect mis-match made in heaven. He has a genuine sweet spirit and knows everyone in Hollywood. The thing I love the most about him is the way he is with people. From the biggest studio-moguls and stars to the valets and waiters, Richard treats everyone the same. We have nothing romantic. He is more Harvey's type, but I do have a room for him in my new home.*
*Working in the film industry, one is either crazy busy or doing absolutely nothing at all. I have started writing a script in my free time. It's the story of a farm girl who meets a gangster. He takes her to the big city to be a singer in his speakeasy and she falls in love. One night he goes into a jealous rage and when he tries to kill her, she escapes. Sound familiar?*
*How fortunate for me to have spent those two wonderful years with you, Miss Pearl. You taught me how to be a lady seductress and how to value myself as a woman. There are so many young, pretty girls in Hollywood who allow themselves to be used with the hopes of becoming a star. Then there are those women who use their sexuality to entrap the men. At least Miss Pearl's Parlor is more honest because everyone knows what to expect. I understand that better now.*
*With unending gratitude,*
*Heather*

CHAPTER 22

# Rio Concho

"Heather, this is Stewart. Can you come over to the hotel? There is someone here I'd like you to meet."

"Sure, Stewart. Do I need to dress up?"

"Something simple will be fine, Heather. You always look nice.

Heather had just returned from spending Christmas with her family. Happy to be back, she was grateful that January in Southern California was nothing like the cold winters Heather had known growing up on the farm in Illinois. Although she would love to have her family close to her, whenever she mentioned the possibility of their coming to California, her father was not in the least bit interested in pulling up his roots.

Walking into the lobby of the Hotel Redondo, Heather felt a rush as two lovely women jumped up from their seats and ran to her with open arms.

"SURPRISE!"

It was Maggie and Sarah.

Arms locked around each other, the three women jumped up and down with excitement.

"I've never been so happy to see anyone in my life. You are staying with me!"

"I figured as much," Stewart said. "Let me get someone to give you a lift and help with the luggage."

As the women walked out to the back deck of the beach house, the ocean seemed to be singing a welcoming song.

"What a fabulous view! Oh, Heather, everyone is so happy for you," Maggie exclaimed.

"Let's call Dusty and Jesse and I want you to meet Richard! He's my new best friend."

The next day, the girls jumped on the Red Car for a day of sightseeing. Showing her favorite places to Maggie and Sarah was like seeing everything for the first time all over again.

First stop was the Pink Palace in Beverly Hills to see Edward. They saw the 45-foot letters that spelled HOLLYWOODLAND spread across Mount Lee in the Santa Monica Mountains. Shopping was fun at Olvera Street where they ate tacos and listened to the music of a mariachi band. The final stop was Universal Studios, where Richard was waiting to give them a personal tour of the movie lots.

As always, Richard was charming, informative and accommodating

"Let's go by the barn where Sport is. Dusty and Jesse said they would meet us there if they don't have to work today."

Standing outside the barn was that familiar older gentleman Heather had fallen in love with a few months before.

"Wyatt!"

"Hello, little darlin," he said, swooping Heather up and giving her a big hug.

"And who are these fine ladies?"

"These are my girlfriends from Texas. Maggie, Sarah, may I present to you my good friend, Wyatt Earp?"

"The Wyatt Earp?" Maggie exclaimed. "I have read all about you, sir," she chirped with her perfect Texas drawl.

"I'm Sarah."

"You girls born in Texas?" Wyatt asked.

"Oh yessir," Maggie sang, trying to catch her breath.

Just then the girls heard two familiar voices coming from the barn. Tall, lean and smiling ear to ear the Texas cowboys were coming their way, looking sexy as ever.

"Dusty!" Maggie yelled

"Hey, Jesse!" Sarah waved.

"Come here to me, Maggie, you good lookin' thang!" Dusty said with his arms stretched out.

The reunion was exhilarating. Laughing like kids at a circus, the group hugged and frolicked with excitement.

"Dang, I didn't realize how much I missed Texas till I saw the two of you," Jesse proclaimed. "Sure is good to see you, Sarah. How are things at Miss Pearl's?"

"Things are good, Jesse. Business is good with the oil boom in San Angelo and all. I miss seeing you there."

Sport joined the group with his wife, Opal, who was carrying his new baby boy.

"Is this Duke?" Heather asked, reaching for the plump little bundle of love. "May I?"

"Anyone want a cold one? My sweet wife just made a fresh batch of bathtub beer," Sport said, opening a chest standing beside the barn.

The next two hours were spent catching up with old friends and sharing stories with the new ones.

"Tex died and left me his ranch, Dusty. I don't know the first thing about ranchin'."

"What are ya gonna do, Maggie?"

"Not sure yet. I have been thinking about fixing up the house. That's about it. Sarah is going to move there with me."

"Jesse and I were just talkin' about goin' back to Texas. We can run that ranch for you. River runs through it as I recall."

"Really? Really, Dusty?"

"California is fun but I'm ready to go home," Jesse said.

"Tell ya what I'll do. You give us half the profits and Jesse and I will run that ranch."

"Ok Dusty, DEAL," Maggie said, reaching out her hand.

Dusty took Maggie's hand and pulled her close, kissing a little at first then passionately. Maggie responded and everyone watched as things got pretty heated up.

"Richard, take my friends over to my bungalow, if you don't mind. I believe they need to freshen up a bit," Heather smiled, setting everyone at ease.

Everyone at Pearl's knew Dusty and Maggie had a special sexual chemistry because of all the noise they made whenever they were together. Although Maggie had told all her lovers they were the best she ever had, Dusty took the prize. He just had a way of setting her womanly parts on fire.

"Lucky man," Wyatt commented as the group watched the couple continue being glad to see each other. "Hope they make it to the bungalow for Richard's sake."

Sport thought it a good time to extend an invitation.

"Opal's going to play piano at the Waterhole tonight. Why don't you girls come on over? Billy's going to make burgers and hot dogs. Hoot Gibson and some of our stuntman friends will be there."

"Sounds great," Heather said.

"I'll go too," Wyatt assured them. "I like the boys at the Waterhole. Sounds like a good time."

That evening Richard took the girls back to the beach house. "I have a surprise for you, Heather. I have arranged a trip to Catalina on my friend's yacht, day after tomorrow. I will be by to pick you girls up at 9 AM sharp."

The next day, the girls stayed close to home. Heather took them to Moonstone Beach. It had become a favorite place for Heather to go explore. A bowl of moonstones she had collected on her walks sat on her dining room table. That evening, Ruby invited the girls to dinner at the La Venta Inn. They enjoyed a delicious meal of fresh seafood and vegetables grown by the local farmers.

Richard had picked a perfect day to go to Catalina. Although Heather had seen Catalina from the mainland, she had no idea the island resort had so much to offer. Walter, who owned the yacht, was a member of the Tuna Club, a private yacht club exclusive to men. Other members included Rudolph Valentino, Charlie Chaplin, Cecil B. DeMille and the famous western author Zane Grey, who served as president of the club.

"What a perfectly charming place," Heather said as they pulled into the harbor. "Who owns the mansion over there?"

"William Wrigley Jr.," Richard informed her. "He bought Catalina Island a few years ago and has made several improvements to make it a first rate resort. Made a fortune packaging chewing gum. He loves nature and beautiful things."

"What's a glass bottom boat?" Maggie asked, pointing to a boat in the harbor.

"Exactly what it says," Richard laughed. "The boat has a glass bottom with benches all around it so you can look at the sea life below. Why don't you girls go for a ride while we go to the Tuna Club? I think you will enjoy it. We'll meet you back here at 2:30. We want to get back to San Pedro before dark."

Maggie, Sarah and Heather enjoyed their day on Catalina Island, laughing, eating, and exploring the coastline. They were walking along the rocky sea when Heather suddenly jumped on a large rock and put her hands on her hips.

"Shiver me timbers, my lassie friends. There is buried treasure on this island, as sure as the sun will come up in the mornin'. It is a secret I possess locked away in the archives of my mind. Yet, if anything should ever happen to me, a map revealing the secret location I reverently refer to as Shark Tooth Cave, shall be revealed to a worthy candidate!"

"Heather, that's really good," Sarah laughed.

"Maybe there is buried treasure on the island," Maggie said. "It certainly is possible."

"There is treasure here, Maggie. It's called whiskey, rum, gin…they bring it in from Canada and Mexico."

"How do you know that?" Sarah asked.

"I know a lot of things I'm probably not supposed to know," Heather grinned.

Heather had not realized how much she had missed her friends until now. Less than a year ago she was living with Maggie and Sarah in San Angelo, Texas, only fantasizing she was a famous actress. She never dreamed her life could change so drastically in such a short time. Youth was on her side and, although she knew there would be challenges along the way, today everything was wonderful.

Pearl always told her girls, "Savor every moment you have with the people you love and live each day as if it were your last time together." Today, being with Maggie and Sarah was a good day.

As they walked back to the yacht, Heather noticed a man sitting in front of a lovely canvas painting of the raw Catalina coastline. His hair was jet black and curly and he was wearing a loose fitting white linen shirt.

"Hey everyone, look at that man over there. I have never seen anyone like him before. He seems so intense but at the same time serene."

"He is good-looking in a Rudolph Valentino kind of way. I like big strong cowboys, myself."

"I can see what you see. He's an artist; a sensitive, passionate man who brings the beauty of nature he sees to life with a canvas, paintbrush and vibrant colors," Sarah teased with a dramatic tone. "I'm with Maggie. I like the manly Tarzan type," she giggled.

"Something about him intrigues me," Heather said. "Ah well, enough of this sightseeing. We need to get back to the boat."

Heather turned around for one more look at the man who had roused her interest. To her surprise he waved at her and smiled, then turned back and resumed his creation.

Halfway between Catalina and the mainland, the yacht met up with a school of dolphins dancing in the last hours of the day's glimmering sunlight shining on the ocean.

"Sometimes the dolphins like to put on a show," Walter said, shutting down the motor of the boat.

"Look," Maggie pointed, squealing with delight.

Right on cue, with the first warm colors of the setting sun serving as a backdrop, one of the dolphins jumped high into the air... then another...then another. Like a choreographed ballet, several dolphins surfaced then descended with a smooth, slow rhythmic stride.

For a long time, everyone on the boat watched in silence as the dolphins danced in the glistening deep blue waters of the Pacific Ocean. It was as if they could sense the appreciation of their audience and wanted to share the beauty of their world that existed below the surface of the water.

It was Sarah who finally broke the silence. "I don't believe I have ever seen anything so magical, so beautiful..."

"It's as if they are dancing just for us," Maggie smiled.

"I have even seen them surf in the waves," Walter commented. "The males are called bulls, the females are cows and the babies are calves. They are considered the most intelligent of all animals and are master communicators."

"Cows? Bulls? Sounds like what I'm going to be raisin' when I get back to Texas," Maggie laughed.

"I've heard dolphins have rescued drowning sailors," Richard said.

"That is correct, Richard. They talk about it in Greek mythology."

"All I know is they are absolutely beautiful," Maggie sighed. "I will never forget this as long as I live."

"I must admit it is probably the best dolphin show I have ever seen," Walter smiled. "I think they wanted to show off for you pretty women. Can't say I blame them."

That evening, Heather made a fire and the three friends reflected on the precious time they had spent together.

"When I first came to Miss Pearl's I didn't understand why it was so important to read every day and walk right and talk right and all that," Maggie said. "I guess it's because I never knew any different."

"Hollywood and meeting the people who work in the movie industry has been fascinating. I didn't realize how much I learned from Pearl until now. Acting like a lady, you just can't lose. Just like at Pearl's Parlor, people don't fall in love with you personally, they fall in love with the fantasy."

"You are right, Heather," Maggie agreed. Then there is that animal-like attraction. I know we might have gotten a little too carried away the other day, but I was so happy to see Dusty. I'm very excited he and Jesse want to come run the ranch."

"Dusty and Jesse are real cowboys, Maggie. Hollywood uses their skills and, believe me, directors and producers love a real cowboy. The truth is, real cowboys like to be real cowboys," Heather said. "I know they miss Texas. They say it all the time."

The day of the premiere, Maggie and Sarah were a great comfort to their excited, but still nervous, friend.

"I can't imagine what this day would have been without you. Thank you so much for coming," Heather said, hugging her friends.

"Would not have missed it for the world! We love you, Heather. It's going to be great. Your first movie! This is so exciting!"

When the limo pulled up to the beach house, Richard, along with two tall, handsome, manly men wearing cowboy hats emerged from the car.

"My God! Look at Dusty," Maggie proclaimed with great appreciation. "Mighty fine, mighty fine!"

"Howdy ma'am," Dusty smiled as he approached her.

"I know I shouldn't, but I am just going to say it anyway. Dusty, I want to tear your clothes off!"

"The feeling is quite mutual, little lady," he smiled. "You look good enough to eat."

Richard was amused. "You ladies look stunning. Are you ready, Heather? They're all going to be there."

"What if…" Heather grimaced.

"Don't even say it. I have seen the film. You are going to light up that screen like a beacon in the night," he said, crooking his arm. "I am so proud of you."

Jesse looked at Sarah. "May I have the honor of being your escort tonight?"

Sarah's smile was radiant. "Delighted."

Richard was right. *Rio Concho* was a huge success. They were all there: Mary Pickford, Douglas Fairbanks, Charlie Chaplin, Wyatt Earp and his wife Josie, Ruby, Edward, Stewart, Marion Morrison, Sport and his wife Opal, and several others Richard had personally asked to attend.

Mary Pickford hosted an intimate gathering at Pickfair to honor Hollywood's newest starlet. She had become fond of Heather and was impressed with her friendship with Richard. There were those who wanted the fame and then there were those who loved the art itself. Mary always knew the difference. Heather had talent and had earned her respect.

Bill Stein had shown up with Sally Jean. Within an hour she had belted down three double martinis and was asking for number four. Heather recognized the secretary's dilemma and approached the bar. Black streaks of eye make-up were smeared down Sally Jean's face.

"What do you want?"

"Let us have a glass of water," Heather told the bartender "Let's go for a walk," she said taking her arm and leading her outside.

"I'll be right back," Maggie told Dusty.

"Where ya goin'?"

"I believe we have a sister who needs some help. I won't be long."

"It should have been me! He promised me!" Sally Jean cried. "Then you and your girlfriend showed up and ruined everything. Did he make you suck it? Did your girlfriend suck it too?"

Heather looked at Maggie and sighed. Sally Jean had said enough for them to know her dilemma.

"Nothing like that happened with Bill Stein, Sally Jean. Where are you from?"

"Iowa," she slurred.

"You seem like a nice kid. Let's go…"

Brrrrrrarf. Sally Jean's martinis were splattered all over Mary Pickford's neatly trimmed hedge.

"Stay with her, Maggie. I will go get a cold washcloth."

Coming out of the restroom, Heather ran into Bill Stein. Her eyes were full of fire making Bill Stein freeze in his tracks.

"Listen to me, you son-of-a-bitch. I know the game you are playing with Sally Jean. She is a mess. Fix it!" she whispered, "Or I will see to it that you wished you had."

Stunned, Bill Stein didn't say a word. It only took one quick glance around the room for Bill Stein to see that Heather Diamond outranked him. The critics loved her, the audience loved her and most important of all, Hollywood loved her.

To his surprise, Heather instantly changed her demeanor, threw her arms around Bill Stein and gave him a huge kiss on the cheek. "Thank you for all you have done for me Mister Stein," she chirped. Richard, who had observed the entire scene, followed Heather outside.

"What was that?"

"Richard, can we find a part for Sally Jean in *Blue Midnight*?"

Richard smiled. "I'll see what I can do."

Being a most gracious hostess, Mary approached the two of them. "Everything alright?"

"I believe Sally Jean has had a little too much excitement," Heather smiled.

"Let's take her to the pool house. There is a place there where she can lay down," Mary offered impressed with Heather's desire to preserve Sally Jean's dignity. "I'll get one of my staff to look after her."

That evening the group returned to Heather's beach house. Maggie and Dusty jumped out of the limo and went straight to Maggie's room. That was the last anyone saw of them until the next afternoon. Sarah changed her clothes and she and Jesse took a warm blanket down to the beach. Heather slipped on a white satin, fur-lined dressing gown and Richard built a fire for the two of them to share.

"I know we had an eclectic guest list this evening, but everyone I invited is part of your journey, Heather, as well as mine. You learn in this business that your friends are your greatest treasures. That's why they came, Heather. You are the celestial virgin, a reminder of their first time, when the business was exciting and all brand new. They loved you."

"I feel like a small fish that has been thrown into a giant pond. I'm looking forward to doing *Blue Midnight*. I love the script. It's very intriguing. Surely you can find a part for Sally Jean."

"Actually I have a part in mind. Consider it done. We will have to change her name of course."

"Poor kid. I can only imagine what she has been through working for that jerk."

"Yeah. Unfortunately there are too many Sally Jeans in Hollywood. At least she didn't try to fly off of the Pasadena Bridge. By the way, have you thought anymore about New York? I think you should go. Christopher is a good man. He can get you a singing part in the Follies tomorrow if you want."

"I must confess, I'd love a shot at playing on stage to a live audience," Heather admitted.

"You will be more respected among your peers. Silent movies evolved from vaudeville and theatre. More and more of New York's most popular entertainers are coming to Hollywood to be in movies. New York just looks good on your resume and the experience will do you good."

"I'd love to go. Pearl is planning a trip in the spring. She has friends there."

"Go for three months. I know after tonight there will be more movie offers and requests for screenplays. You can manage both."

"It sounds wonderful, Richard."

"Congratulations, my dear. You are on your way."

For the next several days, Heather wanted nothing more than to enjoy her friends. She bought a ukulele at the pier and learned to play just enough chords to have fun. The girls sang, laughed and talked about pains of the past and their dreams of the future.

On their last night together, Ruby came over with bottles of wine. The women spent the evening on the deck, wrapped in warm wool blankets, telling stories and enjoying the magical song of the sea. Ruby reminisced about her days in Tombstone. "It was cold and windy on that bloody day at the OK Corral. Josephine was hysterical when she came to

Consuelo's house that morning! Word about the Cowboys wanting to kill the Earps was spreading through the town like wildfire. Consuelo was our rock. She always knew what to do and say. Lord knows what would have happened to me if she had not taken me in. God how I miss that woman."

"She sounds like Miss Pearl," Heather commented.

For a while the ladies sat in silence, watching as the neon white foam of the waves gently break on the sand.

"It's late. I need to get going," Ruby announced.

"Why don't you stay here tonight, Ruby?" Heather invited.

"Thank you anyway, Honey. I need to spend as much time as I can at the Hotel Redondo. The city is taking her down in a couple of months and selling her for scrap wood."

"That is so sad," Sarah commented.

"Tell me about it. Mickey and I sure had some good times there," she smiled.

"Do you need a ride?'

"I can walk there in less than ten minutes. I do it all the time. Mickey and I loved our moonlight walks on the beach. It's when I feel closest to him," she said tearfully. "You girls take care now. It has been a pleasure being in the company of real ladies."

"Ruby really does remind me so much of Miss Pearl," Heather remarked. "I am fortunate to have her as a friend."

Richard showed up the next morning to say "goodbye" and take the girls' luggage to the train station.

"Thank you for everything, Richard. We had a glorious time," Maggie said as she kissed his cheek.

"I hear Dusty and Jesse are going back to Texas to run your ranch," Richard said. "Maybe I can get out there sometime and see it."

"You are welcome anytime, sir," Maggie grinned.

Although she knew she would miss her friends, Heather was anxious to get back to work. In two days, shooting for *Blue Midnight* was going to begin and she was anxious to get back to what she loved to do.

*Blue Midnight* was a much different experience than *Rio Concho*. Sally Jean was given the name, Veronica Snow. She and Heather had a special chemistry. In fact, she played her part as the heroine's best friend so well, two more scenes were written into the script.

Heather especially liked doing the love scenes with Ramon Novarro. Ramon's passionate Latino chemistry was electric and dynamic before the camera; however they maintained a friendly and professional friendship off-camera. It was clear he was more interested in Richard than her in that regard.

"He is handsome," she told Richard one day.

"We had drinks one night," Richard confessed. "We had a very nice evening but it was only one time. Ramon likes to sleep in a coffin…"

"Oh. Enough said."

On the last day of shooting, Richard came to Heather with a huge smile on his face.

"The studio is sending us to New York to promote *Blue Midnight*.

"When do we leave?" Heather asked.

"You can leave next week," Richard said.

The beach had become Heather's playground and solitude. Stepping out to the deck, she decided to practice her ukulele and enjoy the freshness of the salty breeze. The day was coming to an end and it was almost time for God to begin painting another glorious sunset. Looking towards the south, Heather could see an artist on the beach standing before an easel. He was making broad deliberate strokes on a large canvas before him. The man was wearing long dark pants, a white loose fitting shirt, and his long black curls were gently blowing in the breeze.

"Is it him?" she asked herself.

"I believe it is him," she answered.

Quickly changing, Heather hurried down her steps to the beach below. As soon as she hit the sand, she changed to a casual stride in an attempt to not look too eager.

Again to her amazement the man smiled and waved, motioning her to join him.

"*He is gorgeous*," she thought to herself. "*I wonder if he likes women?*" It was a question she had never even considered before she had worked in Hollywood.

# CHAPTER 23

# Lovers

*"Handsome, sexy, strong, olive skin, pearly white teeth, a beautiful smile… he kind of reminds me of Lorenzo or even Tony…uh oh…I wonder if he is Italian."*

The closer she got, the better he looked.

"Hello."

"Bella, so good of you to join me."

"Oh no…he is Italian."

"I am Giorgio," he smiled, "and you are the most beautiful woman I have ever seen in my life."

"Oh no," she groaned. "My name is Heather," she said rolling her eyes.

"What is wrong?"

"You couldn't do better than that?"

"What do you mean?"

"Most beautiful woman? Please…"

"Oh, I see. You must hear that all the time. I am sorry I offended you. Please forgive me… it will not happen again."

Giorgio picked up his brush and continued his masterpiece, acting as if Heather was no longer there. Unsure of what to do, Heather walked towards the shoreline.

*"What just happened? In one stupid moment it went from good to bad. Am I so bitter that I have to attack the most handsome man I have ever met? Why did I react like that? Oh, Heather! You dummy. Maybe I can fix this..."*

When Heather turned around, she saw Giorgio sadly packing up his brushes and paints. Horrified, she realized she had destroyed his joy and bruised his artistic spirit.

"Oh no!"

Quickly she ran towards Giorgio.

"Wait! Wait! Please, Giorgio! Please forgive me!"

Giorgio could only stare. *"I know her. I knew her on Catalina and I know her now. Oh, my heart, how it trembles when I see those eyes. What do I do? She has too much power over my soul. What do I do?"*

All time stood still as Heather locked her gaze into Giorgio's soft brown eyes.

*"Who is this man? Why is my heart dancing in my chest with joy? His joy was my joy. Now his pain is my pain. Please God, give me the right words to say to make this right."*

Softly a tear fell from Heather's eye. Giorgio quickly pulled out a handkerchief and gently dried her cheek. It just seemed like the right thing to do and Heather was a little surprised with how comfortable she felt with his kind gesture.

"Please forgive me, Giorgio. May I watch you paint? Oh my goodness. Look at the sky!" she said, pointing towards the ocean.

Giorgio quickly picked up his pallet, adding white, red, orange and yellow paint. Bright golden rays appeared like beacons flashing throughout the sky, as if the heavens were posing for him.

Heather could feel Giorgio's emotions. Passions flared as the handsome artist dramatically caressed the canvas with the brilliant colors that filled the sky. Making his final stroke, Giorgio was satisfied. Clenching his fists as if declaring a victory, Giorgio raised his arms to the beauty of God's glorious creation before him, and then slowly opened his hands. Turning, he offered Heather an invitation to join him.

Heather's heart was soaring. "I know him. We know each other. He is my love from another time."

Giorgio gently put his arms around her and, as their bodies embraced into a comfortable oneness their souls rejoiced, delighted to be united again. In that moment words were futile. All that was present was the magical feeling that the heart and soul recognize in those sacred moments when love is real.

"I am staying at the Hotel Redondo. Please join me for dinner."

Heather's womanhood was tantalizing with desire and her breasts became firm and hard. In an attempt to appear as if she was in control, Heather made a simple suggestion. "Let's go to my house. I just bought fresh vegetables. I will help you carry your art supplies. Your painting is quite lovely."

"It is not finished."

Without saying a word, Heather and Giorgio made their way to the beach house, each possessing an insatiable craving for the other one's touch.

Adhering to Miss Pearl's advice, Heather attempted to keep the conversation superficial. Being with Giorgio was different than other men. This time she was out of control.

"I just bought the house a few months ago," she said, as she opened the door.

"May I set the easel up in the corner of your room?"

"Of course. Help yourself, Giorgio, while I fix us something to eat. Care for a drink? The decanter over there is full of gin."

"Thank you but I believe I would like to remain alert," he smiled. "I have a few finishing touches to make on the painting that I would like to do while it is fresh in my mind."

"I like the vegetables in California," she said from the kitchen. They seem so vibrant in color and taste out of this world. I especially like the oranges…so many orange groves and the tomatoes… they are simply divine."

Within a few minutes, Heather produced a tray of cheese, bread, freshly cut carrots, avocado and sliced tomatoes. Giorgio was smiling as he made one last little stroke on the canvas.

"There. It is finished," he declared.

"May I see?"

Gazing upon the finished painting, Heather felt a hot rush surge throughout her body like a bolt of lightning.

"Me?"

On the shoreline was a woman looking out into the vast blue water of the ocean. Her hair was gently blowing as she gazed into the glow of the sunset, as if searching for the answer to a complex question.

In that moment, Heather forgot everything Miss Pearl had told her about seeming anxious.

"Oh, Giorgio…don't make me wait a minute more!"

Gently, Giorgio took Heather's face into his hands, softly kissed her forehead and looked deeply into her eyes. With a familiar sense of trust, the two souls surrendered to the passions stirring deep within their hearts.

"Amore... I want to make love to you… I want to taste your sweetness and make you scream with ecstasy," he breathed as he grabbed her buttocks and pulled her up to him, kissing her deeply.

Feeling like a feather, in the strength of Giorgio's powerful arms, Heather wrapped her legs around his waist, responding to his every move.

Giorgio laid Heather on the bed and turned on the small lamp on the bedside table.

"I want to see you, Heather. I want to see all of you."

One by one, Giorgio unbuttoned Heather's blouse. Gently sliding everything covering her torso, back over her shoulders, he tenderly kissed every inch of her creamy white skin as it slowly was revealed. Heather's nipples were hard and erect, offering a delicious invitation for Giorgio's tongue to taste. Softly he sucked on her sweetness, sending her body a rush of desire to her womanhood.

Pulling himself up, Giorgio stood before her and removed his shirt, revealing soft, black chest hair on his slightly browned olive skin. Heather could see his manhood was bulging.

Slowly sliding off the remainder of Heather's clothes Giorgio's breath became heavy.

"Molto bella," he breathed, licking his lips with anticipation. "Lay on the pillow, Amore. I want to drink from the cup of your sweet nectar."

Heather's body was in a state of complete surrender. No one had ever made love to her before. Tony enjoyed her but never made love. Within a minute, Heather's womanhood began to go into orgasmic contractions bringing forth a primordial cry of ecstasy, joining the universal song of love and appreciation. She felt suspended in some sort of timeless dimension as she joyfully celebrated being a woman and feeling alive.

"Do you want me, Heather? If you do, please tell me."

"Please, Giorgio! Please!"

Dripping with love juices, Giorgio entered Heather with a firm thrust, waking up even more sensations deep within her body. Together they performed the lovers' dance in perfect rhythm and perfect time. Giorgio had amazing control. Finally, knowing it was time to retreat, he pulled out of their union and Heather skillfully brought him to his final destination, a fountain of pleasure released in a state of pure erotic ecstasy.

For several minutes the lovers laid on the bed, staring at the ceiling. Heather's knees were trembling. Giorgio couldn't move. Both of them were breathing hard.

Heather finally broke the silence.

"I am hungry."

"I am hungry."

Together they began laughing, a little bit at first then a full-on HA HA HA.

"You are fantastic!" Giorgio said, rolling on top of Heather then rolling back, pulling her up. "Let's go eat."

"I have never shaken like that before, Giorgio," Heather said, offering Giorgio a plate of bread and cheese.

"I think I would like to have that drink now," Giorgio smiled. "I'll get it. Would you like one, Amore?"

"That would be lovely." Heather was full of mixed emotions. She had just broken every one of her rules and was not sure what to think, so she decided not to think at all.

"Where do you live, Giorgio?"

"My home is in Italy. You've heard of Leonardo de Vinci? I live close to Vinci. Our home is over 300 years old."

"Really."

"A cousin of mine owns an art gallery in New York. I decided to come to the west coast to paint the ocean. Southern California reminds me of parts of Italy on the coastline. It is very beautiful here. I have never seen so many waves before. It has been a lovely adventure."

Realizing she knew nothing about this man, all kinds of thoughts began swarming in Heather's mind. How many women has he slept with in America? Is there a wife and children somewhere? Does he really have a cousin in New York and a house in Italy or is he like Lorenzo; a liar that preys on women and bewitches them with his charm? No. He's different. Something about him is familiar, he lights up my heart.

What Heather didn't know was that Giorgio was also having thoughts similar to hers. Does she sleep with just anyone? Is this house really hers, or does she have a husband who is out of town? She's clearly not a virgin, but something about her… she is the only woman I have ever known that has the power to break my heart.

"You are a beautiful girl, Heather. You must have many men who want you."

"No, Giorgio. I only moved to Redondo Beach a few weeks ago. I have two friends, Richard and Ruby."

"Richard?"

"I work with him.

"What about the girls I saw you with on Catalina?"

"They are my friends from Texas."

What happened? Twenty minutes ago they were making passionate love. Now everything seemed so awkward.

"I am leaving on Sunday, Heather."

"Leaving? Where are you going?"

"I have to return to Italy."

All that could be heard was the clock ticking away the seconds and ocean waves breaking on the shore outside.

"That makes me sad," Heather sighed, walking towards the painting to take another look.

"It is a gift, Heather. I want you to have it."

For a long, contemplative moment, Heather stared at the painting. "Thank you, Giorgio. It is beautiful."

Once again, a tear fell from Heather's eye. This time Giorgio kissed it away and swooped Heather up into his arms. He carried her across the threshold of the bedroom and laid her on the bed once again.

And so it was… all night long…and the next day… and the next night… and the next day… and the next night…until Sunday morning finally arrived.

## CHAPTER 24

# New York

Although Victoria knew she would be happy to see Minna and Ada, it wasn't until the moment she stepped off of the train and saw them that she realized how much they meant to her.

"Victoria!"

"Oh, my two darlings," Victoria cried, as she happily embraced the two women who completely changed the course of her life.

"Hello, Madeline," Minna greeted. "Harmony, are you getting excited about your recital?"

"I am thank you."

"She practices for hours every day. She has learned much from Julliard," Madeline bragged.

In a strange way, walking across the threshold of Minna and Ada's New York house, Victoria felt as if she had come home.

"Is this the same mirror that was in the entry hall of the Everleigh mansion?"

"Yes it is," Ada beamed.

"I remember looking in that mirror that first afternoon you invited me to tea and wondering what I had gotten myself into," Victoria laughed. Moving into the main parlor, Victoria's heart was full of sentiment, as she recognized so many decorative things she had formerly enjoyed while working as a courtesan at the world famous Everleigh House in Chicago.

"Oh, look, you still have these gold-framed paintings of the nude women. Quite provocative for the day."

"We kept our favorites. Unfortunately we had to let some of our things go," Ada said.

"Like the full sized statue of Cleopatra that was in the Egyptian room?" Victoria teased.

"Turn around," Minna smiled.

Standing proudly looking out one of the big windows was the familiar effigy of Cleopatra.

"There she is," Victoria smiled. "Still beautiful as ever. I had fun with Miss Cleopatra telling stories about her romantic interludes with Mark Anthony. Is that one of the spittoons?" she laughed.

"We kept five of our solid gold spittoons for sentimental reasons," Minna smiled. "We put a plant in each of them as not to confuse anyone who might think we still employ them for our personal use."

"Look over here, Victoria," Ada invited, leading Victoria to a table in the corner of the room. On it were several photos of beautiful, young women in ornate picture frames. "This is a collection of our favorite butterflies. Here is your picture in front with Maddie's."

"I remember when this was taken. I believe Robert had just left to go back to Texas. So long ago, but yet in a way, it still seems like yesterday."

"That explains why the photo shows a radiant glow on your face," Minna complimented. "You always were stunning, Victoria, but you were especially beautiful when your cowboy was in town."

"Every day I miss him," Victoria sighed. "Losing him has been difficult. I so loved that man."

Proudly, as is the southern custom, the sisters gave a grand tour of their home. Each room was decorated with paintings, statues and other decorative objects from the Everleigh mansion, including one of the perfume fountains that filled the room with an intoxicating scent of fresh roses.

As the women entered the library, Victoria felt her heart leap as she gazed upon the thousands of books the sisters still had in their collection.

"The library was my favorite room in the Everleigh mansion. So many hours I spent there keeping my mind occupied between visits from Robert. Oh look, here is your Charles Dickens collection… Shakespeare… ah…Wuthering Heights." Victoria pulled out the book and began caressing the cover as if it was an old friend.

Minna smiled warmly. "One of my favorites."

"It seems like there are so many wonderful new authors these days. Hemingway… F. Scott Fitzgerald. We have fallen in love with a new author from England. Her name is Agatha Christie," Ada informed.

"Agatha Christie writes murder mysteries. She is a clever one," Minna added. "Her books have a curious character from Belgium by the name of Hercule Poirot."

"I will make a point of adding her to our library."

"Let's show the ladies our music room," Ada offered.

Harmony gasped, "This must be the solid gold piano you told me about, Miss Pearl. I have never seen anything like it before. It is absolutely exquisite."

"My golden Steinway is my pride and joy. I try to play her as often as I can."

"I remember that poor fellow who made fun of your gold piano and you told him he had to leave," Madeline smiled.

"And he was never invited to enjoy the Everleigh Club again. We did not allow men who were disrespectful to anything we loved. Not only that, he had to be of poor breeding because he obviously had no taste at all," Ada proclaimed, putting her hand gently over her heart.

"May I?" Harmony asked, her eyes still fixed on the piano.

"Please do, Harmony," Ada invited. "Ladies, won't you sit down and make yourselves comfortable?"

Harmony respectfully sat on the bench and thought of the amazing journey of this exquisitely beautiful piano. From its creation to the Everleigh mansion and now sitting in a place of honor in one of the finest neighborhoods in New York City, the golden piano had brought joy to those privileged to listen and to play. Like an elegant woman, she was meant to be appreciated and adored.

Gracefully and with great sentiment, Harmony played the first three notes of Debussy's Claire de Lune, sending chills up the arms of everyone in the room. Ada closed her eyes, Minna smiled, Madeline stared and Pearl watched Harmony's performance with loving eyes.

As always, Harmony isolated herself to a private world of her own. She was one with the piano, one with the composer and one with the lovely music that was gently caressing the soul of each person in the room.

Harmony played with such delicate perfection that when she finished, applause seemed inappropriate.

"I have no words, Harmony," Ada whispered.

"Exquisite," Minna said. "Like music from heaven."

"Play Autumn Equinox," Victoria encouraged. "Tell the story of how you came to write it, Harmony. Oh dear, do I sound like a stage mother?"

Harmony smiled affectionately at Victoria Pearl. "I wrote this one day while I was sitting at the piano looking out the window. There was a beautiful oak tree full of bright orange leaves. A soft autumn wind seemed to be taking leaves from the tree and swirling them around making them look as if they were dancing in the air. I wanted to express what I was seeing with music. I began playing from the high notes on the keyboard like this."

Harmony began playing a reverse A minor scale. "These are the leaves falling." She began a series of ascending notes. "This is my expression of leaves swirling," as she played new musical phrases. "I chose a minor scale because although it was a lovely sight to behold, there is a hint of melancholy when trees lose their leaves."

When she finished Minna hugged her. "Simply enchanting, my dear. They are going to love you, Harmony."

Harmony was in love with the golden piano. "May I practice a while?"

"Absolutely," Ada consented.

We have 20 years to catch up on. Sometimes Harmony practices for hours at a time. Her music is divine," Victoria complimented.

"Enjoy yourself, my dear. We are taking you to the Plaza for dinner this evening. It is located on 5th Avenue next to Central Park," Ada said. "Alfred Vanderbilt was the very first guest to sign the register when it opened in 1907. Sometimes we see former clients there, although most of the time we respectfully ignore each other. On many occasions our bill had been picked up anonymously."

"Now it is time for tea," Minna announced.

"Tea," Victoria repeated. "September 27, 1899, I shall never forget it. You invited me to tea. Isn't this the same china?"

"It is the same china, Victoria. I remember Minna and I were very excited about your accepting our invitation. Any regrets, my dear?" Ada asked.

"I must admit I was more than a little surprised when your invitation took me to the Levee District of Chicago. Although I was apprehensive at first, I have never regretted my decision to be part of the Everleigh Club. If not for you dear ladies, I would never have met Robert or experienced so many adventurous things."

"It is simply a matter of understanding human nature, my dear," Ada said in a matter-of-fact tone. "We made good money offering our services in a luxurious fashion."

"Boys will be boys," Minna said.

"I always thought it quite clever how you had those little fire crackers in the Chinese room. It always amused me to watch a grown man instantly transform into a little boy when he lit one and watched it crackle and pop in that big brass container," Madeline laughed.

"Those were good times," Ada smiled.

"I have learned well from you ladies," Pearl said.

"If it weren't for married men, we couldn't have carried on at all, and if it weren't for cheating married women, we could have made another million," Minna said and everyone laughed.

"Such an interesting business," Victoria said. "We all did well, and you were so good about keeping us sheltered from the rough element forever present on the Levee."

"Big Jim Colosimo. I still believe he was part of the reason they shut us down. He always wanted our clientele," Minna said. "After he married Victoria Moresco the two of them opened over 200 brothels," Ada said. "He ran a dirty business."

Minna puffed up. "He was a horrible man. His men would kidnap a girl, rape her for three days and then, after she was ruined, sell her for $50. Most of those poor women died young from drugs or a beating. Sometimes they would just fade away. I don't know what was worse…that or the parents who sold their daughters. That was something we never allowed."

"One of my girls was sold by her mother to a Madame in New Orleans when she was 16. A beautiful girl… her name is Ginger," Victoria shared.

Ada was the more reserved. "We never tolerated drugs, pimps or any of that. Our girls came to us of their own free will. We ran a respectable business with an unrespectable reputation."

"No one was admitted without a formal introduction, an engraved card or a letter of referral," Madeline quoted.

"So what happened?" Victoria asked.

Ada became indignant. "Honestly, I believe we were shut down because we were making so much money. Mayor Harris said it was because someone gave him one of our brochures. However, if immorality and disease prevention were the real reasons they made us close our doors, we would have been the last place on the Levee they would want to shut down. Jim Colosimo's brothels were not bothered at all."

"Ada and I moved to the north side of town. We paid a fortune to Hinky Dink Kenna and Bathhouse John Coughlin. Hinky Dink wanted $40,000 just before we closed our doors. Crooked politicians to be sure."

"That was $40,000 we didn't have to pay. Minna and I testified to the fact we paid the aldermen for protection. We were told if we had any intention of making our testimony public, Big Jim would make sure we were dead first."

"How frightening," Victoria gasped.

"We decided at that point it was best to leave Chicago. After a much deserved European vacation we decided to settle in New York. We changed our last name to Lester and started a poetry circle, although I wish we could have remained Everleigh. It was just too risky," Minna sighed.

"We couldn't compete with the Mafia. Big Jim recruited a gangster from New York, John Torrio, to be his right-hand man. He was known as The Fox. A few months before we were forced to shut down our business, they opened a brothel on South Wabash and called it the Four Deuces. Torrio recruited his man in New York to be his bouncer. His name is Al Capone."

"I think I am beginning to see the big picture," Victoria said, nodding her head.

"Coincidence? I don't think so," Madeline said.

"We heard Big Jim did not want to participate in bootlegging so they got rid of him and took over his whole operation. Someone shot him twice behind the ear in his office. No one was arrested but they are pretty sure Al Capone did the deed," Ada grimaced. "We really did pick a good time to leave Chicago. On a better note, Broadway is simply thrilling. We so love the theatre. As you know, Minna and I had joined a theatre group when we left our husbands. They were such brutes. We ended up in Omaha, Nebraska during the big Expo in 1898."

"The women snubbed us."

"That's because you were so adorable, my dear Minna."

"The men did seem to love our southern accents."

Ada smiled at her sister. "And our southern charm."

"That's when we came up with the idea of a high-class parlor. We knew the husbands would like us," Minna declared.

"You must see the Ziegfeld Follies while you are here, Victoria. We also want you to meet a fascinating woman who we have come to know. We have invited her to Harmony's recital. Her name is Mae West and we absolutely adore her. The woman is brilliant on stage and really knows how to connect with her audience," Ada bragged. "She has written a play she calls SEX."

"Sex?" Victoria exclaimed.

"That is brilliant!" Madeline commented.

"We all know sex sells," Ada sang in a dainty fashion as she took a sip of tea. "We are investing in the production."

"It sounds intriguing," Victoria commented.

All four women smiled, and then simultaneously sipped their tea, each with their own thoughts of days gone by.

"We were so sorry to hear about Robert, Victoria," Ada consoled, "I know how you loved him."

"I am the one who introduced you to him," Minna bragged. "He had his eye on you from the moment he walked into the Everleigh Club. The two of you were like a fairytale romance. The way you looked at each other; I shall never forget it. The Rose Room was always yours when he was in town."

"We had 15 glorious years together on the ranch. Here is a photograph of our twin boys. This is Michael and this is David," Victoria said, pointing to her handsome sons.

"My goodness, they look so much like their father," Minna said. "Look Ada."

"David has your smile, Victoria. They are handsome lads indeed."

"Our sons attend the University in Austin. Robert would be so proud," Victoria sighed. "Mozella has been a godsend. I do not know what would have happened if she had not rescued me from my grief."

"Mozella is a fine woman," Ada remarked. "We would love to see her again."

"We are partners at Pearl's Parlor. Mozella is my best friend."

"Madeline says Miss Pearl's Parlor is a first class operation," Minna complimented.

"I learned from the best," Victoria smiled.

For the next two hours, Harmony's music created a lovely ambience as Madeline, Victoria, Minna and Ada spent their time reminiscing.

"Remember Uncle Ned?" Madeline suggested.

"He is one of my favorite memories!" Minna declared.

"He paid us very well to fill that large bucket full of ice to put his feet in it and watch you girls sing Jingle Bells while he played the tambourine," Ada reminisced.

"It made him so happy. 'Let us go on an old-fashioned sleigh ride,'" Victoria imitated and everyone laughed.

"I remember the beautiful party you gave for the King of Prussia. Someone spilled champagne in Gloria's shoe and one of his men gallantly drank the champagne from it."

"A beautiful woman must not get her dainty foot wet," Madeline imitated in a Prussian accent.

"After that, drinking champagne from a girl's shoe became an Everleigh tradition," Minna smiled.

"My girls love the story of Suzy Poontang!" Victoria said. "Such a clever girl."

"She got a rich husband and we lost a very good client," Minna said. "After all that trouble I went through to get her, she only lasted one night."

"Maddie and I saw her rose tattoo. She was showing it off to some of us before her soon-to-be husband arrived that evening to experience her talents," Victoria shared. "I have never seen anything like it before."

"She called it her 'Gateway to Ecstasy,'" Maddie laughed, and everyone joined her.

"Minna, what really happened with Marshall Field, Jr.?" Victoria asked.

"That was a most unfortunate accident. When we saw he was shot, we wanted to get him help. He told us it was only a flesh wound. He obviously did not want to reveal his location and insisted we not call the doctor. He just wanted to go home. We took him out the back way. Now, in retrospect, I wished I had called the doctor. His wound was more severe than any of us thought. Fortunately, having friends in the press worked to our advantage. The newspapers reported he was shot in his home while cleaning his gun."

It was a memorable visit. Minna and Ada told butterfly stories, Maddie talked about former clients and Victoria shared her experiences at

Miss Pearl's Parlor. With appreciation and respect, the four women understood each other, like Veterans who had survived the Great War.

Finally, at 6 PM Ada looked at the clock and announced, "It is time for champagne, ladies. Our reservations for the Plaza are at 7:30 this evening."

Although Ada and Minna attempted to keep a low profile in New York, whenever they enter a room, heads would turn. Each person would have one question on his mind, "Who are they?" In Chicago, they had treated their servants like family and, always friendly and gracious, the sisters made it a point to be respectful to the staff of any establishment they frequented. Ada always said, "You must give respect, if you expect to receive respect. Everyone is equal in God's eyes."

"How is my boy?" Minna greeted the maître d'.

This had been Minna's standard greeting to every client at the Everleigh Club. Remembering how she would welcome Robert with the same tonal expression, Victoria's heart fluttered.

"Miss Minna and Miss Ada, we have your favorite table ready. Right this way, ladies."

The women followed their guide like ladies of royalty, with heads held high. Minna's always warm smile and Ada's look of approval seemed to satisfy the staff, making their jobs more enjoyable.

"We have taken the liberty to order in advance," Ada announced. "We will begin with mushroom caps stuffed with crab and Parmesan cheese followed by cream of celery soup with toasties. Our main course is breast of chicken a la rose. The vegetables will be served with a superb hollandaise sauce and the Waldorf salad is especially delightful."

"Have you ever heard of the book This Side of Paradise?" Minna asked.

"Actually, I have," Harmony answered. "Miss Pearl checked it out of the library for us to read."

"The author is sitting with his wife Zelda at that table over there. His name is Francis Scott Key Fitzgerald."

"He was named after the writer of the Star Spangled Banner?" Harmony asked.

"Exactly. His pen name is F. Scott Fitzgerald. He has a new book coming out next month called The Great Gatsby. I believe there is talk about making a movie about it," Ada said.

"We attended a private reading. The story appeared to be very similar to his courtship of Zelda. He met her at a country club dance and instantly fell in love. Apparently she was a premiere belle of the south and her family encouraged her not to respond to his affections; he just did not measure up to their standards. When This Side of Paradise was published, Zelda finally agreed to marry him. Not only is she the object of his affection, she is his inspiration as well. When he writes he glorifies Zelda as the first American Flapper," Minna informed.

"I have read some of his short stories in The Saturday Evening Post," Harmony said.

"I believe he is one of the most influential journalists responsible for creating the popularity and carefree lifestyle of the spirited flapper," Madeline said.

"It is amazing to me how magazines and movies have so much influence over our American culture," Victoria commented. "Young girls everywhere want to act and look like Clara Bow."

"Women from all walks of life are certainly becoming more independent and rebellious," Ada remarked. "We live in a much different world now than the days of the Everleigh Club. Nowadays prim and proper is out and sassy and sexy is in."

In so many ways, it felt as if no time had passed. With the success of Pearl's Parlor, Victoria had a great appreciation for Minna and Ada. Being with them again reminded her of just how much she had learned from these remarkable women.

"Miss Pearl talks about you all the time," Harmony complimented, as a tray of puffy cream pastries and chocolates was served. "I am extremely grateful to you for arranging the recital."

"The women in our poetry circle have helped us with the invitations. It is our intention that you be seen by influential people who can assist you in furthering your career," Ada assured her.

"You are where you need to be, Harmony," Pearl assured her. "New York will appreciate your talent, especially the lovely compositions you have created."

"My format is a little different than most recitals. I like to talk about the composers, maybe because I am one."

"I like that," Minna said. "We enjoyed listening to you play this afternoon. Your music is enchanting."

"Thank you."

Just then the waiter appeared. "A gentleman who wishes to remain anonymous has taken care of your check. He told me to give you this note."

Minna opened it and smiled.

The note read:

*A small token of appreciation to*
*two of my favorite ladies.*
*Being "Everleighed" was one of the*
*greatest highlights of my life.*

"It is nice to be remembered," she said, handing the note to her sister.

"A real gentleman," Ada commented. "Please tell Mister Jeffer… I mean, the gentleman, Thank You."

Ada had spotted their former Everleigh client earlier and had avoided any eye contact. There was very little Ada ever missed.

Throughout their dinner, Victoria was especially aware of a couple sitting two tables away. "Something about her seems familiar," Victoria thought. "Her diamond necklace and bracelet are exquisite and her dress looks as if it were custom made. Obviously she was a strikingly beautiful woman in her youth. I wonder how long it has been since she smiled. They have hardly spoken a word. In fact, they seem to be completely ignoring each other. How sad for them."

Sometimes coincidence can be a strange phenomenon. As it turned out, Mister Jefferson decided to approach the table and say hello to Ada and Minna. In order to provide them some private conversation, Victoria and Harmony excused themselves to visit the ladies powder room.

While Victoria was sitting at the vanity, the woman whom she had noticed earlier at the table walked in and sat next to her.

"Oh my, I do need to change this color lipstick to a brighter, deeper red," she said with a southern accent.

"You sound like you could be from Texas," Victoria commented, still curious about the woman she judged to be just about her age.

"Houston," the woman said.

"I live in San Angelo. My name is Victoria Pearl and this is Harmony. She grew up close to Austin."

"So nice to see someone from Texas. My name is Alice. I left Houston years ago to be with that son-of-a-bitch husband of mine. It seems he has this thing about chorus girls. Sometimes he is gone for weeks at a time. Too expensive to divorce me, so I just spend his money."

"We have friends from Houston," Harmony innocently chirped with her adorable Texas accent. "Lucy Armstrong and Linda Donovan. We call Linda, Redbird."

Alice turned white as a ghost. "Oh my. Oh, my, my, my. Linda Donovan is my daughter," she quivered.

Victoria felt a flush of heat rush over her.

"So this is Linda's mother, the woman who left her children and devoted husband with nothing but a cold, heartless note. That must be the man she left her family for. She looks so unhappy."

Trying to maintain composure, she didn't know what to say or do.

"How is Linda?"

Graciously smiling and speaking in a lady-like tone, Victoria fired away and didn't hold back. "She is well now. After you left them she and her brothers had a rough go of it. When her father died from grieving for you, his brother and your sister-in-law moved into that big, beautiful house you used to call home. One night Linda's cousin brought a business associate home. Later that evening, he had sneaked into her room and raped her. Gertrude accused her of being a whore and Linda was kicked out of the house. Your sons were sent to boarding school."

Alice showed no emotion at all. All she did was stare.

"Just last fall, Gertrude chocked to death on a chicken bone and Linda is happy to be back in Houston with her little brothers. I will not tell her we saw you. It would be too disturbing for her."

Alice did not respond. Arrogantly she lifted her chin, reached into her bag, turned to the mirror and began re-applying her lipstick.

"Linda is a beautiful woman. I can see the resemblance in you. We all make mistakes, Alice. Try to forgive yourself."

Linda's mother did not respond.

"Linda has forgiven you. It was the only way she could release the hurt. Come along now, Harmony. We must get back to our friends."

When the door shut, Alice found herself alone again, engulfed in the dark silence of her mind. Pulling a flask from her bag, she swallowed two pills and took a long, hard drink.

Whatever it took… to make her not feel the agony of her pain.

# CHAPTER 25

# A Recital

The first day of Heather's scenic train ride from California to New York was spent staring out the window, contemplating thoughts of Giorgio, Hollywood, her life on the farm, Chicago, Tony the gangster who wanted her dead and Miss Pearl's Parlor. She had bought and laid on the seat next to her a book full of humorous short stories, quotes and poems by Dorothy Parker. She picked up the book and found herself laughing out loud, enjoying the clever wittiness of the author.

*"I require three things in a man: he must be handsome, ruthless and stupid."*

*"It serves me right for putting all my eggs in one bastard."*

*"I don't know much about being a millionaire, but I bet I would be darling at it."*

*"By the time you swear you're his*
*Shivering and sighing*
*And he vows his passion is*
*Infinite, undying -*
*Lady, make a note of this;*
*One of you is lying"*
*~ Dorothy Parker*

On the third day, Heather felt inspired to write. "Why not?" she thought. "Between Chicago, the girls at Miss Pearl's and Hollywood, I have plenty of material. Telling stories is what I do. In fact it is what I have always done."

By the time Heather's train pulled into Grand Central Station, she had written her first short story. She called it, New Orleans Lady, about a young girl whose mother sells her to a brothel on Basin Street and how she rises like a Phoenix from the ashes to overcome her sordid past.

"There she is!" Rosey screamed. "Heather! Ovah here!"

Hearing her name, Heather looked up to see a woman wearing a bright red cloche hat running towards her, wildly waving her hands in the air. It was Aunt Rosey from Joysey, one of the Santa Rita investors who had come with Madeline to visit San Angelo the year before.

"Rosey!" Heather waved. Looking to the woman standing next to her, Heather's heart soared with joy. "Miss Pearl…MISS PEARL!"

Unaware of the strong emotions she would feel, Victoria was surprised at the warmth of her tears that suddenly clouded her vision. In just a few months, Heather had transformed into a beautiful, confidant, strong woman.

In a tearful reunion the two women hugged: Heather with great appreciation and Victoria with a sense of motherly pride. Although no words were exchanged, so much was said.

"Where is Harmony?" Heather asked.

"Harmony is at the recital hall practicing for her Saturday matinee," Pearl answered.

"It is good to see you again, my dear," Madeline said, kissing both of Heather's cheeks.

"How is your sister, Elizabeth? I am so looking forward to speaking with her."

"Elizabeth is anxious to see you as well. She is at the house making preparations for lunch. We have you in a guest room with Harmony. It has been so nice having her with us."

"Oh my goodness, Heather, I saw your movie," Rosey exclaimed with her strong Jersey accent. "You were absolutely fabulous, darling! I tell everybody I know a real movie star from Hollywood."

"You liked it?"

"Liked it? I loved it! Especially after seeing Fort Concho and meeting real live cowboys. Were all those scenes really filmed on the Concho River?"

"Some of them were. The shots of Fort Concho were all filmed in San Angelo. The rest were done on movie sets made to look like the inside of the officer quarters."

"Well they sure did a good job. I really thought I was in West Texas again."

Elizabeth's home was in Chelsea, a section of Manhattan located not too far from where Minna and Ada lived. Chelsea, known for its art galleries and creative spirit, was quiet and clean. Several silent movies, including those by stars such as Mary Pickford, were made in Chelsea before most of the industry moved to Hollywood. Elizabeth had chosen the neighborhood because in many ways it reminded her of England.

Walking into the entry hall, the women could hear the festive sound of Chopin's Valse Op.64 ringing throughout Elizabeth's house.

Stopping in the middle of her piece, Harmony's bright eyes twinkled with delight at the sight of Heather's smile.

"Hey…where's your feather, Heather with her feather?" Harmony laughed.

"Look at you… how pretty you are! You let your hair grow out. I love it; looks like shiny, spun gold," Heather exclaimed, stroking her friend's long blonde hair.

"Long hair is different nowadays and you know I like to be different. Hey, did you hear that Tex died and left his ranch and all his money to Maggie?"

"Yes I did. Dusty and Jesse told me they had had enough of Hollywood and were going back to Texas to run the ranch."

"I think Dusty and Maggie could be the next wedding," Victoria said as she entered the room. "You should see them together now."

"I am not surprised. Sparks were flying everywhere when they were together in California."

Everyone in the house awoke on the morning of the recital to the sweet sound of Claude Debussy's Arabesque.

"Oh dear. Did I wake you?" Harmony asked. "I tried to wait as long as I could. I have been playing with the soft pedal down…it only plays two strings per note instead of three and I…"

Victoria smiled. "I do miss waking up to your lovely music, Harmony. You are a joy. Come here, I want to show you something."

Victoria held a large white box in her arms. "Open it."

"Oh, Miss Pearl. I do not believe I have ever seen a dress so beautiful. Are these real pearls? And the fabric…Is this chiffon?"

"This is the dress I was wearing the first night I met Robert. Minna and Ada bought each of us a gown for opening night. As you can see they spared no expense."

"But Miss Pearl… I…"

"I wore this dress the night my life was forever changed. Today you will begin a brand new chapter of your life. Think of the dress as a butterfly coming out of its cocoon. It is meant to be seen…just as you are meant to be heard. Today you will emerge as a musical butterfly. I want you to have it."

"I do not know what to say…" Harmony gasped, picking up the dress with her delicate hands.

"I believe, Thank you would work," Heather smiled as she entered the room. "I know this dress is special to you, Miss Pearl. The dress is lovely. I can see why Robert fell in love with you. Harmony will be gorgeous."

Harmony could hardly speak. "Thank you, Miss Pearl. My mother died when I was a baby…and…"

Harmony fell into Pearl's tender embrace.

"And you are like a daughter to me, Harmony. I am very proud of you. Today your music will touch their souls."

That afternoon at Steinway Hall, Minna and Ada were gracious as ever as they greeted their guests in the main lobby. Memories of the Everleigh Club flooded Pearl's mind as she watched the sisters smile, charm and welcome each one as if they were the most important person in the room.

There were wealthy people, theatre people and old friends from Chicago. Aware of the importance of being friendly with the press, Minna and Ada had invited members of the famous Algonquin Round Table, including Harold Ross who had released the first issue of his new magazine The New Yorker only a few weeks before.

"Victoria Pearl, may I present to you one of our favorite entertainers, Mae West. She is quite talented. I believe we mentioned that we are looking into investing in her new play," Minna smiled.

"How do you do," Victoria graced.

"Pleased to know you. Any friend of these ladies is a friend of mine," she winked.

"We are bringing Victoria to your show next week."

"Very good," Mae commented. "Come early and we'll open a bottle of champagne in my dressing room."

A middle-aged gentleman with a neatly trimmed beard approached the women with a bow, kissing each of their hands.

"How's my boy?" Minna greeted.

"Very well," he replied. "Is this Victoria Pearl?"

"Victoria Pearl, you remember Mister Christopher Baker?"

"Of course I do. Do you still play golf?"

"As a matter of fact I do," he smiled with appreciation.

"Thank you for coming, Mister Baker," Pearl graced. Of course she remembered him. Minna introduced Christopher to her the evening after she had spent those first magical days with Robert. He had been her first real client at the Everleigh Club."

Madeline handed Victoria a drink. "Hello, Christopher," she smiled. She had also spent time with Christopher Baker.

"Two of my favorite butterflies," he breathed with a beaming boyish grin. "Still beautiful as ever."

"I guess you did not expect that," Madeline chuckled at Victoria as he walked away.

"Minna told me there might be a familiar face or two," Victoria admitted. "Actually, it was kind of nice to be remembered and appreciated."

"Oh good, she came," Minna said as two attractive women entered the lobby. "Look at her, Victoria. Is she not exquisite? Her name is Louise Brooks. She dances in the Louis the 14th Ziegfeld Follies. I personally invited her to meet Heather and Harmony. As it turns out, her mother is an accomplished pianist and she was happy to get the invitation."

Louise waved and approached the welcoming party.

"Louise, so good of you to come. Victoria, may I present to you Miss Louise Brooks."

"Thank you for inviting us," Louise exclaimed. "I really am looking forward to hearing Harmony play. This is my friend Barbara Bennett."

"Ah, yes, Richard's daughter. Welcome, my dear. Louise dances as gracefully as a butterfly on the stage, Victoria," Minna grinned. "Ziegfeld stole her away from the George White Scandals. We saw her dance there as well."

"Butterfly?" Victoria thought, picking up Minna's reference to the exquisite Everleigh butterflies.

"Louise, we would like to invite you and Barbara to a private reception after the recital," Minna graced.

"Sounds good to me," Louise accepted.

"Louise is dancing in the Follies tonight," Barbara said.

"I really do want to meet Harmony," Louise insisted. "I have never met a woman composer before."

The invitation to Harmony's recital said 3 PM. Like the maid-of-honor taking care of the bride's last minute emotional and physical needs, Heather had been sitting with Harmony in the green room.

For several minutes Heather slowly brushed Harmony's long golden hair to relax her.

"It might sound strange, Heather, but I am not at all nervous about this recital. I have prepared for this day my whole life. Miss Pearl was right. I feel like a butterfly breaking free from its cocoon."

"Did I hear my name?" Pearl asked entering the room.

"Oh, Miss Pearl. Thank you for the dress. I feel like a muse on Mount Olympus."

"I brought you this for good luck."

"A diamond solitaire? It is exquisite. You have already done so much…"

"Turn around. Let me put it on you. Twinkle, twinkle little star…" Victoria recited, winking at Heather.

"Like a diamond in the sky…" Heather responded.

"I am going with Miss Pearl. I love you, Harmony," Heather said.

Alone with her thoughts, Harmony went back to all the events that led her to this moment. She thought about her playing the upper keys when she was just a toddler while her grandmother played Bach's Prelude in C. She remembered the mean girls at the Country Club snubbing her and telling her she was "just the help." The memory of David rescuing her from the humiliation made her smile. Her heart felt a stab of pain remembering that horrible moment she learned he was killed in The Great War. Immersed in her emotions, Harmony was ready.

Hearing her name called, Harmony graciously appeared before her audience and bowed. The only people she saw were the women she loved, sitting in the first row.

Sitting at the piano and looking at the keys, Harmony heard the loving voice of her grandmother say, "Play with your soul and their souls will hear it. If you can make them feel, you have accomplished your goal."

With each composer she played, Harmony spoke a little bit about their lives and pointed out characteristics that she appreciated in their music. Then she began to explain the pieces she had written.

"The first composition I will play for you I wrote the evening we buried my sweetheart David, who bravely gave his life for his country in the Great War. I call it *The Yellow Rose*."

As Harmony played with soft tenderness, soft sniffles could be heard from the audience and handkerchiefs were produced from pockets and ladies handbags. When she had finished, Harmony gently laid her hands in her lap and paused. No one made a sound.

"When I was a baby, our house caught on fire. My father brought me out and perished trying to save my mother. My grandmother raised me, and somehow, by God's good grace, I met this wonderful woman I like to call *Mother Pearl*. I wrote this piece for you," Harmony smiled, looking at Victoria.

The composition was simple, short and lovely. The love among the women sitting in the front row spread throughout the audience in Steinway Hall.

"Now, I am going to share something special. I have a friend in the audience who just finished filming her second movie in Hollywood. Unfortunately, because movies are silent, only those who see her in person can enjoy the fact that she sings like a bird. Heather, will you please join me?"

Surprised and honored, Heather made her way to the stage. Like hundreds of times before, Harmony played the familiar introduction and smiled at her friend.

"*Nights are long since you went away, I think about you all through the day, my buddy, my buddy, nobody quite so true…*"

Blinking back the tears, Harmony realized how real the song had become for the two friends. Heather, feeling the same emotions, stayed strong until the end.

"*Miss your voice the touch of your hand, just long to know that you understand, my buddy, my buddy, your buddy misses you.*"

The celebrated applause was deafening. They were cheering for the talent, the friendship but most of all, for the love genuinely displayed by the two women on stage.

"In closing I want to honor one of the greatest composers and songwriters I have ever had the privilege to perform. We lost him only a few months ago, but his music will endure forever. I will pay homage to Giacomo Puccini with a medley of his work. I will begin with the very beautiful Muzetta's Waltz followed by my version of Mio Babino Caro and finally Madama Butterfly that I will dedicate to Minna and Ada Lester, the two very gracious women who made today's recital possible. Thank you all for coming."

Any person whose soul does not respond to Puccini's music does not have one. Chills, thrills, goose bumps, and tears, the audience was moved to great heights. Each one of them had been touched by the beautiful music and presentation given by Harmony that afternoon.

A much-deserved standing ovation was delivered as the audience welcomed New York's newest concert pianist to their fine city. Harmony was a sensation and the buzz of the new composer/musician in town had just begun.

As promised, Louise Brooks and Barbara Bennett attended the reception. Minna graciously introduced the girls.

"Harmony, your recital was absolutely divine," Louise said excitedly. "Your compositions are exquisite, so melodic. I could listen to you for hours."

"Thank you, Louise," Harmony smiled.

"Maybe Barbara and I can show you around town sometime," Louise said. "You must come too, Heather. Now if you'll excuse me, I need to get to the theatre."

"*Beautiful girl,*" Pearl thought. "*Something about her is very sad. I wonder what her story is*?"

CHAPTER 26

# Louise Brooks

Louise burst into the house in tears.

"Mother!" she sobbed.

Annoyed at the interruption, Myra Brooks looked up from her piano to see her nine-year-old daughter hysterically crying. "Whatever is the matter dear? "Did you skin your knee?"

"He hurt me, Mother. I am bleeding," Louise screamed.

"Who hurt you, Louise?"

"Mister Flowers invited me into his house and…"

"Mister Flowers? The man who painted our house? Such a nice man… He leaves popcorn and candy on his porch for all of you children."

"He made me take off my clothes, Mother."

Myra Brooks didn't say a word.

"He touched me on my private parts. Then he made me lie down and told me he was going to give me a present that I would like a lot. He hurt me, Mother! He hurt me and told me not to scream!"

Unwilling to acknowledge her daughter's pain, Myra continued studying the notes on her sheet music without blinking an eye. After a long minute she finally spoke. "This is your fault, Louise. What did you do to make him do this to you?"

"What do you mean??"

"You must have done something to make him do this to you."

"I just wanted some candy. He told me I could come in and pick what I wanted."

Little Louise was sobbing uncontrollably.

"Go take a bath."

"He told me I was his favorite."

"You should have brought your brother and shared the candy. You wanted it all to yourself."

"Mother! It hurts! He hurt me!" Louise bellowed.

"Do as I told you, Louise, and go take a bath. For heaven sakes child, I am trying to memorize Bach."

Frustrated and sore, Louise let out a scream that could wake the dead and began sobbing so hard she lost her breath. Deaf to her daughter's cry for comfort, Louise's mother continued practicing the piano as if she were the only one in the room.

Gradually, Louise's sobs became whimpers and finally, there was only the sound of Bach's Prelude in C.

After completing her piece, Myra paused. "You will not speak of this with anyone, Louise. Remember the time you broke my Havoline china cup?"

"Yes."

"We threw it away. That is what will happen to you if people find out what you did with Mister Flowers. They will throw you away like the garbage. You should be ashamed of yourself. You are worthless now."

"I don't understand."

"You are broken, Louise… damaged goods. You are no longer a virgin. If people find out about this, no man will ever want to marry you. This is why you must keep what happened with Mister Flowers a secret."

"What is a virgin, Mother?"

"I have no time for this, Louise. Go take your bath."

Louise sat in the bathtub for over an hour. Her mother was right. No matter how hard she scrubbed, she still felt dirty.

What did she do wrong?

She liked it when Mister Flowers told her she was pretty and told her she was his favorite and gave her candy.

Mister Flowers hurt her. That is what men do when they think you are pretty. They give you candy then they hurt you and somehow, it was all her fault.

Growing up in Cherryvale, Kansas, Louise Brooks dreamed of being a great dancer. At the age of ten she began studying dance and performed in local theatres and festivals. Although there were times her parents seemed supportive, their parenting skills left much to be desired.

Too busy to discipline his children, her father was an attorney whose collection of books was so large, it literally caused the house's foundation to sink under the library. Myra, Louise's mother, was an accomplished pianist who inspired her children to love music and books. Lost in her private world of music, she spent most of her time studying the classics and learning the latest Debussy and Ravel. Often she would perform for her children. This was the only real attention Myra gave to them. She had determined from the beginning of motherhood that any "squalling brats she produced could take care of themselves."

Louise was a pretty little girl, with soulful dark eyes and short black hair, cut in a pageboy that would later become her trademark. The life changing experience with Mister Flowers would have a major influence on her attitude with men the rest of her life. He was not the only predator in Louise's childhood. Her Sunday school teacher, Mister Vincent, whom Louise adored, also sexually took advantage of the young girl's desperate need for attention. Growing into her teens, she found a new sense of power when she learned that boys liked her and wanted to shower her with kisses. Like a bee going from flower to flower, Louise filled her diary with a different boyfriend every week, having fun and breaking hearts along the way.

Sadly, Louise never saw herself the way the rest of the admiring world sees her. Although extremely talented and lovely, Louise secretly always thought of herself as the broken china cup. Because of her extraordinary beauty, life took her on a journey that most girls only dream about.

Recognized for her remarkable dancing talent, Louise was accepted to the Denishawn School of Dance in New York City at 15 and was chosen to go on tour. The prestigious dance company was well respected and in effect, founded American modern dance. Because of their reputation they attracted such celebrity guest-pupils as Lillian Gish and Myrna Loy.

Joan and Barbara Bennett, daughters of the famous actor-director Richard Bennett, also attended the school. Their mother Adrienne was a celebrated actress and their older sister Constance was a young film actress on the rise. Barbara, the middle daughter, was a free spirited flapper. Richard Bennett sent her to the Denishawn School, hoping she would be guided towards some type of career or at least to obtain some hint of discipline.

Louise and Barbara Bennett shared a cabin at the Denishawn summer dance camp known as Mariarden. "Hello, pie-face," was the first thing Barbara said to Louise after watching Louise devour three pieces of apple pie. Barbara Bennett, a cultivated young woman and the fiery, spirited Louise Brooks became best friends. Although Louise admired her new friend's sophisticated elegance, she made it her mission to inject some excitement into Barbara's otherwise boring life.

Louise did not have many friends but she adored Barbara. One night, ignoring the 9 o'clock curfew, Louise invited some of the Peterborough boys to their cabin. They brought cigarettes and applejack and in return, much to Louise's delighted surprise, Barbara entertained them with funny limericks and dirty songs.

*There was a young man from Kent*
*Whose prick was so long it bent*
*To save himself trouble*
*He put it in double*
*And instead of coming he went*

Louise worked very hard developing her art. For two years, she lived out of a suitcase, travelling from city to city, performing with the Denishawn Dancers.

An exceptional dancer, Louise communicated deep passion from the stage. For this reason, she was given specialty dance numbers. Her advancement excelled when she was chosen to play the little Hopi Indian girl in Feather of the Dawn. In 1923, at the Apollo Theatre in Atlantic City, Louise danced in the world premieres of Denishawn's newest ethnic dances, Ishtar, The Spirit of the Sea, Cuadro Flameco and Feather of the Dawn.

Playful and flirty, and because of her extraordinary beauty and talent, most men found Louise enchanting and many women hated her. Drawn to male attention, she learned to see jealousy as a compliment. While on the road, some of the girls gossiped about her questionable encounters with men. This was threatening to Louise because, in order to maintain a respectable image, the dance company had a strict moral code.

Serving as co-director of the Denishawn dance company, Miss Ruth St. Denis demanded high standards and ran a tight ship. Although Louise had great respect for Miss Ruth's unique talent as a costumer and stage-director, she did not care for her as a dancer or a person. In return, even though Miss Ruth saw Louise as a great value to the show, she did not approve of her attitude.

Confident of her talent and rebellious in nature, Louise did not find the need to sit at Miss Ruth's feet and adore her like the other girls. By the end of the 1923-1924 tour, Louise was convinced that Miss Ruth hated her. Because of this, Louise became silent, wicked looking and declared to herself to do no "ass kissing." When the Denishawn dancers returned to New York, a general feeling was growing throughout the dance company that because of her attitude, Louise was daring not only Miss Ruth but also the entire world to cross her.

St. Denis and her husband and co-director of the company Ted Shawn were hard-nosed professionals and knew the importance of maintaining a clean reputation. If they thought one of their dancers was negatively affecting the company's morale, the offender had to go, with or without just cause. Finally one day, it all came to a head.

Miss Ruth had called an assembly to discuss the following year's tour. Louise sneaked in late with Barbara who was not a member of the company. The two girls stumbled in the dark and when Barbara fell into a seat, she let out her loudest, froggiest, Bennett laugh. Disturbed by even the most polite interruptions, Miss Ruth stopped her speech and began stroking her long, green jade necklace.

"Is that you, Louise?"

"Yes, Miss Ruth," Louise whispered.

"Well, Louise, to be brief and to the point, not to keep you from your more pressing concerns, I am dismissing you from the company because you want life handed to you on a silver salver," she said with icy contempt.

Louise was shocked, embarrassed and humiliated.

Victim to a public display of mortification, Louise felt as if someone had stabbed her in the heart. She was not the only one who was shocked. Although she was not aware of it, Louise was the most beautiful and talented of the dancers and everyone knew it. Terminating Louise in such a fashion made her an example and sent a strong clear message, instilling fear throughout the company; no one was exempt from dismissal.

Isn't it ironic that the Denishawn dancers, who saw themselves as an elite group and better than anyone else, would terminate Louise for believing she was something special. Had all of her hard work and thousands of hours of endless rehearsals gone unnoticed? Train rides from city to city, hundreds of performances and the rigors of the Denishawn discipline; none of it seemed to matter. Stunned by Miss Ruth's words,

Louise walked away from Denishawn for the last time. At seventeen, the demoralizing experience would shatter Louise's self-esteem and leave a deep painful wound she would carry with her the rest of her life.

"Barbara, what's a silver salver?"

"It's a silver tray."

Devastated, Louise burst into tears. "I won't go back to Kansas! I won't! I won't!"

"Don't worry Pie Face. I will get you a job in a moment."

It was just what Louise desperately needed to hear.

As fate would have it, Barbara Bennett was true to her word. Within an hour of expulsion, the two friends found themselves outside the Palace Theatre where Barbara caught sight of the young booking agent and producer Rufus LaMaire. Noticing his eyes widen with appreciation of the beautiful, teary eyed Louise Brooks, Barbara quickly introduced them and wasted no time or words.

"Rufus, you must get Louise a job immediately."

A Bennett had spoken.

Rufus took the girls around the corner to where the chorus for the new George White Scandals was being picked. Learning she had danced for Denishawn, George White hired Louise on the spot.

Started in 1919, the younger, faster George White Scandals gradually were becoming successful in competing with the more opulent Ziegfeld Follies. George liked his costumes scantier than the Follies and there was a greater emphasis on the latest dance styles and crazes. Louise was grateful for the job.

And so, in the summer of 1924, Louise Brooks became George White's newest and youngest chorus girl. She was the only one who was a trained dancer and it didn't take long for the chorines to get jealous. Because of her stunning beauty and presence on the stage, the newspapers were singing her praises. Again, Louise saw the resentment as a compliment and at times could even be mean about it.

One afternoon, Louise walked upon a newspaperman she had gone out with holding Francesca, one of the chorus girls in the show, by her waist. Seeing Louise approaching, he quickly dropped his arms to his side and hustled off.

A few days later, while the girls were lined up to go on stage, Louise confronted Francesca.

"Francesca, about that little argument we were having last night. About Kingsley saying in his column that the most beautiful girl in the show was an exotic black orchid. You, Honey, and the other girls were all saying he meant you?"

All the girls waiting in the chorus line scooted behind Francesca to hear what Louise was going to say.

"Well I called him today at the paper and told him another girl had said she was the black orchid. He told me I was the black orchid but didn't know my name when he wrote the article. He asked if he'd like me to write another article using my name. I told him, no thank you. I just wanted to make sure, that was all. I knew you would believe me."

Walking away, Louise heard Francesca burst into tears.

Behind the scenes, Louise had very few friends. Because of her training with Denishawn she saw everyone as inferior and at times did not take her new job seriously. She drove the stage manager crazy with tardiness, sometimes missing the opening chorus altogether. Rehearsals had to be redone for lack of Louise's participation or just making a mess of her part.

Between her appreciation for good literature, music and dancing with Denishawn, Louise had very high standards and found she had little in common with her peers. With the exception of only a few, she saw the majority of the chorus girls as uneducated morons.

For instance, Louise wore her Chinese headdress the way it should be worn, like a gold helmet covering her hair. The other "illiterate slobs" wore their helmets like hats, making it possible to show off their precious curls. None of them were familiar with great authors such as D.H. Lawrence and, as far as music goes, they probably thought Ravel and Debussy were some kind of bicycle act.

Louise carried the same attitude she had with Denishawn to the Scandals. The chorines could never understand why she was never reprimanded. Somehow, because of her beauty and talent Louise got away with being careless with her job.

Although they were completely opposite in many ways, Barbara and Louise were the best of friends. Louise admired Barbara's elegant upbringing and sophistication and welcomed her sisterly advice. Barbara saw Louise as humorous, talented and adventurous.

By mid-1924, Louise had become an unofficial member of the Bennett household at 950 Park Avenue near 82nd Street and was exposed to a whole new world of speaking, dressing and understanding the etiquette of the social elite. Louise felt it was time to get rid of her Kansas accent and talk more like Barbara, "eyther, nyther, rahther, lahst, cahn't..."

Unable to attend finishing school, Louise found people who were experts in such matters to educate her.

There was a drugstore with a soda fountain on Broadway where Louise liked to go. A young Columbia University student, who worked behind the counter, would hand her a hot fudge sundae then make fun of her Kansas accent.

"It is not hep, you hayseed! It's help, help, help!"

"Instead of making fun of me, why don't you teach me how to say it?"

The young man smiled at the opportunity of becoming a Pygmalion. Louise practiced incessantly and within a month of hot fudge sundaes, Louise accomplished her goal.

Barbara Bennett began introducing Louise to a sophisticated group of wealthy bankers and stockbrokers who loved spoiling beautiful women by taking them to expensive restaurants and buying them extravagant gifts. Louise was thrilled when a wealthy gentleman stockbroker bought her an ermine fur coat and another bought her an exquisite diamond bracelet. Although affairs were generated from these arrangements, sex was not necessarily a requirement. The men enjoyed competing with whose date was prettiest, had the fanciest clothes and most flashy jewelry and the girls benefitted from the competition.

"You mean all I have to do is have dinner with them?" Louise asked her friend.

"That's it. Believe me, they would rather spend their money drinking, dining and buying us expensive presents than getting stuck with a snobby debutante some desperate rich family is trying to marry off. Not only that, Pie Face, it's fun!"

Flappers gone wild, Barbara and Louise loved the New York nightlife. The two friends were part of an elite group of beautiful chorus girls and stars having the time of their lives with wealthy gentlemen at restaurants like the Colony and speakeasies like the 21 Club.

Unlike the Ziegfeld Follies that had several musical composers, the George White Scandals employed a musical songwriting team, the most prominent being George Gershwin.

One day, during a rest period from rehearsal, Gershwin wandered in, sat at the rehearsal piano and began playing through the score of the new show. Louise hopped on a work-table next to him, crossed her legs and silently listened. A few months before, Gershwin wowed an audience at Carnegie Hall with his new classical-jazz composition *Rhapsody in Blue*. A magical evening, he created some of it on the spot. Because of her mother, Louise saw herself as a connoisseur of good music.

"You know the only good thing you have written for the show is Somebody Loves Me."

For a moment he just stared at Louise and then they both burst into laughter.

"I am sailing for Paris on Saturday. What should I bring you?"

"Oh, you'll forget."

"No I won't. What do you want from Paris?'

"One of those wobbly dolls in felt pajamas, smoking a cigarette…but you'll forget."

Indeed, George Gershwin did forget to bring Louise the doll. He always felt bad about disappointing her.

Because of her extraordinary beauty and association with Barbara Bennett, Louise was constantly invited to parties. Wealthy men kept extravagant apartments in New York where they would entertain business associates and beautiful girls. One night, Louise and several of the Scandals girls were invited to Otto Kahn's suite at the Ritz Hotel. That evening the British newspaper baron Lord Beaverbrook befriended a lovely girl Louise actually admired. The two disappeared into a bedroom for a long while. A few days later, the young dancer had a movie contract with MGM. The girl went on to be a famous actress.

"Hooray for Lord Beaverbrook!"

When it came to fashion, Louise was still a novice. One day a sales clerk invited her to buy a little pink dress that made her look as if she were only fourteen. Although Louise faithfully paid her bills at the Algonquin, one afternoon, while wearing the dress, Louise experienced a humiliating eviction.

"We are a respectable hotel. You cannot be more than fourteen-years-old and we have seen you with men…"

Within half an hour, she was escorted out of the hotel.

After spending a few days with Barbara, Louise moved to the Martha Washington, a respectable women's hotel on East 29th Street. Two weeks later she was asked again to leave when people in the next building saw her exercising on the rooftop in flimsy pajamas.

"Within a month, my wearing apparel has gotten me kicked out of two hotels," she complained to Barbara.

The next morning after the second eviction, Louise marched into Milgrim's with $500 cash, determined to look like a photo she had seen of Marilyn Miller, the Ziegfeld star. She walked out with a barebacked white gown made of crystal beads, slashed to the naval, and a silver coat with a fox collar. Within a few days she learned that a well-dressed woman could get just about anything she wants.

A week later Louise was presented the final blow. "Mother and Father are sending me to a private school in Europe, Brooksie," Barbara told her. "I will miss you."

It was the last straw.

"No you won't because I am going with you."

That day without any notice, Louise quit the Scandals. Before she left, she insulted a few of her enemies, including the stage manager, for good measure. Then, with a little sweet talk to a clerk in the Manhattan Federal building, she acquired an emergency passport and set sail to London with her best friend Barbara on the Homeric. The voyage was like a wondrous tonic and Louise was miraculously cured from the Manhattan Blues.

It was December of 1924. During the long voyage, Barbara had been toying with a change of plans. After checking into the Edouard VII Hotel in Paris, as she was eating a ham sandwich with German mustard, Barbara decided to cash her letter of credit and go back to New York on the return trip of the Homeric. Louise decided to stay.

Standing in the hotel lobby, Barbara was reluctant to leave her friend. "What are you going to do for money, Brooksie?"

"I'll figure it out," Louise answered, feeling exhilarated with adventure.

"This is enough to hold you for a few days," Barbara said, handing her a small stack of bills.

"I'll be fine, Barbara," Louise said embracing her friend.

Barbara had not been gone from the lobby for more than a few minutes before the producer Archie Selwyn recognized Louise and came to her rescue. After painting a grim picture of what can happen to a 17-year-old Kansas girl in Paris, Archie persuaded Louise to go with him to London. There he was able to get Louise a job at the famous Café de Paris in the West End's Piccadilly Circus. It was there that Louise Brooks became the first American girl to perform the Charleston in London, England.

Again, the magical essence of Louise Brooks wowed the crowds and after a few days, she found herself in a prominent solo spot at "London's creamiest calling card." To play at the Café de Paris with its lush décor and padded satin walls was comparable in vaudeville to headlining at the Palace. Top stars such as Marlene Dietrich and Tallulah Bankhead graced the famous staircase at the Café de Paris and were paid $5600 a week for their performances.

Although she was not a headliner, Louise bewitched the crowds who jammed the club to watch her shimmy across the dance floor and crisscross her knees. Her dark bob was the rage and women throughout London cut their hair to look like the adorable flapper from America. Although her audience adored her, it did not compensate for Barbara's protective presence.

Louise was lonely and wanted to come home.

Living beyond her means, Louise invested her last pound in a pathetic cable, pleading to Otto Kahn to rescue her from London. Kahn cabled Ed Goulding, who happened to be visiting his mother in London, and instructed him to pay her rent and passage on the Homeric to enable Louise to return to America. So on February 14, 1925 Louise left London to return to New York. Louise's Broadway buddies welcomed her home with opened arms.

Florence Ziegfeld had been looking for Louise since her mysterious disappearance from the Scandals six months before. Ever since he heard his spies rave about the talented Miss Louise Brooks dancing in the Scandals, he wanted her in his show. Although he had an endless number of lovely girls, relatively few of them had any real talent. One of her cronies informed him that Louise Brooks was indeed back in town.

Learning Louise had recently returned from abroad, Ziegfeld asked her to his office.

"I have an opening for a chorus girl."

"I am not a chorus girl. I am a dancer."

"So much the better, Louise. Welcome to the Ziegfeld Follies."

Ziegfeld instantly gave Louise a specialty dance in his new three-hour musical, Louie the 14th. Before presenting the new show on Broadway he decided to give it a trial run in Washington D.C. to see how it would be received. The first performance of Louie the 14th was a huge success and received rave reviews.

In the latest offering from the Ziegfeld laboratories, Louie the 14th, which was presented in the National Theatre last evening, there is a transcendentalism - an exaltation - of beauty over baseness - that far surpasses ever before produced by either Ziegfeld or his rivals of recent years.~ John J. Daly - The Washington Post

Returning to New York, Ziegfeld's publicity agents had done their job well and by the time Louie the 14th opened, both the critics and the public were primed for the new musical showing at the Cosmopolitan Theatre.

On opening night, March 3, 1925, hundreds of stargazers endured the bitter cold to view the crème de la crème of New York City grace the red carpet. They were not disappointed. Arriving in the fanciest of limousines were: Mrs. Randolph Hearst, Mrs. W.K. Vanderbilt, R.S. Rothschild, Paramount's Adolph Zukor and Jesse Lasky, Ruth Chatterton, the queen of the stage and Bea Lillie, New York's comedy's toast of the town.

A triumph in stagecraft. An abundant and gorgeously staged musical show. The results certainly met the expectations of all, and exceeded those of most. ~ The New York

## CHAPTER 27

# The Algonquin

"A pretty girl is like a melody that haunts you night and day." These words, written by the great songwriter Irving Berlin, were first sung in the 1919 Ziegfeld Follies. The song went on to be the theme song of the Follies, Broadway's spectacular productions, famous for Glorifying the American Girl.

In all of Broadway and across America, in 1925, the Ziegfeld Follies was the top show in the business. If you were a privileged performer, you were considered to have reached the pinnacle of theatrical success. The showgirls averaged $275 a week and were dripping in diamonds and furs – not just from their salaries, but from the wealthy men who adored them.

Thousands of young women from all over America came to New York with the dream of becoming a Ziegfeld Girl. When asked, Florence Ziegfeld could never really describe the unique quality he looked for when selecting the long-legged beauties, draped in chiffon and pearls, to walk so elegantly across his stage or down a staircase.

The women Ziegfeld selected for his show were based on pure instinct. "A Ziegfeld girl must deliver the promise of romance and excitement." It was the way they walked across the stage and the convincing smile that said, "I can make all of your dreams come true."

Right leg out, left shoulder in, left leg out, right shoulder in came to be known as, "the walk," but more than that, it was the way a girl suggestively moved her hips. Sometimes, even a plain Jane could be transformed into a Ziegfeld beauty. As long as she glided across the floor and smiled, she communicated a believable invitation of sexual fantasy.

Before a girl was chosen to present herself before the great Ziegfeld, she must be able to wear a large headdress and her figure must meet certain standards: bust 36 – waist 26 – hips 38 the accent was on the hips. As far as he saw it, bare legs were never as enticing as legs sheathed in chiffon or the finest of silks. The illusion of nudes were scattered among the laces, rosebuds and spangles of his fabulous settings. Tights were more seductive than nakedness, creating the art of intimation rather than full disclosure.

Ziegfeld saw himself as a collector of beauty and a connoisseur of charm and grace. Theatre auditions were only one of his methods for finding qualified girls for the Follies. He was always on the watch for a beautiful body, with a lovely face poised on a patrician neck. Most of all he looked for that unique quality of bewitchment. Ziegfeld always had his eye out for beauties, hunting in restaurants, the streets, shops, or wherever his day took him. He also had spies looking for talent in other Broadway theatres and shows competing with him.

In general, a Ziegfeld girl had straight backs, straight brows and straight noses, implying a frigid, pure high school girlishness the American people liked. Ziegfeld's goal was not to present a woman to be as sexually attractive as possible. His goal was to appeal to idealism, first displaying her as a chaste, dewy-eyed vision, and then discreetly disrobing his sexually inviting goddess.

The week after Harmony's recital, Christopher brought Heather to the theatre to sing for the great Florence Ziegfeld. She had never seen anything so grand and her heart soared with the opportunity to sing to a live audience at the world renown Ziegfeld Follies. Taking a deep breath, she filled herself with the fragrance of the theatre, a smell she would remember all her life.

Sitting in the 10th row with Christopher, Florence Ziegfeld watched as Heather slowly and deliberately walked across the stage, like a swan gliding across a crystal, blue pond. She was everything he looked for in a Ziegfeld Girl and more. Although she was obviously stunning, it was Heather's eyes that captivated him the most. Now let's see if she can sing.

Smiling a seductive smile, Heather looked at the piano player. "It Had To Be You, slow and bluesy, key of C, if you please." The piano player smiled back, eager to hear her delivery on one of his favorite popular songs.

Getting in sync with the music, Heather closed her eyes and slightly moved her hips to the musical introduction. Reading his vocalist in her creative dance, the piano player paused.

Slow, rich and husky, Heather delivered. "*It had to be you… it had to be you… I wandered around and finally found somebody who…*"

Bewitching, magical, inviting…seductive…the promise of enchantment, Heather had it all. Nodding with approval, Florence Ziegfeld applauded, and so did everyone else who heard her. Heather responded, nodding with professional appreciation.

"You were right, Charlie. Heather Diamond, I want you in my show and I want you to sing that song the way you just sang it for me."

"Thank you, Mister Ziegfeld. Thank you very much."

Victoria Pearl had been sitting in the last row watching.

"Miss Pearl," Heather exclaimed. "I am going to sing in the Ziegfeld Follies!"

"A pretty girl is like a melody," Pearl smiled. "Let's go tell Minna and Ada."

Broadway, Wall Street, Macy's, Central Park, Madison Square Garden, speakeasies, mobsters and dreamers, the "Big Apple" had it all. In many ways, New York City reminded Heather of Chicago. To Harmony it was like nothing she had ever known. Both girls were excited and at the same time, a bit overwhelmed.

Extremely private and highly selective of anyone crossing their threshold, Ada and Minna Everleigh had succeeded in maintaining a low profile in New York City. Aware of the importance of maintaining influential connections, some of their closest friends included men with fond memories of 2131 Dearborn Street in Chicago, as well as former butterflies like Madeline. Their special bond ignited exciting memories from good times past, like belonging to a secret club whose sacred membership was allowed to only a chosen few.

To those unaware of the sisters' past history, Ada and Minna were perceived to be wealthy, middle-aged ladies, well bred, dainty and refined. This image served them well in finding their place in New York society. At least once a week they attended a show on Broadway and kept up with all the latest reviews. It was their innate love and appreciation of the theatre that filled the void of excitement that had been unfairly taken from them fourteen years before.

After Heather's audition, Victoria phoned Ada and Minna with Heather's good news.

"We must go to lunch and celebrate, Victoria," Ada exclaimed. "Please ask Madeline and her sister to join us."

Strategically, the sisters invited the women to meet them the next afternoon at the Algonquin Hotel, where every day an exclusive clique known as "The Algonquin Round Table" met for lunch. The celebrated group included New York writers, critics, actors and local celebrities. The writings of these popular journalists had a powerful stronghold in influencing culture across America and even some parts of the world.

With notepads and pencils in hand, many times lunch became an exciting brainstorming session filled with new ideas and creative collaborations. As The Round Table grew, they moved into the Algonquin's Rose Room and nicknamed themselves "The Vicious Circle." Outside the hotel, the group gathered socially as well, playing games like cribbage, poker, Wink Murder and croquet.

When the women walked into the Algonquin, the day's meeting of The Round Table was already in session. Recognizing the Everleigh sisters, columnist Franklin Adams, a charter member known by his readers as F.P.A, immediately jumped up from his seat and hurried to greet his old friends from Chicago.

"Minna! Ada! I cannot believe my eyes!"

"How's my boy??" Minna smiled, embracing her old friend.

In 1903, Franklin Adams had signed on with the Chicago Journal to write both a sports and a humor column. Because they knew the importance of maintaining their friendship with the press, the sisters had allowed him honorary admittance into the Everleigh Club.

"Franklin Adams, these are our friends, Victoria Pearl, Elizabeth, Heather, Harmony and I believe you know Madeline."

"How do you do, ladies, Madeline… so nice to see you again," he said, bowing and kissing her hand.

"Merkle's Boner, 1908," Minna declared.

"Frank Merkle," Franklin laughed. "Poor kid. He should have gone to second base. They still call it 'the most controversial game in baseball.'"

"Good thing he didn't. Our Chicago Cubs wouldn't have beat the Giants and won the pennant," Ada exclaimed.

"What a party that was! I'll never forget the champagne corks popping and everyone drinking out of the Butterflies' shoes! Those were good times," Franklin reminisced, shaking his head and smiling.

"These are the saddest of possible words: Tinker to Evers to Chance. Trio of bear cubs, and fleeter than birds, Tinker and Evers and Chance," Ada recited.

Franklin joined her in reciting his famous poem.

"*Ruthlessly pricking our gonfalon bubble.*
*Making a Giant hit into a double*
*Words that are heavy with nothing but trouble:*
*Tinker to Evers to Chance*."

Franklin laughed. "You memorized it?"

"Your poem made those boys famous with their double play," Ada grinned.

"Oh how we loved our Chicago Cubs. Still do. Now that we live in New York, we have become Yankee fans. We like to go to the games," Minna informed.

"Watching The Bambino walk to the plate sends such a wave of excitement throughout the crowd," Ada commented. "It's just thrilling to watch."

"Ahh yes. The Great Babe Ruth. Also known as The Sultan of Swat," Frank said. "He needs to get back in shape. These days he's tipping over 260 lbs. Too many hotdogs and soda pops. They're calling his condition the bellyache."

"I heard he likes to visit children in hospitals," Ada said.

"That is correct. The Babe is quite a generous guy, but unfortunately he parties a little too hard. Too much booze and fast women. Guess it's just part of being famous."

"Heather just got a singing role in the Ziegfeld Summer Follies, Franklin. We are celebrating," Ada said in an effort to focus on the mission at hand.

"I can certainly see why. You are a beauty, my dear."

"Harmony is a composer and concert pianist," she added. "Last Saturday she performed a wonderful recital at the new Steinway Hall and made quite an impression," Minna bragged.

In that moment, Franklin realized there was a purpose for their lunch at the Algonquin. They knew he would be here. Aware of the Everleigh sisters' mission in knowing the importance of proper introductions to the right people, Frank grinned with admiration at his old friends. This was his opportunity to repay his free, regular admittance to the famous Everleigh Club.

"Heather, Harmony, I believe you need to meet my friends."

So much was being said without being said.

Ada nodded her head and smiled with appreciation. "Thank you, Franklin."

As Franklin crooked both arms, Heather and Harmony, responding to his invitation, slipped their hands inside. Approaching the table, they saw the journalists laughing hysterically.

The group was playing a game they had invented called, "I can give you a sentence." Somebody says a word and everyone tries to make the best sentence, using the word.

The word had been horticulture. With uncanny wit, Dorothy Parker had responded, "You can lead a horticulture but you can't make her think."

Frank waited until the group calmed down.

"Everyone…I want to introduce you to Harmony and Heather. Heather is going to be in Ziggy's Summer Follies and Harmony is a concert pianist."

"Hello everyone," Heather smiled.

"Fascinate," someone yelled out.

"Excuse me?" Heather inquired.

"They are playing a game, Heather. Think of a clever sentence using the word fascinate," Frank suggested.

"OK. Let me see," Heather said. "I've got it! How about, "Her boobs were so big, although there were 10 buttons on her sweater, she could only fascinate." (fasten 8)

Again the table roared with laughter.

"Very good, Heather," Dorothy commented. "I am impressed. Beautiful and smart."

"Hey everyone!" a cheerful voice greeted.

It was Louise Brooks, a new honorary member of The Round Table, looking stunning in her new hat.

"Brooksie!" a tall young woman sitting at the table exclaimed.

The woman's name was Lois Long, a columnist for the just newly released magazine New Yorker. To her left sat its founder Harold Ross who along with Franklin Adams had written for Stars and Stripes during World War I.

Lois used the penname *Lipstick* when writing her exciting new column. The daughter of a Connecticut preacher, her assignment was to report on the carefree lifestyle of the American flapper by visiting the most interesting speakeasies in New York City. Lois had an expense account to party hard and spent every dime of it well. She was known to come to the office at all hours of the morning to write about her latest escapade.

"Hi, Lois… Harmony? Heather? This is a surprise. Fancy seeing you here," Louise exclaimed.

"Hello, Louise," Harmony responded.

"I heard Harmony's recital last Saturday and enjoyed it immensely. Harmony plays very well," Louise announced to the group. "How did your meeting with Ziggy go, Heather?"

"It went well, thank you. It looks like I will be singing in the Summer Follies," Heather answered.

"That is fantastic!" Louise exclaimed. "Are you joining us for lunch?"

"We are with friends," Harmony informed her.

"Yes, indeed. In fact, I better get these two ladies back to their table," Franklin said.

"Why don't you come out with us tonight? Lois and I are going to Texas Guinan's."

"Sounds like fun," Heather answered.

"I'm in," Harmony agreed.

"Good. Come to the Cosmopolitan Theatre tonight and I'll show you around backstage," Louise smiled, taking a seat next to Lois.

Mission accomplished; important introductions had been made. Minna and Ada were satisfied.

"So good to see you again, Franklin," Minna said.

Knowing the sisters were cashing in a favor, Frank smiled. He always admired Minna and Ada's business savvy and felt they had gotten a bum rap in Chicago.

"And you as well, dear ladies. Heather and Harmony, it has been a pleasure to have met you. We are here every day at lunch. Come join us anytime. Any friend of Minna and Ada Everleigh is certainly a friend of mine."

Tea had been served and popovers and celery sticks had been placed on the table. Ada ordered everyone the popular chicken hash with pancakes for lunch.

"Heather… Harmony… Ada and I would like to sponsor you during your stay in New York City. We have arranged for you to be here at the Algonquin," Minna offered. "You may stay as long as you like until you know what your next step will be."

"That is incredibly generous, Minna," Victoria commented.

"It is certainly our pleasure to do so, Victoria. Ada and I love the theatre. To us, this is an exciting venture, watching these girls make a name for themselves."

Madeline's sister Elizabeth had been sitting quietly, taking it all in. The women at Miss Pearl's Parlor had experienced Elizabeth's intuitive gift when she had visited San Angelo two years before. One evening she predicted Heather was in grave danger. A few weeks later, Tony, a gangster in Chicago and Heather's ex-boyfriend, had shown up with the intention of killing her.

"Both of you girls are going to experience great success," Elizabeth offered. "If I may suggest, no matter what happens, keep your eyes on your goals and beware of false promises. You have a wonderful support system with the women at this table and for this you are blessed."

"Thank you, Elizabeth," Heather responded.

"I do feel blessed," Harmony added.

"That young man in the uniform is still with you, my dear. I see a kind woman as well. She is a grandmother figure"

"Is it Nana?" Harmony exclaimed.

"I see her sitting on a piano bench with a little girl. Is she the one who taught you to play the piano?"

"Yes…yes!"

"She says your name is not really Harmony."

"Oh my goodness! My real name is Harriett Jane. Nana told me I named myself when I was three. We were playing the piano together and she told me we were making harmony. She said I told her, 'I am harmony.' It has been my name ever since."

"Elizabeth, why don't you go on Houdini's show?" Heather asked. "I heard that besides being an escape artist there is a part of his show that he brings up people who say they are mediums."

"Can you imagine what would happen if I did that, Heather? I like my life the way it is. It was not that long ago women were accused of witchcraft and burned at the stake when even suspected of having the gift of intuition. Besides, Houdini is frustrated because he wishes he had the gift and is quick to discredit those who really do."

"I guess you are right; I never thought of that."

"By the way Heather, what were all those people laughing about?" Victoria asked.

"They were playing a game where someone says a word and you try to make a clever sentence."

"Heather came up with a good one," Harmony bragged. "The word was fascinate and Heather said, 'Her boobs were so big, although there were 10 buttons on her sweater, she could only fascinate.'"

Everyone at the table laughed.

"I have one," Minna offered. "The word is focus. What did the English cow say to the other heifers when the farmer put his prize bull in the pasture? Get ready girls, he is here to focus again."

"Minna!" Ada declared. "That is hysterical!"

*My girlish delight in barrooms received a serious setback a week or so ago in a place which shall not to say should remain nameless. The cause was a good old-fashioned raid. It wasn't one of those refined, modern, things where gentlemen in evening dress arise suavely from ringside tables and depart, arm and arm, towards waiting patrol wagons. It was one of those movie affairs where burly cops kick down the doors and women fall fainting on tables and strong men crawl under them and waiters shriek and start throwing bottles out of windows. ~ Lipstick*

It was after midnight before the girls entered Texas Guinan's 300 Club, located at 151 West 54th Street. Generously serving the who's who of New York, the popular speakeasy was packed full of people willing to be overcharged for ignoring Prohibition. The party was well underway and spirits were flowing like gutters in a rain storm. Jazz music was blaring, the chorus girls were dancing and people were laughing hysterically at silly things that if sober, might be moderately funny at best.

On the stage appeared the Queen of the Night Clubs herself, Mary Louise Cecilia, an eccentric woman from Waco, Texas, known to New Yorkers as Texas Guinan. In 1906 she had moved to New York and began her career as a chorus girl in vaudeville. In 1917, she made her film debut in The Wildcat, a name that suited her well both on and off the silver screen, where she acquired the nickname "Queen of the West." A woman with a heart of gold, Texas Guinan had served her country by going overseas to pick up the spirits of the American soldiers, entertaining the troops during The Great War.

Her smile was huge and her personality was as big as the state of her birth. Fun, fearless and feisty, Texas Guinan was a master at putting butts in the seats and showing people a good time. Seeing Lois and Louise enter the room, she greeted them with a friendly wave and pointed to an empty table she had reserved for them.

"Hello Suckers!!" Guinan yelled with her familiar flare.

Everyone cheered.

Those who went to Texas Guinan's did not go just to have a good time; they went to have a "crazy" good time. Guinan called her patrons "Suckers," probably due to the fact that they gladly paid $25 for a bottle of fake champagne and $1 for a shot of water-downed whiskey. Her partner was Larry Fay, a gangster who recognized the magnetic power of Guinan's personality. People loved her stories of the "old west" and their partnership created what was known as the "Granddaddy of all speakeasies."

Guinan proudly wore a long necklace made of golden padlocks, each one representing a different visit from the paddy wagon. Bending the rules to her advantage, the illegal liquor was kept in the house next door, so it was never technically stored on the premises. Every time the police would raid her business, she would swear her patrons had brought their own booze and, as for her scantily clothed women demonstrating sexual affection, "they were just snuggling up to the customers because the club was so small."

When she was arrested, Guinan turned the event into a ritualistic sideshow. Several times when escorted to the paddy wagon, Guinan would instruct the band to play The Prisoner's Song and the patrons would solemnly sing along. Although her clubs would usually have to relocate within six months, Texas Guinan was never convicted and always came out smelling like a rose.

Tonight the energy at the 300 Club seemed to be soaring exceptionally high. Lois Long was on a mission to tell all and Louise was in her element of flirting, drinking, and dancing. From the minute the two women walked through the door, they were greeted with hugs and kisses by several of the regular customers.

The four women made their way to their reserved table but before they sat down, all four already had a drink waiting on the table for them. Although Lois was attractive enough, Louise, Heather and Harmony had caught the eye of just about every man they passed. Louise seduced, Lois observed and Heather and Harmony maintained their "you can look but do not touch" attitude, a lesson emphasized at Miss Pearl's.

"Don't be too eager girls, men prefer a good hunt."

"Everyone, look who's here. George Gershwin, get on up here and play us a song," Guinan yelled from the stage.

Harmony gasped with delight as the composer made his way to the stage. With an exaggerated bow, he greeted the audience, sat on the piano bench and waited for the crowd to subside. Banging out the first familiar notes of his *Rhapsody in Blue*, Harmony swooned like a schoolgirl with a romantic crush.

Seeing Harmony's reaction, Louise rolled her eyes. "Oh he's a talent all right. He wrote most of the songs for The George White Scandals when I was dancing with them. Unfortunately, like so many other men I've known, he doesn't keep his promises, at least to me. He told me he would buy me a doll when he went to Paris. I told him he'd forget and that's exactly what happened," she pouted.

Harmony didn't hear a word Louise had said. Eyes closed, she was lost in the music. Gershwin was playing his *Rhapsody in Blue* on the modest upright piano standing in the corner of the stage. To her, he was playing a 12-foot Steinway in Carnegie Hall.

Gershwin had first performed his now famous *Rhapsody in Blue* as a musical experiment, mixing jazz with classical music, at Aeolin Hall the year before. On the night of the concert the piece was only partly finished. As the music grew into a crescendo, a magical co-creation with the orchestra occurred and a section of the piece was composed on the spot. In 1924, a time of significant change, the musical collaboration bridging the two genres proved to be a huge success, making *Rhapsody in Blue* the signature melody of the old meeting the new.

Although Harmony was sitting in the midst of a crowd of carefree patrons lit up with liquid spirits, she was in music heaven. Listening with the soul of a composer, Harmony appreciated the genius of the composition.

"Bravo," she whispered when he completed his last note.

Texas Guinan appeared again on the stage. "Thank you George, always a pleasure. Now give the little girls a great big hand," she announced, as a chorus line of young ladies wearing just enough to not get arrested, appeared on the stage.

The crowd resumed its jovial ambiance and once again, the party was on.

Suddenly, Harmony gasped. Making their way to the table was Mae West, the vaudeville entertainer who had attended her recital, leading George Gershwin.

"Hey kid… thought you'd like to meet my friend George. I told him all about your recital. Thought the two of you might have a few things in common," Mae smiled.

"How do you do," George said graciously. "Hello, Louise… Lois…"

"I'm sorry, I don't think I've met your friend," Mae said.

"This is my friend Heather," Harmony chirped. "She's going to be in the Ziegfeld Summer Follies."

"That's good, that's good," Mae said. "Congratulations."

Lois and Louise decided to wander around and mingle with some of the other regulars. George invited Harmony to a quiet table where they could talk about music. "Don't leave without me," she said to Heather.

Mae stayed to visit with Heather. "Best speakeasy in town. Texas Guinan is an old friend of mine. She's a corker all right. Love her. She's quite a gal."

"She reminds me of my friend Katie in San Angelo," Heather smiled.

"So you're gonna be in the Follies? See that skinny little gal with the dark curls dancing on the end up there on the stage? Her real name is Ruby Catherine but we all call her Missy. She used to dance in the Follies."

"What happened?" Heather said.

"Ziggy runs a tight ship. More relaxed around here. Not so much pressure. Poor kid has had a tough go of it. Her mama and daddy died when she was four. She has a little brother. Her older sister tried to raise them, but she worked as a chorus girl so the younger ones got passed around in foster homes. Missy is a feisty little thing. Kept running away from her new 'daddies' when they'd get too friendly. Damn men. I try to look out for her. She really wants to be an actress."

"I've been in a couple of movies. My friend Richard told me I should come to Broadway to experience the real deal."

"Your friend Richard is a smart man. Everyone is in such a hurry to run to Hollywood and be in the movies. Where do ya think they get most of their talent? Clara Bow, Buster Keaton, Charlie Chaplin, they all started on Broadway.

"I grew up in vaudeville. I love a LIVE audience and I do whatever it takes to make them love me. Once I spent a king's ransom on a dress made with 40 lbs. of rhinestones just so I could look good. You're real pretty, honey. You will do well in the Follies."

"Thank you, Mae. I am looking forward to it. I've never performed in live theatre before, although it has always been my biggest dream."

"Ziegfeld is smart when it comes to his costumes and sets. He spares no expense and the audience loves it. It's all about the audience, kid. They gotta love ya or you'll flop. You'll look good on his stage. Ziggy really gets angry when the movies snatch up one of his girls," Mae laughed. "Seems as soon as he makes them a star, next thing he knows they wanna go to Hollywood."

"Hollywood was fun, but I'm looking forward to being on stage in a live theatre."

"There ain't nothing like it, Heather. The lights, the laughter, the applause… there just ain't nothin' like it in the world."

"How well do you know Ada and Minna?" Heather asked. Mae knew what she meant.

"Well enough, I suppose," Mae grinned, nodding her head slowly. Heather smiled back, communicating that she also knew the secret of the Everleigh sisters.

"I just wrote a play and I'm looking for investors. A mutual friend who knew the sisters in Chicago introduced us. Smart ladies… quite a history there. Let's just say, we appreciate each other."

"Ada and Minna are incredible women."

"Harmony's a talented girl," Mae commented, "and quite the lady. She is in good hands with Ada and Minna. They'll take care of her. Like I told Harmony, any friend of Ada and Minna is a friend of mine."

"I guess that makes us friends then," Heather grinned, offering her hand.

Mae took it and gave her a friendly shake. "Friends are important in this city, Heather. New York is a big place and at the same time, a small place, but most of all, it's an exciting place. Come see me sometime," Mae smiled.

Heather watched as all five feet of the Brooklyn bombshell strutted away as if she were the queen of the city.

"Now give the little girls a great big hand," Texas Guinan yelled from the stage as the chorus line disappeared off stage. "HELLO SUCKERS!"

"Hello, Tex!" a table full of rehearsed drunks yelled on cue.

Guinan laughed. "Everyone having a good time?

The crowd cheered.

"Hey, y'all. Look who's here. Louise Brooks, get on up here little darlin'. For those of you who don't know, Louise was the first to perform the Charleston in Merry Old England. Give this little girl a great big hand."

Making her way to the stage, the crowd began chanting, "Louise! Louise! Louise!"

"Play it boys!" Guinan commanded.

Darling, fun and wildly entertaining, Louise Brooks, America's most celebrated flapper, lit up the stage with her rendition of the popular dance that had raged from coast to coast.

Lois returned to the table to watch.

"So what do you think, Heather?" Lois asked.

"About what?" Heather replied.

"All of this craziness. What do you think?"

"I think I am happy I am twenty years old, living in America in 1925," Heather smiled.

"You're different," Lois said. "It's like you are an old person in a young body. What's your story, Heather?"

"I have several," she smiled mysteriously, rousing the natural curiosity of the inquisitive reporter.

"I'll be you do," Lois smiled.

CHAPTER 28

# The Follies

Reconnecting with Ada and Minna had satisfied the emptiness in Victoria that she had not even realized was there. If not for the sisters she would not have met and fallen in love with Robert McKnight, who brought her to Texas to be his bride. If she had not accepted their invitation to tea, she would not have met Mozella or Madeline or helped so many young women find refuge at Miss Pearl's Parlor. Heather would be fish bait and Harmony's talent would never be realized. They were all connected with golden threads of friendship in a beautifully woven tapestry of women helping women.

Now, their legacy was being passed on to Heather and Harmony. Not having children of their own, Ada and Minna were excited to participate in their careers. The next several weeks were filled with moving into the Algonquin, going to the theatre, walking in Central Park and receiving more introductions to highly influential people. Finally it was time for Victoria Pearl to return to Texas.

The day before leaving, Victoria invited Heather and Harmony to visit Ellis Island. Tears streamed down Victoria's face as she thought about her parents coming to America with only a suitcase and a dream. Strangers when they met on a ship headed from Ireland to the New World, Molly O'Connor and Brian McDougal had fallen in love.

"There she stands ladies… the Statue of Liberty. She was not there when my parents came to America. It wasn't until 1886 when France presented her as a gift to the United States. How lovely she is."

Harmony was looking at a brochure. "This says she was named after Libertas, the Roman goddess of freedom. She bears a torch to light their way and holds a tablet with the inscription, 4 July, 1776, the date of the American Declaration of Independence. A broken chain lies at her feet, a welcoming signal intended for immigrants arriving from abroad."

"She is a glorious sight indeed, Miss Pearl," Heather proclaimed, taking Victoria's arm.

"A glorious woman indeed," Pearl sighed.

Although saying good-bye at the train station was difficult, Victoria Pearl was satisfied in knowing Heather and Harmony were in good hands with Ada and Minna.

*"Life is an exciting adventure*," Victoria thought to herself. "*Love is the only thing that really matters, and it is forever."*

Heather fell in love with the stage that evening, and Florence Ziegfeld was more than pleased with his new singer's performance. Although she enjoyed making films, Heather realized that first night singing at the Ziegfeld Follies that performing to a live audience was her greatest joy. "That was good," from the movie crew did not compare with the roar of applause she heard that night from the auditorium full of elated people.

Most importantly, the press was impressed and greatly approved the new Ziegfeld star.

`Silent film star Heather Diamond has found her way from Hollywood to Broadway to appear in Ziegfeld's sensational Summer Follies. If movies had sound, this girl's voice would melt many a heart. ~ The New York Sun`

Meanwhile, across town at the Cosmopolitan Theatre, Louis the 14th continued to be a smashing success and Louise Brooks had been receiving consistently excellent press for her performance. Unfortunately, Louise had a major personality conflict with the stage manager Teddy Royce. To her he was crude, insulting, disrespectful, and drank too much.

Louise always took the approach: a good defense is a good offense. Knowing he could not fire her, she began provoking Teddy by showing up late and wiring the theatre to inform him she was unable to come to the performance. Teddy saw Louise as a spoiled beauty and took the bait. It all came to a head one night. Teddy called a special rehearsal. After taking a stiff shot of gin for courage, he dramatically threw his Oliver Twist scarf over his shoulder and with a hateful glare, focused his dark, beady eyes on Louise, obviously speaking only to her.

"Some girls are breaking down the whole discipline of the company – coming in late, missing performances and in fact using the theatre as only a place to showcase their wares."

Taking great delight in her being called down, all of the girls looked at Louise and grinned. Publicly humiliated, Louise ran to Ziegfeld's private den in tears and brazenly told him what had happened. Although Ziegfeld agreed that Teddy's words had just cause, he knew Louise was a hot property and didn't want to lose her.

Grinning, he gave her his adorable "silver-fox" smile, "Forget Teddy, Louise. How about I feature you in the summer edition of the Follies."

"Thank you, Mister Ziegfeld," she said with a grateful embrace.

When Louise Brooks showed up for rehearsals for the Ziegfeld Summer Follies her reputation had preceded her. Stage manager Billy Strode was not sure what to do with his new 18-year-old rebel. "I have asked them all and there's not a girl in the show willing to dress with you," he said, scratching his head.

The girls within earshot of the conversation were amused, throwing Louise looks of satisfied contempt. Heather was among them.

"She can dress with me."

"Heather?" Louise said, happy to see a familiar face.

"Hi, Louise. It is good to see you again," Heather smiled. "I saw you in Louis the 14th. You were brilliant."

"She needs to dress with the other dancers."

"I believe you just said…" Heather grinned.

"All right, all right. I guess it will be okay for now. Hope you know what you are getting yourself into, Heather," Bill said, as he wrote on his clipboard.

"You are not like most girls I have worked with in the theatre," Louise said with curiosity.

"You are like most girls I have worked with," Heather grinned. "I understand you, Louise. Maybe we can talk about it sometime. For now, just trust me. I know the ropes. Welcome to the show."

From then on Louise saw Heather as a confidant. To her, Heather was someone she could trust and share her secrets with.

On June 27, 1925, newspapers and wire services, anxiously following Ziegfeld's cast changes, reported: Louise Brooks – who until a few weeks ago danced a specialty dance in Louie the 14th – is now one of six new members of Ziegfeld's "beauty chorus."

All the long hours of Denishawn dance training had paid off. Louise was sensational. Not merely a "glorified girl," she had several solos including a Gypsy dance. Ziegfeld himself selected her for the Apache dance. The critics especially were impressed with Louise's dance to Syncopating Baby which went on to become a musical hit from the show.

"Last but not least there is Louise Brooks, a charming brunette, who dances engagingly and has real personality. She would be a welcome addition to any revue." ~ Stephen Rathbun - The New York Sun

Despite her good reviews and performing thrills, Louise was unable to find joy in her own success. One day she confided her frustrations to her new friend.

"I have made some stupid mistakes, Heather. I know I should feel grateful for the opportunity to dance in the great Ziegfeld Follies, but after dancing with Denishawn, these little dances I do for the Follies are boring. It has made me bitter and sometimes I say things and do things…"

"Who hasn't made mistakes?" Heather comforted.

"The only real happy moment for me is at the end of the show when the whole company is on stage."

"I like how Ziegfeld put you on top of the pyramid in the grand finale."

"It's fifteen feet up in the air! He told me it he gave me the position on the pyramid to symbolize my ladder of success."

"That is nice, Louise."

That evening Will Rogers made a small noose in his rope like he always did. Twirling it faster and faster, the rope circle got bigger and bigger until the rope hissed around the chorus girls like an intoxicated snake. The curtain opened for the finale and the audience marveled as the spotlight shone on the girls. Rogers ascended the staircase, expertly twirling his lariat around the very beautiful Louise Brooks. Reaching the top, in an inspiring moment of devilish mischief, the comedian removed gum from his mouth and placed it on Louise's nose.

The audience laughed hysterically.

Louise was furious. Backstage she let him have it.

"You rotten son-of-a-bitch! I will kill you!"

Again she was publicly humiliated.

Rogers apologized to Louise. Although it received a huge laugh, he never did it again. He meant no harm. He was just a simple Oklahoma cowboy. From then on, Louise saw Will Rogers as a hayseed with a gimmick. On the other hand, she saw W.C. Fields as a brilliant comedian.

In the public mind, Will Rogers was the darling and Fields was the eccentric.

Fascinated by the "Great Misanthrope's" humor and delicate timing, she watched Fields from the wings as he performed his act. Most of all she admired his stately procedures and the passionate amount of work he put into his performances.

Louise and Heather would have liked to know him better but Fields was a loner off stage. Although he adored beautiful girls, very few were invited into his dressing room. Morbidly sensitive about the eczema that inflamed his nose and sometimes his hands, he learned how to perform his juggling act with gloves. After several heartbreaking episodes with pretty girls, he restricted his romantic interludes with less attractive women. Most of his experiences with amorous chorus girls ended in rejection and humiliation.

During the Summer Follies, Ziegfeld decided to pair Louise up with another talented dancer, Lina Basquette. The two teenagers received a brilliant review:

Lina Basquette and Louise Brooks were animated things of joy. Both beautiful girls, both remarkable dancers and both so vivacious that one's blood tingles within thirty seconds after either one starts a dance."
~ The New York Sun

One evening before the show, Lina showed up backstage flashing a diamond ring she had received from Sam Warner. Twenty years her senior, Warner had seen Lina first perform in Louis the 14th and instantly fell in love with her. Born in Poland, he and his brothers had formed Warner Bros. and had recently purchased the Vitagraph movie studio in New York City.

"Look everyone! I am getting married!"

Oohs and ahhs rang throughout the room as girls gathered around to see another Ziegfeld girl's victorious leap into marriage.

Thinking of her mother's words, Louise quietly retreated to her dressing room.

"*You are broken, Louise... damaged goods. You are no longer a virgin. If people find out about this, no man will ever want to marry you. This is why you must keep what happened with Mister Flowers a secret.*"

"Are you all right?" Heather asked, following her into the dressing room.

Louise began to cry softly. "I am a horrible person. My mother was right. No one will ever want to marry me. I have done some stupid things, Heather."

"What is wrong with you, Louise?"

"Can I tell you something? I need to tell someone or I think I will die from guilt. I feel like I can trust you.

"One of my best friends has a boyfriend. He's an actor from England. Nice looking, sophisticated, thinks he's God's gift to women."

"I know the type," Heather said, rolling her eyes.

"Every time I would see him, he was always so snooty and liked to make fun of my Kansas accent. It was humiliating, especially when others would laugh.

One night he called me and invited me to dinner. I knew my friend was out of town but I agreed to go. He took me to the Claremont Inn up the Hudson and was ever so sweet. He even taught me how to eat clams. It was the first time he had ever been kind to me. He even said I was beautiful..."

"*Uh oh, I know where this is going,*" Heather thought.

"It was so cold driving home. All I had on was a little red jacket. He took me to his house for a nightcap and built a lovely fire. He sat on a big flowery chair and I was on a polar bear rug looking at the fireplace. He was being so nice to me..." Louise began crying. Heather handed her a handkerchief and sat next to her, rubbing her back in an attempt to comfort her.

"The next morning I awoke to an empty bedroom. After a few minutes he appeared at the bathroom door looking so smug with his hands shoved down into the pockets of his white shantung dressing gown. 'Oh, so you're awake. How do you feel? I hope you're not plotting any crying scenes. I have the devil's hangover and I'm not up to tears this morning'," Louise said, mimicking him.

"What a son-of-a-bitch," Heather exclaimed. "He knew you wouldn't tell your friend and ruin your friendship. Son-of a- bitch…"

"He went to his dressing table and looked in the mirror. "'Christ, what bags…look at my eyes will you…what bags!'" Louise said, mimicking him again. "All I could do was stare at him. I felt dirty and ashamed."

"Son-of-a-bitch," Heather repeated.

"Oh, it gets worse. He slips into his red slippers, and looks down at me. 'It might be a good idea for you to get up and dress. My wife has closed her damn show in Chicago and her maid will be here at eleven to clean the apartment…'"

"He was married?"

"Yes. 'And don't think you've taken me in with that ancient virgin business. You've been had before, my pet… you've been had. Would you like a drink before you go?'

"I told him, 'no thank you.' Then he told me my red jacket was in the living room. I could hear him puking his guts out in the kitchen sink when I left."

"Serves him right," Heather proclaimed.

"He was so sick. And he looked like hell."

Louise started laughing and Heather joined her; a little at first and soon both girls were laughing hysterically

"Oh my goodness, I feel better!" Louise sighed. "My friend broke up with him when she learned he was married."

Heather fixed Louise a glass of water that she gratefully accepted.

"Funny how the world looks different when the sun comes up. He had been so nice to me. I didn't once think of my friend. I just wanted him to like me. Stupid…Stupid…STUPID!"

"So many times a man will quickly change his prince charming persona after his springer has sprung," Heather grinned. Both girls fell into laughter again, this time wiping tears from their eyes.

Louise took another drink of water. Looking down at the glass in her hand she sighed and began telling another confession.

"There's something else, Heather. I made another stupid mistake. There is a man passing out suggestive pictures of me. I don't know what to do."

"What are you talking about, Louise?"

"Two years ago I let a photographer take nude photos of me. I was told a nude shoot was the publicity price every new girl to Broadway must pay. In some I am barely covered. He also took some where I am completely naked."

"Who is he?"

"The photographer is a man named John de Miriam. People know me now…"

"For heaven sakes, Louise. You were sixteen. Take him to court. You can get a cease and desist act against him."

Louise did just that.

In court, John admitted he had "photographed a thousand others, wearing maybe a shoe, maybe a hat, maybe a shawl… and not only the girls of the shows but women of society as well." Although Louise won, the publicity from the court case made the photographer famous overnight. Thanks to Louise Brooks, John de Miriam's work was in high demand and his studio was now one of the most famous and lucrative photography studios in New York.

Louise never made an attempt to be popular with the other girls in the Follies. Because of her love of books and her high standards of appreciation for music and dance, Louise considered herself more sophisticated and culturally superior. She had been featured once on the cover of the Police Gazette. The other chorus girls were jealous. Louise thought it was beneath her dignity.

Although Heather wished many times to be as free-spirited as Louise, she always heeded Miss Pearl's advice. "A lady's actions must be impeccable. Never give it away and whatever you do, never let a gentleman see you intoxicated. It is most unattractive."

Richard had also warned Heather of the pitfalls of stardom. Because of her two mentors, Heather understood the importance of holding on to her boundaries. Although she could also be cute and fun, she managed to maintain a refined attitude making her more interesting to men.

Gloriously passionate, spontaneous, boundless and free, Louise Brooks encompassed the spirit of the New Woman, living in the moment, as if it were her last day on earth. She was the epitome of the 1920s flapper. Journalists loved writing about her lifestyle and her photo was on the cover of major magazines everywhere. Young women across America fantasized what it would be like to be Louise Brooks. They cut their hair like hers, dressed like her and practiced the cool, curious and inviting, "Louise Brooks look" in the mirror.

Men adored her. At least they adored what she was. Louise Brooks, "Brooksie," the beautiful dancer, the glamorous flapper, the exciting Ziegfeld girl. No strings attached, just a lot of fun!

Ring…

"Hello"

"Hi Heather. It's Louise. Tell them I won't be there tonight."

"What do you mean, Louise?"

"Tell them I am sick. I am going to the opening of *No, No, Nanette.*"

"Louise!"

"Herman Mankiewicz is taking me. He's going to critique the show. Everyone is going to be there. It was a huge hit in Chicago. Thank you, darling!"

Click.

Heather shook her head and grinned. Louise definitely marched to the beat of her own drum.

"She'll get away with it. She always does."

When Heather arrived at the Amsterdam, the first person she saw was Billy Strode walking around backstage with his clipboard.

"Louise will not be here tonight."

Billy rolled his eyes and shook his head. "She's going to *No, No, Nanette,* isn't she, Heather?" the stage manager winced.

"She said to tell you she is sick," Heather said, truthfully.

"And I am supposed to believe that?"

"She said to tell you she is sick," Heather said, shrugging her shoulders.

Florence Ziegfeld was an easygoing man. Understanding the nature of artistic people, he had an endless capacity of tolerance for his cast. He knew that Louise's shenanigans were part of her being the lively spirit that she was and for this he was very forgiving.

Learning about her absence from the show that evening, Ziegfeld could not help but smile. To him it was part of the price he paid to have Louise Brooks light up his stage. "That would be our Louise," he sighed. "Oh to be so young, talented and so beautiful…"

CHAPTER 29

# Charlie Chaplin

In 1925 most of the world knew the name Charlie Chaplin. Spanning all seven continents he was the most famous man who had ever lived. No one was more welcomed in the theatre and film world or more adored. For over a decade, the genius of Charlie Chaplin had brought billions of tears and laughter to millions of people across the globe. When he came to New York to promote *The Gold Rush*, he made a point to take in the show at the Ziegfeld Follies. It was there he first set eyes on the very lovely Louise Brooks.

A few days before the premiere, film producer, Walter Wanger threw Chaplin an afternoon cocktail party and invited Louise Brooks to attend. Wanger had given Louise a small part in the movie, *Forgotten Men.*

"Come with me, Heather," Louise begged.

"I would love to come with you. I met Charlie Chaplin in Hollywood a few months ago… a charming man.

"You did?"

"You know I have made two films in Hollywood."

"You did? How did you like it?"

"It was grand. However, I believe I like a live audience better. It is much different performing to the darkness of a theatre, knowing hundreds of people are watching. Although I loved my camera crew and the people I worked with, it is just not the same."

"I totally agree. Theatre trumps filmmaking every time."

Louise Brooks walked into the apartment as if she owned the building. Walter kissed her on both cheeks. "Thank you for coming, dear," he expressed. "And who is this exquisite creature?"

"This is my friend Heather."

"Ah yes. I saw you sing in the Summer Follies. You are quite talented, my dear. Wait a minute…are you Heather Diamond from the movie *Rio Concho*?"

"Yes I…oh my God I don't believe it!"

Coming towards her in a state of frenzy was the most handsome, glorious sight Heather could ever wish for. With arms outstretched, he was grinning from ear to ear.

"Richard! What in the world are you doing here?"

Heather jumped into Richard's arms. He swung her around several times in a joyous reunion.

"I came in for the premiere. My train arrived a few hours ago. I was planning to go to the Amsterdam this evening to surprise you."

Charlie Chaplin had seen the two stunning women enter the room. He specifically asked Wanger to invite Louise to the party after he had seen her dance. With drink in hand, Charlie sauntered over to the group.

"You look wonderful, Heather," Richard exclaimed. "New York obviously agrees with you."

"And you are a sight for lonely eyes, Richard."

"How can anyone be lonely in New York?" Charlie expressed.

"Charlie, you remember my friend, Heather," Richard said in a cordial manner.

"Of course I do. How could anyone forget a woman so lovely and talented?" Charlie charmed, kissing Heather's hand.

"So nice to see you again," Heather said gracefully. "Congratulations on your new movie. I heard it was a great success in Hollywood."

"Thank you, Heather," he said, humbly nodding his head. "By the way, I have been following your career. You were wonderful in *Rio Concho*."

Heather blushed. "Thank you." The great Charlie Chaplin just complimented her. She was stunned at how elated it made her feel knowing the king of comedy had taken interest. "Richard, Charlie, this is my friend Louise Brooks."

"Charmed, my dear," Charlie said, kissing Louise's hand. His glistening, mysterious eyes looked straight into Louise's soul. Never before had a man impressed her like this.

Louise could only stare. "Such exquisiteness he has the screen does not reflect," she thought. "Small, yet perfect; fine, silver streaked hair, ivory skin, teeth like pearls, meticulously dressed, and a glow…a radiant beautiful glow that lights up a room like sunshine."

For the next hour, Richard and Heather played catch-up while Charlie Chaplin made small talk but never wavered too far from the ever-so-stunning Louise Brooks.

"They are taking down the Hotel Redondo, Heather."

Charlie who was within ear shot responded. "Oh, what a horrible shame. I am so very sorry to hear that. I often stayed there when I first arrived in Hollywood. It was my solace, a place of refuge."

"We all need a place of refuge if we want to survive this crazy business," Wanger commented.

Charlie sighed. "There is nothing to compare with the feeling of peace one gets when listening to the ocean waves break softly on the sand... such a grand, yet quaint hotel. So sad to destroy something so beautiful."

Louise and Charlie Chaplin were having a silent conversation of their own. Charlie had an innate love for beautiful women and from the first moment the two laid eyes upon each other, fireworks and flashes of heat lit up their entire beings. Although at thirty-six Chaplin was twice her age, the chemistry between the two was astounding. It was as if a bolt of lightning flashed whenever their eyes met.

The New York premiere of *The Gold Rush* was celebrated as a huge success. The day his assistant took the train back to Hollywood, Charlie moved into the Ambassador Hotel and invited Louise to move in with him.

Louise Brooks enjoyed her fantasy love affair with Charlie Chaplin. When they wanted to be seen, they did it with flare. When they wanted privacy, they would duck into small restaurants to avoid the crowds.

On the day Charlie Chaplin left New York City, an envelope arrived. When Louise opened it, she found a check for $2500 and a card that simply read, *Love Charlie*.

More depressed than she thought she would be, Louise called Heather.

"Please, Heather. Please come over. I need to talk."

By the time Heather got there, Louise had had way too much to drink.

"He's gone… my prince charming is gone."

"Did you fall in love, Louise?"

"I honestly don't know. Such a sophisticated lover and creative too," she smiled. "He never took booze or drugs to enhance his lovemaking or to help him sleep. Sometimes I would wake in the middle of the night and just watch him breathe in his peaceful slumber. Such a beautiful man."

Heather listened to Louise like good friends do.

Louise laughed. "The man actually believed iodine was a preventative for venereal disease. He would paint his pecker bright red with that stuff. The first time I saw it I laughed hysterically... such an ominous sight, seeing that thing come at you. If not for censorship and lack of color in film, I truly believe it would be his funniest gag of all."

Both girls laughed hysterically, tears rolling down their cheeks. When the laughter finally subsided Louise became very quiet, her emotions shifting to a melancholy song.

"I believe the two of us have a lot in common. He truly believes women only want him because he is so successful...because he is Charlie Chaplin. He is very humble, you know. He's a very hard worker and sees his purpose as simply to make people laugh. He really does not realize his greatness... the glorious star that we all see."

"Like a diamond in the sky," Heather said.

"In a way I guess we used each other, but at the same time, in another way, I believe we truly loved each other as well. The truth is, Heather, Charlie Chaplin lives on a plain above pride, jealousy or hate. He never says one bad thing about anyone. The man lives totally without ego. Charlie is such a kind man. Only tenderness and appreciation exists in his heart."

"I can see that," Heather smiled. "I know my friend Richard thinks the world of Charlie Chaplin."

Slipping in and out of her sorrow, Louise chuckled again. "You know he loves his mother's madness. It inspires him to find the humor in tragedy. She spent time in a mental institution in England. Did you know Charlie grew up extremely poor? That is how he created his little tramp persona."

"I believe Richard mentioned that."

"Charlie takes care of her, you know. He brought his mother and his brother who I believe works for him, from England to California. He bought her a home near the ocean. I sure am going to miss him," Louise said as she sucked down the last drop from her glass.

"*Louise and Charlie are very much alike in many ways,*" Heather thought. "*Even with her beauty and talent and all of his fame and success, they both seem so vulnerable.*"

"Heather, did I tell you I am going to be in another film? It is called *The American Venus*. Walter even bought me a fur coat.

"They want to link the film to the Miss America Beauty pageant and the Follies to glorify the American Girl," Louise said sarcastically. "I play the part of the vamp Miss Bayport, destined to lose out to one of the blondes. They're going to film part of it in Atlantic City where the pageant is held."

"That's great, Louise." Heather decided it best to hold back her personal opinion about a contest that lines up women like cattle.

"I really like theatre best but what the hell. Bill Fields will be filming a movie at the Astoria Studios at the same time. He can be my refuge. Bill always has a secret stash of whiskey to calm the nerves."

"I am going back to Hollywood with Richard in a couple of weeks to work on my next film. Who knows, Louise? Maybe you will come to Hollywood and make a movie one day. If you do, you must come to Redondo Beach and visit me."

"Maybe I will," Louise said, as she poured herself another drink.

CHAPTER 30

# Mae West

"I have to have a spotlight."

"All right, you'll get one."

Seven-year-old Mary Jane West had only taken two weeks of dancing lessons. Dressed in a pink and green satin dress with gold spangles, a large white lace picture hat with pink ribbons, pink tights and slippers, this Brooklyn-bred little girl was ready. A big theatre stage, a twelve piece orchestra, two balconies and boxes, pretty little Mary Jane was excited.

Mary Jane asked ten times if she were going to have a spotlight and the stage manager assured her ten times that she was. Backstage, her mother was concerned this was all too much for the little entertainer, but

Mary Jane knew without a shadow of a doubt, this is what she was born to do.

"You've only sung and danced with a piano, honey."

"Mama, you're more nervous than I am."

Papa was in the front row, worrying his little girl might get stage fright. "Tonight is a test for Mae," he had said earlier.

In the dark wings offstage right, little Mary Jane was poised, ready to make her entrance. The announcer stepped into the spotlight, shining bright in the middle of the stage. "Baby-Mae Song and Dance." The spotlight followed him offstage.

The orchestra played the introduction then played it again. This was her cue but there was no Baby-Mae. She was waiting for her spotlight still shining brightly on the other side of the stage. The band played two more introductions. Baby-Mae still waited. Furious, she shouted, "Where is my spotlight??"

"Walk out there Baby-Mae. He will give you the spotlight when he sees you," a stagehand said.

"He'd better! My father is Battling Jack!"

Baby-Mae walked on the stage. Stomping her foot, she yelled at the man in the balcony. "Where is my spotlight?" The spotlight found her wearing a sour look, stomping her foot again and fussing at the spotlight man. Everyone laughed and applauded. The audience absolutely loved her. And so it began.

Mary Jane West was born in Brooklyn to a world of fresh air, horse-drawn carriages, ragtime music and a sense that the coming new century was going to be the biggest and the best. Theatres were full of vaudeville acts and girls in tights. A new kind of music stirring from the brothels in Storyville (the red light district of New Orleans) was making its way to New York. The new genre was called jazz, named after the jasmine perfume that the sporting women wore when entertaining men.

Of English-Irish descent, Mae's father, known as "Battling Jack West,' was the boxing champion of Brooklyn. Mae's mother Matilda immigrated with her family to America from Bavaria in 1882. A lovely woman, she was at one time a corset model. Matilda always had a carriage available and in winter it was lined with deep soft fur; a feeling Mae came to love. Motor-cars were very few and considered a fad known only to those who could afford them. Her parents adored Mae and her favorite memories were of soft-shell crabs and hot corn in Coney Island and picnics in the Brooklyn parks.

Everything about the theatre excited Mae. She inhaled the smells of the stage with its canvas drops, tall wings, footlights and the ropes overhead as if they were sacred odors. Mae loved walking down the stage alley, the big tin-covered stage door, the spotlight and most of all, her adoring audiences.

Mae West learned early on that it took a unique personality to be a real star. Performing as Baby-Mae, she usually won the $10 first place prize at the amateur talent contests singing such songs as *Movin' Day, Doin' the Grizzly Bear* and *My Mariooch-a Make-a da Hoochy-ma-cooch.*

Her voice was deep and rough for a child, and the audience would laugh when they heard her powerful tones. Much different than other child acts, Baby-Mae made up her own moves and dance routines. Her audiences loved her. However, when her fans would throw coins and wadded bills on the stage, she refused to pick it up.

"Why don't you pick up the money they throw at you, Mae?" her father asked. "It's an insult to the audience. You turn up your nose as if they are insulting you. Can't you pick up just one bill to acknowledge their appreciation?"

"Mae doesn't even pick up her clothes," her mother said.

"I won't go on stage if I have to pick up the money, Papa."

"Now don't be rash, Mae. Of course you will go on with your stage work even if my friends have to wear out their derbies picking up the cash they toss at you."

"Don't worry, Papa. I'll buy them new derbies."

When Baby-Mae performed, her mother would hold her muff and scarf and Papa would carry her makeup, costume changes, and dance shoes in a leather grip. Even at a young age, she felt that sharing the dressing room with "the amateurs" was beneath her class. Mae fully expected that it was her destiny to be a sensational star.

Mae's father was always impressed that his little girl never had stage fright. "If they could bottle nerve, Mae would have more than Rockefeller has oil."

Mae wanted to know everything about the theatre. She would stand in the wings and watch the orchestra take cues from great vaudeville stars. She listened to the songs and the patter of the men in their natty suits, straw hats and limber canes performing soft shoe dances. Smiling, they would sing about *Bill Bailey*, gracefully twist their legs and arms then pause for a joke. The dance men were to her the funniest well-dressed people on earth. "You ought to be on the stage…it leaves in 10 minutes."

Still considered an amateur, Mae won the $10 prize one night at the Gotham Theatre in New York. Hal Clarendon, a fine, handsome actor, and his wife came backstage to meet the little girl who had taken first place. They recognized Mae's father as the former Brooklyn prizefighter.

"Everyone is so famous," Hal said.

"I only do amateur contests for practice," Mae bragged.

"How would you like to come with us?"

A professional!! Mae's eyes lit up and she accepted the offer before her father could speak. The Clarendons' show had children roles to play and most of the kids were famous. She went from $18 to $25 and then $30 a week. It was in these stock companies that Mae received proper training in both dramatic and comedy parts.

From age eight to eleven Mae played the Kentucky moonshiner's daughter, stopped the express train with an oil lamp when a bridge was washed out, was the poor little white slave in Chinatown and even did Shakespeare. She learned stage directions, dramatic effects, and most importantly, Mae paid attention to how the audience reacted. Fortunately for her, she did not have to learn the hard way or the wrong way. Mae learned the right way.

When Mae was 17, she was receiving a lot of attention from men and began working with Frank Wallace, a talented, lively, song and dance man. They danced and sang to the song *I Love It.* The dance was sultry, passionate and smooth and their act became a big hit. Frank was desperate to marry Mae.

"I love you."

"That sounds fine."

"Keep away from those men."

"They come to me."

One day an older prima donna on the show approached Mae. "Listen, honey, with all those men tomcatting around sooner or later something is going to happen. Marry Frank and be respectable."

Finally, Mae consented. "I'll marry you with one condition. You cannot tell a soul."

Mae wasn't in love so she slept in a separate bedroom. "It's a physical thing. You don't move my finer instincts."

"What are they, Mae?"

"I don't know yet but I must have them."

"You've got everything, Mae."

"We're talking about different things, Frank."

"But I love you, Mae."

"That's good."

Within weeks Mae ended both the partnership and a very short marriage.

By 1911, Mae had sung and danced on vaudeville tours all over America. It was time for New York. Appearing at a Sunday night concert at the Columbia Theatre, Florence Ziegfeld happened to be in the audience and he was impressed.

"I want you in my New York roof theatre."

"It's too big, too wide. I need people close to me."

"What's wrong with my roof for you?"

"I'm thinking of myself and how I would appear on your stage. I wouldn't be seen by the entire audience at the same time. People on one side of the orchestra floor can't see what was happening on the other side of the stage. The entire effect of my personality depends on audiences being able to see my facial expressions and to hear me properly."

"You intrigue me, Miss West."

"If you ever put the Follies into another theatre, I'd be glad to work for you, Mister Ziegfeld."

"Come up to my theatre during the day, Miss West, when no one is there and try the stage; perhaps you could get used to the place."

Mae said she would but didn't mean it. Her instincts were spot on and she knew she would be a fool to play on a stage that was not right for her. Mae went to see Ned Wayburn who also liked her act.

"What theatre would the show go into?" Mae asked.

"The Fulton Theatre on West 46th Street. Why?"

"Could I see the theatre?"

"Sure, if you wish."

"I'll be right back and let you know."

Ned was mystified. "This is a new one on me, Miss West... previewing a theatre."

"Wait till you get to know me better."

A porter was cleaning up and the doors were open. Mae walked in and saw gilt balconies and deep red boxes that hugged the stage. It was perfect. Mae went back to Wayburn's office.

"The theatre is fine and I'll do your show."

"Well, I better take you before you inspect the city."

Although playing a part on Broadway paid well, Mae was more interested in what her part would be... what material... what kind of songs would she sing?

Ned gave her a part to read.

"It's good, but I'd like to change a few things in it."

"We'll talk about it at rehearsal."

Mae especially liked the song They Are Irish but she wanted more verses than just the one. She decided to write two of them herself then went to the publishing company where another songwriter wrote three more. Because of some prop problems she was unable to rehearse the song, so she rehearsed it at the publisher's.

The show's producer was unaware Mae had significantly lengthened her part. "We decided to use the song as an entrance number for you. Wait until you see the blowtorch bit!"

Mae played dumb. There were going to be more surprises than a blowtorch.

Ned Wayburn called his new beautifully mounted, gorgeous costumed show A la Broadway and Hello Paris. It was opening September 11, 1911 and Mae West was an unknown. One of the producers Jesse Lasky, (who would later be head of Paramount Studios) was unsure if Mae could carry out the part. Mae was anxious for opening night. She wanted to get before an audience before Lasky could say she was out of the show.

Unlike Lasky, Ned was confident in Mae West. "What will you do if you should happen to get an encore performance?" Ned asked at dress rehearsal.

"I have an extra chorus ready for *They Are Irish*. Just tell the orchestra to play the chorus again, same tempo."

"When did we get an extra chorus?"

"You have been very busy, Mister W."

Opening night was wild and confusing. The first scene was a military act with 12 young men and 12 girls wearing spectacular costumes, doing a drill. At the end they would stand at attention for Mae's entrance. As soon as the military drill stopped, Mae West poured herself on stage and went to work, using all the stage tricks she had learned in stock training and vaudeville. No one had much faith in the song until Mae West took seven encores. It was a time of immigration and Mae sang each chorus in a different dialect. English, Dutch, Italian, Jewish and Irish, the crowd went wild as she acknowledged their homeland and welcomed them to America.

After that first number, the audience was booming with applause every time Mae appeared on stage. Ned Wayburn smiled and a dazed Mr. Lasky. Wiping his glasses, he had decided he liked Mae West after all.

Having received raving reviews, Mae was put in a star's dressing room the next evening.

There were some shining lights in the cast, notably Miss Mae West who danced in Turkish harem trousers in a most energetic, amusing and carefree manner. ~The New York Herald

Again there was some color and pretty movement in a Continental march by the chorus, and a girl named Mae West, hitherto unknown, pleased by her grotesquerie and a snappy way of singing and dancing." ~ The New York Times

"Mae West, as Maggie O'Hara, really put a little newness into her ragtime songs. She has a bit of a sense of nonsense, which is the very latest addition to wit." ~New York Tribune

At eighteen years old, Mae West was a smashing hit on Broadway and had a star's dressing room. Gentlemen lined up at the stage door and filled her dressing room with flowers and expensive trinkets that would make most girls swoon. But Mae still was not satisfied. There was a lot more she wanted and a lot more she wanted to try.

In November of 1911, Mae performed at the Winter Garden Theatre in the Schubert show Vera Violetta, where she gained a great deal of attention and excellent press reviews. Two boys from her previous show wanted to partner with Mae and form a vaudeville act. She liked the boys and after much persistence she finally agreed. Together they created Mae West and the Gerard Brothers.

The act required a higher class booking agent so, with a friendly referral, Mae and the boys walked into the office of Frank Bohm. This was the first time since she was ten years old that a man had not removed his hat in a gentlemanly gesture when she entered the room. This annoyed Mae greatly. She was so irritated she lost interest in the meeting altogether.

Without looking at her, Frank penciled her into a spot.

"You open in South Norwalk tomorrow night."

Mae just looked at him. She didn't care how much of a big shot he was; to her, he was just rude.

"I booked you for one night. And you don't get paid for it. I'll bring some theatre managers to look at the act. I will give you ten dollars in travelling expenses."

"You can keep the ten dollars," Mae said, holding her tongue from suggesting a part of his anatomy where he could put it. "We don't need it."

Frank looked directly at Mae.

"South Norwalk," said an anxious Gerard Brother, "tomorrow night… we'll be there!"

Leaving the office, Mae walked behind the agent's chair and, without saying a word, knocked his hat over his eyes.

The Gerard boys shivered in mock horror and looked worried. Frank was a big-time agent. "Gee, Mae, maybe we should have taken the ten dollars."

Mae laughed. "Don't worry boys. That ten will get us more from Mr. Frank Bohm."

The next evening Frank Bohm and Chris Brown, another big vaudeville agent, sat in the front row and watched the show. Later, they were all on the train headed back to New York.

"Mae, you got something," Frank said.

"You can say that again," Brown added.

The act was booked for $100 a week. Frank Bohm gave Mae a beautiful diamond ring and told her he wanted to get to know her better. They all wanted to get to know her better.

They took the act to New Haven, where she was labeled "Trouble" by the local bluenoses. The newspaper called her most outstanding quality, "that enchanting, seductive, sin-promising wriggle." The audience was crazy about Mae, especially the Yale boys who, after seeing her first performance, brought friends. Word spread and by the second performance, fifty hot-blooded male college students charged the stage singing Boola Boola. The plan was to repeat that action all week long.

With pressure from local moralists, Lou Garvey, the theatre manager, called Mae into his office. Firmly, but politely, he explained to the dancer that the act would have to be modified. "That is my act and that is the way I do it." There was no harm in it as far as she could see.

The next performance the Yale boys filled the auditorium threefold. When Mae West came on there was an expectant burst of applause and cries from the gallery. She flashed her dazzling smile and slid into a wriggle. It was the same wicked wriggle Garvey had censored that very afternoon and when the boys went wild, he turned purple with rage.

The act was called in. The Gerard boys looked worried but not Mae. When the management sputtered their anger she listened with a smile and unconcern.

"I couldn't help it," she said. When they fired her, Mae laughed, put her hand on her hip and wriggled out of the room."

The paper read: `Her wriggles cost Mae West her job. Curves in motion shock Lou Garvey at Palace. Whole Act fired.`

Mae never thought of herself as a sex symbol. She was just being her natural, seductive self. As long as her audience liked it, Mae had no intention of changing. Unique in her power, she possessed an instinctive sexual energy that made even the most harmless lines seem suggestive.

After the tour, Frank suggested she go solo. "I can get you $350 a week, Mae."

"I'm not objecting, honey."

Although it was hard for her to break the news to her friends, the Gerard boys took it well. Because of Mae, they were now making more than twice the money as they had before. "You're a great girl and a great act. It isn't what you say and do, Mae. It's how you say and do it."

Now that Mae was making good money, she decided to dress like she had never dressed before. A real show-lady, she went to the best dressmakers in New York. Mae bought a gown, slit dangerously up the thigh, made of solid rhinestones with alluring lines that clung to her body like skin. Shimmering like sparkling diamonds under the spotlight, the $540 dress looked like a million dollars.

Because of her creativity, Mae was becoming more and more popular, she also became more creative. Unlike many vaudeville acts that do the same routine for years, Mae West would perfect an act and then move on to something new when she was bored with it.

An earnest student of audiences, before a show, Mae would peek through the curtain, study her audience and read their temperament. Some audiences were more challenging than others. That's when Mae would turn up her flirting, winking, wriggling, and dazzling smile. Usually by the third song she was giving them encore after encore. Instinctively she knew how to connect, excite and spread a warm feeling throughout the theatre. Mae West genuinely loved her audiences and they adored her.

With the onset of the Great War, Mae recognized the change in what appealed to American audiences. Songs like *My Buddy* and *Over There* became popular. Waving the American flag with a patriotic flare seemed to help lift the spirits of the American people and sell war bonds in the effort to support the young men fighting on foreign soil. Songs about peace were avoided because people thought it favored the Germans. Bravery and courage were the theme of the day.

Comedy acts were more difficult to perform during wartime. Mae always had a nonchalant manner and an air of indifference; it was her style and she couldn't change it. People didn't know that on the inside, she was really worried about the audience's reaction. Mae never lost her patience and continually did her best to entertain. Sometimes she would adjust the mood, tempo and material of her act to comply with the temperament of her audience. A satisfied audience always was her only goal.

Mae was a master at suggestion and allowed her audience to fill in the blanks with their own imagination. She liked to open her act with a song called:

*I've Got A Style All My Own*
We were sitting on the couch – and then
The lights went out – and then

After finishing the song Mae would smile seductively and say, "It isn't what you do, it's how you do it" and the crowd would go crazy with applause.

Although ragtime was still popular, by 1918, jazz was the new sound. Segregation was prominent throughout America. In music and entertainment, white performers were recognizing and even attempting to imitate the unique talent of the "Negroes." Most "colored" folks were not allowed in theatres and when they were, it was to the highest balcony seats. They had dance moves whites could only hope to emulate. As the Roaring 20's emerged, the black folks' musical style and rhythms were becoming more and more popular, especially among the younger generation.

Vaudeville shows were allowed to have only one truly Negro act per night. To maintain their social status, Negroes were not allowed to wear fancy clothes when performing in white theatres. To acknowledge the talent and appeal of the Negro culture, white performers such as Al Jolson began to dress in tattered clothes when they performed. They even painted their faces black and their lips white to accentuate their mouths when they sang.

Mae West had great respect for the great talents of black performers. In October of 1918 she performed the song *Any Kind of Man* in Arthur Hammerstein's *Sometime* at the Schubert Theatre. It was in this show Mae first introduced "the shimmy," a dance the Chicago "colored" community called "the shimmy shawobble". She first saw it performed one night at the Majestic Theatre in Chicago. Although others try to take credit, it was Mae West who first danced the shimmy for a white audience in New York. The shimmy became popular in the 1920's.

By the 1920's, the show business Mae West had come to know and love was changing. With the onset of Prohibition, young Americans seemed to be spinning out of control and gangsters and bootleggers began invading the theatre-movie industry. Chorus girls, nightclubs and the glitter and glow of the theatre were appealing and speakeasies had become the new recreation on Broadway. Money was flowing and reckless living had become the norm.

Seeing the changes on Broadway, Mae had become more and more aware that vaudeville was slowly fading away. She began looking for a play; it couldn't be just any play. Mae was picky and the role had to be a perfect fit... something flirty, suggestive and funny. She looked at script after script. Nothing appealed to her and Mae was becoming more and more frustrated. She had gotten this far by being sexy, entertaining and funny. Mae West was not going to settle for anything less than a spectacular role in a spectacular play.

"Why worry about a play?' Mae's father said one day. "Let the producers find the play and do it. Then if it doesn't turn out too good, it will be their fault not yours. You can always try another one."

"That is just what I don't want to do. Whoever gets two real chances? I want to be sure I do it the first time. The play has got to be right for me or I would rather not do it at all."

Mae's mother was encouraging. "You always change your lines, Mae, and rewrite your songs. Why don't you write a play for yourself?"

Mae began contemplating her mother's words. While riding along Tenth Avenue one day, she thought of the sailors who were illegally importing bird-of-paradise feathers, very popular before they were banned. She saw two women, walking arm in arm with two sailors, wearing worn-out felt hats adorned with the colorful plumage of these tropical birds. This inspired Mae to write her first act.

Mae knew two rules of playwriting; write about what you know and make it entertaining. So she decided to write about her favorite subject SEX. For weeks she would write her ideas down on napkins, brochures or anything else that was handy. She read it to her mother and Jim Timony, Mae's lawyer and manager, when she finished.

"This is too damn good! We won't give it to the Schuberts. We'll do it ourselves," Jim declared. He immediately began making plans with Mae's mother to raise the funds.

Mae felt like she owed it to the Shuberts to at least let them look at it. The play department sent it back. This gave Mae the freedom to produce her new creation about a Montreal prostitute named Margie La Mont and the obstacles she had to overcome to reform and live a respectable life. To separate from her stage name Mae West, Mary Jane West chose Jane Mast as her penname.

Mae's next mission was to find the right director. She wanted a good, tough and seasoned stage director who knew all the staging tricks. Wanting the best, she approached one of Broadway's most successful hit makers.

"Who wrote this?' he asked.

"It's there some place."

He turned back to the title page. "Jane Mast? She's a new one on me; and the play is a new one on me too. You have everything in here but a merry-go-round. I don't get it. There are characters in the first act that don't come back in the second."

"Why should they? They're busy," Mae said.

"I'd like to take this with me and study it carefully. Perhaps suggest some changes."

"I don't want it changed."

"Could I just offer some suggestions?"

"I'm sorry, that's the only copy we have free and we have other appointments for readings."

"If you send me a copy, I'll give it some time."

"Some other time. Sorry."

That afternoon Mae had an appointment with another director. This one was a slow reader, a finger wetter.

"Who wrote this?"

"It's mine," Mae said tired of playing games.

"My dear child, this is a salacious play. Furthermore, you are going to have a jazz band in the second act and the star sings and dances with it? That is never done. You could have a few string instruments playing offstage, and a tenor singing a love song off-stage, while the star does a love scene on stage. You kill all your dramatic scenes."

"If you directed the play."

"I'm rejected??"

"You've done some fine plays, but you're mired in your own ways and it would be too hard for me to change you to my ideas. I know I am doing things in this play you have never done before. Thank you for your advice."

"Don't worry over your play, Miss West. No one will do it your way."

Jim began to worry. "Mae, these men know…"

"No Jim. These men are old-fashioned. We need a young director to do this. A man with… "

"We have one more appointment with a director named Edward Elsner. He has a great reputation."

"What's he done?"

"Henri Bernstein's The Thief, Peter Pan, Pauline Frederick's Within The Law, the Barrymores in a play about Queen Elizabeth…"

"Is he for us?"

"He has worked with some of the biggest stars on Broadway, Mae."

Mae and Jimmy decided to go to Elsner's latest production, a beautifully written play about World War I. They sat in a box overlooking what Mae surmised to be an older, conservative audience. Although she enjoyed the good qualities of the show, Mae did not see it as entertainment.

When Mae was introduced to Elsner during intermission, she thought he looked like a character straight out of Edger Allan Poe. Draped in a black overcoat he wore like a cape, he softly shook Mae's hand. His devilish smile was quirky, turning on and off as they spoke.

"My dear, Miss West, I am looking forward to reading your play tomorrow at 11 AM at the office." Mae half expected a puff of smoke, an odor of brimstone and the clap of a trap door.

"This guy is a good act in himself," Jimmy remarked.

"I've made up my mind. Even if he doesn't like my play or understand it, it won't make any difference to me. I am sure of my play and sure of myself. I haven't read all those scripts offered to me for nothing. My play is fresh, new and exciting. It is different in every way. And if it is directed in the way I have in mind I know I can't miss."

The next day Elsner arrived on time. Reaching into his pocket he grimaced, "Well this is a fine thing. My dear Miss West, without my glasses I just can't read a line. I shall phone home and have them sent over."

"Why bother? Shall I read it for you?"

"Oh would you? That will be fine."

"Sit down," Mae instructed. Mae began reading, looking for reactions at key lines. There would be that quick quirky smile. He even laughed out loud in the first act like Dracula asking for the cost of veal chops.

"Now get ready for Act II. I have a jazz band and I sing and dance to it."

"That should be amusing," he said straight-faced.

After she finished reading the second act, Mae asked, "Shall I read the third act or just explain it?"

"I want to hear every word and every syllable. By all means, read it!"

When she had finished, Elsner stood up and shouted, "By God! You've done it! You've got it! This is it!"

Jimmy entered the office and Mae smiled. "I think Mr. Elsner is our man."

Mae had found her director. Now all she needed was the money to produce what she considered her new hit play. A mutual friend who had worked in the theatre in Chicago introduced Mae to Ada and Minna Everleigh. The sisters had seen Mae West perform prior to their meeting and had been admirers from afar. After listening to Mae read the first act of her play, Minna and Ada agreed to be investors.

Comfortable with the subject of sex, the women understood each other on many different levels. Mae West and the Everleigh sisters immediately hit it off. After listening to Mae read the first act of her play, Minna and Ada were enthralled.

Ada nodded at Minna who was smiling from ear to ear.

"This is going to be sensational!" Minna declared.

"We will be happy to invest in your new play, Miss West," Ada stated with a friendly smile.

"Thank you, ladies. I promise I will not let you down."

CHAPTER 31

# Texas Guinan's

It was the end of The Ziegfeld Summer Follies. Richard had been working on a project for Paramount and Heather was again amazed of all the people he knew. In a few days Heather and Richard would return to California to start on the new picture.

Mae kept her sights on Richard. "Some people say the movie business is heading towards talkies. What do you think, Richard?"

"I think that's very possible, Miss West."

"I'm not interested in doing silent movies. Now talkies, that's a different story. Missy here wants to be an actress."

"Yeah, me and every other dame in this town," Missy laughed.

"Texas Guinan and I know a guy who is looking for someone to play the part of a chorus girl in his new play *The Noose*. He wants a real chorus girl. Guinan and I think Missy here will be perfect. She's going to audition next week."

"Well you're certainly pretty enough to be in movies, Miss Missy," Richard complimented.

"Mae has a unique quality," Heather bragged, turning the attention back to her.

"She's great!" Missy cheered. "I've never seen anyone work an audience like you can, Mae. What's your secret?"

"It's all about personality. That's why I won't do silent movies. If you don't have personality you'll never be a real star. Personality is the glitter that sends your little gleam across the footlights and the orchestra pit into that big black space where the audience is." "It's all about personality. That's why I won't do silent movies. If you don't have personality you'll never be a real star. Personality is the glitter that sends your little gleam across the footlights and the orchestra pit into that big black space where the audience is."

Captivated with Mae West, Richard listened to her with great admiration. She was seasoned, all right. Although his experience had been mostly in movies, he loved the theatre, where he had started his career working as a stagehand.

Mae continued. "Personality is what you as an individual radiates. It's a combination of thoughts and how you express them. A person with a great personality never has to act, he just does what he feels."

Mae looked at Heather. "It's love too. Love and respect for yourself first, then logically for others."

"Well said, my dear," Richard applauded. "Sam Warner is talking about talkies. They think they have found a way to match the voice with the actor. It looks bad when an actor's voice doesn't follow their mouths. Recording music on film isn't a problem because the sound doesn't have to exactly match."

"I won't do pantomime. I hope they figure out how to record the voice. That's the only way I will do movies," Mae expressed. "Right now

I have written a play for Broadway. I couldn't find a script I liked, so I wrote my own."

"What's the name of your play?" Richard asked.

"*The Albatross* is my working title for now. I have some others in mind. I'm thinking about calling it *SEX*," she flirted.

"That would be bold, Miss West," Richard grinned. "Very bold."

"Sex definitely sells," Heather laughed. "Ada and Minna made their millions doing just that. They think it's a great idea."

"What do you think about *SEX,* warm, dark and handsome?" Mae said smiling at Richard.

"I guess it depends on what you like."

Just then Texas Guinan appeared on the stage.

"HELLO SUCKERS! WELCOME TO TEXAS GUINAN'S!"

Everyone cheered.

"I hope all you bread and butter men aren't lettin' the ladies get thirsty. I see my good friend Mae West is here. C'mon up honey and give us a song."

Richard watched as Mae West made her way to the stage. "Heather, I do not believe I have ever seen anyone walk like that! What an intriguing woman."

"She is somethin'," Heather grinned. "It's gonna hurt her feelings when she finds out that you are not available for what she has to offer."

"I wish I could walk like that," he grinned.

Standing in the center of the stage, Mae paused. "*A Good Man Is Hard To Find* key of A," she instructed the band. "Make it sexy. There's a guy here I wanna impress."

Mae waited. She wasn't going to sing a note until she had everyone's attention.

Within a minute the room was quiet. Mae looked at the crowd and turned on her flirty self. "It's not the men in my life, it's the life in my men," she smiled.

Looking at a gentleman standing close to the stage, Mae pointed and grinned. "Is that a pistol in your pocket, honey, or are ya just glad to see me?"

Everyone in the room laughed and cheered.

Mae nodded at the orchestra. Moving her hips to the rhythm of the intro, she looked straight at Richard and smiled her glorious smile. Like a beacon radiating with a pulse, Mae's complete aura was sparkling brighter than her $5,000 diamond bracelet. With her natural seductive flare, Mae West belted out the first few lines of *her* version of the 1919 hit song.

"*A hard man is good to find… you always get the other kind...*"

And the crowd went wild!

## CHAPTER 32

# Back in Hollywood

Returning to her home in California, Heather was disheartened to find that the Hotel Redondo was no longer there. Ruby was at the station to meet her train.

"I knew I would be sad to see that fine hotel go down, Heather… so many wonderful memories of Mickey there. I just didn't realize I would be this sad. I'm glad you're home."

"I appreciate you staying in the house while I was gone," Heather said. "How is the house in Palos Verdes coming along?"

"As good as can be expected, I guess. It probably would go faster if I wasn't so picky," Ruby smiled.

Heather was happy to be back in California; however, she was enamored with the bright lights of Broadway. Singing on a big stage to hundreds of people at a time in the Ziegfeld Summer Follies was far more fulfilling than acting for a camera crew. As a true artist, Heather always felt most purposeful on nights she knew she had prompted an emotional response from the audience hidden within the vast darkness of the theatre.

It was as if there was a magic veil between them, each with an invitation welcoming the other to a special event.

Heather was glad to be working with Richard again. She felt that they were soul mates, both understanding and appreciating the talents of the other. Although she was grateful she was making a living acting in silent films in Hollywood, she knew in her heart that working in New York was where she truly loved to be.

On a crisp cool October afternoon in California after a long day of shooting, Heather found a package waiting for her at her bungalow. She squealed with delight when she opened it and quickly phoned Richard.

"Richard! Quick! Come over here now. Ginger sent her new record." Heather was bubbling over with excitement.

"I'm already on my way. I have something I need to discuss with you."

Heather had already played the record five times when Richard pulled up to Heather's bungalow. Hearing the deep sultry sound of Ginger's voice soulfully singing on the phonograph, he grinned. "It ain't the first time, it ain't the worse time, but it's the last time you'll break my heart…"

"Ginger and Harmony wrote this song, Richard. Listen!"

Gennet Records in Richmond, Indiana had invited Mozella's brother Duke, Ginger and a group of jazz musician friends from New Orleans to record. The company had already made records with other New Orleans artists including Jelly Roll Morton, The Rhythm Kings and a group called Oliver's Creole Jazz Band that featured a coronet player by the name of Louis Armstrong.

"She's really good," Richard said, nodding his head.

"Good? She's amazing! I am so happy for her. She's going on tour with the band. They call themselves Ginger and The Bayou Boys."

"Isn't she the friend who went with you to Bill Stein's office?"

"Yes. The one and only," Heather laughed. "I forgot I told you about that."

"I'd like to meet her someday."

"Richard, I think I would like to go back to New York."

"I knew you would. That's what I want to talk to you about. There is nothing like a live audience."

"Heather, Sam Warner is going to make a talkie with Al Jolson. It's called The Jazz Singer. It's about a Jewish cantor who has to choose between honoring his father's wish to sing in the temple for Yom Kipper or having his big break on Broadway."

"Really? They have the technology? Sounds fantastic."

"If movies do go to talkies, it will change everything, Heather. It will be good for some but others will get left behind. For now, I think Broadway is a good fit for you. I have a friend who has written a new musical he calls *Steamboat Annie*. It's a period story about a southern belle who falls in love with a gambler and their adventures on the Mississippi River."

"Sounds like fun."

"My friend saw you perform at the Summer Follies and you made quite an impression on him. He's pitching the musical now and the Shuberts are interested in producing the project."

"Does that mean I need to learn how to speak southern?" Heather cooed, in a singsong style sounding just like a lady who had grown up on a Georgia plantation.

"Like I said, Heather, you are perfect for the role," Richard laughed.

"Call your friend," Heather gleamed.

## CHAPTER 33

# Gambler's Gold

A bright, blue Southern California morning at Universal Studios welcomed the first day of shooting Heather Diamond's new film *Gambler's Gold*. Heather played the part of Sarah Noble, a woman trying to survive in a Texas cattle town after her husband's death.

Heather had spent the night in her bungalow so she would be ready at dawn for a shoot. As she witnessed the bright orange glow of light appear in the east, Heather took a deep breath and with a gust of stirring emotion bursting from her heart, raised her arms to the sky and whispered, "Thank you!"

Twirling, laughing and imitating some of the dance steps from the Follies, Heather was unaware that someone had been watching her enjoying the show. When she stopped she heard the gentle applause.

"Lovely, my dear. Simply lovely."

"Wyatt Earp, what in the world are you doing here so early? I sure am glad to see you," she said, hugging her friend.

"I've missed you, Heather," he said, kissing her forehead. "Let's go get some breakfast when your shoot is over," he grinned as he put his arm around her. "I want to hear all about your adventures in New York."

"It's so much different in front of a live audience, Wyatt," she said excitedly with her bright eyes shimmering, catching the early morning light. "I sang in the Ziegfeld Follies for hundreds of people at a time. It's amazing how someone on the stage can transfer emotion through music."

"I'm not afraid of much," Wyatt laughed, "but I don't know how I'd feel about hundreds of people watching me on a stage expecting me to entertain them."

"I guess we all do what we do," Heather grinned. "How is Sexy Sadie?"

"She's fine. Have you seen Ruby lately?"

"She just built a house in Palos Verdes. We're like family."

"Ruby's a good woman," Wyatt smiled. You should have seen Ruby in her day. She was a real beauty."

"She still is," Heather smiled. "It's funny… when I'm in New York I like being there and when I'm in California I like being here. Both are so different but I really can't say which one I like better."

"I've been a lot of places, Heather, and I have certainly done a lot of things. Some I'm not real proud of and would never do again. But then there are those glorious moments that make life worth living."

"Like what?"

"Like now. At my age every now is a gift," he laughed.

"You have so many stories, Wyatt."

"Heather, I've been a buffalo hunter, a sheriff, a gambler, a saloon-keeper, a soldier and a constable. I'd like to think I was a pretty good lover, too."

"Any regrets?"

"Not really. Mistakes are the best teachers. Life is a journey, Heather, and mine has been a colorful one. I believe pretty women are my most favorite things of all."

Wyatt's eyes were sparkling. Heather knew he liked her. Although there were many years between them, there was an attraction neither of them could deny.

"Do you believe in past lives, Wyatt?"

"Hmm. Never really thought about it. Sadie says I'm like a cat with nine lives. All those gunfights I've been in, I should be dead. Funny thing about that... every time I was in a rough spot I never once considered that I might not survive. Guess it was just never my time to die."

"Maybe we knew each other in another life, Wyatt. I believe we did. I love you in a familiar kind of way. From the first day we met, I felt like I already knew you."

"I need to think about that one, Heather. Who knows? I like the thought of second chances," he grinned with that gleam Heather had come to love so much.

*Gambler's Gold* was Heather's favorite film to date. Wyatt Earp came every day of filming. His consulting was invaluable to the movie. Not only did he enjoy watching Heather work, he enjoyed the consulting because the plot reminded him so much of his gambling days in Texas when he had befriended Doc Holliday.

"That's a wrap," became Heather's favorite three words. Her part in *Gambler's Gold* was extremely demanding and after long days of hard work and shooting, Heather was exhausted. When her part was finally finished, she decided to go home to Redondo and do nothing but sit by the beach and write for the next three weeks. Putting her make-believe stories on paper had become her favorite past time.

Late that afternoon, as the sun was descending and colorful patterns of yellow and orange began to fill the sky, Heather saw a familiar sight on the beach. It was Giorgio joyfully painting another masterpiece. As if expecting her, he smiled and began waving his arms to join him.

Surprised by how happy she was to see him, Heather ran excitedly down the stairs. The last time she saw him he was going home to Italy and she was on her way to New York.

Genuinely happy to see each other, the two lovers embraced and Giorgio kissed her deeply. It was as if only a moment had passed since they were in each other's arms. Although Heather tried to protect her heart by immersing herself in her work, she had to admit she had thought of Giorgio often, wondering if she would ever see him again.

"Amore!" His dark eyes and glorious smile filled Heather's eyes. To her surprise, heat was flashing throughout her body like lightening in a Texas rainstorm. Overcome with desire, she wanted Giorgio to make love to her and feel his warmth and passion all over her. She wanted it NOW.

"Giorgio! What a lovely painting. Let's go to the house."

"Don't you want to see…?"

"Let's go to the house."

Giorgio and Heather could not get their clothes off fast enough. Within minutes, both bodies simultaneously burst into ecstasy launching their souls somewhere into a cosmic existence. For a seemingly endless moment, the two lovers trembled like a powerful earthquake…then fell away to enjoy the satisfying aftermath of their fiery passion.

"I've missed you, Giorgio. I didn't really know it until now, but I have really missed you."

"Amore. Not one day goes by when I do not breathe a hundred thoughts of you. I want you to come to Italy with me. We'll drink the wine from my family vineyard and explore the beautiful towns and hills of Tuscany. There are so many things I wish to show you, Amore. I love you."

These might be Heather's new three favorite words, at least when she heard Giorgio say them.

"I think I love you too, Giorgio. Strange… but I really think I do."

Giorgio and Heather made love again…then again…then again…then again…then again…then again…as the gentle waves broke along the golden shoreline.

The next morning Heather awoke with Giorgio smiling at her. "Bella, bella," he whispered kissing her on both cheeks. I love to watch you sleep. Today you meet my Aunt Anna."

Needless to say, Heather was more than surprised when the car drove into Ruby's driveway.

"What?? Ruby is your aunt?"

"Ruby? My aunt's name is Anna Maria."

They found Ruby sitting in her favorite chair gazing at the ocean.

"This is the woman I told you about, Zia" Giorgio expressed. "Heather is the woman I love."

*April 5, 1926*
*Dear Miss Pearl,*
*I am in love with the most wonderful Italian man. His name is Giorgio. Handsome, caring, fun, exciting, passionate, being with him fills my heart and soul. He paints. I met him on the beach in California. At first there was no denying we were attracted to each other but I do not believe either of us expected to fall in love. Both of us agree that it happened the very first moment our eyes met.*
*He took me to Italy to meet his family. They have a vineyard in the Tuscan hills that has been in their family for centuries. The train ride from Florence to Rome was breathtaking and we visited Vinci, Assisi, Capri, Sorrento, and the Amalfi Coast. I was pleasantly surprised to learn that Carlo Collodi who wrote "The Adventures of Pinocchio," is a distant cousin of Giorgio's family. It happens to be my favorite children's story! The town of Collodi is named after him.*
*Being in Tuscany filled my soul. I believe the land holds the spirit of the Renaissance. You should see the art! The Della Robias in Pistoia, Leonardo da Vinci's work and Michelangelo's "David" is a sight to behold. Everything was breathtaking.*
*Giorgio's family is partners with his aunt's vineyard in California. His aunt is my best friend in California. It was a strange coincidence. Because of Prohibition the grape business is doing very well. Homemade wine seems to be very popular.*
*When I return to New York I will begin rehearsals for Steamboat Annie. I am very excited about the show. Giorgio has a cousin in New York who has an art gallery in Chelsea, not too far from where Ada and Minna live. He will be having a show for Giorgio this summer. I would love it if you could come.*
*Sometimes I want to pinch myself to see if I am dreaming, Miss Pearl. I am so blessed. Give my love to Mozella and Katie. I miss you all and you are always on my heart.*
*Lovingly yours,*
*Heather*

*May 4, 1926*
*My Dearest Heather,*
*How I enjoyed your letter; in fact it made me cry. I read it several times before I finally laid it down. The same thing happened to me when I met Robert McKnight. It felt as if all time had stopped and we were the only two people in the room. He asked me to dance and when he touched me I felt complete, a feeling I will not forget but will never experience again in this lifetime. We read each other's minds and felt each other's hearts. How I loved him.*
*Our son Michael married Eloise. We just learned she is expecting a baby; now my son David tells us he is also getting married. Both boys are talking about building a new home on the ranch.*
*I have spoken to Mozella about going to New York. She really wants to see Ada and Minna, so we are making plans to see your show and pay the Everleigh sisters a visit. Madeline has invited us to stay with her and Elizabeth again. Sarah's Aunt Katherine will take care of Miss Pearl's while we are gone.*
*Do you remember that funny little lady Miss Comstock? She brought her new baby to the house last week. She has a precious little girl she calls Susie. Although I was happy to hear about my new expected grandchild, looking into Susie's sweet little face made my heart jump knowing I will be holding our grandbaby in my arms next Christmas. I just wish Robert were still here to see.*
*The oil boom is growing by leaps and bounds. Everyone is especially excited about the discovery on the Yates Ranch. New little towns are popping up everywhere in West Texas and it has been exciting to be financially a part of it.*
*Again let me express how very happy I am for your success and the fact you are in love. I will see you soon my dear. Please give my best to Ada and Minna when you see them. Please do not tell them about Mozella coming. We want it to be a surprise. The brightest of blessings to you, my dear.*
*Everly yours, Victoria Pearl*

Mae West - 1926 - Broadway star

CHAPTER 34

# Sex

In the spring of 1926, Heather was in New York rehearsing for *Steamboat Annie*, Harmony was on a concert tour in Europe and Mae West had begun rehearsals for her new play. All the business part and fundraising had been done and the cast had been carefully selected. It was time now for the slow, hard work, the days and nights in a cold empty theatre, the dust, work lights, confusion, run-throughs and the pure agony of preparing a play. Mae found that her director Elsner stimulated her creativity.

"Now right here – we need something."

"Do you mean the first walk-on…new lines?"

Elsner would dramatically raise his hands. "Yes… it's not quite… it has to be…mmm…rrruff! It's got to reach a height. But with no dialogue."

Elsner's challenges always made Mae think. She finally figured out he was hunting for a surprise, the unexpected. He had complete respect and confidence in Mae's talents. The brilliant director craved originality and Mae would produce a brilliant solution.

By the second week Elsner gave Mae the reins to make any new changes she felt could work better. They worked well together, as if they were performing a tango with each aware of the other's lead.

"What should I do here?" Mae asked.

"Just what you are doing, the arms out, the slow sway of the hips… that's great!"

"I didn't do anything I don't usually do."

"Oh yes you did."

"I was not aware of it."

"I want natural acting, your original mannerisms, a particular sultry walk and good timing. You don't even know you have these qualities. I recognize them and I will not change them. I only want to highlight them."

By the third week of rehearsals, Elsner was in full appreciation of Mae's natural talent. "I have directed a good many women. The good ones have a unique quality that makes them a star."

"What have I got?"

"You have a quality – a strangely amusing quality I have never found in any of these other women. You have a definite sexual quality, gay and unrepressed. It evens mocks your personality."

"A self-mocking sexual quality? Does it overshadow the part?"

Elsner grinned his Dracula grin. "You reek with it. You have it all over you."

"All over me?"

"In your eyes, your mouth, your voice, your body movement…"

"That's just my vaudeville style."

"Don't lose it. It's natural with you. You don't have to act it or try to be that way. You are just *it*."

"That's just fine. Let's get on with the play."

By the fourth week they needed a definite title. Mae had made a decision. "I want a one-word title. The title is *SEX*."

"*Sex?* If only we dared." Elsner burst out in laughter.

"We will." Mae had made up her mind.

Broadway was full of hit shows that season and finding a theatre was going to be a challenge. Everything from 39th to 48th Street was already taken. Harry Cort who managed Daly's Theatre on 63rd Street agreed to take the play on a percentage basis.

"That means you like it?"

"That means I'm willing to take a gamble."

"You think we can draw people that far uptown?"

"I can take a loss or make money."

The show was ready for a break-in date. This is when the play is performed before a live audience to work out the rough edges. It was decided that the play would be shown in New London, Connecticut. The theatre was old and had been converted to a movie theatre. It had two balconies, box seats and musty drapes. The company did a full rehearsal with costumes and scenery.

"How are things coming at the box office?" Jimmy asked.

The theatre manager was a surly old grump. "Not coming at all. The title is scaring them away. Nobody in this town will buy tickets for a show with the title *SEX*. You better change that challenge right away. We don't talk about sex hereabouts and we don't put it on signs."

"That's a title for Broadway," Mae informed.

"Well, you better think of something less on people's minds."

It was curtain time. The manager came backstage. "Just as I said, they ain't coming in. About 80 people in the theatre tonight and you can blame it on the New York title."

"Where is the audience…in the orchestra?" Mae asked.

"Nope. They're all over the house."

"Get them all down front so I can see them."

"Give people that bought gallery seats, the first row orchestra??"

"No, give them the third row."

"That is still giving them a $3.00 seat for 85 cents."

"The trouble with you is you have no sense of humor."

"I can't change the house policy just to be funny."

"Jim, go out there and get all those people sitting in the front rows."

"But why? It still will be too empty."

"We'll never get a reaction on this show if they spread all over the theatre like they are now. I want real faces down front."

"This old guy isn't going for it."

"Tell him we won't raise the curtain until he does. I MEAN IT!"

The curtain went up to 85 people. Every laugh or reaction Mae wanted, she got. Among the small group of satisfied customers were two of the top drama critics from New York as well as reporters from New London.

When it was over Jim came backstage. "The show played fine. It's a hit."

"Wait till we see some reviews," Mae said.

"Elsner came in wearing his bat coat. "It needs a little tightening but it's good. It's great! Don't tell me the critics haven't been to bat yet. They'll love it."

The reviews were very good.

"Just wait till word of mouth spreads it around," Jim grinned.

Mae refused to be cheered up. "I have never played to 85 customers before."

The next day was a Saturday matinee. There was a huge line of people two and three deep wrapped around the block. Most of them were sailors.

"What's happening? Is there a war on? What are all these sailors doing here?" Mae exclaimed.

"There must be a naval base in town," Jim said.

"New London? Why of course," Mae smiled.

The theatre manager was looking for every chair he could get his hands on. "Something has happened to this town. We're putting people up in the boxes that don't have any chairs because there hasn't been a box seat sold for ten years."

"Get all the chairs you can," Mae said.

"Some of the stagehands that lived nearby went to get their dining room chairs. I'll hold the show until 3:15."

"And you said it was a bad title."

"I forgot about sailors."

Cheering sailors packed the balconies and brave civilians packed the gallery and the orchestra. The show was a riot when played to a packed house. Harry Cort from Daly's Theatre came to the night show. "I want this as soon as I can get it to New York."

The grumpy old theatre manager begged to keep the show at least another week. Cort paid off his current show and *SEX* began playing the following week.

Opening night was sensational but the newspapers refused to print their ads. The word "sex" was taboo unless in phrases like "opposite sex" or "the fair sex."

Mae suggested they hire "snipers" to paste up posters and pass out one-sheets and brochures. "Paste one of these on anyone you see standing still or looking in a storefront window," Mae instructed.

Taxis carried a sign that read: HEATED MAE WEST IN *SEX* – DALY'S 63rd Street Theatre.

The second week of the show, the Chanin Theatre Corporation offered Harry Cort $50,000 to bring the show to their theatres.

*SEX* was on its way to becoming a cash cow and Ada and Minna Everleigh were thrilled.

CHAPTER 35

# The Art Gallery

"Mozella!"

"Hello, Miss Ada," Mozella said. "Miss Minna."

"I can hardly believe my eyes. Oh my goodness! Mozella!" Minna exclaimed.

Victoria Pearl and Madeline watched as happy tears fell and warm affectionate hugs exchanged among the three women. The friendship dated back to 1898 when the sisters opened their first brothel in Omaha, Nebraska. Ada and Minna had brought Mozella with them to run the staff when they opened the Everleigh Club in Chicago. They always treated her like family.

"*John: Chapter 4, Beloved let us love one another, for love is of God,*" Mozella exclaimed.

"You are still quoting the Bible, Mozella?" Ada laughed. "Oh how I have missed you, my dear."

"Yes Ma'am. Looky here…we brought groceries."

"What? But we wanted to take you out…" Ada said.

"I can't go with you to any restaurants, Miss Ada. Besides, I remembered you always liked my cooking. I brought fixins to make your favorite foods: fried chicken, mashed potatoes, peas and carrots…I even found what I need to make you some cornbread and apple pie."

"We will do it together," Minna insisted. "We are capable women. Let us all go to the kitchen."

"Sounds delightful," Madeline said.

The five women spent all afternoon cooking, drinking champagne, and reminiscing about their days in Chicago. Their hearts were full, laughing and reminiscing. The conversation about Robert was comforting for Victoria and all would remember the day fondly for the rest of their lives.

After enjoying a delicious meal, the ladies retired into the parlor. "I'll clean the dishes," Mozella offered.

"You most certainly will not," Ada said. "We already have someone to take care of that. You are our guest, Mozella."

"Have you seen *Steamboat Annie*?" Victoria asked.

"Yes we have," Ada smiled. "Heather is quite a talent. It has been a joy being involved in her career. I was moved to tears when Heather sang *Shenandoah*; it reminded me of my childhood. Father loved to sing that song."

"Some of the girls are coming to town to see the show," Victoria said.

"Minna smiled. "I would love to meet them."

"Ginger is a recording artist. Lucy and Linda, whom we call Redbird, are in the import business in Houston, Texas."

"Do you remember our friend Mae West from Harmony's recital, Victoria?" Minna asked.

"Mae West is not an easy woman to forget," Victoria commented.

"We have invested in her new play SEX."

"SEX?" Victoria laughed.

"SEX," Ada reaffirmed. "The play is a huge hit and is taking Broadway by storm."

"Because of the show's title the newspapers will not allow them to advertise so Mae made sure her fliers were posted all over town. She told us anyone in the city that would stand still for more than seven seconds just might have a poster glued to their back," Minna laughed.

"Mae is a funny girl. It took just a few weeks of word of mouth for this to spread like wild fire. *SEX* is playing to packed houses now," Ada exclaimed. "It turned out to be a good investment despite the controversy."

"I suppose you can say that we are in the business of selling *SEX* again," Minna laughed. "You must go see it while you are in town. Mae is quite sensational in it."

"We can go this weekend, Victoria," Madeline suggested. "I am sure my sister Elizabeth would like to go."

"Mozella, why don't you spend a few days with us?" Minna invited.

"Oh yes, Mozella, please do," Ada said earnestly.

"That is a lovely idea," Madeline confirmed.

"I will under one condition," Mozella insisted. "That is that I do the cookin!"

The train from Texas pulled into Grand Central Station the next morning. Lucy telephoned Heather to let her know they had arrived.

"Redbird and I are staying at the Drake Hotel."

"Good deal. I will be over in an hour," Heather said.

Standing 21 stories high on the corner of Park Avenue and 56th Street, the brand new Drake Hotel was proud of its spacious, luxurious rooms and suites; it even had refrigeration. Located in central Manhattan, the Drake Hotel would serve the friends perfectly as a glorious place to spend two memorable weeks in New York City.

"Harmony!" Lucy cried, as Heather and Harmony entered the plush suite. "I didn't know you were in town!"

Like schoolgirls at a sorority reunion, the friends danced around the room, squealing and hugging each other. When everyone had settled down, another surprise popped out.

"Hello everyone! Happy Harvey is here!"

"Harvey!" Heather cried and again the squealing and hugging resumed.

"Of course I came. I would not have missed it for the world. Now Heather and Harmony, I insist you stay with us. I have rented two adjoining suites so you can all be together. My room is on the floor below."

"Thank you, Harvey."

"You know how I love my Lady Pearls!"

The next evening Heather had arranged for everyone to sit in a box seat to enjoy *Steamboat Annie*. Harvey laughed hysterically at the funny parts and wept like a baby during the dramatic scenes of the show. By the happy ending his handkerchief was completely soaked with tears. After the show in Heather's dressing room, Harvey was still wiping his eyes.

"I loved it," Harvey said with a sob.

"You were fabulous," Lucy exclaimed.

"I am so proud of you," Redbird exclaimed. "You are good in your movies, Heather, but you absolutely sparkle and shine on the stage."

"Twinkle, twinkle little star, how I wonder what you are, up above the world so high, like a diamond in the sky," Ginger grinned.

"Ginger was the one who gave me the idea to use Diamond as my stage name by reciting that poem," Heather announced.

"So that's why you are known as Heather Diamond," Harvey said. "Very clever and appropriate indeed.

"Too bad Mozella couldn't see this," Ginger said.

"I will give Mozella a private show."

"Mozella is staying with Ada and Minna while we are here," Victoria informed her.

"I guess it's just as well," Harmony said. "The Negroes have their own hotels, restaurants and speakeasies."

"I don't like it," Ginger pouted.

"Let's go back to the hotel," Heather suggested.

"Sounds good to me," Ginger said.

Just then another surprise walked into the dressing room.

"Richard! Everyone, this is my friend and mentor, Richard. He is the reason I am in *Steamboat Annie*. Richard has worked with me on all my films and knows everyone who is anyone in the movie business. Richard, these are my friends: Ginger, Redbird, Lucy, you already know Harmony and this is Harvey Rochester."

"Very nice to meet all of you. Now I can match names with faces. Heather talks about you all the time."

Harvey's heart was beating a little faster and he became unusually quiet. "Calm down, Harvey," he said to himself. "Try to be cool even though he is the most handsome man you have ever had the privilege to feast your eyes upon."

"What are you doing in town?" Heather asked.

"Valentino is here promoting his new movie *Son of the Sheik*. I am here to support him. He hasn't been well lately."

"Rudolph Valentino?" Redbird exclaimed.

"The one and only," Richard smiled. "They are having a party for him at Texas Guinan's this Sunday. You all should go."

"We'll be there," Harvey blurted out.

"I hear your friend Mae West is making a killing with her new play *SEX*," Richard cheered.

"*SEX* is a hit," Heather bragged. "God, I love that woman. She's got more hutzpah than a Marine drill-sergeant."

"I was thinking about going Friday night."

"I'm in!" Harvey exclaimed.

'Let's all go," Ginger laughed. "I wanna see what a woman with balls like a Marine drill-sergeant looks like."

Heather called Mae and reserved orchestra seats at Daly's Theatre for her friends. Harvey made it a point to sit next to Richard. Sexy, sassy and hysterically funny, Mae was especially so on this evening.

"I wish I could walk like that," Richard remarked.

"I wish I could dress like that," Harvey commented. "Oh my goodness, that woman is something. Love her, Love Her, LOVE HER."

"Goodness has nothing to do with it," Richard said.

"What?"

"I heard her say it at Guinan's one night. Goodness has nothing to do with it," he repeated.

Mae made sure the group had backstage passes and a friendly stagehand led them to her dressing room. The room was adorned with huge bouquets of colorful flowers from her many admirers, filling it with a pleasant fragrance of fresh roses.

Mae took Richard to the side. "Hey there, warm, dark and handsome. Heather gave me the lowdown on you, honey. Let me know if you ever decide to like girls. I wanna be first."

"I will keep that in mind, Miss West," Richard smiled.

"Nice to see you again Miss Victoria Pearl," Mae said warmly.

"This is Harmony, Ginger, Lucy and Redbird," Victoria said.

"Hello girls. Glad you're here.

"And this is Harvey Rochester."

"You look familiar, honey."

"I like to visit New York and sing a little..."

"Ah, yes. I have seen you perform. I enjoyed you; however, I believe you were dressed much differently?"

"I love to sparkle and shine," Harvey blushed.

Mae winked at Harvey then turned to Victoria. "You knew Minna and Ada in Chicago, didn't you?"

"I did."

"Like I told Heather, any friend of theirs is a friend of mine," she grinned.

"Thank you, Miss West."

"Call me Mae, Honey."

"Loved your show, Miss West." Harvey exclaimed. "Loved it, Loved It, LOVED IT!"

"That's good."

"Are you going to the party for Rudolph Valentino at Texas Guinan's Sunday night," Richard asked.

"I am. Heather says you are friends with Valentino."

Richard nodded his head.

"Figures," Mae said, winking at Harvey. "See ya on Sunday, everyone."

When Sunday came, Victoria Pearl decided to spend her evening with Ada, Minna and Madeline and Mozella. Everyone else was eager to see the famous heartthrob of the silent screen. When Richard introduced Rudolph Valentino to Heather and her friends, Redbird felt herself swoon into a state of sexual intoxication.

Harvey had the same reaction.

Texas Guinan greeted the crowd with her standard, "HELLO SUCKERS!" Guinan was especially happy to hear that Lucy and Redbird were native Texans and spent much of the night visiting with them like they were old friends.

"Texas is God's country," Guinan told the girls. "I'd go back in a heartbeat if not for the money and the mobsters. In the last year we've made over $700,000 dollars. I don't get it. These suckers come in and pay for watered down whiskey and sparkling cider. I guess it's good for now or at least as long as it lasts. Personally, I'd like to retire and just go back to Texas. I will one day; hopefully it will be sooner than later."

For the next few days, Heather took her friends around the city. They took walks through Central Park and visited Macy's Department Store. Richard's wealthy friend from the Hamptons threw a big party for Valentino. He invited Heather and her friends to join them.

Overlooking the water, the mansion was magnificent and could very well have been the inspiration for F. Scott Fitzgerald's The Great Gatsby. Those who attended were an interesting lot. There were celebrities, movie moguls and local residents, some impressive, some impressed and some wanting to impress by acting bored and unimpressed. Then there were those who were genuinely happy and those who did their best to pretend they were happy and in full control of their lives. Sophisticated and elegantly dressed, the girls were a huge hit at the party, impressed and genuinely happy to be together.

They visited Coney Island and took a drive through the woods outside the city. Although the sightseeing was good, the best moments of the trip were spent in the suites of the Drake Hotel. Harmony, Heather, Lucy, Redbird and Ginger spent most late evenings talking until the sun finally told them it was time to go to bed.

"I miss us," Redbird said one evening.

"Me too," Ginger said.

"I think I'm in love," Heather said.

"In love?" Lucy asked.

"I met him on the beach in California. He's an artist…Italian…handsome and the best lover I have ever known. It's almost magical. He took me to Italy to meet his family. They have a winery and grow grapes. I love him," Heather sighed. "He calls me, Amore."

"What about your career? What about…" Lucy asked.

"Things will work out if they are supposed to, Lucy. All I know is that right now I am in love. I have not told anyone except Miss Pearl and my friend Ruby in California. Richard doesn't even know."

"We can't help who we love, Heather. I'm hopelessly in love with Sam," Ginger sighed.

"You've been in love with Sam for a long time, Ginger," Redbird expressed. "Everyone at Miss Pearl's knows it."

"I remember when he would show up, the two of you would disappear for days. Mozella would leave food outside your door," Redbird laughed.

"Only man in my life who makes me feel like I might have a heart 'cause it leaps when I see him and it aches when he goes away. I try not to think of him too much."

"I'm too busy to be in love," Redbird said.

"And I'm having too much fun traveling around the world with Harvey. He goes on buying trips with me," Lucy said. "We've been everywhere."

"I was in love," Harmony said. When David was killed in the Great War, I thought I would die. Now all I have is my music. The joy of his memory and the pain of missing him has helped me create some of my best compositions."

"I surely was not looking to fall in love with anyone. It just happened. Would you like to meet him?" Heather asked.

"Sure," Lucy said.

"His cousin Eduardo has an art gallery in Chelsea and he is going to give him a show next week."

"Sounds fun," Redbird said. "I want to go."

"We all want to go," Harmony declared.

"I want to go to Harlem," Ginger announced. "I want to take Mozella to the Cotton Club."

"Ginger, the Cotton Club is whites only," Harmony informed her.

"Damn… in Harlem? This black-white thing really gets on my nerves," Ginger fretted. "Jazz music started in Storyville in the brothels. Got its name from the jasmine perfume the sporting ladies used to wear. Jazz music is black and white mix and as far as I'm concerned, mostly black, because they can pull the soul out from deep inside."

"That reminds me, Ginger. Congratulations on your big hit," Redbird complimented. "We are so proud of you."

"Thanks. I wrote it for Sam. Harmony and I wrote it together. Gennet is releasing another song I wrote next month. It's called *This Night Ain't Over Yet.* Wrote that one for him too," she sighed.

"I wrote a song about Suzy Poontang," Harmony chirped trying to lighten the mood.

"Miss Pearl's Suzy Poontang?" Lucy laughed.

"The one and only."

"Sing it, Harmony," Heather requested.

"Ok. Here goes."

*Suzy Poontang came from China to Chicago way*
*When the men would come and see her*
*She would smile and say*
*If you give me five more dollars I will give to you*
*A magnifying glass to gaze upon my rose tattoo*
*Oh Suzy was famous for her roses*
*A clever girl was she*
*Beautiful roses a work of art*
*For the gentlemen callers to see*

(Everyone laughed)

*A wealthy man heard about the talent she possessed*
*She became an Everleigh butterfly at the man's request*

*Susie took the man up the stairs for an hour of delight*
*He was so impressed that he proposed to her that night*
*Suzy Poontang's famous story spread for miles around*
*How the clever girl from China came to live uptown*
*In a mansion in Chicago her dreams had all come true*
*All because she showed the gentlemen her rose tattoo!*

"I love it!" Ginger cried.

"Very clever, Harmony. I remember the day Miss Pearl told us that story," Heather smiled.

"We were on a picnic," Redbird said.

"In Christoval by the river," Lucy added. "Miss Pearl took us to the mineral baths that day,"

"Those were some good times," Ginger reminisced. "I miss us being together. Those were the good old days."

"We're together now," Harmony said, trying to stay positive. "These are the good old days."

The next evening, everyone went to Harlem, including Ada and Minna. Mozella came with them.

"I'll get Mozella in the Cotton Club," Ginger said. "Let me check things out. C'mon, Heather."

When Ginger walked in, she could hardly believe her eyes.

"Satchmo!"

"Oh my Lawdy, Lawd! Ginger! What in the world are you doin' here?"

"I'm in New York with friends. This is Heather."

"How do," he grinned. "Heard your record. It's good, Ginger, real good. Was that Shorty on the clarinet?"

"It sure was."

"I thought so. Man those were some good times. You don't sound like a white girl when you sing. You got the soul – that pure, New Orleans, Storyville soul."

"Being raised in the Bayou and workin' in New Orleans for a time, guess it comes pretty natural," Ginger grinned.

"Will you sing us a few songs?" he asked.

"Sure. Hey, do you remember Duke? You know my piano player?"

"Of course I do. Played with Duke many a time."

"His sister Mozella is with us."

"Bring her round back, Ginger. I'll take care of it.

"They know me as Louis Armstrong here at the club."

"Well you'll always be Satchmo to me."

The chemistry Ginger brought to the stage was electric. A piano player named Duke Ellington was filling in that night. Ginger loved his style and the three produced a musical sound that was magical. It was a perfect combination of each one doing their part, making one sound. At one point Satchmo was singing and forgot the words. He started babbling, "Dee doo dah wee bee jah bah dee dee la…"

Picking up on his music vibe, Ginger did the same. "Dah dah joo bee la la dah jo dee dee…"

Although there were no lyrics the music stayed in motion and never broke stride. This summoned a feeling of endless creativity, strangely harmonic and never missing a beat. The meaningless song continued for fifteen minutes with each instrument including the drum taking a solo. Everyone in the room, black and white, could feel the spirit of oneness, the spirit of jazz.

From then on, every time Louis Armstrong would forget the words he would make up gibberish. They called it "scat."

When they were finished Ginger and Satchmo hugged and hugged. The manager of the club was especially excited. "The night for you and your friends is on us, little lady. You are terrific! We want to book you."

"No thank you. My friend Mozella is with me and she is not allowed in your club. My friends and I are leaving now to find a place where she is welcome."

"I understand. Round the corner there's a speakeasy called Sally's. It's clean and there's usually a mix of fine folks that go there. Mozella will be most welcome."

"Thank you."

"I am proud of you, Ginger," Victoria said.

"Mozella is family, Miss Pearl."

YOU ARE INVITED TO A PRIVATE SHOWING
ITALIAN ARTIST GIORGIO BALDECCHI
EDUARDO'S
AUGUST 2, 1926

As Heather's entourage of friends entered Eduardo's art gallery, the fragrance of tomato, warm cheese and garlic filled the air. In the corner of the room a man with an accordion accompanied by a violinist were playing traditional Italian songs, creating a beautiful Mediterranean ambiance throughout the room. Everyone was pleasantly impressed.

"Do you think she'll come?" Lucy asked.

"She said she would," Redbird answered.

"Amore!"

There he was, wearing a dark blue Italian-made suit, looking more handsome than ever. Heather could feel a familiar warm surge fill her body as she gracefully held out her hands to subdue any excessive display of public affection. There would be plenty of time for that later. Taking her cue, Giorgio tenderly took her hands and kissed her on both cheeks. As always their touch was electric, sending a burning desire to fall into each other's passionate embrace.

"Giorgio Baldecchi, these are my friends." One by one, Heather introduced Richard, Harvey, the girls, Madeline, Elizabeth and Miss Pearl."

"Welcome, welcome. Please, you must have a glass of our family's wine," he said, leading the group to a beautifully decorated table with colorful ceramic vases from Florence filled with bright yellow sunflowers.

"How did you get the wine here?" Lucy asked.

"Easy. We are Italian."

"Yes, we are," Eduardo affirmed with a happy smile.

"You have a lovely gallery," Victoria complimented.

"Thank you. We are very proud of my cousin Giorgio and his fine work. Please, everyone, enjoy yourselves. Now if you will pardon me, I need to speak to that lady over there. She wants to purchase one of Giorgio's paintings."

The gallery was filled with people chatting, socializing and admiring Giorgio's work.

"Look Redbird. There she is. Marcella!" Lucy called.

Marcella Donovan had also grown up in the Houston Heights. Although slightly younger, she had attended the same school and had sung in the choir with Redbird and Lucy. Now she was enjoying New York. Like Louise, she had also studied at the Denishawn dance school and was currently dancing as a chorus girl in the Greenwich Follies.

"Linda! Lucy! Is this just the 'bees' knees'? What are you doing in New York?"

"Linda took over the family business and we are on a buying, pleasure trip. Our friend Heather is starring in the musical *Steamboat Annie* so we all decided to come."

"Heather Diamond is your friend? I'd love to meet her."

Heather was talking to Richard, who was especially interested in Giorgio's paintings of the California coast. "That's Redondo…and that's Catalina Island."

"He's very good, Heather. Is there something you want to tell me?" he grinned.

Heather blushed.

"Heather, this is our friend Marcella Donovan. She is a fan of yours. We grew up with her in Houston," Lucy said.

Marcella eagerly began asking Heather about theatre, movies and how to break into the business. Richard knew Heather had other things on her mind and gently took her arm to lead her away.

"Please excuse us," he smiled.

"That's Richard," Lucy explained. "He's like her business manager and he's very protective."

"I get it," Marcella said, disappointed. "Gee it's good to see the two of you."

"We saw you on that Art and Beauty magazine cover," Lucy said.

"You did? I wasn't wearing any clothes."

"The fan covered your important parts."

"I thought it would help my career. At least that's what I was told."

"A lot of girls are probably told that. I thought you looked pretty."

"Thank you, Lucy."

Giorgio's art was selling well. Elizabeth bought a colorful painting of an Italian farmhouse on a hillside surrounded by red and yellow flowers and tall slender cypress trees. "It reminds me of a place we would visit when I was a little girl. Mother loved Italy and would take Madeline and me there for holiday."

Miss Pearl had a lovely conversation with Giorgio and liked him very much. She could tell he was genuinely in love with Heather. Harvey invited some of his friends and encouraged them to purchase Giorgio's art. He bought three paintings himself. He gave the one with the colorful sunset painted from the balcony of Heather's beach house to Victoria as a gift for the parlor.

It was towards the end of the evening. Most of the clients had come and gone and more than half the paintings had been sold. An attractive dark-haired woman with silver strands of grey, wearing the latest fashion from Coco Chanel, wandered in. Obviously a good customer, Eduardo welcomed her with a glass of ruby red wine.

Redbird turned white.

"What is wrong with you?" Lucy asked.

Recognizing who had walked in, Miss Pearl hurried to Redbird's side and firmly took her arm.

"It's my mother, Miss Pearl." Redbird whispered. "What do I do?"

"Stay cool, honey. Just breathe. Let's go sit down."

The woman looked over at them but thought nothing of it. It was obvious she had been drinking before she arrived. She did not recognize her daughter, probably because the day she walked out on her family, Linda was only nine years old.

"Do you want to talk to your mother?" Victoria asked.

"You are my mother, Miss Pearl. I do not know that woman standing over there."

The woman seemed to recognize Victoria then looked at Redbird. Did she know it was her daughter Linda?

Quickly, Alice finished her wine, raised her chin, breathed in hard and left.

Again, Alice abandoned her little girl.

"Forgive her, honey."

"I already have," Linda sighed heavily. "It is the only thing I can do. Mother has to live with deserting us… I don't."

When it was time to say goodbye to New York, and although everyone was sad, they were grateful for the time well spent making new memories with old friends. Taking the train back to Texas was bittersweet.

"What a glorious two weeks, Mozella. I believe life is all about the people we love."

"And new babies…" Mozella grinned.

"You are right about that. I'm going to be a grandmother, Mozella."

"You sure are."

"I miss Robert, Mo. I miss my cowboy."

"I know you do."

Two weeks after everyone had returned to Texas, Richard was waiting for Heather in her dressing room after her curtain call for *Steamboat Annie*.

"Valentino's dead."

"What?"

Richard began sobbing. "His soul was too tender for this crazy business, Heather. His stomach was eaten up with ulcers."

"Oh, Richard. I am truly sorry."

"I will take care of you, Heather. No one will hurt you as long as I can help it. No one!"

With that, Richard fell into Heather's arms and released his pain. He wept for Rudolph Valentino, Olive Thomas, Fatty Arbuckle and all those weary souls he had known who had suffered for the price of fame.

CHAPTER 36

# Broadway Stars

In the fall of 1926, Heather Diamond's sensational performance in *Steamboat Annie* had made her a star in the theatre world. Mae West's controversial play *SEX* was making Broadway history and thanks to Mae and Texas Guinan's connections, Missy, the skinny little chorus girl from Texas Guinan's, was making her stage debut as the troubled chorus girl, Barbara Frietchie, in Willard Mack's play, *The Noose.*

When Mack first tested *The Noose* the best audience reactions came when Missy was on stage. She was sensational. Seeing this he wrote more dialogue for the new actress, making her part bigger and better.

Ruby Catherine Stevens, whom everyone knew as *Missy* decided to change her stage name by combining the first name of her character, Barbara Frietchie, with the last name of another actress in the play, Jane

Stanwyck. Because of Barbara Stanwyck's powerful performance, *The Noose* went on to be one of the most successful plays of the season, running on Broadway for nine months and 197 performances.

*SEX* was a smash hit, with a winning run of 375 performances. The show was such a huge success that the theatre was getting \$10 for orchestra seats and the first six rows, at a time when the top dollar for a dramatic show was \$2.80. Against all odds, Mae West's theatrical instincts were right on the money. She knew what her audience wanted and she delivered with gusto.

When *SEX* was in its forty-first week, the show fell victim to a puritan campaign. The real problem was that *SEX* was so successful, other producers and playwrights decided to follow suit. Most of those attempts to jump on the bandwagon were nasty, filthy and even repulsive plays.

"You have class, my dear," Minna told Mae. "There is an art to being suggestive and sexy but still within good taste. Ada and I are happy investors to be sure. You have done well."

When told to close her show, Mae West decided instead to stand trial for her play. Mae, Jimmy and Elsner were all arrested. The courtroom was to her just another stage. Because the prosecuting attorney could not find one lewd or obscene line in the entire play, he decided to pursue another tactic.

"Miss West's personality, looks, walk, mannerisms and gestures make the lines and situations in her play suggestive."

Still the court did not find this to be offensive.

Finally in desperation the prosecuting attorney attacked the belly dance performed by Mae West during the second act to the jazz song, *Saint Louis Blues.*

Thinking the whole thing absurd, Mae attempted to explain in truth what she was really doing.

"What I do on stage is nothing more than a stomach exercise. Back in the day, my father was known as Battling Jack the prizefighter. He showed me how to roll my abdominal muscles one by one. It's not easy to do. In fact it takes a lot of practice, discipline and control to be able to roll your stomach muscles. I figured it was a good idea – something different. I never really thought of it as a belly dance."

One of the officers who had seen the show was called to the stand to testify. Blushing, he tried to explain what he saw. "Miss West moved her naval up and down and then from right to left."

"Did you actually see her naval?"

"No… but I saw something in her middle that moved from east to west."

Although the entire courtroom roared with laughter, it was on this testimony that the GUILTY verdict was secured.

Jimmy, Elsner and Mae West were all sentenced to ten days in jail and were each fined $500 for "corrupting the morals of youth." As far as she was concerned, Mae saw those ten days as a well-earned vacation.

Mae thought the prison underwear rough on the body and unacceptable. "I want to wear my silk underwear."

"This ain't Saks Fifth Avenue," said a toothless hag who worked for the prison.

The Warden, clearly a gentleman, blushed at the conversation. "It's all right Miss West. You can wear your own underwear."

Mae was transferred from Tombs Prison to Welfare Island where she received a cotton dress to wear. She had a lovely view of the river and the bridges that crossed it from the large windows in her cell.

"The word has come down to treat you as a special guest, Miss West," the guard told her.

"Thanks. I appreciate that."

The warden came to Mae in the second day with a message. "All the women want to see you."

As she walked into a large dormitory, the women welcomed Mae with a grateful applause. Mae felt that if she could make them a "less miserable mob" she was doing well. One by one, she patiently listened to their pitiful stories. Sometimes, she tried to offer some comfort and advice. Unfortunately there were just too many sad cases.

A few days into her sentence, Mae was asked to write an article for Liberty Magazine for which she was paid a thousand dollars. After eight days in jail, Mae was released for good behavior.

After leaving jail, Mae read an article in Variety Magazine that said, "Vaudeville will go." This prompted her to start thinking seriously about Hollywood. The movie studios were making millions of dollars. Paramount had grossed $21,000,000 the year before. Theatre, as Mae West had known it, was unable to compete with the new Hollywood giant. All over America, vaudeville theatres were closing or converting into movie theatres.

Mae started thinking, "*What is next for me?*"

## CHAPTER 37

# Talkies

By 1927, the Roaring Twenties were ablaze with creativity. The whole world appeared to be on the fast track to change. There was power and money associated with the new technologies and thanks to Prohibition and automobiles, American culture was running wild.

The movies had made a huge impact on America and Clara Bow's phrases such as "the cat's meow" and the "bee's knees" were being used by young people everywhere. Young women who could not afford to go to the speakeasies were living vicariously through films and magazine articles about the flappers. Necking in automobiles had become a favorite pastime when travelling home from dances and sports events.

New inventions were popping up everywhere. Frozen food and electrical appliances such as toasters, irons, refrigerators, washing machines and vacuum cleaners were making life easier for the domestic housewife.

Radio was connecting people from coast to coast, offering news and entertainment in the comfort of one's own home. In England, Philo Taylor Farnsworth was successful in transferring pictures through electrical lines. In May of 1927, Charles Lindbergh made the first successful flight across the Atlantic from New York to Paris, France. That same year the possibility of man actually landing on the moon was conceived when Robert Goddard successfully launched the first fueled rocket in Massachusetts.

In October, Sam Warner's concept of talking movies was finally realized with the release of *The Jazz Singer* starring Al Jolson. Despite the fact there were those who said that the movie would flop because the story was about a Jewish cantor, America loved the film.

Movies would now have a voice. Many were convinced "talkies" would never survive; however, the same thing had been said about the automobile. Just as vaudeville had faded with the onset of movies, talkies would soon replace silent films.

This was an exciting time for those who embraced change. There would be those in the movie industry who would thrive and there would be some who, because of inferior voice quality, sadly would be left behind. Unfortunately, preserving film to prevent deterioration had not been considered. Several silent movies would be forever lost and with them the people and artistic talent that had created them.

Thanks to Richard and his incredible insight, Heather Diamond was at the right place at the right time. Talent scouts in New York were singing her praises. Those in the movie industry familiar with her films recognized her natural ability to light up the screen in a way that could evoke emotion in anyone who had a heart. The fact that she could sing made her even more appealing to the studios.

Currently, most of Heather's films had been westerns. She had developed a close friendship with Wyatt Earp… and even had a small crush on him. Never before had she met a man with so much grit. There had been some interest in Hollywood to tell his story on film, but unfortunately the project had been relegated to a shelf somewhere.

"If I was just 40 years younger…what a time we'd have, Heather Diamond," Earp would say with a mischievous gleam.

By 1928 it was clearly evident that Hollywood was the place to be for anyone wanting to be in on the new trend of talking movies. Although performing on a big stage in front of a live audience was most appealing, Heather was excited about making friends with the camera and the microphone. She decided it was time to stay in California and start a new phase of her career in the talkies.

The autumn afternoon in Redondo Beach felt cool and crisp. Heather was standing alone on her balcony, drinking a cup of hot chamomile tea and watching the waves break gently on the sand. She was thinking about Chicago, Texas, Giorgio, the farmhouse, New York…"

Richard appeared carrying a stack of folders. "We need to find you the perfect script, Heather. The studio wants to try something different with you."

Heather picked up one of the scripts. Flipping through the pages she looked at it for a minute than laid it down.

"I've been thinking. I want to write scripts like Mae West did when she wrote *SEX*."

"Really? I like that idea."

"I can start by telling my story, Richard," Heather said with excitement. "I've already started working on it. I can play the leading role."

"Pitch me your story, Heather," Richard grinned.

"Once upon a time there was a little girl who loved to sing and dance and make up stories of faraway castles and knights in shining armor. The front porch of her farmhouse was her stage, and whenever she could, she would gather her little brothers and sisters, dolls and pets to be her audience. She loved to see them smile, gasp, grimace and most of all, her heart was full when she heard the sound of their applause.

"One day a handsome man took her away to the big city to sing in his nightclub; it was a dream come true. He gave her expensive presents, a fancy apartment, made passionate love to her and treated her like a queen.

"Like an ogre who hides a beautiful princess in a tower, he kept her all to himself. She was unaware that she was being held captive because he had her under his magical spell. The handsome man was really a bad monster, a gangster with a heart of icy stone. One day, the girl innocently broke his rules and left the tower. She did not know this was an act punishable by death. That night after she had sung her set, a strange beautiful woman appeared in her dressing room and rescued the girl. Convincing her of the grave danger she was in, the woman took her far away to Texas where she would be safe.

"After years of searching for the girl the gangster learned where she was and secretly traveled to Texas to kill her. When he discovered he knew the woman who had rescued the girl, he raged with so much anger that he decided he would kill her first. He kidnapped the woman and took her to a secluded place by the river where he tied her up."

"Is this really true? What happens next?"

"You'll have to see the movie," Heather smiled, kissing his cheek. "Can I fix you some tea, Richard?"

"What happens next, Heather?"

"The fact you are asking means it's a good story."

Richard smiled with admiration. "Write it. Now that movies have a voice you can sing in it too."

Just then there was a knock at the door.

"Ginger!"

"I'm pregnant, Heather. Sam and I made a baby."

Returning to her hotel late one evening, Mae West stopped at the front desk to get her messages. Always accommodating, the night manager handed her a small stack of mail and a bouquet of sincere compliments.

"Miss West, your diamonds are the hotel's best advertising. They're really beautiful."

Over the years Mae had received lovely gifts from admirers and grateful male friends. Tonight she was wearing a small diamond dinner set, a diamond brooch with a diamond chain, 2 two-and-a-half diamond-platinum bracelets set with a few emerald stones, a beautiful diamond watch, and a pure white ten-carat diamond ring.

"My, my, they are something to look at."

"I guess that's why I wear them."

"What are you going to do next on stage, Miss West?"

"I am thinking about doing a period play of the turn of the century."

"In those days I was a young police captain in the Bowery. It's still wild and crazy and full of misfits."

"You must have been some kind of guy."

"You wouldn't think it now."

"I would. You look like you have nothing to regret."

"You remind me of a sweetheart I had then. She had a lot of diamonds just like you and how the men did run after her."

Mae immediately went to her suite and started writing ideas down on paper. She thought about how her father would playfully call her mother, who was not a drinker, "Champagne Til" because she would occasionally sip champagne. Mae decided to call her new play, *Diamond Lil.*

The play was tested at Teller's Shubert in Brooklyn during Holy Week, 1928. Traditionally known as the worse week in the year for theatre attendance, *Diamond Lil* played to a packed house, breaking box-office records all week long.

Mae took *Diamond Lil* to Manhattan's Royale Theatre. On opening night, Ada and Minna had orchestra seats. Heather, Harmony and Richard were sitting two rows behind them. Heather was in town promoting her new movie Ruby Red.

"Mae is *Diamond Lil,*" Minna said to her sister. "We and our beautiful butterflies are Diamond Lil. I know the play is going to be a huge success.

"I agree with you, dear sister. I believe Mae has another hit. *Diamond Lil* is every woman's secret fantasy."

Mae West was sensational, introducing her version of the classic story in the song, Frankie and Johnnie. To her delight, the entire audience stood up and cheered the final curtain.

"The Rewards of Virtue… Miss Mae West has become an institution in Broadway drama… The theatre Royale is crowded at each performance of DIAMOND LIL." ~ NY Herald Tribune

After receiving raving reviews and with the great success of *Diamond Lil*, Minna and Ada invited Mae to their home to celebrate with bubbly champagne and a light supper.

"You put so much of yourself into Diamond Lil. Ada and I relate completely to your character. I believe every woman can relate to *Diamond Lil* in one way or another," Ada commented.

"Most of the audience for *SEX* was men. I really wanted to do something that would appeal to women. I believe the biggest difference between the two characters was the diamonds. Diamonds are a gesture of appreciation and every woman wants to be appreciated."

"You have a point," Ada smiled.

"*Diamond Lil* is me, we are each other," Mae said. "It is good, isn't it ladies?"

"Yes it is," Minna answered.

"Truthfully I do have one fear. What am I going to do next? *Diamond Lil* is going to be a hard act to follow. In this business you're only as good as your last show. The public will expect bigger and better things from me. I don't want to let them down."

"Right now you are a success, Mae. Savor it. You'll know when it's time to walk away – just like Minna and I did."

"Success is a two-bladed golden sword, ladies. It knights one and stabs one at the same time."

The friends sipped and shared. Ada and Minna told Mae stories of their days at the Everleigh Club and Mae revealed some of her greatest moments on stage. The conversation gave the women a new appreciation for each other. By the end of the evening Mae West and the Everleigh sisters were friends for life.

Since opening night Heather could not get *Diamond Lil* out of her mind. The play was exciting and Mae was outstanding in her part. Mae's timing was perfect. Heather watched as the audience reacted appropriately to every line. So much of the overall message of the play reminded her of how her life had been at Miss Pearl's Parlor.

"Harmony, I keep thinking of *Diamond Lil*. Remember that song you wrote about Suzy Poontang?"

"I was just goofing off, Heather. It was a song I had written for fun," Harmony smiled.

"Yes, but do you remember how we all reacted to your song?"

"Sure I do. We all laughed."

"Exactly! And do you know why we all laughed?"

"It was funny?"

"It was hilarious! Tears in the eyes hilarious! Harmony, let's write a musical. We can write about Miss Pearl's. We have so many characters! We can put Miss Comstock, Happy Harvey, the church ladies…"

"Miss Pearl…Tommy Lee, Emma Grace…"

"Betsy… Dusty… Texas… Katie… Suzy… Poontang… Doctor Gedderoffe…Holy cow, Harmony…We can make it a musical and call it, *Pearl*!"

"Let's do it!" Harmony exclaimed.

"Ginger can help us. Now that she has little Luke she has really settled down."

"How is that going for her, Heather? It's hard for me to imagine Ginger with a little baby."

"You should see her, Harmony. Ginger is the sweetest Mommy. They live with my friend Ruby in Palos Verdes. Ruby is crazy about that baby. The three of them are really happy."

"What about Sam?"

"He doesn't know. Little Luke looks just like his daddy. Ginger said it happened the night before she went on her last music tour; she says that she knew the minute it happened. He's the only one she ever let inside of her. She told me she had some concerns with Sam before. There was a couple of other times she thought she might be pregnant.

"She once told me, 'Sometimes we get too much in a hurry to slip that condom on.' Anyway, she doesn't want him to know. I think she's afraid of how he might react."

"I think Sam loves Ginger, Heather, at least in his own way. Who knows what he would do. I like your idea of writing Pearl. I will be free after the first of the year."

"Good, you can come out and stay with me. By then I can at least have an outline. Ginger can be one of our songwriters."

"We've already written one hit together," Harmony said.

"I love writing, Harmony. Richard is helping me make my story into a screenplay. I've already put it in book form. It is a suspense thriller about a girl singer and her gangster boyfriend."

"That sounds familiar."

"I've had to change some of the details to protect the guilty," Heather grinned. We're calling it, *Once Upon A Moon.* Right now the studios are looking for scripts for talkies. I am going to be able to sing in it."

"It sounds like a winner to me. By the way, what is happening with Giorgio these days?"

"We are in love and busy at the same time. Right now he is in Italy with his family. His paintings are getting more and more popular and he has a show in Chicago next month. He has his career and I have mine but he is my one and only and I am his. It may turn into marriage one day, but for now we are passionate lovers who adore each other."

Although there were still some silent movies being made, by 1928 production in Hollywood was becoming more and more focused on the talkies. Louise Brooks had made eleven silent movies and Heather Diamond had made eight. Both had become famous.

Louise occasionally would visit Heather at her beach house. Heather could see that Louise Brooks was on a road to self-destruction. She drank heavily, partied hard and was careless with her affairs, including her rendezvous with Greta Garbo. Louise was living as if there were no tomorrow, unaware that youth and beauty are only temporary assets in the grand scheme of things, especially in Hollywood.

In 1928 Louise Brooks starred in the crime/mystery film, *The Canary Murder Case*, with William Powell. It would be the last film she would do under her contract with Paramount pictures.

Because Paramount would not give Louise a raise, she left when her contract came up and went to Germany. There she made two films for Georg der Pabst's. In Pabst's silent film *Pandora's Box*, Louise Brooks became the biggest international star of the day playing the role of Lulu. Some regard Pandora's Box as one of the best silent films ever made.

Lulu turned out to be the perfect role for Louise Brooks. Just as *Diamond Lil* was the persona of Mae West, Lulu was in essence, Louise Brooks, a beautiful temptress who uses men and, in the end, is destroyed.

With the popularity of talkies, Paramount decided to reshoot scenes from *Canary Murder Case* with recorded dialogue. The studio cabled Louise in Germany, demanding that she return and record her lines. Feeling that she no longer had an obligation to Paramount, Louise refused their request. When told she would never work in Hollywood again, Louise's response was, "Who wants to work in Hollywood?"

This fateful decision destroyed her status as a mega-star and would be the biggest mistake of her life. The beautiful, talented, exciting, vibrant Louise Brooks from Kansas would forever be blacklisted from working in any major film in Hollywood. In one careless moment, Louise Brooks had sabotaged her own career.

# CHAPTER 38

# Texas Reunion

The sky and the ocean were gray the morning Richard came to Heather's house to deliver the bad news.

"What's wrong, Richard? You look so sad."

"He's dead, Heather. Wyatt Earp is dead."

"Oh no! No…no…no! I just saw him a few weeks ago at Christmas. What happened?"

"Some kind of infection. William Hart and Tom Mix are going to be pallbearers. Tom is pretty shook up about it."

Heather put her face into Richard's chest and wept for her friend.

"I loved Wyatt," she sobbed.

"I know, Heather. We all did. Such a great man," he said, stroking her hair.

"I've got to call Ruby."

When Ginger answered the phone, Heather could hear Ruby and little Luke laughing in the background.

"Wyatt Earp died, Ginger. I'll let you tell Ruby at a better time. Sounds like she is having too much fun with that baby right now."

Heather, consumed with sadness, went to her closet and grabbed her coat "Let's take a walk on the beach, Richard. It always makes me feel better."

Richard put his arm around Heather and the two friends walked along the shoreline. Heather was grieving and Richard was there to comfort her. For a long time neither one of them said a word. Richard left Heather to her thoughts.

Finally he spoke. "I pitched *Once Upon a Moon* to the studio. I think they want to do it; they loved the plot. That's where I was when I learned about Wyatt."

"Now I don't know if I should laugh or cry," Heather said, astonished by the news. "Oh my God, Richard! That's fantastic!"

"Thought I'd deliver the bad news first."

"Harmony is coming out next week to work on our new musical. I have it in storybook form right now."

"Don't tell me anything about it. I want to see it when it is finished."

"Deal. Richard, you have been a good friend to me."

"You're my best friend, that's for sure."

"Ahh…look at the clouds, Richard. Look how the sun is casting those vibrant colors on the fluffy parts."

"It really is lovely"

"I have never seen the sunset so glorious. It makes me think of heaven. Maybe it is heaven and Wyatt is telling God to show me he is in his bliss. He is with his brothers again."

"Maybe."

"I choose to believe it's true."

This was the first time Heather had ever been to a funeral for someone she loved. Seeing Wyatt in his casket, part of her expected him to wink at her as he always had done. The other part realized she was not seeing Wyatt at all. He had a new body now and somehow she felt as though he was in the room.

Heather was a little surprised that Wyatt's wife Josephine had refused to come. She sat next to Ruby and held her hand. Tom Mix, the famous cowboy star, cried.

"Maybe one day they'll tell his story, Miss Ruby. Maybe you'll be in it," Heather said.

"I don't know, honey. All I know is he was a good man. Lots of memories there. Did I ever tell you about the time when he saved my life in San Francisco?"

"No."

"It's a long story. Remind me to tell you about it. I'll go see Josephine tomorrow. She can probably use an old friend about now. Funerals are tough. I was a mess at Mickey's. I hardly remember it."

"Harmony's going to be here in a couple of days. Ginger will be working with us on our new musical. Guess you're going to be babysitting," Heather smiled.

"I sure do love that baby, little Luke Michael. She chose Michael because Michelangelo was Mickey's real name and Luke is biblical. Isn't that just like Ginger?" Ruby laughed. "Little Luke is my happiness, Heather. I believe I am in love again."

When Harmony arrived, she was a sight for sad eyes to be sure. Heather bought a piano and the three girls went to work.

The next few days were a roller coaster of emotions. The girls laughed when they wrote about Miss Comstock and Happy Harvey. They cried when they talked about Betsy, so desperate to be loved. They wrote about Maggie, the girl who told every man she saw that he was the best she ever had and Susan, the spinster schoolteacher who had to be convinced that she was not a sinner for having natural thoughts about sex.

"Remember getting so excited when the cowboys came to town?" Heather exclaimed. "We'd see that dust cloud getting bigger and bigger…"

"Men on a mission," Ginger said.

"I've got it," Heather exclaimed running to the piano. "Listen here…it's Friday night we're all getting ready, the cowboys are comin' to town, look at that dust cloud getting bigger and bigger as the sun is going down…"

Within an hour the friends had written the opening number. "I can see the curtain opening and all the girls are dancing and singing, *The Cowboys Are Coming To Town*," Heather exclaimed.

Heather, Ginger and Harmony had formed a powerful songwriting team that had connected as one mind. In the next few days they wrote, *Nobody Hears When She Cries* for Betsy, *You Make Beautiful Love With Your Eyes* for Tommy Lee and Emma Grace to sing as a duet and *Deep Pockets* in honor of Happy Harvey.

"I want to write a song about Texas," Harmony said.

"Yeah, that Texas thang," Heather agreed.

"Texas is like a good woman," Ginger said. "Kind of like Miss Pearl…beautiful… comforting… mysterious… loving…"

"If Texas was a woman I'd marvel at her beauty like the colors of a sunset lighting up the western sky", Harmony recited.

"That's lovely," Ginger said. Within half an hour the girls finished *If Texas Was a Woman.*

"We need a good finale song," Heather said. "A real kicker that will make the audience leave happy. It has to be something that will make them want to dance in the aisles."

Harmony began playing a "walking bass lick" on the piano.

"Every time Sam would come see me he'd always tell me I was good medicine. 'Baby, you are a magic cure for the blues,' he'd say."

"A cure for the blues!" Heather exclaimed. "Just come down to Pearl's, we got a cure for the blues!"

Harmony was playing, lyrics were flying and Ginger was writing as fast as she could. In a matter of minutes the writing team had finished the first chorus. Ginger and Heather were dancing and singing while Harmony played. They had their finale and it was upbeat, sassy and fun.

For three weeks Harmony, Ginger and Heather worked on Pearl. When the scenes and songs were finally in place, Heather called Richard. "I think we have written a hit. When can you come over?"

Heather had each scene laid out on the dining room table. Heather would explain the scene and the three girls took turns reading the parts.

Then she and Ginger took turns singing the songs. Totally immersed in the energy and vibe of each musical number, Richard laughed, cried and sometimes even applauded in the exact places the girls intended.

"You've really got something here, Heather. You really do! I am behind you all the way."

"You really think so?" Harmony squealed.

"I really do, Harmony. It needs work, but your ideas are good. I want to be part of this."

"Would you like to direct it?"

"I was thinking more of producing it," he grinned. "We'll get you a good director. By the way, the studio wants to talk to you next week about *Once Upon a Moon*. Looks like you are on your way to being a writer, my dear.

Speaking of which, they just announced the winners of the first Academy Awards show. The ceremonies will be held at the Roosevelt Hotel in May. They are giving Chaplin an honorary award. You are going with me."

"We should go to San Angelo, Ginger. Richard, you need to come with us. After all that's where all of this got started. Miss Pearl says the new Hilton Hotel is opening at the end of May. According to her, it's supposed to be real nice."

"I think I'll pass," Ginger said.

"Why?"

"What if Sam…"

"What if Sam?" Harmony said. "Don't you think he has the right to know he has a son? Besides, everyone knows he loves you."

"Is that what you call it?" Ginger rolled her eyes in an attempt to cover up her heart.

"Well, I certainly want to go," Richard proclaimed. "I want to visit Miss Pearl's Parlor."

"I want to see Katie," Harmony exclaimed. "I will let Lucy and Redbird know we are coming."

"I will tell Pearl to reserve a dozen rooms at the hotel," Heather exclaimed.

"A dozen?" Harmony asked.

"Yes, a dozen. We are going to have a reunion" Heather grinned.

Ginger finally agreed to go to San Angelo but not with her baby. Ruby was more than happy to have little Luke to herself.

It was a happy day. Everyone was there. Redbird, Lucy, Harvey, Richard, Heather, Harmony and Ginger were all expected. The ladies from New York were a surprise.

Pearl was sitting on the front porch when the cars pulled up to the mansion.

"Mozella! Mozella!! Come quick! Look who's here!"

Maggie and Sarah came running from inside the house. Katie was hurrying from the barn with Rusty eagerly wagging his tail.

Mozella appeared holding Maggie's baby in her arms. "Lord have mercy! I don't believe it! It's Miss Minna and Miss Ada. Oh happy day! Oh happy day!"

Hugs and tears and more hugs and tears were exchanged. One by one, beautiful unfamiliar faces appeared on the porch, curious to meet the legendary, original Lady Pearls.

Richard was touched by the genuine love and appreciation these women had for each other. He thought about the many colorful stories Heather had told him about the Lady Pearls at Miss Pearl's Parlor, the Everleigh sisters, Mozella and the passionate love story of a cowboy and his beautiful butterfly, Victoria Pearl. Every one of them was a movie with a potential happy ending.

As the group made their way into the mansion, Richard was greeted with several pairs of flirtatious eyes.

"Sorry girls. He's with me," Harvey said to their great disappointment.

"Thanks," Richard said.

"You are welcome," Harvey said. "No use getting their little ol' hopes up."

That evening Ginger, Heather and Harmony performed their new songs from the musical they called Pearl. Dusty and Jesse were there as well as Sarah's Aunt Katherine. They laughed when Ginger sang Deep Pockets.

*"You've got deep pockets I can tell in a flash; you've deep pockets and a mighty fine ASK me how I know you are the man for me, Hey Mr. Deep Pockets are you lookin' for some company?"*

"We wrote this one for Betsy," Heather said. "In fact we wrote it for all of us. It's called Nobody Hears When She Cries."

Harmony picked up her guitar and Heather sang.

"She knows so many men; they tell her their troubles and she understands; looking for comfort they hold her tight; a friendly face in the night; but Nobody Hears When She Cries; they kiss a lonely girl goodbye…"

There wasn't a dry eye in the house.

The finale song tied it all together and by the second verse everyone in the room was singing the line, "Just come down to Pearl's, we've got a cure for the blues!"

*"When you're all by your only, feelin kind of lonely*
*Life gets too hard to bear*
*When you want a woman a special kind of woman*
*To give you comfort and care*
*Just come down to Pearl's*
*We've got a cure for the blues"*

"What do you think?" Richard asked Ada.

"I think I like it," Ada smiled.

"This needs to be on Broadway," Minna said. "Mae West has blazed the trail. We can make this happen. *Pearl* has everything. It's funny, touching and the songs are good. I believe Pearl is a hit."

"Count us in," Ada said.

"I'm definitely interested," Pearl said. "How about you, Madeline? Elizabeth?"

"Oh yes," Madeline agreed, with Elizabeth nodding her head.

"Don't forget me. After all she wrote a whole scene in my honor," Aunt Rosey sparked. "I was so moved. Talkin 'bout Joey and that crazy dame who moved in right next door to us! I'll never forget her hangin' up my husband's green striped underwear on her clothes line…clothes pins in her teeth, waving to me like we were old friends!"

"And me!" Harvey exclaimed. "That's just how it happened the time daddy took me to Miss Hattie's to make me a man. I just love *Deep Pockets*."

After the girl's performance, Victoria Pearl took Ada, Minna and two bottles of chilled champagne to the gazebo by the river. The night was warm and the sparkling moonlight glistened on the water, making a perfect setting for old friends to reminisce.

"So this is the Concho River," Minna said. "I remember those pink pearls Robert would send you. They were so pretty… so feminine," Minna said.

"The only river in the world that produces pink freshwater pearls," Victoria smiled with some melancholy.

"You have a lovely place here, Victoria," Ada complimented. "I am quite impressed."

"I learned from the best," Victoria smiled.

"Your girls are quite lovely and well mannered. You have done a good job with them."

"I am selling the parlor. Harvey is going to buy it and Katie and my friend Katherine will take it over."

"What? Why?"

"I have plenty of money now and two of the most adorable grandchildren in the world. Little Amy is two and little Robert is just starting to walk. They call me Nana and they totally have my heart. I want to be with them and travel a little. Mozella is going to come with me."

"Another Robert McKnight?" Minna smiled.

"Yes, and he looks just like him," Victoria bragged. "It was hard being at the ranch after I lost my cowboy. Now I love going. My grandchildren are my happiness."

"You are most fortunate, my dear," Ada smiled.

"Would you like to see the ranch while you are here?"

"That would be lovely," Ada smiled.

"We would absolutely love to see where Robert McKnight gallantly took one of our favorite butterflies to be his bride," Minna concurred. "Anyone for more champagne?"

When Victoria and her friends from New York pulled up to the Five Star Ranch, Amy and her mother were playing outside the main house.

"Nana! Nana!" she squealed, running with arms stretched out the way toddlers do.

"Hello, my happiness!" Victoria exclaimed, sweeping the little girl up in her arms. "This is Michael's wife, Eloise."

"Oh my, this is absolutely breathtaking," Minna marveled.

"Look at those springs…and the lily pads. Oh, Victoria how happy you must have been when Robert brought you here."

"Our sons, Michael and David have built their homes on the ranch. That one is Michael's and David's house is over that bluff," she said, pointing. "Oh look, here comes David now with his wife and little Robert."

"My goodness, David looks just like Robert," Ada exclaimed.

"Honey, these are my dear friends, Ada and Minna Lester. They knew your daddy. Minna was the one who first introduced us. And this is Madeline, her sister Elizabeth and Aunt Rosey."

David smiled and removed his hat. "Pleased to meet you, ladies" he smiled.

"It's uncanny how much you look like your handsome father," Ada commented. "Oh my, there's another one!"

Just then Michael, riding a chestnut mare he called Trixie appeared. His smile was bright and Minna and Ada's hearts were filled knowing their butterfly had found a home.

"I love little girls," Rosey said to Amy. "Is that your doll over there?"

Elizabeth's eyes were shining bright. "Let's go to the springs, Victoria. "Just you and me," she said, taking her hand.

Taking her sister's cue, Madeline spoke next. "Is this where we are staying tonight?"

Eloise stepped forward. "I can show them to their rooms. Maria has made enchiladas for everyone."

"What is an enchilada?" Ada asked.

"Delicious," Victoria laughed.

"I'd like to hold little Robert," Minna declared. Michael's wife Estelle handed her baby to Minna's outstretched arms, and when she pulled him close to her, he grabbed her nose and giggled.

The springs were especially beautiful and the land was dark green from the much appreciated rain that had fallen the week before.

"He's here, Victoria. He's always with you but this is his favorite place," Elizabeth said.

"I know," Victoria said. "I can feel Robert the most when I am by the springs."

To her surprise, a bright orange monarch landed on Victoria's arm. "Very often I see butterflies when I come here. This is the first time one has actually landed on me."

"He loves you, Victoria. The love is pure. I can see sparkles all around you. He is happy you are coming home to the ranch. He wants you to know he will always be here when you need to feel close to him. Robert is your eternal love. You will be together again; just like lifetimes before, he will always find you. You will find each other."

Meanwhile, back in San Angelo, Sam showed up.

"Where have you been, Ginger?"

"Around," she said.

"No one would tell me where you were."

"I've been here and there, singing…you know."

Avoiding any eye contact, Ginger's heart was beating like a timpani drum.

"I've been going crazy, Ginger, not knowin' where you were and all. Let's get married."

"Married?"

"I love you."

"You've never said that before."

"Well I do. I love you, Ginger. I don't want anyone but you. I want to marry you now."

"I live in California, Sam. I'm not movin'"

"California? What! You got another fella?"

"I like it there and I'm not movin'"

"Dang, Ginger. You are stubborn as a mule! Guess I'll have to move to California then."

"Who says your invited, Sam?"

Ginger knew this would happen. She just knew it. Sam always knew when to show up. Her heart was saying *yes*, but her mind was saying *no*. Sam just wasn't the type to settle down.

Ten days later, everyone was on a train to wherever they called home. Redbird and Lucy moved into a brand new mansion in River Oaks, a fancy suburb in Houston, Texas. The New York ladies returned to New York, excited to be involved as investors in *Pearl*. Harmony was scheduled to do another concert tour in Europe and Heather, Ginger and Richard returned to California. Ginger had been hired to sing on radio programs and Heather and Richard were negotiating the terms of Heather's new movie *Once Upon a Moon*.

Richard had fallen in love with Redondo Beach and considered Heather, Ruby and Ginger his family. He decided to build a home in the Hollywood Riviera, a new real estate development between Redondo and Palos Verdes named with the intention of attracting the Hollywood elite. The terrain was similar to the French Riviera and there were plans to build a fancy beach club right on the beach.

Life was good. At least that's what they all thought. Little did they know that the world they had known soon would be drastically changed.

CHAPTER 39

# Goodbye Ruby

The day was October 29, 1929, forever to be known as Black Tuesday. Wealthy people lost millions and modest people lost hundreds, leveling the entire economic status to owning zero or less, depending on how much they owed.

Brokers and bankers were jumping out of windows or "eating their guns." Broadway theatres were eerily quiet and as one vaudeville comedian said, "The place was so empty you could shoot elk in the balcony."

Another asked his friend, "You got change for a match?"

Broadway was stunned; everything seemed to have stopped overnight. Former actors who owed fancy hotels $500,000 in back room rent were selling apples on street corners.

Six million people across the nation were out of work. President Hoover assured Americans everywhere, "Conditions are fundamentally sound."

It was a time when having friends mattered. Each day, after Sport had been laid off from his position taking care of the horses at Universal City, he would say to his wife, "Let's just get through today and worry about tomorrow when it gets here."

Most of America's wealth was on paper. Linda's (Redbird's) mother's husband lost everything. Two days after the crash, Alice found him slumped over his desk in a puddle of blood, with a bullet wound in his temple. She humbly returned to Houston and showed up at Linda's front door in River Oaks. Linda took her in and settled Alice in the small apartment Linda had built over her garage. After a year of healing and reconciliation, Alice had a fatal heart attack. Miss Pearl was there for Redbird – to comfort and help her through the grief.

Those who had cash stowed away and valuable diamonds and gold would survive the Depression. Land was a valued asset as well, as long as it was paid for. Mae West had her diamonds. Ada and Minna Everleigh had mountains of cash hidden away in a safe. They had learned well from their days in Chicago, "Don't ever let them see your hand."

Victoria Pearl was receiving royalties from the oil business and The Five Star Ranch in Menard County was completely paid for. Wisdom from the Everleigh sisters had been passed down. Victoria also had diamonds and a safe full of cash. The Lady Pearls all had hidden money away and Heather's mother in Illinois now had over $50,000 hidden in the basement of their farmhouse.

Harvey kept a safe full of money secured in an old barn. He never did trust banks since that day his father's banker took them through the secret tunnel from the bank to Miss Hattie's Bordello in San Angelo.

Ruby had seen too many bank robberies in her day. Between the diamonds Mickey had bought her and her safe, she had several million dollars hiding in her house in Palos Verdes that she had paid for in cash.

Some places did not feel the drastic effects of the Great Depression. One was San Angelo, Texas, where the oil boom was still thriving and men still wanted the services offered by Miss Pearl's Parlor.

Although the movie industry was stung, talking films were now the norm and producers found creative ways to lessen the cost of production. Even when times were hard, people still wanted to be entertained. Radio was the newest pastime, connecting Americans from coast to coast. It was the first time all were offered the same news broadcasts and entertainment every day. This would prove to be a great asset in building the future of the country.

It was a Tuesday afternoon when Heather received a call from Ruby. "You better come up here, honey. Ginger has a radio show and I'm not feelin' so pretty good. I need you to come look after Little Luke."

When Heather entered the front door, Ruby could barely walk."

"Let me call the doctor."

"I'll be okay. I think it's just somethin' I ate. I'm going to lay down now."

"I'm calling the doctor."

An hour later, while Heather was building towers with Luke's ABC blocks, the doctor carrying a big black bag arrived.

"She's in there, Doctor," Heather directed.

"Hey, you're Heather Diamond. I saw you in *Once Upon a Moon*. It's my favorite movie. I heard it's a true story."

"I heard that as well."

Heather wrote under the name, Victor McKnight, in honor of Victoria Pearl. "I'm glad you liked it," she smiled.

The room was quiet when the two walked in. The doctor looked at Ruby then gravely shook his head. There was no heartbeat. Ruby was in her new body, dancing with her beloved Mickey in heaven.

The sun was setting when they took Ruby away. Beautiful warm colors cast a golden glow across the ocean.

"It reminds me of how the sunset looked when Wyatt passed away."

That evening, when Ginger came home she found Heather reading *Goldilocks and the Three Bears* to little Luke.

"Where's Ruby?" she asked.

"Ruby is with Mickey," Heather whispered and the two friends held each other and cried.

Ginger went into her room to change and wash-up for dinner. Heather poured two glasses of red wine. Now that Prohibition was over, it was easier for Giorgio to supply his favorite girls with the rich red wines from his family's California vineyards.

A minute later, Ginger walked out of her room, carrying an envelope. "It's a letter addressed to you and me. It's from Ruby. She must have known…"

*Dear Heather and Ginger,*

*I was a lonely, miserable woman after I lost my Mickey. Then one magical evening at the Hotel Redondo, I began a friendship with two of the most remarkable women I had ever known. Since that night, knowing you has given me a reason to want to get up in the morning. In the last two years with Little Luke, I have experienced complete joy. I am giving all that I own to the two of you and I have set up a trust for Luke. Enclosed are simple instructions to claim my fortune. Take good care of the ruby necklace. It belonged to my mother. The journal will explain the beautiful love story associated with the necklace. Most of it was written by my mother and then I added some things in later years. Know that I love the three of you with all my heart and I am eternally grateful for the precious time we have shared together. If you are reading this, you know I am dancing in heaven and singing Italian songs with my Mickey again.*

*With love, eternally,*

*Ruby*

Salty Dog, Ginger, Heather, Giorgio and Richard took Ruby's ashes to the tide pools by the Palos Verdes cliffs where Ruby liked to explore. After each one said something to honor her memory, Ginger sang *Amazing Grace* as Heather reverently sent Ruby's ashes off to be carried away into the vast blueness of the sea that she and Mickey loved.

In that moment two dolphins appeared, dancing and jumping in the sun. Not a word was said. Finally it was little Luke who broke the silence.

"Wuby! Wuby!" he cheered, pointing with glee at the glorious sight.

"They are together again," Salty Dog said. "Goodbye, old friends."

Six months after Ruby's passing, Ginger was singing her new hit *Nobody Loves You Like Me* to a live audience at the radio station. In the middle of the song she recognized a familiar face watching her. It was hot blooded, good lookin' sexy as hell Sam. In his hands he held a bouquet of fresh flowers.

"What are you doing?" Ginger asked.

"Looking for you."

"How are you?"

"Better now."

"What do you want, Sam?"

"You. I love you, Ginger."

"Do you want to come home with me?"

"Sure I do."

"Ok, then."

Ginger's housekeeper Mandy was knitting a blanket and listening to the radio when Sam and Ginger walked into the living room. Mandy lived in the small cottage that overlooked the ocean located behind the house. Mandy took the flowers in the kitchen and put them in a crystal vase.

"Thank you, Mandy," Ginger said.

"Yes Ma'am. See you tomorrow," she grinned.

"I've got something to show you, Sam."

Ginger led Sam into Luke's bedroom. He looked like a cherub, holding on tight to his teddy bear."

"Meet your son."

"What??"

"Your son, Sam. This is little Luke."

Tears rolled down his face as he gazed upon the little boy who looked exactly like a photo of him when he was three.

"If you ask me if he's yours, I will shoot you."

"Why didn't you tell me?"

"I don't know."

"Marry me, Ginger."

"Ok."

Heather was about to begin working on her new film, *New Orleans Lady*. It was a story about a girl named Jean Louise whose Mama sells her to a Madame in New Orleans. She falls in love with a Texas rancher who marries her and they live happily ever after. Heather would receive a nomination at the Academy Awards for best actress and screenplay. She would win both.

It was a lovely Saturday afternoon in Redondo Beach, California. *New Orleans Lady* was breaking records at the box office and life was good. Ginger and Heather were sitting on the sand watching Luke giggle and laugh as he played along the shoreline.

"Do you want to go with me to the premiere of Mae West's movie *Night After Night* next week? She told me she rewrote a scene and added a couple of lines. The scene happens when she checks in a luxurious white fur at a nightclub. The girl takes it and says, "Oh my goodness what a lovely fur. Mae's response, 'Goodness had nothin' to do with it, dearie.'"

"Mae is brilliant," Ginger said. "I believe she's going to take Hollywood by storm."

"Mae West really made a name for herself when she took *Diamond Lil* on the road. I heard she even received the red carpet and the key to some of the big cities. She's working on a new movie now. It's called, *She Done Him Wrong*. It's a takeoff of *Diamond* Lil; the studio is excited about her."

"I like Mae," Ginger said.

"How do you like being married, Ginger?"

"Most days are good. I think Sam likes being a daddy. He's real good with Luke."

"I'm going to marry Giorgio, Ginger. We're going to do it in Italy with his family."

Ginger hugged Heather. "Good. He's a good man, Heather, and there is no question he loves you."

"We're going to workshop *Pearl* at the Pasadena Playhouse. Now that the economy is picking up, I think it's a good time. Richard is taking care of the details."

"That's good, Heather."

"Thank God for Miss Pearl. She has been such a blessing to both of us. I am so happy she is living on the ranch with her sons and grandbabies now. Victoria Pearl is quite a woman."

"Ruby reminded me so much of her. I wonder what is in the journal? I cannot wait to read it!"

For a few minutes the two friends listened to the sounds of the surf, breathing in the fresh salty air.

"Remember that day we wrote our wishes in the sand?" Ginger smiled.

"I do. I wrote FAMOUS ACTRESS and you wrote LOVE. I guess we both got what we wanted."

"Mozella always says, 'All things are possible with God.'"

"It's kind of funny, Ginger. When it's all said and done, I am still that little girl that grew up on a farm in Illinois that likes to tell stories. Being a star doesn't change who you are deep inside. This business can be hard and to tell you the truth, I really like writing. I want to have children and live happily ever after with the man I love."

"I understand," Ginger smiled.

"With everything I have done the most important lesson I have learned is that *real* happiness is found in the heart. Life is about those you love and the people who *truly* love you. Like little Luke here," Heather grinned.

Ginger reached for Heather's hand. With peaceful contentment, the two friends watched the happy toddler squeal with delight as the white foam swirled around his dancing feet and then slid back to once again unite with the oneness of the deep, blue sea.

CHAPTER 40

# Hello My Beloved

Victoria went to the springs at the Five Star Ranch and sat below the live oak, where dark green leaves cascading down created a comfortable cool shade. The fresh scent of roses seemed to be especially fragrant this day. Victoria listened intently to the soft, gentle flow of water and the breeze dancing in the leaves. The sound of happy birds chirping created a soothing orchestrated melody making Victoria's spirit feel light.

As always, Victoria closed her eyes and allowed the memories of her loving days with Robert fill her heart, mind and soul. For a long time, Victoria relished the peacefulness of the springs.

Suddenly everything was quiet and still. Steadily, from a distance, Victoria could hear the galloping trod of horses approaching her. Opening her eyes she saw a man who looked like Robert coming towards her, leading two magnificent white stallions that were pulling a fancy carriage. As the carriage came closer, Victoria gasped in amazement and her heart jumped with joy. It was Robert!

Handsome and virile as ever, Robert's smile was soft and loving. He was wearing a white hat and suit, and an iridescent glow of light surrounded him like a mystic halo around the moon.

"I knew I would find you here," he grinned.

"Robert?" Victoria asked. "Oh, Robert, my love. How I have missed you, my darling."

"I have never left you, Victoria. Our love is eternal and strong. I have always been close."

"You look like you did the first night I met you."

"And you are beautiful as ever, Victoria."

"I am old, Robert."

"You are beautiful."

"The roses are especially lush and fragrant this year. I love coming here. I feel close to you at the springs. I believe it is truly my heaven on earth."

"It is heaven, Victoria, because it is a place of beauty, peace and love. It is our magical place. We spent many happy times here."

"I am drawn to the enchantment of the springs."

Victoria could hear beautiful music and saw bright vibrant colors shimmering like diamonds in the sun.

"Is this real? Am I dreaming, Robert?"

Robert smiled at his bride. "Yes, Victoria, this is real. It is time for you to come home with me now, my love. I have come for you."

"You mean I can be with you forever?"

"Yes, forever."

To her amazement, Victoria watched as a beautiful mahogany full-length mirror appeared. It looked just like the one that stood in the Rose Room of the Everleigh Club where Robert and Victoria Pearl first made love.

"Look, Victoria."

Gazing into the looking glass, Victoria smiled in disbelief. Her reflection revealed an image she had seen 60 years before, the night the Everleigh Club opened in Chicago.

"I am young again! This is the dress I wore the night I met you. We danced a waltz. It was the night I fell in love with my cowboy."

Robert reached for Victoria's hand and helped her into the fancy carriage made of gold, diamonds and pearls.

"Listen," he smiled.

A celestial orchestra began performing *Meet Me in St. Louis, Louis* – the song that was playing when Robert proposed marriage on top of the Ferris wheel at the St. Louis Fair.

"Are you ready?"

"I will go anywhere with you, my love," Victoria smiled, putting her arm in his."

"I love you, Victoria Pearl."

"And I love you, Robert McKnight."

Snuggled together in the beautiful carriage led by two magnificent white steeds, Robert and Victoria Pearl McKnight rode into the most glorious light, inviting them to a magical paradise where all that exists is Love.

## Cynthia Jordan

Cynthia Jordan calls herself a storyteller. She began her career in the music industry and is best known for writing the 1983 Country music song of the year, *Jose Cuervo you are a friend of mine*. In 1998 she signed a record deal with Page music and before 2000 had over 5 million downloads of her ambient piano compositions and instrumental productions. In 2002, Cynthia wrote her first book, an autobiography she calls, *Butterfly Moments*, that tells her story as a composer of music. Her book *If This Was Heaven* is a non-fictional compilation of short stories about spirituality and appreciation of life. Her most recent novels are historical fictions she calls, *The Gem Series*. The books are full of fascinating history and memorable characters. The stories address challenges for women from the 1800s to 1929 with humor and sentiment. Cynthia is an entertainer at heart and guarantees her audiences will never be bored! If you happen to get one of her books, make sure you have a box of Kleenex nearby and prepare to laugh out loud.

For more information and discounts visit www.cynthiamusic.com

# Books by Cynthia

Talking points guide available for book clubs

Available on cynthiaproductions.com

and
Amazon.com

Made in the USA
Columbia, SC
05 June 2023